PARTICULAR STONES

DAVID J. KIRK

WWW.MARTINSISTERSPUBLISHING.COM

Published by

Mudfoot Books, a division of Martin Sisters Publishing, LLC

www.martinsisterspublishing.com

ISBN: 978-1-937273-06-4
Young Adult/Science Fiction
Editor Brittani Wolanin

Printed in the United States of America
Martin Sisters Publishing, LLC

DEDICATION

For Dawne.

ACKNOWLEDGEMENTS

Linda Blakkan.

Ivan Boszormenyi-Nagy, MD, *Intensive Family Therapy*, Hoeber Medical Division, Harper & Row, Lippincott Williams & Wilkins: Philadelphia, 1965

Eknath Easwaran, founder of the Blue Mountain Center of Mediation, *A More Ardent Fire*, copyright 2000, reprinted by permission of Nilgiri Press, P.O. Box 256, Tomales, CA 94971, www.easwaran.org

Mudfoot Books
An imprint of Martin Sisters Publishing, LLC

CHAPTER ONE

It had been nearly a millennium since the human race almost ceased to exist, but my time was chaotic just the same. I guess I should be thankful I wasn't born a thousand years earlier.

When I was twelve years old I had to move into my second orphanage, the one for the older kids. It was Labor Day and school started the very next day. I cried my eyes out as I walked across the yard and looked up at that massive building called Delk Hall. I dragged along an old sea bag with my clothes in it, too heavy for me to lift off the ground.

Why do things have to change? Life was good at the other orphanage. We played a lot and were constantly supervised by nannies that were caring, for the most part. We slept in a huge dorm room, a complete open floor of one of the large buildings. I remember great pillow fights and ice cream at night. But all that was before Delk Hall.

I stopped at the large doors, wiped off the tears, and walked inside. Seated at one of those drab green government metal desks was a man with his feet propped up, reading a comic book.

"Excuse me, I was told to move in here." I placed my records on the desk. He remained behind the comic and silent for several minutes.

"You got a name, pig?" he finally muttered.

"I'm not a pig."

He looked around the comic book at me and laughed, "Oh, a new pig." He picked up my records and looked through them. He was in high school, with big elephant ears. What a goof. "I asked your name!" he yelled.

"Daniel."

"Daniel who?"

"Daniel Kelley."

"That your real name?" he asked with a smirk on his face.

"That's the one they gave me," my voice becoming a bit sarcastic.

"That makes you an orphan," he hissed. "Well, orphan, here's the schedule. Wake up is at six, chore time's at six fifteen, breakfast at seven, clean up at seven thirty, school bus leaves at eight fifteen sharp, don't miss it! You get back from school at two, chore time's right after you change, then game time, then supper at six, then study time, then TV maybe, then showers, then bedtime at nine. Got it? Here, stupid, here's the whole thing in writing, your life and welcome to it. Wait here, I'll call Monica." He pushed a button on the desk and sat reading my records.

"Where you from, orphan Dan?" His eyes followed down the sheet of paper and then suddenly he broke into laughter. "Central Illinois Territory? What happened, you fall out of an airplane? Know what?" he looked up at me, "You'd be better off if they let you freeze down there!"

The last words echoed. Big Ears returned to his comic book. I hated this guy.

"Daniel Kelley?" A soft, female voice asked. I turned around to see Monica smiling. She held out her hand. "Here is your lock and key. Keep the key on this chain around your neck at all times, even in the shower. Come on."

I followed her down a creaky wooden hallway to a storage room full of boxes and another old desk. She gave me a new shower kit and took my old one. Then she heaped clothes on me: a coat, sweatshirts, two pairs of industrially laundered blue jeans, socks, and underwear. Lastly she handed me a pair of walking shoes for school and some work boots.

We sat up on the desk while she reviewed my records. I was a bit cheered up by all the new stuff. Monica had a smile on her face as she checked off my inventory list. Then she reviewed my history and the smile suddenly disappeared. She jumped down from the desk and appeared a bit nervous.

"What's wrong?" I asked, a bit puzzled.

"Oh, nothing. Nothing at all. Looks like you will be in the north wing. I can't go there, but you can find your room yourself. It's straight down that hall at the end." She left the room.

I became sad. Alone as usual. People in my life just seemed to come and go, like Monica.

After a while, I decided no one was going to help me, so I started to haul my stuff down to my room. I grabbed an armful of clothes and walked down the long hall. There were other rooms on my right and left but very few of the beds were made up. No one was around.

I opened the door at the end of the hall and saw nothing. In complete darkness I stumbled in and found a switch, but the overhead light didn't work. Then I found a small desk with a lamp and turned it on. As I looked around, I saw that the walls, ceiling and floor were all dark painted wood, the same color as the outside of the building. There were four bunk beds and one bunk without a top bed. Tall wooden twin lockers stood next to each bunk. The air was stale. There was a fire escape door with a metal bar across it and a sign that read, "Emergency Use Only, alarm will sound when opened." Noticing two windows at the rear of the room and one on each side, I went to one, unlocked and raised the glass pane. I then found a latch on the shutter, unlocked it and swung it open. I walked around the room and opened all four of the windows, then turned and looked at my new living quarters. Even with the additional light, the atmosphere was still depressing. Only one of the bunks looked occupied, an upper, as it was made up with a brown ripped army blanket. The door to the adjacent locker was broken in and only a few raggedy clothes hung inside. I threw my clothes on one of the lower bunks.

I went out of the room and down the hall and found a locker with blankets and sheets, brought some back, and made up my bed. I returned for the rest of my clothes, making about four trips, then folded and stored them in my locker, attaching my lock. Since it was already after five o'clock, I decided to go over my class schedule for the next day. I took all my new school supplies out of my bag and set up the desk next to my bunk.

In front of the building at 6 p.m., I got my first clear look at Centura Orphanage. Set in about a forty-acre field were six large, wooden structures, two-storied, all covered in the same dark wood. My hall, Delk, was on the north end. Next to it was a dining hall, next to that Price Hall, then another dining hall, then Anthony Hall. All of these buildings were in a straight line and all facing the administration/counselors' dorm building. The courtyard was packed with hundreds of kids. The grass was too tall and the bushes needed trimming.

I walked to the nearest dining hall and stood in line. The line was long but moved quickly. There were some bullies up ahead pushing around kids. I just looked down. Although it was crowded and noisy, I ate my supper of greasy steak, and didn't look at or talk to anyone.

Back in my dorm room, I decided to skip recreation time and just went to bed. "Things can only get better tomorrow," I said to myself. So went my first day, the seventh of September, the year of our Lord 3063.

"Good morning!" this booming voice came from the hallway. My cheap, digital watch read 5:55 a.m. and I felt robbed of the five minutes of sleep. I could hear the same voice as the speaker walked up and down the north wing corridor. I noticed my roommate had not returned last night.

I ignored the chores as listed on my schedule and just walked down to the bath with my shower kit and towel. I headed right for the sinks and saw another kid. He was tall with a fat stomach and short hair that was already thinning. Strangely, he was standing at attention in his underwear. He held his shower kit up on one shoulder and had the other arm down at his side, staring straight ahead like an army sentry. He was at a sink on the far end of the room.

I took a sink next to another guy who was shaving. He must have been in high school as he had a dark beard. I began brushing my teeth.

Then at the end of the room I heard, "Prepare to brush teeth, Corky! Brush teeth!"

The guy next to me looked toward the commotion, then back to the mirror smiling. Then he looked over at me. "I'm Frank Davis," he said as he held out his hand.

I shook it, "Dan Kelley."

"You new?"

"Yea, seventh-grader," I responded. "So, who's Corky?"

He laughed, "Oh, don't mind him. That's Crazy Ben. Corky is some auditory hallucination Ben talks to."

Frank sounded smart. He was also the first person to talk to me.

We were interrupted by another guy who came storming in, yelling, "Ben Holden! Don't scare the new kids, you wacko! And I hear you're skipping your showers, so take one, now." His was the voice I had heard giving the wake-up call earlier.

"Aye, aye, sir!" Ben stood at attention, did a military about face and marched toward the showers. The well-built Black guy smiled and then looked down at a list he was holding, "I'm looking for a Daniel Kelley."

I raised my hand.

"Kelley," he said, "you need to see ..." Then he suddenly stopped and looked down at my bare feet. "Where the heck are your shower shoes?" He reached in a bag he had dangling from a shoulder strap, took out a pair of shower shoes and threw them at my feet. "Don't ever let me see you in here without these. You might get fungal rot. So, I need to see you in my office. Davis, show him around today, okay?" Frank nodded with his toothbrush in his mouth. The Black guy left the room.

"Wow, is he the dorm police?" I asked Frank.

"He's not a bad guy, he acts mean all the time but I think you'll like him. His name's Bossard. Always call him Mr. Bossard. He'll be okay after that. I'll see you out front and then we'll go to breakfast."

On my way out I stopped by Bossard's office at the front end of the corridor next to the lobby. Taking Frank's advice, I decided to ham it up a little. I walked in and stood straight saying loudly, "Mr. Bossard, you wanted to see me, sir."

I thought I saw the corners of his mouth turn up a bit. "Kelley, I think we're going to get along. So here's the deal. Sit down."

He rambled through all the rules of the place in his military manner, but I got the impression he really cared about my doing well here. He told me to talk with Frank Davis about what chore details to get on, and then named some guys to stay away from. "That Ben Holden's crazy; stay away from him." And then he looked directly at me and continued, "Kelley, this place is the absolute pits. You can cry and whine about your situation, take a bad attitude toward school, then end up being a farmhand and slop hogs all your life. I've seen it. Plus I've been through it; I was a resident in Delk Hall as well. There are some very bad kids in here and a few good ones. Find the good ones; Davis is a good start. Hang out with them. Stay away from those bad ones; they will bully and threaten you, just walk away. You can come and get me if you need help but I'm not here all the time. You have to learn how to survive." He looked down at some papers on his desk. "I know they only give pass/fail for grades for the first four years in elementary school, but they start giving letter grades out in fifth and sixth grades. I see you got all A's both years. Can you explain that?"

"No," I said, "I'm not sure how that happened."

"There's a note here by your sixth-grade teacher that you used to do all your homework in a one hour study period at school."

"Yes, Mr. Bossard, I never had to take anything back to the dorm. I found the work very easy."

He smiled, "I think you have a gift. I'm going to call the school this morning and recommend they put you in some advanced classes. Okay, get to chow. After school today, tell the guy at the front desk which chore detail you want. You know who I mean?"

"The guy with the big ears?"

Mr. Bossard chuckled, then he shook his head, "Yea, that one, but don't ever say that to his face; he's awful sensitive about that. Now march!"

I gave him a smart, "Yes, sir!" and walked out front to meet Frank.

Frank Davis was friendly but very serious and quiet. He did give me some advice on teachers, however, at breakfast. He told me to be sure to get Principi for history. I wouldn't be bored because "Principi made one feel like they were there." He said all the rest of the teachers were equally bad so it didn't matter which ones I got. He wouldn't recommend a chore detail at first, then upon prodding, slowly released some information, "Don't choose laundry." That was the way Frank was, you never really knew how you stood with him. He still wouldn't tell me which detail to take so I asked him which one he was on. He told me the farm, but then added he didn't like it much.

After breakfast we walked back to the dorm. Frank was in my wing but on the second floor. I ran to my room to get ready, still no roommate, then back out front to wait for the bus. I figured I would meet Frank, but didn't see him. That was Frank.

All of the seventh-graders of Delk Hall piled on to the bus and luckily I got a window seat. True to my limited social skills, I looked out the window and ignored everyone. The diesel engine roared to life as we took off toward the schools. This was my first good look at Centura.

The Township of Centura only existed to support Thompson Defense Base, a northern, isolated outpost that provided national defense. It was isolated in the sense that 99.9 percent of the population of the United States now lived in the southeast. While the Army, Navy, and Air Force still existed separately, they usually operated out of one shared set of facilities in isolated areas. The place was named after two governors of the same name from Wisconsin and Illinois back when they were states and located on the coast of Lake Michigan, somewhere between the abandon cities of Chicago and Milwaukee.

The years of freezing and melting of the lake created large areas of erosion on the once smooth shoreline. Thompson sat on the shoreline above a small bay protected by a T-shaped peninsula. A large glacier-created lake was west of the military complex and to the north was a field of jagged rocks and cliffs that measured more than ten square miles. I had heard they had defensive missile sites up there. Some people said the base had an ideal geographic defense being so situated, although I never could understand what it had to defend against. The base was virtually self-sufficient with housing, utility plants, and an airfield. Most officers and married enlisted personnel lived on the base and few were overjoyed to be stationed here. Military people considered Thompson the poorest base to live.

I never learned how Centura got its name. For the most part, the town existed to support the base. It had stores, banks and entertainment. Although "the strip," a small area of tattoo parlors and sleazy bars, was located just outside the main bridge to the base, the majority of the north side of Centura consisted of finer stores, finer residences and, in the opinion of some, finer people. North Shore Drive, a large boulevard that ran from the bridge to the base eastward, was the primary route of the military kids to the schools out on the peninsula.

The "little kids" orphanage was there, along with an elementary school. Also, the junior/senior high school, junior college/tech school, and college were located together all in one big campus. There were residential classes for the younger kids but as one advanced, most classes were via satellite so a student could attend anywhere in the area via a computer.

And then there was the south side, where the "older kids" orphanage was located and where I now lived. South Centura had more modest houses, only a few stores, and was a little rougher. Some of the single military personnel rented there. Several farms existed south and west of town to support the area and rough farmhands inhabited that end of town as well. There was a little shantytown outside Centura where the real poor lived.

The bus ride only took about a half an hour up South Shore Drive, into the "nicer" part of town, and then out onto the peninsula. I began to get a little nervous as we drove up to the junior high section of the school.

We filed out of the bus and into the school, walking down a short hallway and down a few steps; we were herded into the gymnasium. The place was packed with kids and noise. There were tables around the perimeter of the gym with lines of kids at each one. My bus mates and I were put there, and as others walked in behind us, I was pushed further into the gym and given no instructions on where to go or what to do. I just started walking slowly in the hopes I would get a clue.

I later found out that fall registration should have been completed via computer but input errors, missing phone numbers or addresses, or other such omissions lead to the annual pandemonium.

A girl caught my eye (a phenomenon that was beginning to happen with increased regularity) as she strode across the gym floor carrying a handful of papers. She had round facial features and this flyaway, fuzzy black hair that always seem to lay just right at the end of her walk. She must have been in college. She laid the papers down on a table and then looked right at me. I suddenly turned my head and pretended I was just scanning the room. When I looked back she was walking toward me. This time I was the one caught staring.

"You wouldn't be Dan Kelley, would you?" she smiled.

"Yea."

"Bossard from the home called me. Come with me."

I followed her to a small desk in the back of the gym. Her name was Diane Win, an advanced high school work-study student. Work-study students worked for an employer, in her case the school, but the money they paid her was from a federal grant provided by the Department of Education. She was also enrolled in some college classes. She went over my class schedule on her computer and switched me to Mr. Principi's history class upon my request. Then she looked at my schedule again.

"Okay, you got one open period, how about Intro to Philosophy?"

"What the heck's that?" I asked her.

She didn't bother to respond, just said, "Okay, so there, already enrolled. You also have last hour in study hall like you wanted." She looked up at me and got a serious expression on her face.

"You have any trouble at that place where you live, you see Bossard. You have any trouble at this school, you see me, okay?"

I smiled and thanked her then left for my first period homeroom, wondering why everyone seemed to be warning me of trouble.

Homeroom was English, a very large class with what seemed like forty students. I saw a pretty girl and sat by her. The teacher was Mrs. Merick, a petite-framed, frail woman who could easily yell above the noise in the room. As she went through the roll, I did not see anyone that I knew. She handed out a take-home test to check our composition level, a test that I finished before she got done handing them all out. Then she rattled on for the rest of the time about the benefits of being a good communicator. She let us out ten minutes early so we could find our lockers. Mine was in one of the enclosed hallways leading to another wing, pretty far away from any classroom or hall monitor. Several lockers down the row from me there was a fight between two kids.

My next class was Mr. Principi's history. He was an interesting character. He talked like a college professor and looked a lot like Albert Einstein with gray, fuzzy hair flying all over. He had some sort of disease as he had to walk with a cane and had trouble getting up from and back down into his chair.

"This semester we will be discussing the Old World and the New World. Other history courses address them separately, but this one concentrates on the transition. Like the industrial revolution, this transition changed everything and shaped the future for centuries. A lot of these changes are still in practice today. Welcome to the journey.

"History is the best subject in the world and I enjoy teaching it more than anything else. I suggest you come with me on this journey and for those who choose not to, I expect you will withdraw from class or I will fail you."

That was the extent of Principi's comments on student responsibility for the class. There were no papers and any readings were supplemental in nature. There were only his lectures and exams, all students who did not come or did not participate were merely dismissed from his attention and allowed to fail. Principi took no prisoners. This was going to be a difficult class.

The rest of the day lacked anything of significance, a day of endless roll calls and discovering scores of kids who were in the wrong classroom. Lunch was the best. The food was much better than the dining hall fare at the orphanage and you could have all you wanted. I also ended the day with a new set of books.

After school I found Frank Davis waiting for my bus. He was standing facing the road and I walked up behind him. "Hey, Frank, I thought you took another bus … Man! What happened to you?" As he turned I saw Frank's eye was red and swollen, and he had a dried up cut on his lip.

He just huffed, "I'm not going to talk about it."

We got on the bus and sat together. I tried again, "You know, you need to see somebody if,"

"It's just a couple of guys I don't agree with," he snapped, "and I said I'm not talking about it."

I let it go and talked about my day, especially Principi's class. He chatted with me, but I could tell he was troubled.

Back home we changed and headed for our chores. I told Big Ears that I wanted to go to the farm with Frank and he just mumbled something about it being a good place for me. We walked west of the orphanage and crossed a little creek up to the dairy barn of Milt Frazer's farm. He had dairy, beef cattle, and hogs. He also had acres of pasture and crop land. While the dairy barn was at this sight, the hogs and other cattle were housed just south of it. Frank left me to go pitch manure while I went to orientation with Milt.

Milt Frazer was standing next to one of the work-study students. There were only me and one other new orphanage kid in this orientation class. Milt was a farmer from head to toe. A seed company ball cap sat on his head and he was dressed in overalls, a plaid shirt, and boots with manure all over them. He looked at the other new kid.

"You been here before?"

"Yea," the kid replied, "you sent me back and they put me in the laundry. They got rid of me, too. Looks like you're stuck."

"Looks like I'm not," Milt snapped, "get out of here. Go tell Big Ears at Delk 'nice try.'" The kid stormed out. Milt looked at me but pointed at the work-study student, "This is Clyde; he'll show you what to do. My name's Milt. You ever call me Milton and I'll break your neck." He walked out.

Clyde just looked at me and smiled. "Milt's not in a very good mood today."

"I guess not." I replied.

"He will give you a try and if he gets to like you, he'll go to the wall for you. I know he saved me many times. Come on, I'll show you around."

Clyde showed me the two enclosed wings of the barn that housed the dairy herd. I saw Frank in one scraping the floor with a shovel. He showed me the dirty change room while he grabbed a new pair of rubber boots and wrote my name on them with a black marker. Then through a large window he showed me the clean changing room and the milking room beyond that. "We can't go in there because you need to don those white scrubs and shoe booties. I'll show you when you need to go in there." Clyde told me that ground feed was moved into the housing barns automatically through the use of a conveyor, but that we pitched hay by hand from the loft. We went aloft and I saw this huge room filling the whole of the barn way up to a high ceiling. It was crammed with hay bales. "Come on," he said, "I'll get some papers for you; we don't need to do anything today." We came upon this little space between the bales that had a lamp, a made-up hay bed, and a chair. "This is where I'm staying."

"You don't live in the orphanage?" I asked.

"Naw, I kind of got thrown out of there. I was in Delk Hall, too. So how's Big Ears?"

"A moron, as usual, from what I gather."

"He's the one got me kicked out of there. And he's crafty as well. He got me in trouble with the school, which wasn't real fond of me at the time. So I had to do a week at the fort."

"What's the fort?"

"You never heard of the Irish Fort? It's actually the school's detention center, reform school. It's up at the north end of the peninsula, north of the school. You get time up there for being bad. It adds up. You get a month and they kick you out of school and deport you. Big Ears called them and said I was pulling stunts down here. He's a Mustang wannabe."

"Not sure who the Mustangs are, either," I added.

"They are a south side gang who bully around the kids at the orphanage. Big Ears was a pledge but he failed his bully probation so they kicked him out. The clown can't even join a gang of delinquents without screwing it up. Holy Cross is the only good group of guys down here who fight back. I wanted to join them but they only take Catholics. Anyway, I got tired of the fistfights and the bullying so I left. I'm staying here temporarily until I can figure something out. I got back into school now and I'm doing well and that's the way I want to keep it. School is the only way out of here."

"It doesn't seem like this building is heated. What are you going to do in the winter?"

"Oh, sometimes Milt lets me stay in the bunkhouse with the farmhands, sometimes in the clean room downstairs, it's heated.

"Any family around?"

"Naw. Parents were alcoholics. My sister ran away. I was taken by the court and put here. Dad drowned in Lake Michigan and my mom got sent south. I hope to find my sister someday. What about your parents?"

"Never knew them. Both dead."

"Man, sorry to hear that. I guess it's a hard life at times, eh?" He gave me some papers, a map of the farm and said to report tomorrow. "Good luck to you, Dan, hang in there. There's just one thing about Milt, don't steal anything from here. Gosh, if you get hard up tell me or tell him."

Frank must have left without me so I walked back alone. Near the little bridge over the creek, I found a book in the grass. I picked it up and read the cover, *Living in the Woods* by Thomas Pine. I looked at the inside of the front cover and saw a strange handwritten inscription, Governor Viche. When I got back to Delk and gave it to Big Ears, he put it in the lost and found box. He didn't have a remark for me; too deep into his comic book.

After dinner I studied in the lobby with Frank Davis. His eye was becoming nice and black now, but I did not mention it. I had all my homework done already but decided to get a jump on the readings for English. I started reading *Catcher in the Rye*, until Frank interrupted me.

"There are no pictures in that book if that's what you're looking for," he laughed.

"I know. I was reading it."

"You trying to tell me you read that fast?"

"Yea. Didn't you learn how to speed read in elementary school?" I asked.

He sighed, "You know, Dan, I didn't go to that special university school that you did, I went to the town school on the south side."

"So you must have lived in a home? What happened to your family?"

"Killed in a car accident. Sorry if I'm a bit of a twit lately, it only happened last month."

This time I sighed, "Oh, Frank, I'm sorry. Do you have any relatives down South?"

"There's a few. Of course no one could make it up here for the funeral. Now they are conveniently stalling to decide which one is going to take me. I don't know any of them, never even met them. And I don't want to go anyway, so I hope they take forever. I have a twin sister in the girls' dorm. I worry about her. I want to try and find someplace where we can live together. I'm afraid they will send us to different relatives and we won't see each other ever again."

"Well, I'll help you, for sure," I promised. Frank smiled and thanked me; I think he was finally warming up. "I'll even teach you how to speed read. Hey, why do you use the john on our floor if you live upstairs?"

"Because most of the toilets and sinks in our bathroom are broken, because this place is a dump. I use the first floor john because nobody uses yours, since they use to put all the blue kids on your floor."

"What do you mean, 'blue kids'?"

"Never heard of the blue? Principi will go over it in history. Don't worry, it's an old urban legend but smart thinking doesn't really thrive around here. Besides, if I didn't use yours, I wouldn't get to see my buddy, Ben." He smiled, "I think he's faking it, by the way."

"Being crazy?"

"Yes. Bossard, who thinks he is crazy by the way, told me the school psychologist thought he was psychotic so they sent him up to the base for a military shrink to check out his brain. They didn't think anything was wrong with him. But they put him on meds anyway. You'll see; you'll catch him sooner or later. I can't figure out his reason though."

We went back to studying and I finished my book about the time they turned on the TV in the big room. Frank told me to always jump ahead on the schedule we were supposed to follow to avoid the crowds. So I went down my wing to take a shower.

Done with the shower and back at the sink to brush my teeth, I saw Crazy Ben standing by the far wall. This time he was pointing right at me. His voice boomed out, "Do you see the light, Corky? Do you see that light, Corky old boy?" I finished quickly and split. I didn't care what Frank had said, this guy was nuts.

Back in my room I began writing in my journal about a long and eventful day. As I switched off my desk lamp at 9 p.m., I heard a voice that sent me about two feet off my chair.

"Lights out at nine only means the overhead light; you can keep your desk lamp on."

I switched it back on and stood up. Sitting on the top bunk and escaping my notice until now was a dark figure. "You scared the crap out of me!" I chuckled, a bit embarrassed. "I suppose you are my phantom roommate?" As I walked closer to him I stopped, my mouth dropped open and I let out an audible gasp, "Oh my gosh!" The kid was obviously deformed or something. His trunk and limbs were crooked and pointing out at odd angles. He had a rash of some kind on the left side of his face and down his body. I could tell as he had his shirt off. "I'm ..."

"No, I'm sorry," he said, "I'm not too easy to look at. Sorry to startle you but I wanted you to know I was here. My name is Gov."

"Oh, short for Governor?" I didn't know what to say.

"Yes, Governor Viche. I know, crazy name, huh? Don't worry. I'm not here much. I'm only here tonight because they found out what barn I was staying in and are looking for me there. I'll just be here tonight; I found another place I can go to tomorrow."

I walked back to my chair and sat down; figuring the further away the better. "I found a book of yours today; I gave it to lost and found."

"Thanks. You can have it. I couldn't understand it anyway."

"Who's after you, Gov?"

"A couple of bullies."

"Why don't you tell somebody?" I asked. Why didn't Frank for that matter. What was wrong with this place? Who were these bullies?

"I'm not really the type that gets a lot of sympathy around here."

"Where do you eat? How do you get to school?"

"I eat where I can; I don't go to school; and, I'm twenty four years old. It's a long story. Ask Bossard. I'm going to sleep now; I'm awful tired." He lay back down. I switched off my light and lay down as well, keeping one eye open and on that bunk.

I awoke to Bossard yelling in the hall again. I sat up and saw, true to his word, the Governor had already split.

The day at school was less hectic than the first day. The cute girl I sat by in homeroom actually spoke to me.

"Are you Dan Kelley?" she smiled.

"Yea."

"I'm Betsy Barney; I'm pretty much the center of things around here. The teacher said you were pretty smart."

"I try," I responded. Gosh, talk about an ego.

"You should join our study group. Oh, you see those two girls in the back of the room? They are Melissa and Clairessa Popover. They are identical twins. You can call them Mel and Claire. Claire is not going with anyone, you should ask her out."

I just nodded, not knowing what to say. Both twin girls were cute but I had no idea which was which. Luckily the teacher called the class to order and I didn't have to respond.

Principi's history class was great. I recorded some of the classes, especially the ones where he summarized specific periods.

"The Old World was a more hectic time. Overpopulation and depleting resources were major concerns. The population of the world in 2095 was approximately 7.3 billion. One could say that it was a more civilized time, as society was more globally interactive and cooperative. International travel and commerce ruled the day. Large corporations operated across national boundaries to an extent unheard of today. A fragile balance of power was maintained.

"However, we are interested in the transition from old to new so I won't bore you with Old World statistics. A noteworthy event was in 2096 when an odd drought occurred; not that drought was that uncommon. This one occurred around the equator in a usually tropical climate. This affected the areas of north central South America, central Africa, and the Far East. The drought had little economic impact but was a clue that something drastic was soon to happen to the climate.

"There was also a Middle East conflict in 2101 which had similar results as all the others during the previous four thousand years. The national boundaries changed a little, many people were killed and wounded, and absolutely nothing was resolved.

"Other than those events, the world went through its usual business until the year 2110. Then a strange thing happened. It got cold. This week, starting tomorrow, we will take a look at the ice age."

Philosophy class was definitely hard. We were going to go over the history, which included ancient, medieval, renaissance, early modern, nineteenth century, and contemporary. Then we would look at the main theories, eastern versus western, and the main branches. I found it hard to understand but could read the book and memorize what I needed for taking the tests.

That night I was headed from the showers to brush my teeth and found only one sink open. Unfortunately, it was next to Ben Holden. He was shaving, and I hoped he would ignore me. Then we had the oddest exchange.

"Psst, Kelley," he whispered, "I'm not really crazy ya know." I ignored him. "What happened to Davis' eye?"

"Why don't you ask him?" I whispered back.

"He won't talk to me. I have been keeping tabs on some of the guys here, some of the good ones. I'm going have a meeting next week. I want you to come and bring Davis. Something has to be done here."

I decided to be a little sarcastic with him, "I'll come, but only if Corky comes too."

Ben didn't bat an eye or call me a smart aleck or anything. He just whispered, "I'll have Cork there, just you be sure to bring Davis. I'll tell you more about it later." He left the room.

I got right into bed after getting back to my room and started thinking. Gosh, that would be some meeting. I could see me there with Frank while Ben took the roll, calling out Corky's name and then Ben responding, "Present." What a nut case. I slowly drifted off.

It started off in blackness; I couldn't see anything. Then slowly a faint whirling sound became more audible and it grew louder, then very loud. Then I began to see a dim light that slowly became brighter. I was cold, huddled in a blanket, seated. Soon the light became bright enough that I started to see figures. Some were seated, but one was walking. They all had on these white space suits and shaded helmets. I couldn't see their faces. I looked around my shoulder to my left and saw a round window; outside of it was a black night sky and blowing snow. Then I jumped as I felt a jolt of turbulence and I knew I was flying in something. One of the space men saw me and walked over to me. He bent down. I could not see his face, only my own scared reflection in the mask. He spoke a distorted, haunting line from out of a speaker on his helmet, "We're takin' you to Centura, kid, although we'd be doin' you a bigger favor if we'd left ya to freeze down on the ice!"

I sat right up in bed, breathing heavily, only to realize that I was dreaming. I knew the dream well, all too well. I looked at my watch; it was 2 a.m. Then I let out a faint chuckle as I fantasized that the man in the space suit was Big Ear's father.

When I got to Principi's history class later that morning I realized that all the other students looked older. Eavesdropping on some conversations I learned that most of them were high schoolers. Then Mr. Principi walked in and started.

"The winter beginning in December, 2109 was not so unusual. The strange thing was that the spring of 2110 took so long to arrive. There was a foot of snow on the ground during the first week of June in Chicago. Besides a few farmers complaining, everyone sort of ignored it and thought it to be a temporary freak of nature. The winter beginning in 2110 was also not unusual. What was unusual was the fact that the summer of 2111 never arrived.

"The city of St. Louis celebrated its last Fourth-of-July with a fireworks display that was prematurely ended by a two-foot snow storm. People began to get worried. Successive winters and summers showed no relief and we had the beginnings of a mini ice age.

"By 2114, the continents of Asia and North America were once again fused together by an enlarging northern polar ice cap. The countries of Canada, Greenland, Norway, Sweden, and Finland closed down and moved their governments to embassies in southern Europe or South America. Larger countries fared a little better, such as Russia, since their populations had room to move south within their own borders.

"The United States took longer to react than most countries. It seemed that our pioneer spirit of facing adversity was the cause of thousands of frozen bodies. Water resources froze, power plants began to fail, and food shortages were common. In the year 2116, the mayor of Chicago grabbed the city charter, closed down the government, and headed south. Seattle, Minneapolis, Milwaukee, Detroit, Buffalo, and Boston soon followed suit. Other cities further south, like St. Louis, Indianapolis, Pittsburg, and New York closed up as well.

"People streamed south. It was the largest exodus ever recorded. Although some military bases remained in the north, the general population crammed into the Sunbelt. People in the west headed for the southwest, only to find that the geography and climate couldn't support such numbers, so they then pressed east. The masses from the north were not used to the land or the culture and also space was becoming problematic. Resources were dwindling; riots broke out.

"But it seems that every time humankind faced a dilemma, something also happened to provide relief, although in this case rather drastic relief. In the frenzy of the climate change, scientists were frantically attempting to come up with solutions for the advancing climate problems. A group developed a liquid agent, which they called 'Blue Solution.' The stuff was projected to be a miracle. It thrived at relatively low temperatures and melted ice rapidly. The problem was that it had properties of living tissue. It was tested extensively on some frozen areas to retrieve military records and equipment left in the mad dash south. It was also tried on relatively large areas in west central Illinois and Iowa to determine if it would be useful in large area reclamation. It apparently worked for a while and then 'died,' becoming an inert, harmless powder. Snow and ice quickly reclaimed the treated areas. Although the Blue Solution was considered 'alive' in some aspects, it had no animal or vegetable characteristics. All except one. It got sick.

"Yet another 'accident' was going to change the plight of the human race. With the Blue Solution being developed in the United States, some countries in South America talked our government into letting them try the stuff in their similar fight in the southern high latitudes. A plane filled with the Blue Solution heading for Argentina, developed engine trouble over the equator and crashed. Then all hell broke loose.

"It appeared that while the Blue Solution was quite tame in colder climates, the high altitude and warm air of the area of the crash allowed the development of a horrible, deadly virus. The virus jumped to human hosts quickly and spread around the world in a number of weeks. Massive panic resulted. Thousands, millions began dying. It reached the United States in about ten days and was equally as lethal."

The entire class and especially Mr. Principi were surprised to see my hand raised in the air.

He looked down on his seating plan, then raised his head and removed his glasses, "Well, Mr. Kelley, do you have a question?"

"Yes. You said the solution was tested on some large areas in the north. Did this cause any problems with anyone exposed to it?"

"No. It appears that the virus was the only thing that developed. It has been suggested that it created some genetic problems with human fertility, but that has never been proven. After time, the stuff turned into a harmless blue powder. Even the survivors of the plague developed immunity to the original virus. Does that answer your question?"

"Yes, sir, thank you."

He put his glasses back on but looked over the top of them at me, then began again, "So, the overpopulation problem caused by the great migrations south was solved. The population of the U.S. was estimated at around 270 million before the climate change to around 2.7 million in ten years' time. Those ten years were America's, and the worlds, darkest hour. People went wild and crazy. Most of the survivors banded together in rude gangs and wandered about, in fear of getting sick and searching for food. The military even lost control. I'm not going to go through the extensive and gory details of 'The Chaos' in this course. More information can be obtained from my course on that subject or from my book. The period lasted about a decade. Okay, tomorrow we get into getting the situation under control."

On the bus on the way back that afternoon, I told Frank about my dream. He seemed genuinely concerned since it was related to the situation he was going through.

"So your parents died down there?" Frank asked.

"I assume. They never found them anyway."

"And you didn't remember your own name so they gave you one?"

"Yea. They couldn't even give me a birth certificate since they had no proof. They issued me a Certificate of Discovery and gave me a name. They didn't put a birth date on it, just a range of dates based on a guess.

"You know," Frank said thoughtfully, "our whole wing in Delk is full of guys with stories like these. But no one wants to talk about them. For one, I'm lost. I don't know what I'm doing, I don't know how orphans are supposed to feel, but right now I feel like cow manure. What's going on, Dan?" I saw his eyes start to get watery.

"You need to see your sister more often, Frank; you guys are going to need each other. I'll go down to the girls' dorm with you and we can talk to them and set up some times for you guys to be together more."

"What do you do, Dan, you don't have any family?"

"I don't know. But I've been at this a lot longer; you just lost your family. And I don't really know how orphans are supposed to feel either. People always ask me that, how it feels to be an orphan. I don't know. I want to ask them how it feels to have a family. It's always been this way for me. Your brothers are your bunkmates; your father is the Resident Assistant. But not really, are they?"

Frank laughed, "And Big Ears is the black sheep of our family." We both laughed as the tension faded away for the moment. Frank was really starting to open up, and I think he felt better being able to do so.

"Ben Holden talked to me last night. He wants to have a meeting with some of the guys and he asked me to bring you. I wonder if his medication will kick in by then?" I laughed, trying to be sarcastic, but Frank didn't get the humor.

"I think we should at least talk to him. I believe you'll see the guy's faking it and I think I know the reason."

We agreed to meet out front after changing for chore times and walk there together. We were supposed to get some sort of money for this, but I had not seen any yet. Both the orphanage and the schools had a lot of financial incentives for teenagers in order for them to develop proper work habits. This work-study program allowed business people like the farmers and nearby retailers get free labor and in return they had to provide occupational counseling and supervision. The population was too fragile to support many freeloaders. I was supposed to meet with Diane Win to discuss my educational stipend, the amount of which depended on what major one declared.

When I came back down to the entrance, I hesitated at the door as I saw two big guys out front talking to Frank. One was a tall, lanky goof who was pointing a finger in Frank's face. The other was shorter and stocky, had a mop of hair, and was wearing a new school letter jacket. Both looked dumb. I wondered if they were the two who gave him that black eye. I pushed open the door and headed down the steps but they quickly walked away before I got there. Frank looked okay but gave me this, "I don't want to talk about it," look so we just quietly walked to the farm.

We joined a group of kids from the orphanage standing in front of the barn. Milt was going on with them about how he could never get students when he needed the labor, like during milking or feeding time. When he was finished, he just turned and left.

Clyde took Frank and me out to spread manure on harvested cropland and also to teach us how to drive a tractor. He told us that tractor driving was a good skill to have out here, as it was much nicer work than pitching hay bales or getting pushed around by cows. The tractor was pretty big and scary, but Clyde assured us it was a snap once we learned. It had an enclosed cab. Clyde took us in for loading as Frank and I leaned against the wheel guards.

An older farmhand, a cool guy that smiled and waved at us, filled our spreader with a front-end loader from a manure pile they had stacked up outside the cow barn. Then Clyde took us down a trail about a half mile long out to a harvested oat field. We passed another spreader coming in, driven by another student with a farmhand as instructor. All waved to each other.

It was great being out in the open. A nice warm fall day and lots of space was a welcomed change from that dark orphanage. I felt free.

After getting to the field, Clyde stopped and got out of the seat. "Kelley, no time like the present."

I was somewhat scared at first and killed the engine the first time taking off. But Clyde was patient and I finally got going. Once I managed driving it in a straight line it was rather easy. Clyde told me to hit it so the big diesel roared to life as I moved the throttle. It was a blast. I had a little trouble on the first turn around, taking it a little wide, but my subsequent ones were fine. After we were empty, Clyde let me drive it in for a refill.

Next it was Frank's turn and I think he did much better than I did. Then Clyde did a turn; then we all rotated. I liked driving, but also liked observing. We didn't even notice the time. Milt met us at the loader and told us it was 6:10 p.m. He told us to go to the bunkhouse to eat and that whenever we put in four hours in any one day we could eat the next meal there. We ate a very hardy supper and then hit the field again. We laughed, told jokes, and had a ball. It was good to forget our lives for a while.

Finally, at about 8:40 p.m., we came in for a reload only to find the loader driver had gone. We drove our rig next to the loader under the canopy and shut it down. Frank and I walked back to Delk dead tired.

When we came in the main door, Monica was at the front desk. She barely managed a "Hi" as we walked past her. I went down to my room and noticed it was after nine and lights out. The room was pitch black but I managed to get to my desk lamp and switch it on to get ready for bed. Walking out to go brush my teeth I noticed my roommate had returned. I said hello but he must have been asleep.

I finished quickly, returned and climbed into bed. It wasn't long before I heard a moan coming from Gov. "Gov? Is that you?"

I heard it again, then again as it became louder. I jumped up, turned on the light, and walked over to his bed. Then I saw him. "Holy cow," I gasped. His face was covered in blood along with his pillowcase. "Gov! Holy cow man, you need a doctor!"

He tried to answer but only gasped. I took off down the hall yelling, finally getting to the front desk with Monica turning around to face me.

"Keep it down!" she said to me, "do you know what time …"

"It's my roommate, he's hurt, come quickly!" I yelled.

She reluctantly came down to the room with me. When she saw him she screamed, then turned and started heading down the hall. "I'll call the ambulance!"

I got a towel and put it on the long gash on his temple. His eyes were open but he wasn't talking or making any facial expressions.

The military ambulance guys got there very quickly. They took his pulse and vital signs and yelled out some numbers, but I didn't make anything out of them. Then the town police showed up. I told them what I knew as they loaded Gov on a stretcher and started pulling him down the hall. Finally everybody suddenly left and I sat at my desk alone. Stupid Monica didn't even come back down and talk to me. I put on some pants, grabbed my blanket and pillow and was headed down to the lobby to sleep when I saw a small piece of paper on the floor. I picked it up and read it, "Inspected by #16, Athletic Wear, Inc." I put it in my pocket.

When I returned to the room the next morning, Gov's mattress and pillow were gone, only his empty bunk bed remained. I went down to Bossard's, but he wasn't there. When I showered in the john, even crazy Ben wasn't around. I skipped breakfast and took the early bus to school. The school was crammed with kids, but I was alone all day with my thoughts.

Frank wasn't on the bus on the way home that afternoon. I slowly walked up the steps and through the front doors of Delk only to see Big Ears sitting at the desk sans his usual scientific reading material. He saw me and mumbled something, then flipped me Gov's book that I had turned in. "There are two cops down in your room. And it looks like you got a free book, Kelley."

"Have you heard how he is?"

"Dead."

CHAPTER TWO

I was pretty close to smacking Big Ears as I walked to my room. I later found out the jurisdictions of authority were a bit confusing here in Centura. Of course the militarized Department of Education had their own security with investigators and truancy squad. The township police mainly handled traffic and minor violations and were only armed with tasers and nightsticks. The military, the Army in this location, had armed units and of course the SWAT team. They handled all homicides and serious crimes. Investigators were provided by whichever branch of the military was assigned the case. Homicides were rare, usually domestic squabbles gone badly or the occasional bar fight. Big crimes like bank robberies or grand theft did not happen very often because there were no get-away routes. Most of the remaining authorities assigned to the states down south were split between the town and the Federal government at our location.

When I got to my room this young guy was walking around. A younger women and Mr. Bossard were seated at desks. The strangers had civilian clothes on.

"Danny Kelley?" the gentleman asked.

"Yes sir."

"I'm Lieutenant Cummings and this is Petty Officer Kowalski. We're with the Naval Investigative Service. We asked Mr. Bossard to join us, since you are a minor. We would like to ask you a few questions."

"Yes sir."

"Sit down." I sat at my desk chair.

The gentleman walked up and down as he spoke, but the woman watched my face at all times. "You found Mr. Viche last night, is that correct"?

"Yes sir. I came in late, after lights out. I didn't even notice he was there at first. He was in bed. It was dark in here."

"Why didn't you turn the light on?"

"I did turn on my desk lamp; I didn't turn on the big light because it doesn't work."

"Okay," he said, looking up at the light in the ceiling, "tell me the rest."

"I went to bed and then heard him moaning. That's when I jumped up and looked at him and saw he was hurt. I went and got Monica at the front desk."

"Where were you all last evening?"

"Over working at the farm, Milt Frazer's farm."

"You didn't come back here at all?"

"No, sir."

"Were you with someone who could verify that?"

"Yes. I was working with my friend, Frank Davis; he lives on the floor above us. Also, Clyde was there."

"Clyde who?"

"Not sure he ever said his last name, just Clyde. He doesn't live here; he stays in a barn over there."

Mr. Bossard added, "That's probably Clyde Hastings. He used to stay here."

Mr. Cummings got a little testy, "Why is one of your wards living in a barn, Mr. Bossard?"

"He said he was scared here," Mr. Bossard replied, a little embarrassed.

"Open your locker," Mr. Cummings ordered me and I complied. I sat back down and he had the woman look through it. "How well did you know Governor?"

"I only talked to him once. He doesn't stay here often, he … a … said he was afraid."

Mr. Cummings gave Mr. Bossard a dirty look, and then looked at me, "Did you hit Mr. Viche on the head?"

"No, sir!"

"Do you know if he had any enemies?"

"He told me there were a couple of kids bullying him. He didn't say anything more about it. I had no idea it was this serious. Is that how he died?"

"Yes. He was pronounced dead upon arrival at the hospital but he died in the ambulance. Mr. Kelley?" he asked, and then paused for a minute, "How the heck can you live here?" He looked around at the place making a sour face. He was obviously unhappy with the conditions at the orphanage.

He might as well have asked me what it was like to be an orphan. "I've been an orphan since I was four. It's all I know. I've always lived in these places." My testy interrogator then softened his tough demeanor.

"I know. I've read your record. Sorry to hear about your folks. And Mr. Bossard, I'm sorry to you as well; I know you are only a work-study here. I'll speak to the administrator. It's just that this place is so dirty and unkempt. By the way, you work out?"

"Yes sir," Mr. Bossard responded, "south intramural football."

"Sir, look at this locker," Ms. Kowalski added, "It could pass boot camp inspection." They both looked at it and smiled.

"Dan, I hear you're an A-student as well. You keep it up. Oh, one more thing, did you see anything in the room when you returned last night, a club or something?"

"No. Oh, there was this." I retrieved that inspection sticker I had found and gave it to him. "It was on the floor; I noticed it when they took Gov out."

He looked at it and then frowned, "Well, can't prove much with this. This could have been dropped by anyone." He put it in his notebook. "Mr. Bossard, let's go talk to Mr. Davis and then can you take me to the administration building. Dan, you take care. You can call me with anything."

Ms. Kowalski gave me a card with their numbers on it and then all three departed. Mr. Bossard gave me a pat on the back as he left.

I changed into my chore clothes, waited a while, and then went up to Frank's room. His room only had three bunks made up in it. He was a nervous wreck while he told me they questioned him about where I was the day before and if I had left him for any of the time. They had also told him what had happened to Gov.

The next day Principi gave another excellent lecture and I recorded it.

"By 2130, the United States of America was a fraction of its former self. Only the southeastern states had any resemblance to what once was. The north and west were a massive snow and ice field and practically uninhabited.

"The Federal government was in a real mess. Their lack of action in the first few years was no doubt a product of the false belief that the plague would end, the weather would warm up, and everyone would move back home. But as ice and bodies piled up, the need for drastic action soon became apparent. Luckily, we had a young, aggressive president at the time, Campbell Arthur (no relation to the Old World President Arthur).

"It so happened there existed an obscure set of Federal regulations created only for situations like this. Not much attention had been paid to these regulations since the Old World cold war years. Congress met in joint session and passed a resolution declaring a 'significant national disaster' had occurred to the extent these emergency regulations should be followed. And drastic they were.

"First, the declaration suspended all elections and all elected officials would remain in office, including the president, with only Congress being able to remove them and elect new ones. This would remain the rule until 'such time general elections could be practically resumed.'

"Second, martial law was declared and absolutely required. The new president ordered the immediate return of all overseas military and civilian personnel (many never making it home due to similar problems in the rest of the world). She also cancelled military discharges and retirements as well as instituted a national draft. She stationed many of the functional military units around Washington and Atlanta.

"Fearing the approaching cold weather would take Washington as well, President Arthur developed a bold plan to move the capital to Atlanta. She stationed a number of troops along the route to keep Interstates 20, 85, and 95 open as well as major rail lines. Several office complexes in Atlanta were seized. The White House, Congress, and the Pentagon moved rather quickly with the rest moving within a year.

"Next, the President reorganized the military and sent available forces to retake those military installations throughout the south which had been abandon or taken over by hostile groups. Although some gun battles took place in this process, when the military in the south got organized, most armed resistance faded away. Martial law meant all looters and robbers were shot on sight. She also sent units north to retrieve military materials left there and to close those bases. Of course, many military units were given the awful job of burying or burning the dead.

"Her next target was the healthcare system which needed quick attention. The military system provided some public outreach while, after hostilities subsided, the Department of Veterans Affairs took over public healthcare since their physical structure was still intact. The Public and Indian Health services were then restarted and private hospitals and clinics reopened as they could. All health care became free of charge, as the economy and insurance industry were a total mess. Next week, more on our country's comeback."

I later had to stop in the office of Diane Win to get my finances in order. She had heard about the incident with Gov and talked to me a long time, I guess to get a feeling about how I was reacting to it all. She set up my credit account so all my chore allowance and educational stipend would be deposited directly. Since there was no paper currency, she gave me a debit card. She was an amazing girl, always with a big smile on her face and always nice to me.

I rode home on the bus with Frank and we stopped at my room first. Things had changed. Gov's bunk had been removed and a new one placed there. Two new mattresses were laid on it, still in their plastic covers. A new lock was installed on the room door. Bossard came down and gave me keys for the door and told us there would be a mandatory weekly "field day" at Delk from now on to sweep, mop and dust the rooms. Paint had been ordered for the walls and they would get an electrician to fix my light.

Before I could ask Bossard if I could move, Frank asked him if he could move in with me. Mr. Bossard quickly said okay, probably thinking I didn't want to be alone. I was thinking it was actually Frank that was scared and I suddenly had a feeling that those "couple of guys" who were shaking down Frank had something to do with Governor.

Frank and I decided to switch the new bunk with mine and use the new mattresses. When we were about to move mine I noticed a note on my pillow. It read: "Meeting today, 3 p.m., North Wing second floor john." It was signed, "Corky."

"Geez," Frank reacted, "Ben's even using his hallucination name."

We ripped the plastic off the mattresses and made up my bed. Since we had a little time before the meeting, we decided to move Frank down. I could tell he wanted to get it done as soon as he could. He had less stuff than I did so it only took us one trip. Even with a large room with nine total beds, Frank decided to take the upper bunk above mine. He made up his bed. Then we headed up to the meeting on Frank's old floor.

When we got to the shower room, Ben was standing there looking rather spiffy in his school clothes and conversing very lucidly. There were several guys there who I didn't know.

"Thanks for coming," Ben began. "I called this meeting because I'm tired of putting up with all this crap around here. I have been here for two years now and nothing ever changes. Oh, I know that some things are getting done today; there are locks being put on the doors and other changes. But it only seems they do this when something bad happens, like the other night for instance. You guys might not know Dan Kelley here, but he's the kid whose roommate died. Now, nobody is saying anything but I'm sure we can tell, with all the cops running around here, that somebody wacked him too hard. We've got these Mustangs running around here shaking down kids for money. I've seen them. I know who they are, but nobody's saying anything because they got us all scared."

Frank spoke up, "What are their names?"

A short but well-built guy standing next to Ben said, "They rotate, but the ones down here now are Bus Quint, a tall, ugly dude, and Matt Fuller, his dummy friend. I'm sure you've seen them around."

From Frank's sudden look of shock, I could tell he knew them and that they were the same ones bothering him.

Ben Holden went on, "Like I said, I have been here a while and I've tried everything. I tried complaining, but nothing ever happens. I wrote a letter to the school, no answer. I've tried running away, and the truant officers always bring me back. When they brought me back from my last jaunt around town they told me I was a ward of the state, and I have to live in the orphanage. Well, why? What am I doing here? Why does a town this size have such a big orphanage anyway?

"Like I said, I've been here a while and I have been keeping my eyes open for good guys, guys like you, guys that are tired of being scared. I think we need to start a secret brotherhood, a club. Why should the Mustangs run things here? Why don't we? We could look after each other because believe me, nobody else is going to do it!"

We all sort of looked around at each other and I could tell everyone thought it was a good idea. Then we all looked down and were quiet.

Finally, this rather tall, good-looking guy spoke up, "I'm Jim Donovan and I have a question. Most of us have noticed, Ben, that you're kind of a ..." He broke off his sentence as if he were trying to think of the right word. "Well, a nut job."

All of us laughed at his unrestrained honesty. Ben added, "I assure you I'm not. Certain trouble with the truancy officers made me resort to an insanity defense. It became so natural that I just kept doing it." Frank elbowed me.

Jim asked again, "If you've been here for two years that must make you a ninth-grader?"

"No, I'm in the eighth. I was suspended for a while for truancy and flunked a grade."

I added, "Everyone with any sense around here has told me that doing well in school gets us a ticket south and out of this dump. I would support a club only if we keep our minds on school and make it a priority."

"I couldn't agree more, that's why I picked all you guys," Ben went on. "Most of us do well, heck, Dan, you've got nothing but A's all during school, Bossard told me that. Let me introduce everyone.

"Here's Bo Schlitz, the funny guy." Bo was chubby and had a big grin on his face. "This is Jim, who you've met already. He's the ladies' man." Jim smiled. "This big lug next to me is Empire Murdock, the only exception to the smart rule." Murdock was quietly standing off to the side of Ben and he looked the part. He was big and muscular but shyly smiled and looked down. Ben pointed to the remaining guy and said, "Finally, this is Corky Wall, otherwise known as 'Corky-of-the-Wall.'"

We all laughed, Frank Davis the most of all, as we learned Ben's auditory hallucination was actually someone real and when people thought Ben was talking to himself, he was really talking to Corky. We also learned that Corky was a run-away and often hid in the insulation space between the walls, dead air space designed during construction to help the wooden buildings stay warm when the winters were colder.

Ben then introduced Frank and me. He added also, "I have a couple of more nominations. They couldn't be here now but are Albert Myers, not much in the physical area but a wizard with computers and math. Also, Frank Miller, a steady and smart guy that would also be of value in the toughness area. Anyone else?"

I suggested, "Clyde Hastings, he lives in the barn now." Frank nodded in agreement.

"Good choice," Ben said, "and Clyde's a boxer, good with his fists. Okay, so let's meet again soon. I want you guys to bring suggestions for two things, a name of the group and how we're going to work things out so we can live near each other. Let's meet again Sunday afternoon, same place."

We stood around and talked together for a while. I was happy with the guys; they seemed nice. And since we were all Delk north-wingers, we had a lot in common. We started walking out when we met a group of plumbers coming in to fix the toilets and sinks.

Frank and I went back to our room and discussed the meeting. We were both excited about the club and we both knew why. This was a new place for us, big and scary, and our life around here was anything but fun. We simply went through the motions, getting up, going to school, coming home, doing chores, and so on. We huddled in our separate rooms at night keeping one eye out for bullies and now that there was a suspicious death in the dorm, we were scared.

Frank stated, "I apologize for this since I just moved in here, but I think we should offer this room for our club. These end rooms are the biggest and there are what, ten of us now? We could fix it up and all."

"I agree," I responded, "Let's bring it up on Sunday. There would be more of us around and we wouldn't have to worry about our stuff or our lives."

Frank and I were inseparable now. We went to chores together and pitched manure for a while. That evening we came back for chow only to find our dining hall wasn't open. We went to the south one but the line was so long we had to wait for an hour and then they had run out of some of the selections. We had meatloaf and it was horrible.

There were no classes scheduled on Fridays at the schools although it was a day to go in for tutoring and extra credit, so the school buildings were open and the buses ran. Since the orphans were not known for their high academic achievements, most everyone went to school on Friday and the orphanage was almost completely empty. Certainly neither Frank nor I had anything to go in for, and remembering our wonderful meal, we decided to go out to the farm and hang out there.

Clyde was so pleased with his nomination to the club that he almost got teary-eyed. He did tell us that he had to straighten out a few matters before they would let him back in the dorm. The orphanage was a rather ominous place but it had a few good points. Primarily, there was not much they could do to misbehaving orphanage inmates; they could not kick them out because there was no place for them to go. The school detention center was mostly for school infractions. Unless the safety of students or staff was in jeopardy, punishment usually consisted of extra chores or being put in the miscreant room right behind the front desk at each of the halls. For more serious matters, the town had a jail, but all convicted serious offenders were sent to prisons in the South.

Since we didn't have to be back until Sunday morning for some religious thing, we decided to stay out on the farm and work. Local businesses having work-study agreements with the school could not work kids more than four hours a day at our age, but Milt let us hang out the rest of the time. He had just purchased a herd of young cows from one of the other farms and wanted us to take them out in a far pasture, watch them, and bring them back in at dark.

Clyde made sure he got staffs for all of us. They were just long sticks; we looked like a bunch of sheep-herders. We proceeded to the "cow barn," and herded the skittish calves down a fenced in lane to a far field. Once out there, the cattle just grazed and there was really no work involved.

Clyde pointed us to a small grove of trees, fenced off to protect it from livestock. Hopping the fence, we made our way to a small circle of stones on the ground.

"I come here a lot," Clyde said, dumping his backpack containing a small kettle, a water bottle, tin cups, and some coffee.

We gathered twigs and larger branches on the ground and built a small fire. Then Clyde proceeded to boil the coffee, in "real cowboy style."

So we sat, sipping coffee and letting the breeze blow at our backs. The September wind was beginning to get chilly; a sure sign fall was coming. We were content, sitting there and listening to the birds and the trees rustling.

Frank broke the silence, "Why can't all of life be like this?"

"I know," I added. "It's funny that even though this is a small town in the middle of a wide open space, it seems like this is the first time in my life I've been outside."

"Weren't you in that orphanage out on the peninsula; isn't it rather open out there?" Clyde asked.

"Yea, but we were always fenced in and it was rocky. No grass or trees out there."

After a couple hours of near silence, Clyde announced that he was going into the farmhands' galley and getting us some sandwiches. When Frank asked if that counted as our one meal for the day, Clyde assured him that the cook quite often let him in the back to get leftovers. He instructed us to keep an eye on the cows.

I'm not sure if it was the tranquil surroundings or not, but Frank then opened up to me some more. He told me that the accident his parents were killed in was in the newspaper. He added that they had set up trust funds for him and his sister that provided them an allowance, with lump sums to be provided when they were sixteen and again at eighteen. The two guys bullying him had read about it and wanted a portion of the allowance. He said he had resisted at first but then gave in after they hit him. Insisting that they leave his sister alone, Frank said they agreed as long as he kept paying them. I asked him if they were the mutt brothers, Bus Quint and Matt Fuller, to which he nodded.

"Frank, this is the type of stuff you need to talk to the club about," I insisted, "since Ben said that we look out for each other. That's your money, money your parents worked for."

"I know," Frank responded, "I feel so ashamed about it. I shouldn't have given in so easy. But I'd still rather have them on me instead of my sister."

"They shouldn't be on either one of you. Those guys try that again you get a cop. Get Bossard. Get me for that matter. They shouldn't even be on the orphanage grounds."

We were so involved with the discussion that we just then noticed the cattle were acting up. They were bucking and running to a far fence to try to jump it. Although they could jump pretty high, none of them made it over. Frank and I ran to the fence.

"What do we do?" Frank yelled.

"I don't know," I responded and then yelled, "Saa boss! Saa boss!" Then the funniest thing happened, they stopped, looked at me, and then started running at us.

"Okay, cowboy," Frank laughed nervously, "what now?"

The odd experience continued. They ran right over to us, stopped right by us, and started sniffing with their noses stuck out. I put my hand out and they sniffed it. Sensing I held no treats, they immediately started grazing again right there.

"Kelley! So when did you learn how to talk to cows?"

"I don't know, must have heard Milt or Clyde do it," I said, even stunned myself over the whole ordeal. Could this have been something from one of my dreams?

Clyde returned and we ate these great roast beef sandwiches and drank ice-cold water. Frank excitedly told Clyde about the alleged psychic powers I had with animals.

After lunch, Clyde set up a target on a tree with a sandwich bag and we took turns chucking our staffs at it. We were getting pretty good at it until after a couple of hours our arms began to get sore. After taking the cattle back in around four, we ate a great supper with the farmhands. Having so much fun that Friday, we went back out to the pasture on Saturday and did the same thing.

Sundays were lazy days at the orphanage. Being that most people slept in, the only open dining hall service was swift and the food wasn't really that bad. I guess it's hard to screw up breakfast. Frank and I were there because new residents had to go to church, at least for one time. Bossard told us it was a law or something.

Frank said he used to go to the Methodist church but didn't really care for it. The only religion I got in the kid orphanage was whichever local church sent over a youth minister that particular Sunday. So we decided to attend the Dylanian Christian Church, mainly because we heard they served lunch and it was close. We did not have to go ever again, just needed to sign in so the orphanage would be able to comply with the law.

It really wasn't too bad. The whole congregation met in the large lobby while the minister said a prayer; then we went with a youth group in which we just discussed our problems. Most all the kids had families and lived on the south side. Frank and I didn't talk at all but as we listened to the rather lame problems of the kids, we traded elbow bumps to communicate the fact that we would put up with all those problems to have our parents back. Then we ate about four sloppy Joes at the luncheon, crammed two each in our jacket pockets, and split.

At the meeting that afternoon, all ten of us showed up. As Frank and I walked in, this new guy, Bo, and Clyde were mocking a pretend New Orphan/Big Ears orientation at the front desk. They were a hoot, all the guys were laughing. Ben then called the meeting to order and had all of us, in alphabetical order, introduce ourselves.

Frank Davis went first. He told the story about his family and his altercation with the mutt brothers. Mentioning the remark they made about his sister, Frank also indicated his current fear for her safety. He went on to say he had a desire to go to law school someday, but was afraid he wouldn't make it with these new burdens in his life.

Second, Jim Donovan spoke. He was a lifer like me (someone who never knew their parents) whose mom left him in the hospital nursery and took a flight south. He was lucky, if one could call it that, to be in a few foster homes before landing here last year. He admitted to being sort of a con man but just did it to get food or new clothes. Jim was tall, handsome, and a smooth talker.

Clyde Hastings did admit to some problems he had with the orphanage, but vowed to clear things up and get readmitted as a resident. He didn't set any school academic records but did realize the significance of a good education. Boxing was his passion; he had a ring set up in the barn out on Milt's farm. He had a troubled childhood and used to get beaten by his alcoholic father.

Ben Holden then repeated his story. Also a lifer, he was left on the mayor's front porch as an infant. "My mom must have been from the other political party," he joked, and we all laughed.

Retelling my story, I added my feelings about academics and my fear for Frank.

Frank Miller was of average height and weight and appeared to be a nice guy. His story was rather sad. He lived with a foster family for several years. When his foster dad got his military orders south, they prepared to move and they left without Frank. They had told him they were catching a flight on a Thursday morning and when he returned from school on Wednesday afternoon, they were gone. He took a bus to the airstrip and the officials confirmed that they had already left. He appeared very bitter about it.

An interesting guy, big Empire Murdock, spoke next. His speech was a bit slow and he admitted problems in school due to a learning disability. He was always an orphan, never knew his parents or what had happened to them. Admitting being rather slow in the head, he promised he would personally strangle anyone who harmed any of us. His wink toward Frank told us his statement did not have a literal meaning. "I'm not good at school and stuff, but I take care of my friends." He also seemed lonely.

Albert Myers was very smart, tall, and chubby and seemed to be somewhat socially inept. A perfect A-student, he had a passion for math and computers.

Equally chubby but shorter, was Bo Schlitz. He did well in school and admitted to be a "prankster with a passion." An inability to fight left him only with getting even. He was picked on a lot and liked the idea of the club.

Finishing up was Corky Wall. Cork was small but wiry and loved to spy since he could hide just about anywhere. Being with a series of foster parents, some treating him with cruelty, he had a big problem trusting grown-ups. He admitted to being a discipline problem, but also saw the futility in acting that way. He really needed good friends and help with schoolwork. When Frank told him he would get both, he smiled.

"Okay," Ben spoke, "we vote on everything, right?" We nodded. "What about a club name?"

Of the names thrown out, most were gang-related: The Mad Orphans, The Blue Devils, North Wing Revenge, The Fist, and so on. Some of the guys spoke up to say our name should be about pride, a statement about honor and to reflect that we wanted to change the image of the orphanage and the south side. After thinking about it, we all agreed. Names like the Falcons, Eagles, Lions, and Buffalo were suggested. After a long discussion narrowed it down to two, the Eagles was voted in.

"Now President," Ben went on.

"Noting his excellent record as a mental patient," Al Myers laughed, "I nominate Ben Holden." There was no need for a formal vote as we all yelled in agreement.

"Master-at-Arms and Minister of Defense?" Ben continued.

"Murdock!" everyone yelled.

Ben was a little taken aback with the results of the vote and he promised to serve well. He said as time went on we could rotate presidents. He continued with setting up an intelligence group and named Al Myers and Corky to the posts. I raised my hand and wanted to be in that group as well since I was still interested in what happened to Gov Viche. All agreed.

Ben Holden had a knack for saying the right things, that's for sure. He started with, "Okay, Davis, first of all, your sister rides the bus with us up to school and back from now on. Those clowns will know better than to pull something on the school grounds. Second, I'm going to be seeing Bossard this afternoon about our group and I am going to have him notify the guards that Fuller and Quint are not to be on these grounds. And finally, you've made your last payment to those guys. Let me know when your next meeting is, and me and Murdock will go have a chat with them."

One could almost see the worry and anxiety drain out of Frank Davis after hearing that. I thought the guy was going to cry. It was then that Frank brought up the suggestion of moving into our room, since it had the space for ten guys and since Bossard would be our Resident Assistant. A vote by the group settled the issue.

While Ben went to see Bossard, the rest of us went down to our room to check it out. All seemed to like it; guys even started picking out bunks. We made sure Ben and Murdock got lowers.

Upon his return, Ben indicated all went well. Bossard approved the room arrangements with the exceptions of Clyde and Corky Wall. Holden told Clyde he thought he could get out of any extra chores by just submitting to a scolding by Bossard; Clyde agreed. Corky, on the other hand, had some serious run-away issues to deal with and had to submit to a formal hearing. Fearing some time in the Irish Fort, Corky said he would stay hidden until he could think it over. Ben also said that the staff had some cleaning and painting to do, but the guys could start moving in next weekend.

Frank and I spent a lot of the next week over at the farm, since our room was being painted and new furniture set up. Keeping with the administration's established sense of style, they painted our room in the same stupid green as before; however, at least they used a semi-gloss this time so we could get a little shine with buffing. The new bunks, enough to sleep ten, were wooden instead of military metal, and the new mattresses were thicker. An electrician, having to run new wire to the ceiling light anyway, installed a new multi-bulb fixture that really helped brighten up the room. He let me help him some and was a really cool guy. Friday moving day came. Frank and I helped the other guys move their stuff. Although the new improvements brightened up the place, nothing did more for the room atmosphere than the laughter, fellowship, and the feeling we were watching each other's backs. We arranged the furniture with the bunks against walls, so that guys could at least face the wall if they wanted to go to sleep early. The desks were placed to allow guys to stay up later and study without their desk lamps bothering anyone. Clyde had his meeting with Bossard and was allowed to join us. While still officially persona non grata, Corky always seemed to pop in whenever he wanted, and even slept there, entering after lights out. We discovered that the alarm on the emergency exit door didn't work and we could use it as a second way out if we chose.

The rest of that weekend and subsequent school week revealed the accommodations certainly improved our lives. Jokes and pranks were common and we always had enough for a game of soccer or touch football. We ate and did chores in shifts, allowing us to always have someone in the room. Study groups were held each night with Frank and me providing tutor sessions for Empire and Corky. Diane Win helped get us an online reading program for Empire to work on with a computer in the lobby lounge.

There were a few flaws. Noise, snoring and dirty clothes strewn about caused some complaints. Although an A-student as well,

Frank had to work at it a lot harder than I did. Sometimes he would go to the lobby to study when the rest of us were raising heck. However, we got by. We could, for the first time, relax and just grow up like normal boys.

Frank's sister, Libby, was a cool person. She had the same small build and dark hair that Frank had. Intelligent as well, she simply gushed at having six or seven guys escorting her on the bus. Frank's mood also seemed to rise as he had some extra time to talk with her. She did, however, once complain to me, "I don't know how I'm going to get any boys to talk to me with all these big brothers around."

Then one day as we all got on the bus after school, Empire and Ben Holden came on at the last minute. Ben had his head shaved. I mean he was completely bald. Empire and he sat down on the same seat Libby Davis was in, squeezing her in the middle of them. Empire was looking out the window and laughing uncontrollably. A wide-eyed Libby was looking up at Ben with astonishment, "What the heck did you do?"

"Libby," Ben joked, although one could never be sure, "why don't you just admit that you love me?"

She countered, rolling her eyes, "Because I need a boyfriend with a few more marbles than you got."

"Don't you like what I've done with my hair?"

"Geez," she said, throwing her hands up in the air.

None of us had ever seen Murdock laugh like that; tears were rolling down his cheeks.

"Ben, what happened?" I asked.

"Shhh," he whispered, "can't tell ya here."

After walking Libby down to her hall, we came back to the room and Empire fell onto his bunk, laughing hysterically. After restoring some composure, he told us the story. "So, we go to meet Quint and Fuller near the gym about Davis' payment. Only they didn't show up, they sent some other clown we've never seen.

Only he don't know Holden. So we approach him and he wants to know where Davis is and the money. So Baldy here pulls these pills out of his pocket and says he's Frank's cousin, and that Frank is going to need all his money to buy this special medication for Ben and he won't be paying any more shake-down money. Holden said he was sorry but the last time he stopped taking his medication he beat his parents to death with a baseball bat while they were lying in bed. The guy just freaks out, mumbles something, then just walks away shaking his head."

One of the guys asked, "Who the heck shaved your head?"

Ben replied, "Oh, over at the tech school, at the barber college, they did it for free. Kind of makes me look more psychotic, does it not?"

We all laughed. Frank then explained that while Murdock would fight anyone, Quint and Fuller were pretty big and had a couple of years on both of them. We needed to come up with a plan that would both notify them that payments were ending and hopefully put a little fear in them. Ben wasn't too sure about the latter, and said we needed to watch Frank and his sister because we would probably hear from the Mustangs again.

One morning in homeroom, Betsy Barney attacked me again, "I thought you were going to ask Claire out? You'd better hurry up, other guys are starting to ask her and she likes you. There's a dance this Thursday night, ask her and meet her there."

I felt pretty comfortable about everything else, so I decided to ask out Claire Popover. She seemed happy about it. The dance was at the community recreation center on the north side. Not having any idea how to get there, Corky gave me directions and told me which bus to take.

On Thursday evening, the guys all gave me advice on what to do on a date, as I had no idea. Jim Donovan held the expertise in that area. I had a good shirt, but Frank Miller loaned me his dress jacket. I decided to skip the tie.

So I caught the bus up to the north side and met Claire at the dance. She looked real cute in her dress. We danced some, mainly slow ones, and drank awful punch. She was nice, but quiet. I guess we were both awkward. She whispered a lot of stuff to her friend. Neither Betsy Barney nor Claire's sister were about. When the music was over I walked her out to a car with her mother sitting in it. Mom called me Daniel. Daniel, can you believe it? Nobody called me that.

I walked up to the bus stop only to see Corky Wall standing inside the shelter, trying to remain unnoticed by looking the other way. I walked over to him, "Cork, taking a bus tour of the north side?"

He put his head down, a little embarrassed, "Yea, all of us orphans just love it up here 'cause we're so appreciated."

"What are you doing here?"

"Holden asked me to keep an eye on you," Cork admitted.

"You didn't need to do that, Cork."

He looked up at me, a totally serious look on his face, "And you're an A-student who doesn't need to teach Murdock how to read and help me with dummy math either. Let's just say I take care of my friends."

We rode back in silence, which is good because I had tears in my eyes.

Mr. Principi's classes weren't always great. Sometimes he would have us do small group discussions on a particular concept. They had little value as he never graded them at all, even telling us so in the first class. He worked on his next book while we talked about everything other than history. Being the youngest kid in there, I didn't have a lot to talk about with the high schoolers. Cheri, this total babe of a junior, who sat next to me, would go on and on about her boyfriend and her life. As we got to know each other, however, she became friendly and nice. We usually talked to each other and not to the rest of our group.

But this day Principi did do a lecture that I recorded on my wristwatch. "With the import/export system in complete disarray, the government then reorganized agriculture. Those southern residents lucky enough to still control their farms were required to get them up and running. Abandoned land was taken over by the Department of Agriculture, staffed with Federal employees, and put to work. All farming in the north and west ceased.

"I cannot overstate the positive impact Campbell Arthur had on this country.

"Next she took on education. Faced with a remaining population of about ten percent of its former numbers, she 'militarized' the Department of Education, assigning all teachers as civil service employees in the non-uniformed 'Teacher Corps.' Elementary education remained much the same, but high school and college students needed to be directed into certain shortage occupations that were vital to the survival of the nation. They accomplished this by an elaborate system of financial incentives. For example, if a student wanted to be a pipefitter, he or she would receive free tuition and books as well as a living allowance. If one chose to be a philosopher, they would get nothing and pay a hefty tuition.

"Probably the most significant non-governmental contribution was made by the faith-based organizations. They assisted in the elimination of violence in The Chaos and gave people a sense of moral community. Their parochial schools cooperated with, and supplemented, the nationalized public school system.

"President Arthur died in office, being the only U.S. president to serve thirty-one years. The following year general elections resumed.

"The political subdivisions of the United States went through quite a change. The northern and western states maintained 'governments in exile' throughout the south and still sent people to Congress. Critics soon complained these representatives did not represent anyone. As northwestern immigrants either died in the plague or from old age, geographical and emotional ties to these areas died as well. States were eventually redesigned as territories and lost the power to be represented in Congress. The presidents appointed territorial governors for years but this practice was eventually stopped as well. The states now consisted of South Virginia, North Carolina, South Carolina, Georgia, Florida, Tennessee, Alabama, Mississippi, Arkansas, Louisiana, and East Texas. All other territories were assigned to the Department of the Interior."

We held formal club meetings every Wednesday night and Sunday afternoon. Starting out as general complaint sessions either about orphanage conditions or a dirty room, the meetings slowly began to formally develop our association. We started a bank account and all members paid ten percent of their earnings into it. Being good with both local regulations and banking, we made Frank Davis, "The Attorney," treasurer. Clyde was asked to develop and schedule boxing lessons for all of us. Master-at-Arms Empire was told by Ben that Bossard was unhappy about the appearance of our room and that he was to organize clean up before we left for school.

After one formal meeting, Ben met with Al Myers, Corky and me to discuss our intelligence plans. The most pressing issue was Frank Davis.

"Nobody's even tried to mess with Libby Davis," Cork added.

"Yea," Ben said, "that's what bothers me. Bossard told me today that Quint and Fuller have not even been seen on the grounds since. I've been putting two and two together and something bothers me about this whole deal."

"What?" Al asked.

Ben went on, "These Mustangs are a bunch of bullies who shake down school kids for lunch money. They hit Frank, but I don't think they want to kidnap or kill anybody. I think if they did that to Viche, as Kelley thinks, then it was a mistake. Heck, the kid had all kinds of bone deformities, they probably lightly bopped him, but he was so fragile they crushed his skull. And since then they dropped out of sight, I think they're scared and are waiting for this to blow over."

I interjected rather harshly, "If they hit him with a sledge hammer or if they hit him with a feather, Ben, and crushed his skull, then it's still murder."

"I'm not trying to make excuses for them, Dan," Ben defended himself, "I'm just looking at what they're going to do next and how we can prove they did that to Gov. Why don't you call that military investigator and get an update?"

"Okay," I calmed down.

"My only fear is if they're not allowed on the grounds, they may try to recruit some residents here, which would make it easier to get at Libby or Frank. Cork, you know a lot of guys in this and the other male hall; ask around."

"Will do," Corky replied.

"Al Myers, you can get into school records and such?" Al smiled. "Start with the two mutt brothers, check them out, and then find out who else is in this gang. Let's get some dirt on these guys."

After our meeting broke up, I lay on my bunk and thought for a while. Sure, I worried about Frank, but I also didn't want anyone to forget Governor Viche.

One day I borrowed Myers' handheld computer and called Mr. Cummings. While he didn't appear to share my passion for the case, I was surprised he even discussed it with me. He admitted he was at a dead end. They found no "blunt instrument" weapon, no witnesses and no clues. At first he thought someone entered my room and did the crime, but the desk people indicated no strangers entered. Taking the angle that someone hit Gov outside the building and he walked in later and went to bed, Cummings found no one who saw the bleeding kid enter the hall. Now he was concentrating on one of the staff or residents possibly doing it. He indicated that, while everyone thought Gov Viche was "creepy," he found no one who had a grudge against the kid. I asked about Quint and Fuller, and Cummings indicated that Quint's dad swore the two were at the Quint residence all afternoon and evening. He concluded by telling me to keep my ears open and to report to him any suspicious information. I hung up. Something didn't seem right.

A few days later Al Myers, Corky and I met near my bunk and went over the information we had so far. I summarized my talk with Cummings and added that things didn't appear to add up.

Frank Davis was seated at his desk and spoke up right away, "I can tell you what doesn't add up. How can Quint's dad say he was home all afternoon when those two goons met me out in front of Delk Hall?"

"When?" I asked.

"Just before we went out to the farm."

I was stunned, "Darn! I forgot about that." I made a note of it while the meeting continued.

Corky Wall reported that the Mustangs were talking to guys over in the west wing of Delk and also at Price Hall. They were approaching them at school where the buses unloaded. He knew of no takers so far, as most of the guys knew of the Mustangs and didn't like them. He also named off some other members people knew about and had given those names to Myers.

Al Myers went over a lot of information he obtained on the goofy twins. Matt Fuller was some sort of rebellious teen from a middle-class good family. Quint was from a broken home, his dad an unemployed alcoholic, and had countless school disciplinary actions and a town police record. Al was a genius; he knew their birthdates, birthplaces, school grades since kindergarten, school activities, police records and addresses. Tall and ugly Quint didn't date anyone, big surprise, but Fuller was a big time ladies' man. Al even knew where they ordered pizza. He finished by stating he was going to learn everything he could about the Mustangs as an organization, mentioning the difficulties of such an endeavor since this stuff didn't exist in written or computerized records.

The weeks wore on. Al learned more about the Mustangs, but progress was slow. I was at a dead end as well with my analysis of the Governor affair. However, we were all getting into a rhythm with schoolwork and life in general. Claire became my "almost steady" girlfriend although we never did talk that much. We never went to any more dances, and our social engagements consisted of standing next to each other in the hall while she whispered to her girlfriend. The day I celebrated my birthday was coming up in December.

The week of Thanksgiving a most unfortunate incident occurred. Orphans don't get the same thrill out of the family holidays that is experienced by the general population. We tend to be a bit quiet and annoyed during those times. The orphanage, I'm sure, would have a turkey dinner on Thursday and maybe arrange a gift exchange on Christmas, but most holiday cheer was wasted on us.

So, it was Thanksgiving week and most of us were pretty irritable anyway, when on Monday both dining halls were somehow closed for the evening meal. There was no warning or any such announcement, just a handwritten note on the door saying sorry. So Frank, Corky, Bo Schlitz and I were walking back to the dorm fuming.

When we entered the lobby, Ben Holden was standing at attention in the lobby, continuing his crazy routine. Incensed, I walked up to the desk only to find Big Ears reading his comic book. Although I spoke in a low volume, the tone of my voice gave away my anger.

"Both of the dining halls are closed. Can you please tell us what we are going to eat?"

Big Ears snipped, "You can check the garbage can by the vending machines for all I care."

"I don't think you're hearing me, and that's kind of surprising with those ears of yours!"

He put his comic book down and stared at me, "They probably can't staff the dining halls if that's any consolation; you pigs are lucky …"

Suddenly, Ben Holden was standing right next to me, and it startled Big Ears. "Now look here!" With a rapid quick movement, Ben reached out with his right arm, grabbed Big Ears by the collar, and pulled him up and across the desk; his feet were dangling off the ground.

Ben swung his left arm around, stopping just before the kid's nose, put his thumb and forefinger about an inch apart, and said, "I'm about this close to goin' off right now. The 'pig' didn't ask to be here. Now tell him where he can get a meal!"

Big Ears began squirming and his face turned red, "I'm an official of this …"

"And I'm a mental patient," Ben snapped, "Who do you think's gonna come out ahead here, short term?"

"You let me go, you loony nut cake!" he begged.

"When you tell the kid where he can eat!"

"Tell him to take his darn meal pass to Monical's Pizza, two blocks north. They'll give him a couple slices."

Ben let Big Ears go. He slid down the side of the desk, fell back into his chair, and toppled over backwards. He jumped up to his feet and ran for the main door, yelling something about getting the cops.

Later the five of us were walking up to the pizza place. Everyone was chuckling, except Frank, who warned, "There's going to be the devil to pay for this one, big guy."

CHAPTER THREE

The week after Thanksgiving, Ben got his formal notice to appear before an orphanage disciplinary board for the charge of assault in what was hereafter referred to as the Big Ears Incident. Ben asked Frank Davis to represent him, which Frank certainly became nervous about. When I told Ben this would put a lot of pressure on Frank, he replied, "Dan, here's a lesson on survival. Whenever you need help with a problem and no one around has any experience, always pick someone who cares about you."

Frank studied the written disciplinary board process until he had it memorized, and then started working on his presentation. His legal experience consisted of watching lawyer shows on satellite. Of course, he wanted me to assist him.

The day of the hearing, over in the orphanage administration building, found Frank, Ben, and me in our best clothes, seated at a table. At the next table sat Big Ears and some female pre-law student.

When the board came in, we stood up. Frank was going to use every trick he could. Taking their seats, the board consisted of:

some tall thin dude none of us knew, this mean looking lady with glasses, and, surprisingly, Monica from the front desk.

As we sat, Frank leaned over and whispered to me, "What the heck is she doing here; I thought she was a work-study student?" I shook my head.

The mean lady, sitting in the middle, read the charges, "Mr. Holden, you have been charged with assault on Mr. Montague Fisher, an official of the orphanage. Mr. Davis, you are representing Mr. Holden. Do you want a formal reading of the charges?"

"No, your honor," Frank replied, "Mr. Holden will not be contesting the charges, but we would like to present mitigating circumstances."

The lady said her name was Mrs. Cass and we did not have to call her "honor", but Frank kept doing it anyway and she never mentioned it again.

"Since the charge of assault will not be contested, we will not have Mr. Fisher testify at this time, but he can be present to respond to the circumstances," Mrs. Cass said. The pre-law student nodded.

Frank started to go over the disciplinary board regulations, but Mrs. Cass told him they were well aware of the regulations and there was no need for him reciting them to her.

Frank called me as a witness. After going over my encounter with Big Ears upon checking in, I talked about the Gov Viche incident and the dining halls being closed, as indications of building stress in Delk Hall.

Ben was then questioned about his mental status as Frank was going after an emotional state defense. He indicated he had been to the base psychiatrist where he had been prescribed medication. After Ben was dismissed, Frank leaned down to me and whispered, "He should have gotten a law student to defend him."

When her honor asked Big Ears' counsel to comment, she surprisingly said that since no one is contesting that the assault happened, she had nothing to gain by calling Big Ears as a witness. Equally surprising, Monica spoke up.

"I have a few things. Mr. Davis, I have Mr. Holden's medical report here, the one that the psychiatrist wrote to the orphanage, and I would like to read from it. It says, 'While I have prescribed a neuroleptic for complaints of auditory hallucinations, Mr. Holden's clinical picture is inconsistent with psychosis and a strong argument for malingering exists.' How can you say Mr. Holden assaulted Mr. Fisher because of mental illness when the doctor says he is faking?"

Frank, as well as both Ben and I, was caught off guard by the obvious leading question. Frank hung in there, "He didn't say he was faking, he said maybe. There's still a good maybe he isn't." Then he got a little testy, "Maybe you think you can substitute your extensive knowledge for a board certified psychiatrist, but I don't think her honor would go for that. I'm not sure what a work-study student is doing on this panel anyway and ..."

Mrs. Cass snapped, "Mr. Davis! That's enough. She is an official of the orphanage now and her membership on this panel was approved by me."

Frank immediately quieted, but he had made Ben and me proud with his outburst. Monica's presence here today, and her question, certainly raised some concerns in my mind. What was going on?

Ben was found guilty and given a week in the detention center. Her honor said she could have given him a month, but since there were circumstances related to the situation, she would be lenient. As the three panel members exited, I thought I noticed a faint grin on Monica's face.

Taking it in stride, Ben announced to a contrite Frank Davis the fact that he could have gotten a month was a sign of Frank's success. Frank had done well for his age. Ben went in on a Friday morning. Since no visitors are allowed during one's first week of incarceration, we were restricted to walking over from school and making obscene gestures to an orange jump-suited Ben in the cyclone-fenced exercise yard. He returned the favor. Once Bo Schlitz bought a cake, put a file in it, and tried, unsuccessfully, to visit Ben. This stunt did not sit well with the guards.

During that week, I had an unfortunate incident in homeroom. Upon taking my seat, I was bombarded by a nasty Betsy Barney, "Hey, when you left that dance, the one that you took Claire to, a friend of mine saw you taking the bus home. Why didn't your parents pick you up?"

"They haven't been too good at keeping appointments lately," was my sarcastic response.

"Where do you live?"

"The Centura Orphanage."

"I thought you said your parents didn't …"

"They died when I was four."

Expecting a "sorry to hear that," Betsy plastered me, "Why did you lie to Claire about that? That's not funny."

"I didn't lie to her; it never came up."

"Why didn't you tell her?"

"Why does it matter?"

"You are smart; we just figured you were from the north side. We had no idea you lived in the orphanage. Her mom won't go for that; she's on the town council you know. You should have thought about misleading Claire like that."

"Well, why don't we let Claire decide that? Who gives a flip what you or her mom thinks?"

"We don't want you in our study group," she snapped, although she had never told me when or where the stupid study group met.

So, I lost my first girlfriend in a classic case of orphan prejudice. It was terrible of me, how I could fake being smart and cool while not having any parents or living on the south side of town. She wasn't really much of a girlfriend, I guess. No more long, passionate moments of me standing next to her in the hall while she whispered to her friend. The Eagles never let up on me about it. Bo and Clyde put on a skit with Bo putting on a blonde wig and playing the role of Claire. He referred to me as a "dirty orphan" in this high-pitched voice and how peoples' brains don't develop until after age four. Empire and Corky put fake love notes from Claire under my pillow saying that despite Betsy and her mom, she really desired a dumb orphan boy.

One day at the bus stop outside of school, I was looking down the long line of waiting students, and at the far end of the line I saw Monica, arm-in-arm, with Matt Fuller.

History class continued one day with a great lecture. "There is no definite, agreed upon date the 'Big Thaw' commenced, but signs of the end of the mini ice age started showing up around 2700. Aerial photos showed the ice sheet retreating rapidly north. Most signs of civilization were already gone. Any structures less than three stories tall had been knocked flat by the ice and during the century after the melt. Taller structures, like skyscrapers in large cities, and more permanent ones, like bridges, toppled as well. Wind and water borne soil covered all and vegetation reclaimed the landscape. It began to resemble the landscape as it looked when Columbus arrived.

"But the plague and the extended cold snap had other consequences. The population of this and other countries of the world retreated into small pockets of civilization, the people isolated into tiny geographical areas. There was a mood of profound disappointment. The technology that the human race had relied so heavily on and was so proud of did nothing to prevent catastrophe. Since such a great deal of our technological effort began to be diverted to mere survival, we entered yet another dark age. Research funding came to a halt; professional journals by the thousands began to stop publication; and we became a species of dopes.

"About 2950, it became a popular issue to protect the entire United States from any yet-to-be-defined threat, so a few military outposts were approved by the government. Bases were constructed on Long Island, and in Washington, D.C., Thompson, San Antonio, and Southern California. One was considered in Oregon Territory but was cancelled due to cost. The base in California had and still has only active duty personnel stationed there due to the distance. Only Washington had overland access as Long Island, Southern California, and Thompson could only be supplied by air. The latter three were constructed to be as self-sufficient as possible.

"The current status in 3063 is much as it has been for the past three centuries. The government as always supported resettlement of the west and north, but only half-heartedly. There are several reasons for this.

"The U.S. never regained the population base needed to expand. The plague allegedly caused some genetic problems in the surviving human population that drastically reduced the fertility rate. The population has not increased in over 9 years. We also cannot maintain a sufficient number of active duty military personnel to provide appropriate protection for pioneers. Also, being outside the service area of public utilities and emergency services means no help for stranded people in jeopardy. Being beyond the distance a helicopter can reach on a half tank of gas means doom for someone in need.

"With so few people, everyone had enough food to eat and money to spend in the area we now occupy. There was no longer a pressing need to wean off of fossil fuel since demand had drastically fallen. Oh, there were a few nut cases who took off into the wilderness, only to perish or limp back home, since there were no roads or train tracks or gas stations out there either. There were a few privately funded expeditions. One company created a settlement near Old Saint Louis on the Illinois side of the Mississippi river. It lasted about five years, got into problems with its creditors, and finally got wiped out by a flood. The government even instituted a revised homestead act, increasing the land grant to one square mile if people developed the land for five years. Few took the offer. The summers are warmer now, but the winters are still hard in the north, as you all well know. The large snow and ice sheets melted, but our spirit to live and advance has yet to thaw out."

Ben got out the next Friday. We had a special meeting in the room to discuss what he had learned there, and it was interesting.

Holden said he did not have it too bad. Besides the lack of freedom, he indicated that the facility was in good shape and the food was actually better than the orphanage. He also lost no school time as all the courses were presented via satellite in the center. He said everyone should spend at least a week there. He was given a wealth of information regarding the street life by fellow inmates.

It seems the Mustangs were about the most powerful gang here, and we were facing a formidable enemy with over thirty-five members. They have a clubhouse at an abandon warehouse on the south side with an old barn out west of town where they store cars, weapons, and contraband. They earn money by shaking down kids, petty theft, and confidence scams they pull on the elderly. Consisting of mainly junior high, and high school students, and dropouts, their current president is a guy named Marv Greene.

Another south side gang was Holy Cross. They were thought to have a membership of only Roman Catholic kids, and their numbers, location, philosophy and source of income were unknown. A third group known as The Range, inhabited a neighborhood of the same name on the far east edge of the south side, near the lake. Believed to mainly stick to themselves and stay near home, they would fight anyone at the drop of a hat. They wore gothic clothing.

The groups on the north side were not very organized. There was a jock group, a school political group, and a group of radical feminists. Only the jocks would fight if threatened and they certainly were in a physical shape to cause some damage.

Ben had the addresses of the Mustang headquarters and the barn, as well as names of most members. The mutt brothers were supposedly assigned to shake down the orphanage as we expected. Ben gave all the names to Al Myers to start developing files on them.

We decided to break for supper, so we all headed to the dining hall to eat. About half way there, Clyde mentioned he forgot his meal pass and went back to the dorm to get it. We all proceeded to the hall to get in line.

During our meal, we all joined in teasing Ben. We asked him if he learned how to hot wire cars, if he learned any burglary skills, and if he was working on a plan to bust out. Through it all, Ben just smiled and shook his head. Then he dropped his fork, his smile faded, "Where the heck is Clyde?"

We left everything on the table instead of bussing our plates, and rushed out the door and back to Delk. When we got there, the door was wide open and the room was a mess. A couple of locker doors had been pried open, some mattresses pulled off the bunks, and some desks had open drawers with papers strewn about. Clyde was sitting on a desk chair, his face red, his eye puffy, and his fists bleeding. He looked up at us and said quietly, "Well, heck, you should see the other guys."

We rushed over to him, "What happened?"

"I guess I came in and interrupted the panty raid," Clyde moaned, "There were three of them."

"Did you recognize them?"

"No, they had masks on. We might be able to spot them. I smacked two pretty hard. I'd know the third; he led with his right, pretty good punch, he got me good. They split when I started yelling at them."

We stood Clyde up and brushed him off; Ben suggested we take him to the nurse. Clyde then looked right at Ben, "You know, someday I'm going to burn this place down."

We took Clyde to the administration building. The nurse cleaned him up and put a bandage on his right hand. Bossard then came in and Ben read him the riot act. Ben asked him if he wanted us to carry around nightsticks, like an armed gang, and be ready to fight anytime and anywhere. He got pretty riled, saying the Eagles were doing their schoolwork, doing their chores, keeping their space clean, and not causing any trouble. If we were going to be continually punished for being orphans, then we didn't want anything to do with the stupid orphanage. We were all in agreement and poor Bossard let us pour out our rage and frustration, and just stood there nodding.

We spent the evening in our room discussing the situation and coming up with a plan while a locksmith fixed the door and added a deadbolt to the lockset. Security came in and made out a report. After all had cleared out, Ben's characteristic rationality returned. He said they must have been watching our room since they had known we had all left for the dining hall, and obviously weren't expecting Clyde to return so soon. Corky said how interesting it was that no one was on duty at the front desk that afternoon. Frank Miller added, since security had been doing a pretty good job at keeping strangers off the grounds, it appeared the intruders may be Delk Hall inmates or even north wingers. Frank Davis proposed it was all about him and retaliation for not paying them.

Ben then said what we were all thinking, but didn't want to hear, "So, they'll give us a new lock, add extra security, and so on and so on. Then things will go back to the same old crap.

Nobody's gonna do anything, guys, and we have no retreat. I don't want to do this anymore than you guys do, but we're going to have to confront them. There's gonna be a fight here, soon enough. We'll plan, we'll train, and we'll take it to them straight on. And if they beat the crap out of us, we'll patch up, retrain, and hit them again. And we'll keep doing it until we get some respect around here. Anybody want to vote on that?"

Nobody did.

Ben, Clyde, and Jim Donovan met with Milt Frazer the following morning and worked out a great deal. They offered him ten good workers who could put in four-hour days, more on weekends, for the one meal a day and a place to bunk up. We would even stagger our hours so guys would be available for morning cattle feedings, milking, and evening feedings.

Milt was surprisingly interested. He said the farmers' association had been giving him heck about his herd lowering the price of milk paid by the military, by competing against the two larger dairy operations in the area. He agreed to stop dairy if they would let him expand his beef herd and crop acreage. He was also getting heck from his wife for the demanding schedule it took to run the dairy and how he could never take a day off. What this boiled down to was, we could use the heated dairy "clean" rooms for a dorm and would still be needed for help with the beef herd. Milt hit us with strict rules: the orphanage had to approve, our schoolwork had to get done, no parties, no fighting, and no visitors spending the nights. We agreed.

We spent the rest of the weekend moving over to the barn. Bossard reluctantly agreed with our plan and said he would keep it off the record as long as we kept the orphanage beds made and the room clean, to look like we lived there. He even gave us some furniture the orphanage was getting get rid of.

The accommodations were a little rough at first while Milt slowly sold off the herd and had to keep the equipment installed and working. We had a rather small sleeping room for ten guys and it had a cement floor. We did have both a male and female restroom with showers that we could use. Since we had the evening meal in the farmhand chow hall and lunch at school, we made do with dried cereal and a toaster for breakfast. As time went on and the equipment was removed, we could eventually expand our sleeping rooms and add desks and couches. Corky even found an old satellite monitor being thrown out and Al Myers hooked it up to Milt's satellite feed.

Meanwhile, Clyde put us to work in his makeshift boxing gym. He even got one of the farmhands, an ex-boxer, to show us some moves. "First of all, if this gets back to Milt, I'll take all ten of you on." He showed us defense, how to block and redirect punches. Then he went over some offensive strategy. He said most of us, including me, had some promise, but when Al Myers and Bo Schlitz put on their exhibition, he turned to Clyde and said, "Put those two in the back." Continuing, he went over the two major mistakes young kids make with boxing. "First, they come at you wildly throwing hay-makers. Just back up or step aside, let them wail at air; they'll either make themselves tired or throw out a shoulder joint. Next is they might try to get cute, try kicking you or pulling your coat over your head. Never do that. If you get off balance someone will knock you on your ass. Stay on both feet, stay balanced, and keep your guard up. You don't always have to be punching, keep watching and wait. Ninety percent of your most damaging punches will be right after they throw one, when they throw out an arm they leave an entry open. When you land one that stuns them, go in and go in hard. Don't be afraid to step to the side or back up, in fact, do that more than moving forward. When you charge someone you tend to lean in, that's not being balanced, you're face moves out in front of your guard someone will smack it." He then sparred with Clyde and went over all these aspects with us. Despite being an old, little man; he sure could swing.

After the demonstration, Ben went over his formation. Cork would remain out front, in front of Murdock, but he could always drop back into the line if the situation called for it. The next line would be me, Murdock, and Clyde. Behind them would be Frank Davis, Ben and Jim Donovan, with Davis and Donovan fanning out to extend the first line if needed. Myers, Schlitz, and Miller would be in the back to protect the rear, help with the wounded, or push up to the second line if someone went down. We practiced shadow boxing in formation while several scenarios were acted out. With Frank Davis not getting it, Ben switched him with Frank Miller. We finished with each of us punching a hanging bale of hay for a few minutes.

We practiced for the next few days while we sent Corky to get a fight started. It turned out to be a pretty easy job for him. Not being enrolled in school, he had to wait for the mutt brothers out by the buses. The fight was on, out back of the north dining hall, just off the orphanage grounds and on the Tuesday before school let out for the holidays. When we asked Cork how he did it, he explained, "There's two sure fire ways to get a fight started, either insult the guy's mother or question his sexual orientation. I just told them they were good at picking us off, one by one; let's see how you sissies do in a real fight."

So on Tuesday we donned our old clothes and headed over from the barn. Everyone was nervous. When we arrived, we noticed a large crowd had formed around the famous Mustangs. We weren't surprised, but rather dismayed, to see they outnumbered us at least three to one and some of them were pretty big. We saw Fuller and Quint, but they were standing way in the rear. Our only hope was that we saw two security guards from the orphanage on the back patio of the dining hall. They looked like they were on their radios, calling something in. We walked up as Ben came out front and turned around.

"Okay, form up," he said. "Cork, see that small guy on the left? Go straight at him. Okay, guys, on my word, we take off right into them. No parley, no negotiations, no show for the crowd. Everybody goes." Ben got in his place in line and yelled, "Go!"

We ran at them like mad. Corky ran right up to the guy who was talking and hit him so hard the sound echoed in the tall trees. Then he ran at another, swinging wildly. I ran into one big guy, bounced right off him, recovered, swung a left and missed his face by an inch. I could tell he was more startled than anything else. Coming back with a right I suddenly saw a forearm swing into sight, not seeing who it came from. He knocked me so hard I instantly fell to the ground. I heard punches, and swearing, and saw the guy I had run into grab my shirt and get ready to throw a right at me, when Ben ran into him and knocked him to the ground. I was in a daze. Things appeared in slow motion. Someone else grabbed my shirt; I looked up to see a security guard pulling me to my feet.

Gradually, as my sight returned, I saw a gang of security guards and resident assistants holding onto us. The Mustangs and most of the crowd were running into the trees. Suddenly, my head felt like someone had hit me with a four by four.

The guards yelled at us for several minutes, and then told us to go back to our rooms. We shuffled back to Milt's farm, my arm around Murdock's shoulder. The guys were whipped. We underestimated the energy even a brief fight would take. But we were certainly not depressed. Some even cracked jokes.

When we got back to our barn, a good deal of excited talk began. Ben summarized, "Well, we didn't do that bad."

"Who won?" I asked.

"Oh," Ben replied, "can't say we really won, but we hung in there." He went on to say that Cork and Empire and Clyde were awesome. Cork and Empire caused the most damage, actually drawing some blood, and they just couldn't touch Clyde. He danced around, avoided punches, and landed several himself. Even pretty boy Donovan went out wide and had a pretty good slugfest with one guy. Donovan was bloody but was smiling and joking. I think we felt good just fighting back.

Then Ben looked at me, "Oh, gosh, Kelley, you look like you got in a fight with a bull dozer and guess who won?" Schlitz arrived with an ice bag and pressed it against the side of my face.

When I looked into the mirror the next morning, the whole right side of my face was totally black and blue. But nothing was going to stop me from going to school, proudly displaying my badge of courage.

Even school was interesting. Instead of me being teased and laughed at, people were getting out of my way. I'd lost the fight, but I was there, and that was what was important.

An upper classman in History put his hand on my shoulder and laughed, "Who got the best of you, man?"

I reached up and knocked his arm away, "You wanna give it try right now?"

He jumped back and apologized, "Just kidding, man, no problem, and no I don't."

Mr. Principi called the class to order, when he looked at me he frowned, "Mr. Kelley, I need to see you after class." He then began his final lecture.

"So, my students, this leaves us with our present situation, and present questions. The U.S. remains internationally isolated. The import/export business is only a trickle compared to what it once was. International flights still take place to southern Europe, although no U.S. airlines fly there any longer, so international travel is pretty minimal as well. A ship or plane disaster crossing the Atlantic means no survivors. No one could get there to save them. We have put a few more satellites into orbit to reestablish our communications and they are the only way we can keep track of our former enemies. Manned space flights exist only in the Old World history books.

"Harold Mast was the previous Secretary of Defense, who at his retirement gave a speech containing this quote: 'I have had the easiest job in the world. U.S. Navy ships patrol and protect our coasts against an enemy navy which cannot sail here. The Air Force flies over our country to protect against an enemy air force which cannot fly here. And the Army protects us against an enemy who cannot march here.'

"We teach our young nuclear physics and plumbing, but hardly anyone in history and the arts. My question to you, class, is our species crawling toward re-enlightenment or limping toward extinction?"

Those words just cut right into me, I wanted to applaud, but the rest of the class just got up and filed out. The smart aleck behind me apologized again before he left. He was threatened by my propensity to fight when he should have been afraid of Mr. Principi's question.

Mr. Principi stood cleaning his glasses and smiling. Obviously, we were the only two in the class who were proud of the course he just taught. He picked up some stuff on his desk and slowly shuffled his way over to my desk with his walker. He dropped a package on my desk, saying, "We'll get to this later." Then he threw my final exam on the desk, a big red A+ was written on it.

"On the final essay question here, you answered the question I just asked, you know?" he pointed at the paper, "But it bothers me. You took the extinction approach, didn't you? Your answer was formulated in a grand manner, with examples as well from your personal life. This is college-level work. But you have baggage, dear sir."

I put my head down, "The plague, The Chaos, the Blue Solution, all examples, Doctor. I don't know where we're going or where I'm going."

"You forgot to add your parents leaving you stranded in the middle of the wilderness, how fate put you in that orphanage, and why your roommate died." He certainly knew more than I had thought. "You see these fingers, Mr. Kelley?" He stuck out two bent and disfigured index fingers. "I typed a 188-page doctoral thesis with these two fingers. I should be on faculty at Florida State, yet I'm teaching high school history in God-help-us, Illinois. I see you can fight, or should I say, I see you are not afraid to fight, not sure you're too good at it yet. But do me two favors; don't learn how to fight too well. Find another path to rage in. That's all, see you in January."

He turned and shuffled away; I stood up, grabbed my books and package, and headed for the door. "Oh, Doctor, what's the second favor?"

He smiled, "Why, to take my course in Old World history next semester, what else?"

When I got to my locker, I opened the package to see a state-of-the-art handheld computer of my very own. I stuffed it in my orphanage-issue coat.

Finally, Christmas break was here. As I indicated earlier, orphans never get too excited over the holidays. We did go over to the dining hall on Christmas Eve and ate our turkey dinner. We then visited our dorm to see actual uniformed security guards watching the front desk. On Christmas day we just fed cows and laid in bed reading or playing games. I played with my computer. It had a fully functioning computer, a phone, and an independent GPS locator; these were sometimes given by teachers to a student with the highest GPA in the class. We could access local web services, including the school's satellite campus, and local phone calls. Long distance emails or calls had to go through a local server, and then to a satellite that electronically deducted the cost from your savings account.

Frank Davis then returned from his visit with his sister. Frank wore a new school letter jacket that his sister had bought him. We didn't really have formal athletics since we couldn't compete with any other school, but guys usually attached intramural sports or academic achievement patches on them. Frank put his hands in his pockets and modeled the coat for us while we hooted and hollered like he was a model on a runway. When he pulled his hand out of his pocket, a slip of paper fell to the ground. Frank picked it up, "Inspected by #21 – Athletic Wear, Inc.," he read, "I wonder if number twenty one knew that a totally handsome guy would be wearing this coat?"

As Frank opened the coat, Jim Donavon asked, "What's that pocket for?" He pointed at the inside, right hand side. There was a usual inside pocket for wallets or phones, but another smaller pocket with a buttoned closure was just above it.

"I don't know," Frank replied, "for a watch, or a small cell phone?" He opened it up and pulled out another slip of paper. "Oh, #21 again, another inspection sticker."

I suddenly jumped up from my bed and looked at the pocket. I walked to the other side of the room to where Corky Wall was sitting and asked, "Cork, I need a favor."

"Anything, Dan, just ask."

"Can you get me into someone's locker at school?"

"Those cheap things, I have a passkey," he smiled, "whose locker?"

"Matt Fuller."

School started in January and I knew I had to do this on the first day. I actually discovered Fuller's locker was not too far from mine, only down the hall. Not taking a chance to do this between classes and get caught, I got a yellow library pass and snuck down there when no one was around. Using Cork's passkey, I opened the door, saw the coat, and found the inspection tag in that rarely used pocket. Just as I though, number sixteen. I put it in my pocket and split.

Spring semester went well; I knew my way around a little better. All my new classes were great that first day, but my mind was on the fact that Matt Fuller had been in my room the night Governor Viche was killed.

I had to declare a sports activity to get out of gym class, so I picked cross country. Only the practices were much like gym class anyway, as in the winter we had to run laps in the gym. We met four days a week. Frank took it with me. Our upper classman squad leader, a guy already in the sport for a while, organized our workouts. He was a red haired, freckled faced guy named Tom Crosby and he was one of the funniest guys I had ever met. He did imitations of our alcoholic coach and many of the teachers. The varsity captain and best runner was Mario Wonton, said to be a descendant of the Tarahumara of Mexico.

We learned the custom of spin in adolescent gang fights; both sides go back and brag to friends that they each kicked the others' butt. We started hearing rumors that the Mustangs murdered the Eagles. I mean we didn't even begin to destroy all the guys out there, but we knocked a few down and bloodied some noses. True to his word, Ben sent a note to their clubhouse that we noticed how good they were at running, but are they ever going to fight us? He demanded a rematch. They did not respond.

Cork pulled a couple of stunts. First, he filled three boxes full of cow feces from the farm, packed them up, and mailed one to the clubhouse and one to each parent of the mutt brothers. He signed the notes: Montague "Big Ears" Fisher.

Noticing a rather isolated hallway at school where the Mustangs, those who went to school, hung out with their girlfriends, Corky opened an empty locker and assembled a cluster of cherry bomb firecrackers and a remote detonation device. After getting us all into inconspicuous observation spots, Cork waited until a whole pack of Mustangs were there listening to music and then set it off. The blasts, timed about a second apart, were so loud it hurt our ears. It even blew the locker door clear off its hinges. There were fifteen or twenty scared twits running.

All attempts to set up another fight failed, and for Frank and me it was sort of a relief. Ben wasn't sure, but he saw the cause of their immediate isolation as a product of: (1) increased attention being paid by the orphanage and school toward their gang-related activities with other students; (2) other kids, orphans and regulars alike, saw what we did and were beginning to stand up to them; and (3) police and parents were notified because Clyde and Corky wrote out an anonymous letter of gang activities along with the addresses of the clubhouse and storage barn and sent it to the town police chief and every parent of the Mustangs we knew about. So the famous Mustangs backed off, not even hanging out in groups at school. We still saw individual members here and there, and we got a strict warning from Empire to avoid any confrontation. Since Frank's sister, Libby, recently had a boyfriend from Price Hall, we backed off on our escort service because she rode with him on the bus. Also, while gangs could sometimes be vicious, harming a girl was still taboo in the pirates' code.

Frank Davis and I took a bus up to the defense base to meet with Mr. Cummings and Petty Officer Kowalski. We had hoped for a better outcome.

I began by telling them I had evidence that Matt Fuller and Bus Quint were in my room the night Gov was killed. I told him I had found a second inspection sticker in Fuller's coat that matched the one dropped on the floor that night. Then Mr. C began beating the heck out of my detective work.

"How do you know Quint was there?" he asked

"They always hang out together, it's a good assumption," I responded.

"So you assumed it? How do you know both slips were from Fuller's coat?"

"They matched."

"Both inspector #16, eh? How many coats, let's say per month, do you think #16 inspects?"

"No idea."

"How did you observe the second sticker?"

"I looked in his locker at school."

"Oh, so the door was left open and you saw the sticker drop on the floor?"

"No," I sort of stumbled a little, "a, a friend of mine jacked his locker door."

Ms. Kowalski started to giggle as Mr. Cummings laid his head down on his desk and started to moan. Without looking up he continued, "How do you know the slip is still in the coat?"

"It isn't, I got it right here."

He moaned again, "So you stole the slip from his personal property and now you have it?" Even Frank moaned now, both of us knew we were in the toilet with this.

Mr. C sat back up and summarized, "So, Mr. Kelley, how do you think I'm going to handle this with a judge? Well, your honor, #16 only inspected one coat in the lot sent up to Thompson. Fuller and Quint always hung out together, why wouldn't one assume they were together that night? Oh, how did I get my evidence, your honor? Well, Mr. Kelley broke into the locker and stole it. I got a puny handful of illegally obtained evidence here, Dan, how am I going to go to the District Attorney with this crap." The meeting ended there.

Out in the reception area, Ms. Kowalski thanked us. She said she would talk with Mr. Cummings more about this and get back to us. She also told me to report any innocently noticed evidence to her and not go all Sherlock Holmes on them again.

For the next couple of years, things were pretty quiet. Gang activity was virtually nonexistent. The Eagles thrived on Milt's farm, living in the dairy barn. After Milt took out all the dairy equipment, we had room to expand. We assembled some office cubicles that allowed us each a private sleeping quarter. A desk, lamp, and single bed were installed in each one. Some throw rugs helped with the cold floor. Cork and Frank Miller found an area on the base from which they sold excess furniture and we fixed up our home for cheap. Milt, after a while, even let us eat all three meals in the farmhand chow hall if we wanted. He found us a cheap labor force for routine chores, since he had only a few full-time farmhands in the winter.

They closed the north dining hall at the orphanage as the census dropped at the end of the school year, and turned it into a satellite school building. We ate at the remaining one sometimes, usually Saturday lunch with Libby Davis, but the lines were long.

I ran on the cross country team that next spring. It was not very much fun, but at least Frank and I could jog together and talk. The coach was a mean guy so we didn't put too much effort into it.

Albert Myers stunned us that spring. As he invited all of us to his graduation, we normally assumed he was graduating junior high school. We found out later he was getting a bachelor's degree from college. A 15-year-old college graduate. He even started graduate school the next week in computer science. We made it a point to do more talking about our personal situations. I was lucky to announce straight A's again for me that spring semester.

With school out for the summer, we got into farm work, helping Milt with putting in crops and with the cattle. We all became experts with the tractors and trucks, Milt even letting us drive the planters. I didn't even bother taking driver's education that summer. I did declare a training major, at the behest of Diane Win, deciding on electricity due to my experience with the electrician rewiring our room in Delk. It wasn't set in stone, as I could always switch, but it did open up some money for me. Since I was out of school for the summer, I enrolled in the first two electrical classes via satellite.

Boxing and spear tossing were also daily activities. We were getting proficient with both as time went on. Although our quarters were much cheerier then Delk Hall, with light and plenty of windows, we spent as much time outdoors as possible.

As the summer wore on, the guys started reflecting about some sort of operating philosophy or style of life we wanted to pursue. I know that sounds rather heavy for a band of teenagers, but we were of a special background. Most of us had been ironing our own clothes, taking care of academics independently, watching out for our safety, and reflecting on how we might have been short-changed by life, for several years now. This was stuff most people didn't go through until their twenties. We certainly wanted to be good examples; no one was into using our misfortune to seek pity or be considered handicapped in some way. We were looking to be equals. We wanted to check into a dorm without being called "pig." We wanted to ask a girl out, and not have to hear a lecture on how rude it was for a south side orphan to assume a classy girl might want to dance with them. We didn't necessarily want to be street fighters, but we also wanted to keep our lunch money, as we had earned that just as much as a kid whose parents gave him his.

We decided to do some reading and discuss it, like a book discussion group. First we did *Catcher in the Rye*, which we all had read and of course is every teen boy's handbook. Then Clyde suggested *Living in the Woods*, the book Gov had given me.

We were floored by that text; the words seemed to jump out off the pages. Thomas Pine was a young philosopher, who happened to be from Centura and also a grad from our own orphanage. Writing in those pages many of the thoughts we were having, Pine suggested a respite from society. The story goes, after he became disillusioned with society, he went off into the wilderness and learned how to survive on his own. He learned to like society again, but only after he put it into perspective. We decided to do a chapter a week, meeting out in the grove of trees, just off the far pasture. Sometimes, when the weather was suitable, we would stay out there all night.

I wouldn't say that my eighth- and ninth-grade school years were uninteresting; rather, it was a time of calm, a time when things were going well for both me and the guys. Obviously, I didn't keep up with my daily journal as I should have. Academics, sports, and our part-time jobs were keeping us distracted. Our social lives started to pick up. The national economy was thriving and many improvements at Thompson and in the town of Centura were being made.

None of Frank Davis' relatives ever came after him, his sister, or their inheritance. I guess in the good economy, people were content. While his sister was becoming a popular person at school, Frank just kept his nose in his books and maintained loyalty to the Eagles.

Jim Donovan had so many girlfriends; none of us could keep track of them all. I didn't think even he could. He always seemed to be out on his cell phone or out on a date. During this time he received a phone message at the orphanage from a lady claiming to be the mother who left him in the maternity ward. He never called back.

Clyde began to put on a little weight and muscle, and his boxing skills had improved so much that he became a varsity starter on the school's boxing team. He never could get a killer, knockout punch developed, but he could dance and punch an incredibly long time and would wear guys out. He and Corky were inseparable.

Ben, totally dropping his mental patient persona, continued to thrive as our fearless leader. Although he kept saying we should rotate the presidency, we always voted him back in. He was our club spokesperson, and I think a major reason we were doing so well is that other gangs actually liked him. Although we protested his putting himself in danger, he met with The Range, that small group of gothic Huns on the south side, who offered a mutual support treaty with the Eagles. So, if hostilities with the Mustangs ever redeveloped, they said they would fight them with us. I think The Range admired Ben and the orphans, as both groups had been looked down upon and they saw how we were overcoming those odds. Ben also started going with a girl who we liked. Angie, a teeny, tiny girl, all of four foot two, completed the odd looking couple. With the appearance of a shy, farmer's daughter, Angie had a mouth on her that could make a dead man blush. We used to love to see her go off on Ben, looking up at him and shaking her finger. But Ben loved her. Even in the midst of a complicated conversation on some philosophical matter, he would suddenly blush and announce, "I have to go call Angie on this."

A very quiet and shy Frank Miller was a good worker and loyal member of the club. He did okay in school. Being an excellent writer and poet, we all loved reading his stuff.

Empire Murdock (I'm not sure any of us knew his real first name and we were afraid to ask) did get his reading level up and started doing better in school. He still got C's and D's in English but the rest of his grades slowly improved. No one, either our gang or outsider, either serious or just kidding, ever said a bad word about Ben Holden within earshot of Empire.

Al Myers just kept advancing. He got a master's in computer science within a year. When we all ganged up on him to get his Ph.D. and teach us, he declined, instead starting on his second master's in mathematics. Although still a likable guy, he was a social zero. Donovan even fixed him up on a date, and he spent the evening boring the poor girl with an argument about which type of board material held the longest lasting printed circuit.

It's funny how experiences we have when we are very young sometimes direct us to a certain occupations. When Bo Schlitz was assigned to taking care of the wounded in that first fight, he took it to heart and wanted to be a Registered Nurse. He first became certified in first aid, then went on to complete all the technical requirements for Emergency Medical Technician by the time he finished his ninth grade. He couldn't be certified until he finished his junior college general studies, but at least he was on his way. Bo was odd, and relied on the club for social and emotional support.

Corky Wall, super spy, was optimistic, funny, and often lifted the mood of the group. He had a knack I have never seen in a person for finding out stuff. If I mentioned a cute girl I was interested in, the next day Cork would come in with her address, phone number, what her parents did for a living, who she was dating, her grade point average, and, even what stores she shopped in. I know he got a lot of stuff from Al Myers, but some of it I just don't know. Cork was so loyal to the group; he would have sunk a navy patrol boat in Lake Michigan if we had asked him to.

I had few complaints myself. At some time during my eighth-grade year, girls hit me. I liked looking at them, talking with them (well, more like listening), joking with them, being serious with them, etc. I liked the way their hair smelled and the way they danced. I asked a lot of girls out, most declined, but I kept trying. However, Betsy Barney and the Popover twins were three I never asked out.

I got my driver's license on my fourteenth birthday. As more of us did, we were allowed to haul grain into the elevator at harvest time or run other errands for the farm. Milt had this small fleet of gigantic diesel army trucks he let us drive, and, being a farmer, always had plenty of gas stored on the property. They weighed tons and were loud, smoky, and terribly uncomfortable. He even let us use them for dates or personal errands as long as we didn't abuse it. We soon found out that girls had to like us for more than just what we drove.

Like Bo Schlitz, I finished all my electrician technical requirements by the end of my ninth grade, which meant I could apprentice but couldn't be licensed until after junior college. However, since I could use the advanced placement general studies courses I was taking in high school as substitutes for those, I was well on my way to becoming an electrician sooner rather than later. The on-campus classes were held in the old north dining hall which made it convenient. As much as I thought I knew from academics, however, I soon found out that book learning and doing the job were two different things. I would have to work on getting an apprenticeship.

I did the cross country thing again in my eighth and ninth grades, but Frank Davis finally dropped it. It was hard to keep it up, especially with the daily boxing workouts. I kept at it, totally enjoying Tom Crosby's antics and some other friends I had made on the team. We only had a few actual meets per season.

I did not believe that things could get any better.

CHAPTER FOUR

Delk Hall burned down the last week of summer vacation, just before I started the tenth grade. The fire marshal's report didn't use the word "arson," but instead indicated "suspicious circumstances." What was odd was the building had been evacuated and sealed for fumigation the day before. Nobody was inside, and everybody knew that. Since all of us remembered Clyde's threat long ago, we repeatedly questioned him about it. He never answered, just smiled. We also knew Mr. Corky Wall was proficient with timed detonators, but he vehemently denied any involvement. In Clyde's defense, Frank Davis, not being able to sleep that night, had been up all night reading, and recalled Clyde snoring throughout the night. He was also sound asleep when Frank woke everyone up to run outside to see the fire. We never did find out for sure, and I think that's what Clyde wanted.

High morale was evident as Corky, Frank Davis, and I stood by our lockers on the first day of our tenth year of school. It was after lunch. All the Eagles had good grades, undergone some physical development, and had some money in the bank. We were on top of the world.

Standing there, we noticed my cross country squad leader, Tom Crosby, leading this totally cute babe down the hall. Old Tom was hanging on; he had an arm around her back and an arm out front, directing to one side anyone walking into her in the crowd. She was a peach, long reddish-brown hair, cute bangs, and a figure that was perfect. Having a bright face, her slight smile did give the impression that she was hemmed in. One couldn't blame Tom, I would have held on to that too.

"Why can't we ever get women like that?" Corky lamented.

I asked, "Who is that?"

"Her last name's Dubois," Cork responded, "I know because she's in my study hall, and the creepy teacher only calls out the last names during roll."

"There are certain leagues in the world," Frank added, "And we aren't in hers."

Then Cheri, that awesome blonde upperclassman from Principi's history class, who still sent me emails sometimes, walks by, smiles, and flirts, "Hey, handsome, don't let any of those goons hurt that pretty face of yours again, okay?"

"No," I smiled back, "I only get in fights now if I need to defend your honor."

She and the other older girls with her laughed. I knew she was just kidding, but a guy needs that every now and then.

So the three of us walked off to class together, in stride, thinking this was a beautiful world.

My class schedule was fairly light this semester. I had taken most of the difficult, mandatory classes my last three years. With my electrical classes out of the way, now I could have a little more free time, hopefully for a social life. I was in Spanish II, geometry, another philosophy course, and some English courses. Most of the first day I asked out cute girls that sat by me, but again, all declined.

During last hour study hall, I got a library pass and got to go to the library for the hour. I hated to use my yellow pass so early in the week, but I was bored. Students could get a yellow pass only once a week. Although blue passes to the library could be obtained more frequently, you had to get those from a class teacher to work on a specific assignment.

I was browsing the books on a shelf when I became the victim of a practical joke. The clowns taking summer school use to pull this one prank where they would remove a peg holding up a shelf, and carefully replace it with a short toothpick. When someone either pulled a book off or replaced one, the whole shelf would go crashing down. That's what happened to me, and a roar of laugher arose from the usually quiet students.

I heard this female voice, "Absolute morons!" as she came rushing around the end of a book row and ran right into me. She was a tall, studious looking library helper who wore these scholarly glasses. "Oh, sorry."

She squatted down and starting picking up the books; I helped her. She told me her name was Lisa Richardson and that I didn't have to help her with this; she knew I didn't cause it. Watching her put the books on a stacking cart; I noticed she was tall and pretty. I didn't get the glasses as most eye problems could be corrected at a young age with laser surgery. I then went to a table and pretended to look at a book, but looked at her instead. I think I caught her looking back once. At the end of the hour, I stopped by the desk and asked her to get a cup of coffee with me.

She smiled, "You know, with the kind of day I've had, I think I'd like that."

So I blew off cross country practice and had coffee with Lisa. She was amazingly smart and witty, if only in a high brow way. This one had class. We talked for a long time and before we got on our separate busses, she asked me to go to a poetry reading with her next Sunday afternoon. I said yes right away, although I never even asked who was reading.

One afternoon, I gave Mr. Cummings a call to see how the case was going, an act I repeated every three months or so. Only Ms. Kowalski answered and told me Mr. Cummings had been transferred. Unfortunately, she told me the case had been transferred to the cold case files. It had been closed, and would only be reopened if significant new evidence came to light.

I totally lost it with her. After blasting her for several good minutes, I ended with a sarcastic rampage, "Well, no problem. He was only a poor, blue orphan boy with severe birth defects. And heck, no family to notify. No big deal, right? If you find me dead in a ditch tomorrow, I hope you'll keep my case open that long!" I hit the "delete call" button. I turned over in my bed, shutting my eyes.

"What's your name, son?" the snobby old man asked, never looking at me.

"Danny," I said.

"Danny who?"

"Don't know."

"Do you have parents, Danny?"

"Yea."

"What are their names?"

"Mom and Dad."

The old man looked at the woman standing next to him. He went on, "Where are they?"

"Don't know."

"Are they back out in that big snow storm, Danny?"

"Don't know. Where are they?"

"What were you and your parents doing out there?"

"Don't know. Can I go back home now?"

"We're not sure where you are from," he went on. "You can help us by trying to remember what happened. What happened just before the helicopter picked you up? Try, son."

"It was snowing, bad. Someone was holding on to me by my coat. They just let go, they just let me go sliding down a hill."

"Who was holding on to you?"

"Don't know."

"Try harder."

"I told you I didn't know! Don't you baboons know I'm four years old! How do you ever expect someone ..." I found myself sitting up in bed, sweating buckets, half in the dream, half out. Murdock was shaking me.

"Kelley! Wake up! What's the matter?" he looked scared and concerned. Ben, Clyde, and Davis were standing behind him. Through the window I could see it was night.

"Bad dream?" Frank Davis added.

I just sat there shaking for a minute. "Bad dream for sure," I shuttered.

Frank said, "Come on. It's nearly 5 a.m.; you've been sleeping since dinnertime. Let's sit up and drink some coffee, no use going back to sleep now."

Ben told everyone to go back to bed. Frank and I just sat in our study room, watching a very early satellite transmission of cable news. He didn't ask any questions, just sat there and commented on the news. He was there for me.

I took Lisa to the poetry reading the next Sunday afternoon. I guess the poet was funny because Lisa laughed a lot; I had no idea what he said. She lived on the base, in the officers' section, and I was getting dirty looks in my diesel farm truck with manure dropping here and there on the streets. After taking her to her house and upon walking her to the door, she said she never kissed on the first date. I kissed her anyway. She turned to walk in but she was smiling. Once she got inside, I heard a male voice yelling.

Standing by our lockers after lunch was becoming a standard practice for Frank, Corky and me. One day Jim Donovan walked up, said hello to us and started talking to a guy standing next to Cork about some math assignment; tagging along was his latest girlfriend. So the three drool brothers had another religious experience; yet another beauty had fallen from the sky. This girl was so hot she needed a license to walk in the halls. Long, blonde hair fell to her shoulders and beyond, slightly separated bangs, fair but with some darker eye makeup, she could have been a model. To make matters worse, brain-absent Donovan didn't introduce her, so she had to stand there, holding up her books with both arms, while these three sailors on shore leave stared at her. Frank had his mouth open.

Unable to bear the discomfort any longer, she finally nudged Donovan, "Jim! Are you going to introduce me to your friends?"

Since Donovan kept talking, Corky just jumped in, "Don't worry, he doesn't talk to us either. Hi, I'm Corky Wall."

"Rose Russo," she smiled.

"Dan Kelley, glad to meet you." She smiled at me. "This is Frank Davis." She said hello to Frank, but he couldn't talk yet.

She looked back at me, "Dan Kelley? I've heard about you. Do you have a sister named Wendy?"

"I don't have any sisters, no," I responded.

"So, what are you guys up to?"

"Just …" Frank tried to add something, but it came out in a high, squeaky voice. He cleared his throat and did better, "Just hanging out between classes. I see you're taking el Español there." He looked at her textbook.

"Yea, Spanish. I hate it."

Jim finally joined the conversation and we chatted a while. As they left, she said she was glad to have met us. All three of us watched her as she walked with Donovan down the hall and around the corner. "You know, there is a lot of scientific evidence for evolution," Frank said, "but there was no way she evolved. Something like that had to be created by God."

Final hour saw me once again in the library. Lovely Lisa Richardson was checking books back in, was in a coy mood, and tried to be very business-like with me. "I'm very busy right now, I don't have time for any of your testosterone driven advances, Mr. Kelley. By the way, don't you think you got a little out of hand with me on Sunday?"

"I think I was pretty tame for having to look at you all afternoon," I shot back while she fought to keep the corners of her mouth from turning up.

"Smooth talk won't work on me. I call tell you that right now."

"I was hoping it would work just enough to get you to go back behind the bookshelves with me."

She flung a book on the desk hard, with a scowl on her face, and said, "Okay!"

So she took me by the hand, led me behind the shelves, and started to kiss me. It was turning out to be a great day.

We went back out to the circulation desk, after several minutes, she going back to work while I sat at a table and looked at a magazine. After a while, she came over and joined me. She was serious this time, "Dan, I need a favor."

"Sure."

"Do you mind? I mean, the next time you come over, could you park behind the house?"

I was a little surprised, "I guess. Problem?"

"Well, dad is sort of a Navy big shot on the base, and he, well, he doesn't want the farm truck parked out in front of the house. Would you mind?"

"No problem," I responded. That was probably why her dad was yelling at her when I left.

Fall semester continued on. I kept seeing Lisa, although the kissing sessions were few and far between. I went over to her house a few times, but I took the bus. Most of the time, we just met after school and had coffee. Rose and Jim got pretty serious. One time, we pulled a stunt on them with a home visit to Rose's house. We looked forward to any opportunity to see her.

Corky, Frank, and I dropped Jim off at Rose's house while the rest of us did some errands for the farm. Of course when we picked Jim up, we all got out and rang the doorbell. Rose, holding a baby, answered the door. This got old Cork going.

"Hi, Rose!" Cork greeted her, pushing his way in. We all followed behind him into the foyer. "Oh, how cute, I didn't know you guys had a baby already," Cork cooed at the baby, "So this is Jim Donovan, Junior?"

Rose sighed, "No, you blockhead, this is my baby brother."

"Well, he looks just like Jim; I think that's his ..."

"Corky!" Rose yelled to get him to shut up, "Have you met my mother?"

We all turned to see mom and dad sitting in the living room, the former with a fowl look on her face. "I'm sorry, Mrs. Russo, just kidding, of course."

"Yes, you're very funny," she responded, sarcastically. Next to her sat a frowning Jim Donovan.

Rose introduced all of us to her parents. Mom was a little quiet, dad was totally so. In fact, he sat staring at a fish tank on the wall, deep in his thoughts.

Rose showed us she could handle the wisecracking Cork, "So, I see you guys brought the good manure truck. Tell me, did you have any luck trolling for girls with that thing?"

"No," Cork came back, "we were taking a fresh load up to the north side, but they wouldn't let us in. Do you guys need any for the lawn?"

"I think we're good."

We all sat, letting Corky take the lead in the conversation. Then, Rose's two younger sisters came in, and let me tell you, things just keep getting better with this Russo clan. Two more living dolls came walking in and said hello. I'd seen the older at school; she was a baton twirler in the band and a total cutie. The younger, probably still junior high, had that characteristic doll face of her oldest sister. We sat and talked for an hour or so. Despite their knockout looks, all three girls were friendly and approachable.

We said our goodbyes, the girls vocally, mom waived, and dad didn't do anything as he was still looking at the fish. Rose said goodbye to all of us at the door, smiling. I think she liked us. All three of us now knew why Jim liked spending time at the Russo's.

As Christmas break approached, I decided it was time to make a move with Lisa. I was longing for something more serious and wanted to bring it further than just the coffee chats and stolen kisses. Going to a north side jewelry store, I bought a rather expensive initial ring and even added some sizing yarn to match the background. I made a coffee date with Lisa and told her I had something special to say to her.

We sat down, we ordered our usuals, then I began, "Lisa, I'm falling head over heels for you, and now ..."

"I'm glad you brought that up," she cut me off, "I need a very big favor."

I cringed, oh gosh, another favor? "What?"

"I know this may sound weird, but I'm in a jam. I'm going to have to break up with you, but just temporarily, just for the holidays. You see, I've not been totally up front with you and I feel I need to be honest, so this is just being honest, okay? I have a boyfriend. He goes to the military academy in Tampa, and he's flying in for Christmas. Dad loves him and he'll be staying at our house over the break."

"Let me guess," I interjected, "he'll be sleeping in your room?"

"That's not funny, Dan! Don't you think two people should be honest with each other?"

"Whatever." I certainly wouldn't have objected if she lied right then. She paused as the waiter delivered the coffees.

"If you'll let me finish. Anyway, I'm going to break up with him, when he's here. But with Dad and him here, I just can't have you around, okay? So, if he asks me if it's another boy, I can honestly say no. See?"

I just stared at her in disbelief. I couldn't find any words to say.

"Well, I hope you'll understand. Anyway, I'll tell him, let Dad yell for a week or two, and then I want you to call me in January. Okay? Awe, you're a peach. There's my ride, Merry Christmas." She ran out of the shop. I just sat and stared into space, and then the waiter brought me the bill for the coffees.

So, I got to hang out all Christmas break and admire my shiny new ring. Was a good relationship with a girl this hard to get? I mean, people do it all the time. Look at Donovan. Look at Libby Davis. Look at Ben. Thank goodness my year ended building a good relationship with a woman.

"Yo, Dan Kelley," I heard a woman's voice as I slowly awoke. "You awake?"

I yawned, turned my head and saw Ms. Kowalski sitting on my desk chair, looking at me. I rubbed my eyes and focused. I then looked down to see myself lying in bed, no covers on, in just my underwear. "Dang!" I yelled, covering myself up, "Ever heard of knocking?"

"Sorry," she said, "but your roommates are not too fond of me right now. Clyde Hastings told me where you were, but that you were sleeping, and he wasn't going to wake you for me. So I just waited, because I didn't want to touch … a … oh, you know."

As I slowly came to, I sat up, and looked at her, "Wow, someone got promoted." I noticed her in dress navy black with some new hardware on her collar. "I guess it should be good morning, Lieutenant JG Kowalski."

"Yes, I got my commission. I wanted to talk to you. That was a pretty rude thing you said to me back then, you know?"

"Rude to you, yes, and I'm sorry; rude to the government, no."

"It's been bothering me," she said.

"Is that why it's taken you four months to come and see me? There's no way that case should have been closed, Ms. K. There were two guys after that kid, Mr. Cummings even said …"

"Mr. Cummings got a reprimand on that case. He was onto Quint's dad about lying under oath about that phony alibi he set up for those two boys. Quint's old man called Atlanta; the Navy Department closed that case, reprimanded Cummings and had him sent away. They said Gov could have fell down and hit his head. We couldn't tell you that. Answer me this, you only talked to Gov one time, why is this so important to you?"

"Because of what that helicopter pilot told me, the one that picked me up, that I'd be better off if they left me down on the ice." And then I yelled again, "And that's just what they did to Governor Viche. They let the poor orphan freeze to death in a snow bank, and that ain't right!"

She nodded, water filling her eyes, and I felt bad again. I tried to lighten the mood because I knew I needed Ms. K as an ally; she was all I had. "Are you married, Ms. K?"

She sighed, "No, and I've had the same idiot fiancée for the past six years. And thanks for bringing that up, Mr. Kelley."

"Does he know you hang out with naked teenage boys?"

"Shut up!" but she laughed, "You're not naked. Why the heck did you ask me that? Gonna try to appeal to my sense of motherhood?"

"No, I was going to put a move on you. I figured you've already seen me naked, we should get engaged."

"Shut up!" she laughed again, stood up, "I'm getting the heck out of here. I should know better than to try and interview a hormonal teenager." She walked over to the door, "I'm not going to let him freeze, Danny. I'll keep an eye on the case." She left. I believed her.

Christmas day found Ben, Jim, and even Frank Davis spending the day with girls. Libby Davis set up old Frank with some bookworm friend of hers. The rest of us were on computers all day or listening to music. On New Year's Eve, a blizzard hit the area and the whole town was closed down.

Another spring semester started. I was in the locker room, getting ready for my running, when word got around that Tom Crosby's mother had died over the holidays. I saw him a few days later, cleaning out his locker, announcing that he was going to quit the team. Nothing like his former self, Tom was quiet and hardly spoke. I felt bad for him.

School was going well. I was into social sciences that semester with psychology (college-level intro), sociology, and child development. The club was getting a little notoriety as well, orphans were becoming trendy, and I was even asked to speak at the sociology club meeting. Rose Russo would even see me standing at my locker and stop to talk to me. Boy, was I ever milking that relationship, being seen with her was good for my reputation. I just loved everyone seeing me with that girl.

March came around, the weather was starting to improve, and our lives were picking up. One evening Jim Donovan came walking through our sleeping area and announced, "Hey, Kelley, I heard this girl really thinks you're cuter than heck, and wants to go out with you."

Very used to constant teasing from the guys, I huffed, "Now just who the heck is that?"

He stopped, paused, and then said, "Somebody named Sharon, I think."

"Sharon who?" I didn't know any Sharon.

"Can't remember, Rose was telling me about it."

I was getting curious, "Well, call Rose and ask her."

"She's working, can't right now."

"Can I call her?"

"No!"

"Why not?"

"Because she's my girlfriend, and she's working. Ask her at school."

I didn't waste any time. After a night of total preoccupation doing chores and tossing and turning in bed, I jumped on poor Rose the next day. "So, who's this girl?"

Rose smiled, "Sharon, Sharon Dubois."

My heart, or it could have been my hormones, jumped. "Dubois? That little freshman beauty queen? That one?"

Rose giggled, "She's cute. I'm not sure about the beauty queen part, but, yes, that's her and she wants to meet you."

"Isn't she going with Tom Crosby?"

"They broke up. Okay, here's the deal. Two weeks from now I'm having a sleepover. Jim's getting a van and we're all going out for burgers. Ask her to go with you. Then you can all drop us off at my house. Okay?"

No problem. The only thing I forgot to ask Rose was how to find this girl. I spent the rest of the week trolling the halls for her. Then one day, over in the freshman wing, I saw her loading books into her locker. I was shaking like a leaf as I approached her. "Sharon?" She turned and my throat dropped to my stomach. She looked at me with that big, bright face, a smile that was out of this world. "I … I'm Dan Kelley."

"I know," she said. "Hello, Danny." She called me Danny forever after that.

"So," I nervously asked, "I heard about the big sleepover and was wondering if I could be your escort for the food run?"

"Sure, that would be nice." She still smiled but put her face down, blushing ever so slightly.

"Jim Donovan's my roommate so I'll … I mean I'll just ride up with him … I mean I'll already be with him."

"That will be nice."

"So, see you then I guess."

"I'll be looking forward to it."

"Okay, bye."

"Bye."

I had no idea what I was walking on for the next two weeks because my feet never touched the ground. Gosh, was she gorgeous! I had to rein myself in at times, promising myself that I wouldn't rush her or get all goofy on her. I had to be cool. Of course, I had to put up with two weeks of constant teasing from the guys. The Eagles had no mercy.

One Saturday morning, Donovan started it, "Frank Davis, hey, guess who Kelley got a date with? Sharon Dubois."

"Kelley did?" Frank smarted off, "No kidding?" He then looked at me, "You got a date with Sharon Dubois?"

"Kelley," Corky joined in, "did she lose a bet?"

"I'm thinking maybe she has some mental problems," Ben added.

"Does she drink a lot or what?"

"Does she think you got money?"

"Are you going to pick her up in the poop truck?"

"Maybe it's 'be nice to an orphan' week. I heard the French club is doing that. She is French, right?"

"And she's okay with this, I mean you being a homosexual and all?"

"Maybe she has a screw loose."

I had to get away from those clowns, so I went out and spent some time with the cows. At least they were happy to hear about my news.

A lot must've happened in those weeks, but who the heck remembers? As I stood in front of the mirror in the john right before my big date, I had to work at calming my nerves. Jim Donovan stopped in and actually gave me some pointers and said I had really gotten lucky. Just before leaving, I looked at the calendar. It was March 18th.

Jim drove with Ben and me to pick up the dates. Would Sharon chicken out? Donovan had borrowed Milt's big van to haul the crowd. When we got there, Sharon did show. I grabbed her hand to help her into the vehicle, that big smile lighting up the interior. Her hand was warm and sweaty which calmed me down. She was nervous too. She had on slacks and a leather jacket and looked amazing.

Rose sat on the console next to Donovan and they whispered sweet nothings in each other's ears while Ben and Angie sat in the far back seat. Glad that Angie was along, I felt more comfortable, since she kept the party rolling. She had us all laughing with her verbal antics.

We didn't stay out too long, since they mentioned there were a few other girls back at the party who didn't have dates. We talked as couples during the burgers.

"I don't think I've seen you around much before now," I told Sharon.

"I was in a private junior high school last year," she told me, "we haven't really been here too long, my dad's in the Air Force.

"How do you like the north country?"

"The winters are hard to get use to, but I like it. I went sledding for the first time in my life."

"How did you know me?"

"Saw you in the hall," she dipped her head and blushed, "Saw you out on the track last fall, in those shorts …" Really blushing this time, she had no idea she sent my self-esteem index up about six thousand points.

During the ride back, we kissed. She wouldn't kiss me a long time, just little smacks at a time, and then turned her head. But she looked up at me with that big grin and those dreamy eyes. Gosh, was this one special girl.

The other couples were ahead of us, said goodbyes, kissed, and the guys on their way back to the van as we got to the door. Then we shared a long kiss.

"I had a great time with you," she said, smiling, "I hope we go out again soon."

"You can count on that," I replied. Then, in a totally automatic reflex, without thinking, I pulled my new ring off my finger and pushed it into her hands. "Sharon, please?"

Surprised, she looked down at it, and managed a weak, "Oh no, you hardly know me."

"I know, but it's enough, enough for me."

"Are you sure?"

"Yes," I kissed her, and then she took the ring inside.

We wouldn't use the word "love" for several weeks, but it had hit me in the burger joint and was in my mind from then on. I didn't sleep that night, or the next. I could not get the picture of that face out of my mind. It did not matter what I was doing: chores, schoolwork, running, or boxing; I was continuously thinking of Sharon.

I approached her locker on Monday morning while she was engaged in a discussion with a friend. She was showing him my ring, wrapped in yarn, on her left hand finger. Her face was glowing; she was smiling. After he left, I approached her and we greeted. Then we both started laughing at the fact we hardly knew each other at all.

"Gee, I hope we're compatible," she laughed.

"Did I tell you I was married?" and we both laughed.

"Are you having any second thoughts about this?" she asked.

I shook my head, "No, I'm crazy about you."

"Whew," she exhaled, "I was hoping you'd say that."

"I remember when I saw you, last fall, walking with Tom Crosby."

"Oh, we broke up," she hurriedly added.

"My first question for you, steady girl, do you have any idea how good looking you are?"

Her grin got bigger, "No, but you can remind me all you want."

We had a ball, in school and at lunch. Public displays of affection were frowned upon at school, so sometimes she would walk by my locker and stand several feet away, pretending not to know me. Sometimes I would slip her a note as she walked by; then she would stop and read it, letting me watch her expression. I would write things like, "Smile, you're a dreamboat." Or "I don't know how you leave home in the morning. If I were you, I'd get up, look in the mirror, and not be able to move for the rest of the day."

As the weeks went on, my feelings toward Sharon grew. After the initial shock wore off, the rest of the guys were supportive. Even Frank told me in a serious manner that he was happy for us. All seemed happy with the arrangement, all with the exception of Clyde Hastings. He wasn't nasty or anything, but just mentioned that he had a sense of something about her. He even admitted he was probably mistaken.

Then came time to meet the folks and check out her home. I drove the "poop truck," but parked a few blocks away since I was in officers' country. Dad, not looking French at all, was a colonel, but wore his civilian clothes that Saturday afternoon. He stood quietly a lot, hands locked behind his back, staring out into space, like he was planning a major battle or something. Her little brother seemed normal, although he never talked to me. Mom was this gorgeous French lady who looked like a movie star. She even spoke with an accent. No need to wonder where her daughter got her looks from. With all of us in sneakers and shorts, Mom was dressed to the hilt in a tight dress, high heels, and earrings.

Colonel Dad finally broke the ice with me, "So, Danny, is your family enjoying this unusually warm weather?"

I didn't hear him and responded, "Huh?" which I soon found out was not the way to address a colonel in the Air Force. He gave me a wicked scowl.

The family had some friends over, military I imagined. Then the visitor dad walked up to Sharon, pulled her close to him, and started whispering something in her ear. Sharon smiled, apparently at what he was saying, but he was so creepy about it. She even started trying to pull herself away from him, but he kept tugging on her. I was almost ready to step in there when she finally got out of his grasp.

When she walked over to stand by me, I questioned her, "What's so funny?"

"What he said," she responded, but wouldn't say what it was.

We ate hot dogs and drank punch while the folks poured down white wine. I joked to Sharon, "Isn't the proper choice red wine with hotdogs?" I don't think she got it.

Sharon and I then walked through their back yard, out into the open common, shared with all the other officers' houses. It had a horseshoe shape, with the open end pointing toward the end of the runway. Going around the runway, along the edge of the base, was Perimeter Road, as we saw a car driving out there. "That's a cool little road," Sharon said.

"Your parents seem nice," I added.

"I love my mom," Sharon said, "Dad's okay, kind of stiff if you hadn't noticed. He's a little distracted today; something's up with the Air Force, something big. He's all military; I think he sleeps in Air Force underwear."

I teased, "What do you sleep in?"

"Never you mind, mister!" she laughed.

"What's your mom sleep in?"

"Danny Kelley, you have a one track mind! If my dad had heard that, he would have you marching around this field for a week." She giggled, then got serious, "Danny, what happened to your parents?"

"You knew I was an orphan?" I asked.

"Yes, Rose told me. It's okay with me, and my folks. You just never seem to talk about it and I didn't know if it was too painful."

"No, honey, not at all. Well, the military seems to think they froze to death. We were somewhere in the uninhabited land, south of here."

"What the heck were they doing out there?"

"If I knew that, baby, it would certainly answer a lot of my questions."

"How'd they find you?"

"Well, we got separated, somehow. I was only four so I don't know how. There was a snowstorm and I guess they found me wandering around. They took me by helicopter here. They never found my parents."

I don't know if she felt bad or if we were beyond sight of the house, but she grasped my hand, "I think you are incredible. I can't imagine what I would do without my parents."

"Well, there's not much incredible about it. You just exist only with no family. You wonder about them, pray they're in heaven, and try and make a life."

She stepped in front of me, facing me, "Danny, I want to be good for you. I want to make you happy about life. I'm so crazy in love with you, I can't believe myself sometimes." She hugged me and I hugged back. "Okay, take me for a ride around Perimeter Road."

It was getting dark as we got to my truck and went for a spin on the little road. They turned on the runway lights and I said, "Hey, the stars are out." It was a quaint road; they had these stones placed along the side of it, every twenty feet or so, all exactly spaced. When we got out of sight of the officers' neighborhood, I pulled over and we kissed for a while. I don't think Sharon had ever kissed me so hard.

Frank and I were watching the early morning news when we heard about the problem with Mexico. For some insane reason, the Mexican army was forming a force just south of the border with the uninhabited portion of Texas, and was threatening to move north. Worried about the isolated base in southern California, the U.S. began building up troops in San Antonio. No one saw a good reason for either of the countries to continue these hostilities. Northern Mexico was just as uninhabited as western Texas. If Mexico drove north, who would they be conquering, some armadillos and tumbleweeds? Also, both countries would pay a fortune to keep large armies in a ready state while they sat out in the middle of the desert. The argument started with the diplomatic folks over some old land claims. In any event, Thompson, and some other bases, began sending equipment and troops down there. Rumors of a war with Mexico were in full bloom.

Closer to home, Marv Greene had some sort of epiphany or vision quest or other sort of religious experience and resigned from the Mustangs. He wanted to help the poor, barefoot homeless (sarcasm supplied by Dan Kelley), finish school, and move south. Corky Wall also heard that factions within the Mustangs were arguing about which direction they wanted to move.

Well, I had Sharon Dubois and cared less about either of those situations. I got a yellow library pass one day as a reason to get out of study hall, but headed straight for the gym because Sharon and a group of girls were decorating it for some event. When I got there, I stood in the doorway and spotted her. She was in heaven; she loved this stuff. A big grin on her face, she was busy putting up posters with intricate borders. They must have worked hard on the artwork. When she spotted me, her face lit up and she yelled to me,

"Hey, baby!" I walked up to her and she hugged me, and then stood by me.

Sharon did two unique things. When she stood next to me, she touched me with the whole side of her body. Not in a decadent way or anything like that. It was just her side, but she maintained contact. And when she took me around and introduced me to her fellow interior design club members, she always said, "This is my boyfriend, Danny." She didn't say, "This is Danny" or "This is my friend," it was always right out and unashamed.

I told her we were getting a ride down to the farm with Cork and where she should meet me. Then I went downstairs to get something out of my cross country locker. There, folding clothes and putting them in a locker, was Tom Crosby.

I stopped, and then approached with caution. I had been afraid of this; afraid I might have to fight Tom over Sharon. I certainly didn't want to, but there was no way I was going to lose this girl over him, or over him and ten others for that matter. I broke the silence, "Hi, Tom."

He turned to look at me, and then went back to his folding, "Kelley, I'm rejoining the team."

"I think you should, I think the workout will do you good. Sorry to hear about your mom, Tom."

"I hear you got a new girlfriend? Going steady after the first night?"

"Yes. Tom, are we going to have a problem over this?"

He huffed and I braced myself. Then he said, "Naw. She gave me the axe long ago."

I exhaled, relieved. I went into my locker, closed it up, and started to walk out.

As I walked past him he uttered, "Beware the axe." I stopped, but he had no further comment.

Sharon was a hit with the guys back at Milt's. They did manage to get the place cleaned up and were on their best behavior. We walked all around, saw the cows and farm equipment. She even got to meet Milt who seemed very impressed. Of course he just had to ask her, "How did this little punk manage to land you?" We ate at the dining hall at the orphanage with Libby Davis. She just talked Sharon's head off about how me and my friends took care of her and her brother, how we bravely rousted the bad boys, and how we had been the reason for so many improvements at the orphanage.

We walked back to the farm, hand in hand. "Danny, I am so proud of you, I can't believe all the good things I heard about you today."

"You just met my family today, Sharon. These folks are my brothers and sisters, Milt's my dad, and the cows are the friends I grew up with."

When we got back to the barn, we went up to my cubicle. Sharon, who never ceased to amaze me, lay on my bed, winked at me, and teased, "How about a few kisses, sailor?"

I took her home in one of the trucks. She told me that right after I entered the base, if I took a sharp right, the road would lead out to Perimeter Road, which led around the airstrip and to her neighborhood. So once more we checked out the lights and the stones along the road.

***

"Yes, Angie ... Yes, Angie ... Yes, Angie ... Bye Angie," finally getting the girl off the phone, Ben finished writing out checks while Al Myers, Corky, and Clyde Hastings came in the room to start the meeting. He usually enjoyed being president of the Eagles, but not today.

"Thanks for coming guys," Ben began, "I wanted to have this meeting with just us. I wanted to talk a minute about Dan Kelley."

"If we're going to talk about Dan, shouldn't he be here?" Corky asked.

Ben nodded, but added, "I think if we talk about him because we care about him, then it's justified. As you all know, Dan has it bad for this new girlfriend."

"'Ends-of-the-earth' type stuff?" Cork asked.

"What the heck is that?" Al added.

Ben explained, "When a guy has it so bad for a girl he becomes blind. A guy will blindly follow a girl to the ends-of-the-earth, even when it may not be good for him. It's love for sure, but crazy love. I know he's the happiest he's ever been and I like seeing him this way, but something is nagging at me. Clyde, you were the only one ever to mention caution to Dan about this girl."

Clyde looked down. "Let me start by saying, I love Dan Kelley. He nominated me to this club at a time in my life when I had to go through the garbage cans behind the dining hall to get dinner. Heck, before Kelley and Davis, my best friend was one of Milt's cows."

Cork, even during serious moments, had the knack for placing just the right joke, "I think I can speak for all of us, Clyde, that we didn't mind your sexual attraction to the barnyard animals. But when you sent a dozen roses to that dairy cow, well, that got me thinking."

Clyde shot back, "You said you wouldn't mention that, ever again." Then he got serious again, "But yes, I had doubts. I did soften it a bit by retracting my statement after Dan seemed upset about it. And, yes, I may be a little jealous about all the time he's spending with her. But here is my original concern. I mean, look at her, guys, this girl is in the top five percent of girls. I mean, she's up there with Rose Russo and Angie. Besides her killer looks, she's charismatic. I noticed it when she was down here the other day. That girl can capture a room just by walking into it, and she's probably been used to that ever since she started growing boobs. I'm not saying she's out to take Dan's money or his soul. But what is she doing with him?

"You remember that one girl, what's her name? The library girl?"

"Lisa Richardson," Cork added.

"Yea, Lisa, I know she beat the hell out of Dan, but she was always honest with him. Dad didn't want him parking his truck in front of the house, she told him. She had to get rid of this additional boyfriend, she told him. She handled it badly. She hurt Dan and she's a complete witch, but she's always been an honest witch.

"We're trendy right now. Orphans are cool. There's been a sudden interest in us from the social scientists at the university. Sharon's dad is an up and coming military star, could be a general soon. Mom's a mail order bride from France and probably has a soft spot for people who are looked down upon. At her garden parties, she probably refers to Dan as 'Sharon's little orphan friend,' but when it's time to shape their prize daughter's future, Dan won't be in the cards. This problem with Mexico and the recent instability within the Mustangs, the wind could change direction in a heartbeat, and we all know it. We've all seen it happen.

"To partially answer my previous question, what Sharon Dubois wants with Dan, I'm not sure. But I've always been cautious, and pessimistic, I know. I only feel she's not being completely genuine with him and she does have a history of bailing out."

Ben looked at Al and Cork, "Can you guys do the usual checks on her? And, by the way, all reports come directly to me. If someone has to have a long chat with Dan, then it should be my job."

***

Although spring was track season, we had one special cross country meet in honor of the graduating seniors. With Tom not being back up to speed and with a few other seniors graduating, I moved up significantly in the field of cross country runners. I was now in the top seven and maybe could even earn a varsity letter. So for our big meet, I got Sharon to come out and watch.

The meet probably turned out to be a waste of her time. I did finish seventh, earned a letter, but in cross country the runners are so separated the finish is anticlimactic. No one was in sight, either in front of or behind me. But Sharon was there, clapping and cheering me on. After catching my breath, I went over to her on the bleachers to put on my sweats. That's when I noticed the letter jacket she was wearing.

"You looked pretty good in those shorts, sweetheart," she giggled.

"Sharon, what are you wearing?" I asked.

"Oh, this? I wanted to show my school spirit, you know, get in the mood."

Being either an oversight or innocent ignorance of the custom, she didn't appear to have a clue that a girl only wore her boyfriend's letter jacket. "Whose letter jacket is that?"

"This? Well, it's ..." Then she put her hand to her mouth and gasped, "Oh, shoot! Danny, I'm sorry, I completely forgot about this. This is Tom's old jacket. Oh, honey, oh gosh, I had no idea."

"Well, why do you still have it?"

"I tried to give it back to him, he didn't want it. Honest!"

We started walking back to the school together and I began to realize that it was probably an honest mistake. I was fine, but Sharon was upset.

"Here, I'll take it off," she said as she started to unbutton it.

"No, hon," I countered, buttoning it back up. "Don't be silly, the sun's going down and it's getting chilly. It just caught me off guard; I know I don't have one to give you. In fact, I talked to Tom already about us, and he and I came to an understanding."

"Don't forget, you are the only boy in my life now."

Any doubts the letter jacket incident raised were wiped out by what Sharon wrote in my yearbook. I did buy one that year, mainly because I had a girlfriend who would follow the custom of writing a note and signing the back page. She wrote a long note, and maintained her knack for saying the right things. First, she thanked me for allowing her to be the first signer. Then she included some key phrases such as, "I will never forget you," and "I'm proud to be going with you." "I will always love you" didn't hurt either. She closed with "All my love." These are always good things to hear, and even better to have in writing. She also gave me one of those little yearbook pictures, you know the ones the photographer gives you a few of because it's included in the price? She wrote the usual mushy stuff on the back.

Summer was here, tenth grade over with, and I only wanted to think about warm sunshine, no school, and Sharon Dubois. However, a few dark clouds were forming in the west.

Things started to get a little tense when Corky spoke at a Wednesday night meeting in the tree grove and announced that the Mustangs elected Bus Quint as their new president. To make matters worse, Bus got word out on the street to all the "creeps" out there, and especially The Range, Holy Cross, and the Eagles, that hostilities are on again and "all unfinished business will be dealt with." We assumed that meant our second call for a fight. The message contained a reference to Marv Greene being a "pansy" toward the other south side groups and that Quint would be assuming an iron fist leadership role in the area.

We discussed the situation at length. Ben said he would meet with The Range, renew our pledge, and he would try to get a similar arrangement set up with Holy Cross. He admitted that finding one of those guys, let alone someone with authority to strike up a treaty, would be difficult. He strongly suggested we continue our boxing and staff-throwing practices.

I spoke, "Can anyone tell me about this mysterious, Marv Greene, what's he like, I've never even seen the guy?"

"I saw him just recently," Corky replied, "at some function at the little kids' orphanage on the peninsula. He was handing out candy to the kids. No kidding, he's made a 180 degree transformation, found the Lord, is even running for student body president next fall."

"What's he look like?" I asked.

"Greene? Oh, man, he's a buffy, an avid body builder and weight lifter. I hear, since he's reformed, they have to shovel the girls off him. Plus he's running this organized PR campaign, passing himself off as one of the south side, down trodden youth, who reformed himself. He even speaks at these ladies luncheon groups, especially on the north side and out on the base. Have you ever seen that light green classic car he drives around? It's a puky lime green, so people who see the color of his car will associate it with his name. I'm now trying to prove he bought it with the lunch money he ripped off from all the orphans, but it's turning out harder than it looks."

I didn't like anything about this situation. The country was getting ready for war with Mexico and the Eagles were getting ready for war with the Mustangs. I just wanted to sit under the stars with my arm around Sharon and look at her.

CHAPTER FIVE

Angie, Rose Russo, and Sharon Dubois, lying on a beach in bikini swimsuits, now tell me God doesn't exist.

Jim, Ben, and I took the three girls to North Lake one hot and sunny summer afternoon. We spent the day swimming and sunning at the popular lake out west of Thompson Defense Base. Because we picked a workday, hardly anyone was there. We cooked burgers on a grill, ate, drank, and talked most of the day.

At the end of the day, we dropped the girls off in order of where they lived, Sharon first. I left because the group was my ride, and I think it was a good idea. I'm sure that a combination of the Dubois empty house, the Dubois family couch, and the Dubois family daughter in that swimsuit only meant trouble for me.

Sharon and I went out a lot and she did her best to keep up with me. We interchanged eating out and movies with going dancing and the arcade. I talked to her about schoolwork, club related matters and the national news. She listened. Although I didn't want to admit it out loud, she was becoming part of me, not just standing close, but becoming part of me as a person. I was getting a lot of respect, not a tough-guy respect, but sort of a "star quarterback" type of respect. Guys were complimenting me about her; other girls were telling me what a babe I had and to take care of her. They were writing it in my yearbook. People like Milt Frazer and even old Mr. Principi commented on my girlfriend. Sharon was a major part of my ego.

Orphan integrity continued to build. The Sociology Club had me speak at one of their meetings on "what it was like." I wanted Libby Davis to speak with me but she refused, citing a severe fear of public speaking. I had the usual barrage of questions like: "What do you do on Father's and Mother's Day? Who do you ask about sex? What's it like on Christmas?"

As I was scanning the group for raised hands, a girl in the back caught my eye. It was Mel Popover. Already staring at each other, I had no choice, "Yes, the girl in the back."

"Did you burn down Delk Hall?" she stunned the crowd into silence.

"No."

"Do you know who did?" continuing to harass me.

"I think it was your sister," I joked. Boy, what a dumb thing to say. Nobody laughed. I'm sure Mel, Claire, and Betsy would have a field day with this one. It was only the first in a long line of things not to say.

Ben took me with him to meet with The Range. Although polite and friendly, their looks could certainly strike terror in any foe they faced. These guys looked like the rogue street gangs that roamed the big cities during The Chaos. The president had so many tattoos he was hard to look at, but he pledged total support and renewed his promise to fight side by side with us. Raising some concern in us, he said that gang fighting had progressed, that this wouldn't be a seventh-grade fistfight. The Range scouts had observed that baseball bats and chains were appearing on the Mustangs in some south side areas. He suggested not taking the weapons into a fight, in case it was a set up and they had the cops watching, but he said it would be wise to have them pretty handy. Reminding us to keep valuables in safe places, he also suggested alternating our daily routines. The Mustangs were good at guerrilla raids.

Ben raised his concern about his failed attempts to bring Holy Cross into the alliance. They had recently said, “Thanks, but no thanks,” to his offer, indicating they didn’t do well in coordinated offensive actions with other clubs. They were not impolite or rude, but stated that the nature of their fighting did not fit with ours. The Range boys told us not to take offense with their refusal, that Holy Cross was “funny” that way, their style was kind of similar to ninja fighting so popular in Old World movies. He said you may only see one of them in a year, and then all of a sudden you’ll see twenty of them jumping out of trees on a rival gang. He said their longevity was mainly due to never knowing where they were. Who knew, if we have to fight the Mustangs, they just might show up.

Getting back to the dairy barn, I was greeted by an irate Frank Davis, “What the heck did you say to Mel Popover at that sociology meeting?”

“Frank,” I pleaded, “it was just a bad joke. She asked me if I burned down Delk Hall.”

“What did you say?”

“I might have implied that her sister may have done it.”

“Well that was stupid,” I had never seen Frank so upset with me.

“Why?”

“Because we got a notice today that her mom wants to see us and school officials over it. Did you know Mrs. Popover is on the town council?”

“I heard that, yes.”

“Did you know she was recently voted President of the Town Council?”

"That I didn't know," I put my head down, "I'm sorry, Frank, I thought it was funny at the time."

He finally calmed down. "Okay, I'll get with Ben and we'll figure out a strategy. Don't do any more of those functions."

Sharon wanted to go the arts and crafts swap meet the Base Exchange was having, and get supplies to decorate the front of the school for summer orientation. She said she could get some quality supplies for very little money at those things. I explained to her as we drove over and shopped, of my concerns about her safety with all this gang stuff going on. She listened intently, but said she was not worried. Not planning to go down to the south side, and with her dad in such a critical position at the base, the military police would come down hard on anyone causing her any grief. She said they watched the school pretty closely and if she came down to my place, we could use the far west route through the farms. When I told her about the Popover incident, she laughed.

"The Popover twins are a couple of Pop twits, and like it or not, the town of Centura exists to support the base, not the other way around," she told me. "So hey, let's take this stuff over to the school, and find a shade tree where you can show me the meaning to life."

Along the eastern route of Perimeter Road, north of the Navy Piers, a small cove was situated bordering Lake Michigan. I had never seen it before. Only a small gravel lot, next to the road, could be used as a parking area, then visitors had a short walk through a grove of trees to the lakefront. When we stopped and got out, I noticed one of the little stones along the road. It was octagon shaped, machine cut, not natural, set into the ground. Now I knew why they all looked the same; they were manufactured. They were only about a foot or so across and, once white, now showed a grayish, weathered surface.

Sharon had to show her ID card to the MP sitting in the jeep in the lot. He nodded her through. We walked over to the shore. No one else was there. We found a shade tree and made out for a while, then took a cool-off break.

"Oh Sharon," I said. "The Grand Dance is coming up in about a week. Do you want to go?"

"Oh yea, that's the outside dance, at the drive-in burger joint we went to on our first date. Sure, I'd love to go. They're having a live band too. I can't wait."

This was the first Grand Dance, which the owner wanted to make a monthly event in the summer to promote his restaurant. The joint was more of a hangout; kids just drove in, hung out, and then left, not buying any food. He wanted to keep people there, hopefully long enough to get hungry.

"Sweetheart," Sharon snuggled up to me, "you're awfully preoccupied today, are you going to get all gloomy on me?"

"Oh, it's just all this stuff going on. The war with Mexico, the Mustangs are acting up. I can't seem to find a good electrical apprenticeship. Most of those deals are made by fathers in the business and my father is out of business. Then there's the draft facing me, and with a war on, I fear they will have a bigger need for foot soldiers."

"Do you want me to see if Dad can get you on at the base? Then you could come over to my house and rewire me," she flirted.

"I don't want to put him out, I'm sure he's busy enough."

"Well, let me just ask him. Can't hurt to ask."

"Okay. So is there a schematic I could follow, on that rewiring job?"

"Not that I know of, guess you'll just have to eyeball it, find your own way around. You see? This is how I like you, cheer up, I can't stand it when you get all gloomy."

"People get serious at times, Sharon."

"I know. I just don't like it."

We stayed out there until it got dark, talking and kissing. After about the third check on us by the military police, I took her home.

On the way home, I decided I was going to contact Diane Win and see if I could get into French I this fall. Then I could really impress Sharon's mom.

Our group discussions on Pine's book continued as well, usually in the grove of trees, with a raging campfire going. The first part of the book dealt with his unhappiness with society, the orphanage, and school. It was like our lives. Then later on, he discusses his philosophy and how he "busted out" of his orphan role. Number one was self-reliance.

When Ben told me he and Angie were pre-engaged, I began to think about discussing such a thing with Sharon. The term actually began to take its current meaning after The Chaos. Since fertility was becoming a crapshoot and fertility tests had advanced to the point that almost everyone knew after reaching puberty if they could have kids, serious couples would often pre-engage. This basically meant, "If we're still together and still getting along, in five or ten years we will get engaged." This "reserved" appropriate partners if having children was important. It did not carry a legal obligation and either party could opt out at any time. Both Ben and Angie could not have kids, but decided to pre-engage for romantic reasons. It would be nice to consider with Sharon.

Both the Mexican and American armies soon began patrols out in the desert. Contact was almost a sure thing. Artillery and missile sites were erected; bombers and fighters were put into the air along the line of troops twenty-four hours a day. The largest Army barracks at Thompson deployed; the soldiers and equipment taken out on these huge cargo planes. Despite the military buildup, the stock market took a nosedive dropping so low that it tripped the automatic market close safety three days in a row, and by 10 a.m. each day. To top it off, the anti-war movement created political unrest. We feared all hell was going to break lose.

I was in need of a mood elevator, and I couldn't think of a more timely remedy than taking my baby to the big dance under the stars. I washed my jeans, borrowed Milt's personal pickup truck, and headed north toward the base. Jim Donovan and Ben Holden, going separately, would be there as well with Rose and Angie. Loud music, pizza, and Sharon Dubois were all the therapy I needed.

When Sharon came out the side door, under the carport, she almost knocked me over. She had a new outfit, one I had never seen before. It was a white dress, clingy and short. When I opened her door and helped her in the truck, I almost had a heart attack. Although it seemed a little over the top for an outside, parking lot dance, I didn't mind.

When I got in and started off, her perfume hit me. After I could finally stop looking at her legs, I saw a new hairstyle and perfect makeup. "Whoa baby, you look amazing. New outfit?"

"Oh, this old thing?" she teased. "By the way, when my dad saw the bill for this dress, mom and I had to peel him off the ceiling. Which means we have to talk, Dan."

As I shifted through the gears, and picked up speed out on Perimeter Road, I said, "Sure, what's up."

"Well, my parents have been on me for a while about getting my grades up and getting a job. This new dress sort of brought the matter to the front burner. They can get a lot of babysitting jobs for me but I always complained I didn't have time. So with more time I need to study and all these dates we go on, I don't know how I can do it. I really need to work more, honey."

I thought the solution was simple, "Sharon, people in love always find a way, that's what keeps them together. If you have to work, then work. We'll work it out."

"But that's not fair to you. You like to go out."

"I like to see you. For example, if you have to babysit, and put the kids to bed at 9:30, call me at 9:45 and I'll stop by for a few minutes."

"I'm not so sure they'll like me having a boy over."

"Then just call me at 9:45, and talk to me for ten minutes or so. Can't call, don't worry about it, write me a note and give it to me the next day. Heck, if you can't do any of that, just think of me for ten minutes. We don't always have to be on formal dates, it's the thought that counts."

She pushed over to the middle of the seat and gave me a big kiss on the cheek, "You sure make it hard for a girl not to love you." She remained sitting next to me.

Everything was going perfectly, except the weather. By the time we reached the gate and turned down North Shore Drive, it started to rain. It was raining buckets when we turned into the lot of the restaurant, only to see the place deserted, only a handful of cars in the lot.

"Darn," Sharon said, "they must have cancelled it."

I slowly trolled around the parking lot, trying to find if Ben and Jim were there. Of the few cars there, I noticed a bright, lime green classic parked in a space. "Hey, that's the famous Marv Greene's car; I've heard of it but never seen it." I pulled right behind it and stopped, looking across Sharon out the right side of the truck.

"Dan, move please," Sharon said, putting her hand up next to her face as if hiding from view. "Dan, there's someone in that car, please move."

"He doesn't know us, so what?" I protested, but slowly pulled ahead and into an empty parking space.

"I heard he's amazing," Sharon said, "Mom heard him speak once. He's an orphan, you know. Used to be mixed up with gangs and all, but he reformed and is now helping kids."

I just looked at Sharon in awe, "Marv Greene's not an orphan; he grew up in a house, on the south side. He has a mother, a father, and two sisters. I've seen the house. His dad's an engineer."

"That's what Mom said."

"Sharon, I grew up in the only two orphanages in town, never saw him there."

After the second, "That's what Mom said," I just let it go. If Mrs. Dubois wanted to get the wool pulled over her eyes by that clown, then fine. Sharon's comments did concern me, however.

"What do you want to do? Want to go in and get a drink or go check out the movies."

Sharon thought for a minute, and then said, "Shoot. No dance, I guess. Okay, let's go check out a movie."

We drove to the movie theater, the north side one, and the rain showed no signs of stopping. Sharon guided me to sit in the back row, figuring I would be all over her. She was so thoughtful. Like most movies I saw with her, I had no idea what it was about because I was looking at her. We kissed a little, but as people who had been bound for the dance started to drift in, she seemed awful interested in looking around to see who was there. Jim, Rose, Ben, and Angie walked in; they waived to us but went down front.

Getting pretty late, we started out to take Sharon home. The rain had let up a little, but it was still coming down lightly. As we went around Perimeter Road, planes were still taking off. Troops were headed to Texas no doubt.

I pulled into Sharon's drive and walked her to the side door. She quickly hugged me, kissed me on the lips, then pulled her head back and said, "I love you more than any other boy," and I felt a slight tug on my shirt pocket. She turned to the right as I reached up and patted my pocket, only to feel my initial ring. As I looked up, I saw her form slip through the door. The main door shut, the deadbolt clicked, and Sharon Dubois was gone forever.

***

Clyde didn't know what time it was. Much too early for a Sunday, however, he had to feed the cows this morning so he stumbled out to the study room and the coffee pot.

That's when he first saw Dan sitting there, alone in the dark, the coffee pot already turned on. He was staring at the ceiling.

"Up kind of early?" Clyde mumbled, sitting in the chair next to him.

Dan said, "Never been to bed."

"Kelley? What's wrong?"

"Sharon broke up with me tonight?"

"Oh, man. Just tonight? Why?"

He just shrugged his shoulders, "No idea why, she didn't explain."

"Oh, she didn't mean it," Clyde added, trying to console him, "you two just had a fight, right? No way, call her later and …" Dan just took the ring out of his shirt pocket and plopped it on the table, it bounced, rolled, and then came to a stop.

"And you were the only one that called it, Clyde," he added, "We should all take advice from you. You get things right all the time."

"Oh no, Dan, heck no. It was just a feeling I had, a hunch. I should have never said anything about it. I would trade in that stupid hunch to make this not happen."

Dan got up, poured himself some coffee in a paper cup, and started to leave. "I'll be out in the grove of trees." He left. Clyde then ran to wake Ben up.

Ben said, half asleep, "What? You know what time it …"

"Get up," Clyde added, "emergency meeting."

When Ben finally came in the study room, Al, Cork, and Clyde were already there. "What?"

"Sharon broke up with Kelley last night."

"You're kidding. No way."

Clyde pointed to the ring on the table. Cork picked it up and looked at it.

"Where is he?" Ben asked.

"Out in the grove."

Ben rolled into action, like he usually does, "Okay, I'll get Davis up to go talk to him. Clyde, after the cows, why don't you go out there as well? I'll see if Donovan knows anything. Anybody know any details?" Al and Clyde shrugged their shoulders but Cork was looking at the ring.

"Interesting," Cork said. They all looked at him, "she always wears yarn around this, so it fits on her finger. There's none on here, which means it wasn't on the spur of the moment; it was premeditated."

Ben looked at the three of them, "What the heck is wrong with that girl?"

***

I don't really recall the next few days because I just don't remember much. Stupor is a good word. I could have, should have seen it coming but didn't. I just walked around in a daze. But a nagging reality started to churn up; I had to do something, as this was a totally unacceptable situation. I had to talk to her.

I called her, every hour, that first day, until her voice message inbox became full. That evening, I took a drive up there but was stopped at the gate. I even knew the young airman guarding it. I had been through there so often he knew both of us.

"Sorry, due to the hostilities with Mexico, we have to check ID cards."

"Sharon Dubois, please," I indicated.

"Yea. Sorry about this, man. The colonel's wife called and told us they don't want you visiting."

"Look, we had a fight. Help me out. What if you turned around and I drove through anyway?"

"Then I'd have to arrest you. Hey look, Dan, why don't you go home and call her. She'll come around. You know how young girls get."

"Yes, I know how young girls get." I had no idea how young girls get. I turned around and started back. Well, this certainly was a way for Sharon to handle it. The next day, Sharon had her number changed.

I'll give you a few observations about how one is treated after getting dumped by someone. First of all, when you're cut off at the knees, lying on the floor castrated, kicked in the groin by the most beautiful girl in the world, people don't want anything to do with you. Your friends pat you on the back or say "Oh, sorry," then grab a book or go on their computer. People are afraid to talk to you because they may "set you off." Nobody wants to hear you sulk or talk about what her smile actually did for you. The worst was, "Well, who you gonna go out with now?" It makes you want to grab them by the throat and yell, "Well, who else is there? Is there a girl somewhere who is at least ten percent as good as this one was?"

Frank and Libby Davis were good to me, listened to me at times. Angie was great; she was pretty angry about it. Ben and Jim Donovan didn't say much and I could tell they were thinking, "Man, could this happen to me?" Rose Russo never mentioned it; I think it had to do with her and Sharon being friends.

The fight with the Mustangs came sooner than expected. The timing was excellent for me. I was itching for a good fight and had an overload of emotion I needed to take out on some guy's head. They wanted to meet us at an elementary schoolyard near their clubhouse. Cork sat out in a tree, hours ahead of time, and communicated with Ben as to where they were forming. When they began to assemble on the baseball field, we decided to deploy our group in the trees on the east of them, with The Range just across the road in the tree line to the north. This way we could flank them on each side and use the backstop to protect the center. We met The Range about two blocks away, Ben and their president talked, and then we jogged ahead to our separate lines.

Ben decided to do another quick charge; the more we sat around and thought about it, the more chicken we got. He got in front again, but whispered, "Okay, same formation as last time. If we need bats or clubs, we rush back here, get them, and then charge again."

These clowns must have had some sort of romantic view of street fighting because they were standing around in small groups, talking. Dogface Bus Quint was standing there, flexing his muscles, when we jumped the fence. We didn't yell or scream, just ran quietly, and smacked right into them. One big bruiser saw us and starting running right at our center. Corky managed to trip him and he fell down on his knees. Murdock came flying in, brought up his foot, and kicked him hard in the groin. He was all done, squealing on the ground. Without losing a stride we all made contact, fists flying.

Within a second, The Range ran across the road, through the Mustangs' parked cars, and rushed their left. And let me tell you, these guys brought the main dish to the potluck. Figuring they only had five or six guys, nearly twenty guys came running at them. They must have gotten all their uncles out on a weekend pass from prison; these guys were longshoremen, adults.

There turned out to be no weapons. We were boxing, and advancing. The Range was involved in a massacre. They were not only smashing guys, but also kicking, twisting arms until they cracked, and karate chopping. We were pushing them back; the other side had Mustangs lying on the ground, screaming in pain.

Cork suddenly got too far out in front and got in the middle of about four of them. Empire yelled, "Cork!" and took off ahead to help. Clyde and I just closed in, and continued. Then I started to get nuts, I was getting hit but I loved it, punching back even more fiercely. I had a guy start to go over on me, leaning forward, and I just kept punching. I soon had his blood flying all around me.

I felt a big hand grab my shoulder, it was Ben, "Kelley, stop it! He's done."

Just then, we saw the red lights flashing, only this time we all took off the way we came, The Range right along with us, hopping the fence and sprinting through the neighborhoods. And this time, the Mustangs ran toward their cars and were grabbed by the police. They must have had fifteen guys lying on the ball field, some in obvious pain. There was no way they were going to lie their way out of this beating.

We all got back to the farm intact, only a few scrapes and bruises. We did it this time. Ben sent off another message, asking them for another rematch, only to show our fortitude. We later heard they had two broken hands, one broken leg, two broken jaws and three broken ribs. They did not respond to our offer to fight again.

School was starting in a couple of weeks and we mainly kept to the farm. Ben thought it would be good to keep a low profile on the streets. The police were getting fed up with the street fights and more patrols were put out. Ben was also worried about it. While he had been worried about us getting hurt, he was now starting to fear us getting so good, that we might seriously hurt somebody. He had a personal meeting with me, saying he really got scared watching me in that fight, thought I was going to kill that kid. I was a bit snippy with him.

School finally started. I certainly wasn't looking forward to it. Sharon's absence in my life made the routine sort of boring and frustrating. I was impolite, easily angered, and for some reason food didn't taste very good anymore. I didn't joke or flirt with girls, ask any out, or even like talking to them. As I saw it, Sharon didn't like me when I was nice, why bother. I was a tough gang member during the day, with the Eagles or my female friends. At night I would cry, yes, cry like a baby, sometimes for thirty or forty minutes. Sometimes I had to hold onto my gut it hurt so badly. I was between the proverbial rock and a hard place. One minute I wanted to smash everybody's face in, and another I wanted to get down on my knees and beg her to come back to me. I was a lonely orphan once again.

All my courses this semester were at the college, which meant I was only at my locker at the beginning and end of the school day. Frank and I had many classes together. The college was connected to the high school by a long hallway, and it was a long walk. Juniors now, we stood and watched the girls walk by. We joked and laughed, but somehow it wasn't the same as before Sharon, but then hardly anything was. Cheri from history walked by and we traded pretend flirts, she was in college as well. I certainly didn't mind being in high school and taking college courses; it got me away from my old haunts. I was surprised when I looked up on the wall to see a welcome-back-to-school poster from the newly elected student body president, my old flame, lovely library Lisa.

Having a few minutes, this was Frank's first opportunity to tell me about the meeting he had with school officials and the Chair of the Town Council. Frank didn't want me there because, well honestly, I was a bit of a loose cannon, citing my comments about Mrs. Popover's daughter at the sociology club meeting and the way I had been acting after Sharon dumped me. He said Mrs. Popover was furious with us, that she had heard about the street fight. Frank had denied it. He also said she didn't have any proof that we were connected to the Delk Hall burning, but was "keeping an eye on us." The only thing that saved us was that Diane Win was there, and she made reference to our good grades and advanced levels in school.

Frank was emphatic, and Ben agreed with him, that we were headed for trouble if the Eagles remained on this road of fighting and revenge. This was not the reason we started the club and I had to agree with him on that. More or less, Frank was telling me there were more important issues here then some little French girl ditching me. I felt like I was getting a good scolding, but Frank was my best friend and he was the only one who could get away with it in my present state of mind.

My first day of school was great, I didn't know anybody and everyone was interested in knowledge, and I jumped right in.

At our next club meeting, Ben hinted that something big was up with Holy Cross and the Mustangs. He felt the Cross was going to move on the Mustangs soon. The Mustangs were hurting for sure, we saw a couple of them in the halls and they still had casts on. We were all hoping for a terminal blow. Of course, despite their poor showing, the spin around the hallways was they kicked our butts again and they were going to smash Holy Cross next. Like I said earlier, the true outcome of a fight hardly ever matters. I was beginning to see Frank's viewpoint, fighting at all hardly ever matters.

After the meeting, Ben had me and Frank stay and, joined by Al and Cork, he discussed some new intelligence. "Cork, why don't you explain this to Dan."

"You sure you want me to go over this?" Cork asked Ben.

But Frank answered, "Gosh guys, Dan is a big boy now, let him handle it."

"Okay," Cork went on, "Dan, we lifted an email which includes some stuff about Sharon."

"Whose email?" I asked.

"Betsy Barney."

"How did you get that? How can we get into email accounts?"

"Never mind," Al Myers added, which was a warning to leave it alone.

Cork went on, "Anyway, we've been keeping an eye on her because she's pretty much in the know about everything that's going on. And we weren't spying on Sharon, rather Barney, it just happened to have stuff about her. I'll read this email; it was actually a reply to one she sent." Cork read from a sheet of paper his hand, "'and yes, it was a pretty wild party last Saturday. I guess the girl's parents were out of town and about forty showed up … no, I didn't see Candi there … but OMG, guess who showed up, Marv Greene, and you'll never guess what happened … He brought his latest chicky pie … no, I don't know her, some freshman named Sharon Dubois … so, listen to this … they go into one of the rooms together and then we hear a lot of screaming. Anyway, this Sharon girl comes running out and is screaming … in her underwear! Can you believe that? Running around the whole house in her underwear. Well, nobody knew exactly what had happened but we figured she was trying to set him up or something … I mean Marv Greene wouldn't harm a girl that way … we think she was up to something.' And that's where it ends," Cork finished. All fours guys looked at me.

"Oh, no way," I said, "Sharon's about as popular with me right now as Adolf Hitler, but I know that girl and there is no way she'd pull a stunt like that with Marv Greene."

"We're not implying she did, Dan," Ben interjected.

"Good gosh!" I pounded my fist on the table, "I was trying to tell her about that guy, I told her he was full of crap. Why the heck did she go out with that clown? Shoot, am I going to have to fight Marv Greene now?"

Ben and Cork laughed, Frank joined in and then said, "Kelley, there's chivalry, and then there's suicide. You ain't gonna fight Greene and live."

Ben added, "If it was before Sharon did that to you, I'd help you, but not now. Sorry, buddy, consider this is a direct presidential order not to start anything with Greene, she went out with him, and she has to pay the fiddler."

"What's the date on that email?" I asked, Cork showed me, "This is unbelievable! This makes it the Saturday night a week after she broke up with me. So much for babysitting! You know, Sharon would have been better off if she'd drawn a gun, rather than my ring, out of her pocket and shot me dead right there in the carport! She could have had her mom call the MPs and they could have thrown my body in the lake. A shotgun would have been better. No, my little French sweetie has to take a knife and stab me in the heart, slowly, and a month later she's still doing it."

Ben admitted, "Well, we did run a check on her before, Dan. We didn't find much of anything; most everything she told you was the truth. Her only problem seemed to be that her grades were awful; she's on academic probation this semester. That's all."

The guys waited until I calmed down, which I did, and thanked them for the news. I didn't drink alcohol before or after that, but that day sure did seem like a good day to start.

The school administration wanted to change a library policy, because there had been so many disciplinary incidents in the library. They decided to drop the yellow library passes and make students use the blue ones only. They informed the student council, which set up a public hearing session to obtain student views on the matter. I made a note to attend.

About a week later, I was at my locker at the start of the day. Frank was with me. I heard the faint sound of some girl's shoes clicking down the hall, turned around to check it out, and came face to face with Sharon Dubois.

She stopped, "Hi, Dan," she said, attempting a faint smile. I turned around and got some more books out of my locker. "I said, hello, Dan," I heard again. I ignored it. "Dan, I'd like to at least be friends. Are you going to talk to me?"

I just huffed, not turning around, "Take my ring back, then we can discuss being friends."

"I'm sorry. I just can't do that," keeping her voice low.

"Then I guess you don't have a new friend," I snipped. Oh no, the dreaded "I just want to be friends" speech. Shoot, I was half hoping she wanted to apologize and discuss getting back together. I was hoping she would break down, cry, apologize about Greene, and beg my forgiveness. I woke up from my dream as she slowly walked a few feet away, stopped next to the wall in a space between the lockers, and just stood there.

So I just continued to mess around in my locker. Frank was dying to run away somewhere. Then the worst thing happened, Ben showed up with his little pistol, Angie.

Angie said hello and hugged me, then saw Sharon standing a few feet away. "What the heck is she doing here?"

I just shrugged my shoulders, "Says she wants to be friends."

"Oh no," Angie went on, "she wants to be 'just friends?' That's a death notice, Danny. Did you tell her no? What's she still doing there?"

"Beats me, free country I guess."

"Well, since it's a free country and all, I'll go have a chat with her."

As Angie walked over to her, Frank looked at Ben and me and said, "There's about three or four things that can happen right now, and none of them are any good."

Then we saw little Angie in Sharon's face, "You want to be my friend? I'll talk to you." Then she made a fist and stuck it up to Sharon's nose, "I'll also give you a fat lip. How would like that, Frenchie?"

Ben mumbled, "Oh, no," and then walked over there, picked up Angie around the waist, sort of tucking her under his arm. He started to carry her out, stopped by us, and announced, "I'm going to take Angie outside for a little talk. We'll be outside if you need us."

He continued to carry the struggling girl, almost horizontal, as she kicked and said, "I can take her. Let me down, you big dope. I can take her."

Sharon was standing alone, her face beet-red.

Frank grabbed my arm, "I'm going to class. Hey, take five or ten minutes and go talk to her. Come on, it can't hurt. I'll square it with the professor. Go on. That's an order."

After Frank departed, I closed my locker and walked over to a now hostile Sharon who said to me, her voice cracking, "Is your tiny friend done with me now?"

I shrugged my shoulders, "You know her; nobody tells Angie what to do."

"I want to be friends. That's all I want to do."

"I have a deal for you," I said, but still busy trying to put something together on the spur of the moment.

"I don't make deals. We broke up. People do it all the time. Sometimes it's just over, married people get divorced, boyfriends and girlfriends ..."

"Do you want to hear it or not?"

"Go ahead."

"You take my ring back ..."

"Dan, I can't take a ring from a boy I don't love. I can't ..."

"Are you going to let me finish?"

"Go ahead."

"You take my ring back for a month. You don't have to wear it. Put it in your dresser if you want. You don't have to go out with me and I won't try and kiss you. You can date whoever you want. But you have to talk to me, not just say no to everything I suggest."

"What's that going to accomplish? Why do I have to take your ring back just to talk?"

"Because you won't talk to me!" I almost yelled. "I can't get on the base. You changed your phone number. I need a chance, Sharon," tears filled my eyes, "a chance to make a case for you. Without a keepsake on your dresser I'll spend the next six months trying to make a darn appointment with you."

"It won't solve anything. Friends can talk just as easily as anyone else."

"Then go away, come back and talk to me when you are ready to seriously discuss this. Beat it!"

She turned and strode quickly down the hall for about twenty feet. Then, realizing she was going the wrong way, had to embarrassingly turn around and walk back past me again. As she passed, I didn't see the Sharon Dubois I once knew.

I walked down to statistics class. The top of the hour had passed and the halls were empty. But as I approached my lecture hall, I once again heard the click-clack of Sharon's shoes behind me. "Dan, wait," but I quickly ducked into my classroom.

Statistics class was boring. I sat next to Frank. We were taking notes on our handhelds when Frank, probably bored as well, sent me a text message. It read, "Honey, I'm sorry, but I just want to be friends." I texted back, "Shut up! I can't be friends with you because I'm at my limit. Sharon is my new friend now which makes me one over, and I have to dump you." Another came back to me, "I'm trying to be civil here and you're such a dolt." My response, "I could very easily substitute another word for civil!" That was my best friend; he could yell at me one minute and make me laugh at the next.

Frank and I stayed late to talk to the professor. As we departed the classroom, the halls were empty again. And there, standing by a wall a few feet away, was Sharon. From what I could gather, she had been there the whole two-hour class period. Frank gave me a pat on the back and just left. As I approached her, except for being beet-red from the neck up, there stood the amazing girl with a face and figure that could turn a dead man's head. Her mood, however, was a different matter.

"Dan Kelley. You just have to explain to me why you can't be my friend." There were tears in her eyes and she was visible shaking.

As I stood there, trying to come up with something witty, I realized that something was very wrong with her. What the heck was the matter here? It was as if something wasn't following her arrangements, like something wasn't going according to script. Didn't she know about ninety percent of my heart was still lying on the floor of her carport? Didn't she see it every time she came home from school, all squished from when they ran over it with the car? I knew her. She couldn't be that stupid. "I told you, I can't explain it. I've tried, I tried imagining it, how I would handle seeing that darling smile aimed at another guy. How would you greet me when you saw me from afar, 'Hello, baby,' or 'Hello, Mr. Kelley?' I think the explaining is something you need to be doing right now."

"You didn't answer my question!"

I just shrugged my shoulders and shook my head. I didn't know what else could be said. And true to her character, she stomped off down the hall. I quietly spoke the words, although she was already out of earshot, "I can only be … what I was."

One day, around noon I think, Cork had asked me if I would man a post he was monitoring. Seems he found this dark space, up on the utility balcony above the hallway our lockers were on, only further down. He went up there because it was just above the area where the Mustangs hung out after lunch and before classes started again. He could plainly hear them from there but they could not see him. Cork was a rascal.

So I'm hiding up there as Matt Fuller and Bus Quint were at their lockers. Suddenly this little freshman kid walks up, and with Quint standing right in front of his locker, the kid takes his forearm and pushes Dogface to the right. Quint mouths off, "Hey, what do you think you're doing, I'll stuff your head right in that locker." Quint laughed as the kid scampered off.

I also see these two strange guys, watching the whole thing. They looked kind of weird. I'd never seen them before as they had on dark green work shirts and heavy jeans. So, one of the guys, walks over to Quint and pushes him in a similar manner as the kid had just done, only I know this guy didn't have a locker there. He was trying to start a fight.

"You, too?" Bus spoke right up, "Looks like I'm gonna have to bust some heads today."

Then the kid made Bus jump, "Okay then. Let's go!" he threw his books down and started to square off into a boxing stance. "Come on, Quint, let's go, you and me, right here." A crowd was starting to form.

You had never seen the big gang leader backpedal so quickly, "What, a, yea right. I fight you and your buddy jumps me, right?"

"Okay, hey," he yelled to his friend, "you take Fuller, that will even things up."

The second green kid yells at Matt, "Fuller. You're girlfriend here won't fight my friend. So looks like you and me need to go for a roll." The second kid walked right over to Fuller and took a vicious swing at him, only he missed, smashing into and denting a locker door. The sound was so loud, everyone looked at them. Fuller quickly backed up the hall a few feet. He never hit back.

Quint yelled, "Do you guys know who you're messing with?"

First green guy, "From what I can tell, a couple of scared cowards."

"Okay, that's it. You guys are Holy Cross, huh? Okay, freaks, this is on, you have to fight us now. We'll be in touch."

I could tell what they were up to. They wanted to get a fight started. Then a funny thing happened. One of the Cross kids looked right up at me standing above him, almost knowing I was there, and winked. Both picked up their books and left.

I had not seen Ben and Angie for a few days and I finally did, standing by my locker. I walked right up to Angie and hugged her. As I backed up, she exclaimed, "Wow, bet I would'a got a kiss if I'd have clocked her."

I asked her, “Angie, do you understand where I’m coming from here? I mean, doesn’t she realize how I feel?”

“Oh, man,” she replied, “She’s so weird about this; it’s almost like she wanted to dump you and now wants you to feel good about it. She threw you in the hamper with her dirty clothes, Danny. She knows how you feel. She’s not that stupid; a moron could see it.”

Angie provides a good reality check, she never has a filter working, and everything that comes out comes straight from the heart. Then I headed down to the locker room. Finally quitting the cross country team, I had to go down and clean my stuff out. There was my old friend, Tom Crosby. He was seated on the bench, staring off into space. “Tom.”

“Hey, Kelley,” he mumbled. “So, now I hear you lost a girlfriend?”

I stopped behind him, clenched my fists, and decided that if one wise crack comes out of his mouth his head was coming off. “Yea.”

“She did the same thing to me and in the same way,” he began, at first in a wise guy tone, but then softened, “She did it to the both of us, just when we needed her most.”

I relaxed the fists and sat down next to him. “So, you dating again now?”

He looked at me and huffed, “How can you date anyone else after a girl like her?”

“Good point,” I added. “Tom, the letter jacket you gave her, those are expensive, how come you never took it back?”

“After she wore it, it didn’t mean anything to me anymore.”

The student council hearing on the library pass issue began at 7:30 a.m., before classes started. Jim Donovan and I attended, sitting in the back of the room. Ironically, the hearing was held in the library. Lovely Lisa sat in the center of the long table along the windows, everyone facing her. Mr. “Puke Face” Carter, administration representative, stood behind her. Several heated questions were asked; Mr. Carter handled all of them, not even letting Lisa respond. In summary, his main point was that this was a security issue. Administration has the final say over security, and this is the way it's going to be. Case closed. Donovan raised his hand and spoke.

"Mr. Carter, many students who do behave themselves use those passes, many don't have a particular assignment to get a blue pass for, and isn't time spent reading a positive thing?"

"Mr. Donovan," the old creep replied, "maybe those students could read their books up in study hall, rather than sit in the library and have to listen to you and your hoodlum friends hatch a plan for your next street brawl."

He really got old Donnie Boy ripped then, "Or, sir, this may be an administration plot to continue the asinine policy of mandatory study halls, to save jobs for outdated and unproductive faculty, much like yourself."

A loud round of cheers broke out, several students jumping up and yelling. The meeting was turning into a jailbreak. You could almost see Lisa's skin crawl as she sat there, fuming at Jim and me. Carter called off the hearing and then called security. Most everyone filed out in a calm manner. Outside, in the main hall, a student TV crew was interviewing participants. Someone handed me a packet of yellow three by five cards. Not seeing the camera, I held them up and flipped them up in the air. Then everyone else started doing it, Donovan as well.

As you have probably guessed by now, the student TV channel ran the whole tape, several times, with Donovan and I shown flipping yellow cards. The next week, the school newspaper had a wonderful still of us doing the same thing, under the headline, "Students Support Yellow Pass Riot." And of course, Frank Davis was just thrilled to death.

"You stupid, irresponsible, near-sighted, wing nuts!" Frank Davis yelled, throwing a copy of the newspaper article he had printed off the computer down on the table in our study room. Ben was seated at the head, Cork standing behind him, Jim and I sat across from Frank. Rose and Angie were standing as well, now almost a part of the club. Frank took off on us, "We can't send you to a student council meeting without pictures on the front page? Jim, I would expect something like this from Kelley, but you? You're one of the most elegant speakers we got. Did you two morons know that Mr. Carter is the president of the teachers' union at this place? And Kelley, you're gonna get expelled; you don't have your apprenticeship done or have your associate's degree. You're eighteen next year; you're gonna get drafted. This time next year, you're going to be living in a hole in the ground in Mexico, eating sand, while federales take pot shots at that bone head of yours!" Frank sat down, breathed hard, and said, "Okay, sorry guys, now I feel better. Ben, we need Al and Cork to get some inside information on this rally or exhibition or riot," he shot a wicked glance at Jim and I, "that is supposed to be happening. And if it goes down, we all need to be somewhere else with witnesses around."

"Okay," Ben said, he nodded at Corky Wall who then left the room. "Guys, next meeting let's come up with a plan. If some sort of riot breaks out at the school, we're going to get blamed for this, especially since we have our TV stars right on the front page."

Things were becoming a little rough at school. Despite our high achievement levels, some of the teachers were picking on us in classes. We got citations for being a minute late, and we rarely got any library passes. The integrity of the Eagles was disintegrating.

Ben Holden had a long talk with me. Referring to my recent behavior, he said a few guys were even questioning my membership in the club. I really needed these guys so I took it to heart.

I was eating lunch over in the high school when the student body president's office called me. Informing me of the president's desire to meet with me, her assistant wanted to schedule something. Trying to put her off by indicating I was clear over at the college, I tried to stall for time in order to meet with Frank. Frank didn't come to school that day so I had to call him at home. He didn't have much to say through his stuffy nose, only to be careful on what I would say. I called Lisa's office back right away and made an appointment after classes.

Lisa had a pretty nice office on the second floor of the administration building. A young woman had seated me in front of her desk, but when Lisa came in she motioned me over to a couch. As usual, Lisa looked great, even better than before. She wore her hair up and formal.

"How are you, Dan," Lisa smiled, then treated me to a hug and kiss on the cheek, something I certainly wasn't expecting. We sat.

"Good, how are you?"

She smiled, "Dan, the main purpose of this meeting isn't personal, but I need to get some old baggage out of the way. I treated you pretty badly, back in the day, and I want to apologize. I was pretty cruel. Can you consider forgiving me?"

"Oh, already forgiven long ago," I lied right through my teeth. "I was a pretty fast kid back then. I tried not only rushing this relationship too fast, but also some others. I had different expectations I guess. And when you didn't match those, I got frustrated."

"What expectations?" she asked.

"I didn't respect your father for his wishes. I didn't believe that he would be socially crippled if I parked my manure hauling truck outside his house, only that he didn't want the dirty orphan boy parking there. I never assumed you had a boyfriend, I figured since we had made out, you didn't have one and I thought you loved me.

Plus that day we met for coffee, and you put me on hold for your real boyfriend, well, I had bought a ring to give you that day."

She put her face in her hands and just sat there. "I'm sorry."

"So, how did it go with your cadet, did you cut him loose?"

"Not exactly," she said, still buried in her hands, "He asked me for a pre-engagement and I accepted."

We both just sat there, staring at the room. It was funny, although the outcome was a disaster. It felt good just telling her the truth. Clyde had told me about his talk with Ben and Cork about, although a witch, Lisa being honest with me. I was beginning to think these little hitches came with relationships, and being truthful was the best strategy in the long run.

"So," recomposing and moving on, "I need a favor, not a personal one."

"Oh, I thought you were going to dump the guy and go steady with me," getting no reaction, I added, "Lisa, that was a joke."

She finally laughed, "Be careful, you got me thinking about it now. No, my favor is, I need you to call off this riot."

I was stunned, "Lisa, that picture in the paper? Donovan and I just went to the meeting. We didn't know a thing about any stupid riot."

"So, you or your group has had no hand in organizing this thing?"

"What thing?"

"The protest scheduled for this Thursday afternoon in front of the administration building."

"No way!"

"That's funny; some of the information coming in indicates that some of the south side gangs are behind this."

"This one isn't."

She sat, thinking for a minute. Then she said, "Okay, good enough. Any ideas as to who is behind it?"

"No, but I'll check around."

We both got up. “Thanks for coming. So, Dan, do you want to get together sometime? Things don’t have to be all formal for us, do they?”

I was a bit confused, especially in light of her recent decision to keep the army guy. I shuffled my feet back and forth. What was going on? “I’m not sure what you mean.”

“I mean, sometimes people need to make decisions on the spur of the moment for what they think is best for them. Sometimes they have to be decided very quickly, and sometimes we question our logic regarding those decisions.”

So in other words she’s saying I got my guy, now I need to think if it’s really what I want to do. I wondered if ends-of-the-earth type stuff was just a condition only a few people got. “I’d better go.”

“Do you have a girlfriend?”

“Did, but I just lost her. I guess you could say I’m still carrying a torch.”

“Fair enough,” she said, “Good bye.”

As I caught a ride and rode home with Clyde, I knew there was no way she was ever going to dump her army stud. That was her future, for her and her dad. Although she would love the compliments and kisses, next Christmas I would be back on the “will call” list. I also wasn’t so sure of her absolute honesty anymore.

At the Wednesday night meeting, I gave the guys my intelligence. We decided to all help the cook with Thursday supper, starting at 2 p.m., so he would be able to verify where we were. Ben announced a slight setback in the Mustang affair. It seems the Cross set up a fight with them but didn’t show on the field. The Mustangs were advertising the fact that Cross had chickened out. Complicating matters, the town paper had two interesting articles in it. In one, it appeared a fire had taken place at the Mustang’s storage barn, the one out west. Several of their custom streetcars were burned, and they say miracles don't happen; one of the cars was Marv Greene's green machine. Also, there was evidence of drugs being stored in the building, and all registered members were charged with possession. Although no connection to the Mustangs was reported, another article indicated the old warehouse used by the gang had a serious sewer backup, causing an incredible amount of damage. So even if the Holy Cross final blow was never delivered, these other events could mean the end of the famous Mustangs.

We all left school early on Thursday to be back on the farm and with the cook. Milt also joined us because he wanted to help. It was a good thing, the demonstration at the school turned ugly, and I estimate I was peeling my second batch of potatoes when the riot broke out.

CHAPTER SIX

No one could say we didn't have a nice fall day for a riot. It was sunny, with very little wind, and the foliage was beautiful. The students should have been gathering for an intramural football game or maybe a bus trip to the apple orchard. Personally, I was peeling potatoes.

As students exited the school, small groups formed and individuals took turns leading discussions on the library pass regulation. As the small groups got bigger, a loudspeaker was used. It was innocent enough, the speakers mostly encouraged the students to stop at the library Monday morning and sign a petition to save the yellow passes. There were no chants, calls to arms, or directions given for civil disobedience. I heard even Lisa, student body president, joined as a speaker supporting the status quo. However, an antiwar group joined in, and then the feminists sent a contingent, which added to the crowd. I was told that it was close to breaking up when things got out of hand.

Someone had set charges, nothing deadly, probably untraceable and legal fireworks, along the large windows on the second floor of the building, right above the crowd. This floor was almost totally made up of student government offices; even Lisa's office was there. When the charges went off, the big windows shattered, and the broken glass fell on the crowd.

Seems like everyone did what I would have done; they ran. Since the building faced west, the people ran north, south, and west. Resembling an out of control mob for a brief few minutes, most people then just caught busses or went to the parking lot to get their cars and go home. There was no stone throwing or effigy burning. The police were called, but there were no injuries or arrests. In all, it was a rather sedate riot.

The reason the "Yellow Pass Riot" name stuck, was one of popular spin. Incidents of civil disobedience in these times were becoming a national trend. The local town newspaper, along with the school paper, was eager to promote a local slant to the nationwide antiwar movement and general unrest due to the economy.

We did okay. The police came down, talked to all of us, checked out our alibi, and looked at some financial and phone records. Then we were visited by the investigator from the Department of Education. Even being rather pleasant, he only talked to a few of us and then left, saying he would read the police report. In any event, we didn't get arrested.

School returned to normal, except for the plywood over the space where the big front windows used to be. Things were calm. I spent most all of my time over at the college and since most of us rode in one of the trucks together, I was never out by the bus loading area, never by the buses that took the military kids back to the base.

I was playing it cool with Sharon. Making what I thought was a good compromise to her, she had the next move. I was never going to say that this was all over, smile and be her friend, and I hoped to get little clues from her on what went wrong. I didn't think what I had proposed was that bad of a deal for her; there were no major requirements other than listening. Although, maybe listening was the one thing she didn't want to do. She may be embarrassed about the Marv Greene fiasco or, similar to Lisa, maybe gave in to her father's wishes for her to be dating a better class of guys. What I had said to her earlier that evening was bothering me, "People in love find a way." Would the opposite be true? And the last words she said to me, was it for distraction purposes? I began to formulate a philosophical dilemma: If she loved me, she wouldn't have broken up; if she broke up, she must have been lying. It can't be switched on and off that fast.

In the back of my mind, I still had a faint hope that she might call, or stop by my locker, or even pass me a note. I wasn't a bad guy. I would let her explain to me her reasoning. I would even listen if she wanted to list off the things I was doing wrong and allow me to change. Whenever the phone on my handheld went off, I quickly pulled it out, hoping to see her name on the caller ID screen.

One day, for some reason, I skipped the usual long hall route back to my locker and cut through the area of the school I knew she was in most. And suddenly, there she was, talking to a group of friends. Ducking into a doorway, I stayed hidden and watched. I imagined it was the interior design crew, going over some big project. Then I saw it, she flashed that smile, that big dimpled smile that used to set me on fire. That's why I didn't want to be a buddy and hang with her crew in the hall. I didn't want to be around, see that smile, and be part of the background. I dashed down the hall in the opposite direction and slipped away.

Back at the old bunkhouse, Ben stopped Frank Davis and me saying he had a meeting with a couple of kids who had some information for us. He didn't want to appear to be ganging up on them, so he wanted just Frank and me there. I felt good about being asked, finally gaining back some trust from the big guy and the others.

Merlin Kingsford was the local chapter president of the Academic Society, the cream of the crop scholars of the school system. In other words, he was the head geek. Fitting the bill, Mr. Kingsford was a small, undernourished sophomore in high school, but working on his master's degree in physics; he wore thick glasses and had thin, blonde hair. Chloe Rankin was the head of the Equal Treatment League, an interest group into diversity and equal opportunity. Whatever the title said, Ms. Rankin and her group were dye-in-the-wool feminists. Expecting a tongue lashing from two clowns, we were pleasantly surprised to find them both personable and helpful.

The five of us sat at the table in our study room as Rankin began, "We think you guys are getting set up for this yellow pass riot thing. We usually wouldn't give a darn about some south-side gang like you, but some interesting things are going on."

Ben asked, "So you know we didn't do it?"

Kingsford took over, "We don't think you did it, because we know who did."

"Do you know a person by the name of Betsy Barney?" Rankin asked. When she saw me raise my hand, she went on, "What did you do to her, Kelley, beat her up?"

I let the sarcastic comment go, "No, I went out with a friend of hers, gosh, back in the seventh grade. For some reason, they took issue with my background. I didn't advertise being an orphan back then, so I never told her. Then she found out."

"I don't think that was the total cause of this," Chloe went on, "but I know Barney and her Popover buddies despise the southsiders."

"Chloe, this seems awful petty for Betsy, let alone the Popovers," Frank added, "I can't believe in this day and age people still have these thoughts."

"Welcome to our world," Merlin added. "Chloe and I are both gay; yes, all the jokes are true. Do you guys think you have a monopoly on being put down?"

We had heard all the jokes, even made a few of them, and for the first time realized how much these two were hurt by them.

Chloe lamented, "Sensing the media sensation with these south side gang fights, those girls set up the yellow pass thing. I have a good idea what happened."

Ben asked, "Who actually set the fireworks?"

"We think it was the jocks; we know it was them," Merlin added.

"I have an office in that area of the building. With all the people in and out of there, no way those things were set ahead of time," Chloe went on. "They found no timers; those fuses were set with a match. I left my office after the demonstration began, after the student body president had already gone down there. I saw Barney's jock buddies running down the north stairs. I was on my way down them as well when I heard them go off. Now, I can't testify that I saw them lighting fuses, but the offices were empty when I left, and I didn't see anyone else around.

"Mrs. Popover wants you guys out of here. She threw a fit when the town attorney said he didn't have enough evidence to charge you guys with the riot. But she's going to get you somehow. Rumor has it she turned this over to the Department of Education and told them she wants something done about you guys."

"Any suggestions on what to do?" Ben asked.

Chloe got a little hard on this one, "First of all, you have to watch yourselves. The truancy officers will be keeping a close eye on you. Most importantly, you guys need to stop this macho, grade-school-boy street fighting that's been going on. Grow up!"

Ben became a little testy with that but handled it nicely, "Understood. But, like you, we've had some trouble down here as well. A couple of my boys got beat up. Kelley's roommate got killed when one of those extortionist Mustangs hit him too hard. They threatened my one friend's sister. We have a right to be here, Chloe, and a right to live. If anyone or any group tries to take that away, we will fight them. And if we lose we will come back and fight them again."

"Understood as well, Ben," Chloe smiled.

After the meeting concluded and our guests had left, Frank Davis, of all people, started to laugh. He then stopped a minute, and then started again.

"If this was Kelley, Frank, I would understand, but you?" Ben said, fearing a homosexual joke was about to be delivered. "What is it?"

"The head nerd of Centura," Frank laughed.

"What about him?"

"His name is 'Merlin!'"

We all three laughed.

Frank Davis, now fully into pre-law at the college level, scored a big hit by being voted in as a member of the Law Club. This was a group of mostly law students at the law school, who, upon careful consideration, allowed high-achieving pre-law students into their organization. He was the youngest member to be admitted. Taking into consideration our current poor reputation, this was a major feat. We had a party for him. All the guys, girlfriends, Libby, and even Frank's now steady girl, attended. We drank toasts of Vitamin C water.

During Christmas break, I needed to go to the base so I called Lisa.

"Hello," she said.

"Hi, Lisa. This is Dan Kelley."

"Dan, what's up?"

"I need to get onto the base."

"Why?" she asked.

"I want to run a load of manure up to your dad." There was silence on the other end. "Lisa, that was just a joke. I need to go to an excess equipment giveaway at the Army warehouse."

"Sure. Okay, why don't you just go? What do you need me for?"

"They won't let me on the base anymore unless I'm invited. You need to tell the guy at the gate I'm coming."

"So, you're using me?"

"Yes."

"Okay. When you coming?"

"Thursday afternoon."

"Okay."

"You'll tell the guy at the gate?"

"Yea. I'll do it when I go home tonight. Dan?"

"What?"

"Don't screw around up here."

I was trying to like her but she had absolutely no sense of humor. When I went through the gate that Thursday, my old friend the airman was there. He was impressed at my new invitation to the base, teasing me on how I always chose daughters of high-ranking officers. I told him they liked me for my aristocratic background. There was one major change in his appearance; he was carrying a rifle.

I had no intention of going to the warehouse. I just wanted, ignoring the order of my former girlfriend, to screw around. Going around on Perimeter Road, I noticed more big cargo planes landing. Since most of the experienced soldiers and airman were sent to Texas, Thompson was being staffed by new recruits. Perimeter Road had not changed much; the stones were still there.

When I went into Sharon's old neighborhood, I made sure to go slow and keep the rumble of the big diesel truck down. I halted at the stop sign, a couple of houses from Sharon's, and just sat there for a minute. I didn't see anyone outside, no big surprise in this cold weather. Finally, I turned away from the house and started my return trip. Gosh, I hoped I wasn't becoming a stalker. As months wore on since that summer night in her carport, a creeping fear started to overcome me, one that was telling me this girl was never going to come back to me.

When Frank and Libby Davis turned eighteen in January, they received their trust payment. Although I had never known this before, their parents' home was still in the estate and they got ownership of that as well. The fiduciary had rented out the house to an Army couple, and since the lease was good for another year, Frank decided to allow them to stay until then. Their eighteenth birthday also meant they could bail out of the orphanage, if they desired.

Our book discussion group, meeting inside now, continued with Pine's *Living in the Woods.* One of my all-time favorite quotes was, "answers only come after great peace of mind." I became obsessed with the book, much more than the other guys. It must have been my particular stage of life, having so many questions and no peace of mind to answer them because the questions kept my mind from being peaceful. It was a dilemma. I could think of nothing better than meeting Tom Pine, sitting down and talking to him.

Our discussion finally turned to the author. Corky said that he heard the guy was a cult leader, that he lived out in the woods, did live animal sacrifices, and ate pine trees. The latter was how he had gotten his name. Bo Schlitz said he was a wizard, a mystic who lived with the wolves. I didn't believe them, as the book mentioned none of that stuff. He did sound like a loner, but also a wise teacher, a modern day Socrates. All in all, he sounded like he was a guy who figured out how to answer philosophical questions, and I had a lot of those.

We had a snowstorm one school day, a monster. Although they finally called off school, a bunch of us were already in one of

Milt's trucks halfway there when we heard. Vehicles were getting stuck all over, but we had no problem with the big diesel. So we had returned and were sitting in the study room, all of us into individual activities, when Angie came in. She must have gotten tired of picking on Ben, so she started on me. I wasn't in the mood.

She sat down by me, "Danny, you look skinny. Are you eating enough?"

"Yea," I mumbled.

"You been to the doctor lately?"

"Yea, up at the base clinic, last month."

"What did he say?"

"He said there's too much stress in my life. He told me to restrict the people I hang out with to those who are over two and half feet tall."

"You know, Kelley, you're not too big for me to give a fat lip either, just as quickly as I would have that blockhead girl you used to go out with." Angie was the only one who could say anything derogatory about Sharon; none of the Eagles dared.

Clyde looked up from his reading, "Kelley, we told you not to get her going; it only makes it worse on the rest of us."

"Shut up as well, Clyde," Angie said, and then turned back to me, "Danny, I know what you need. You need a girlfriend. You need to stop moping around, quit thinking about …"

I glared at her, "Angie, you're approaching the limit of our friendship here!"

Uncharacteristic for her, she calmed down, "Sorry. I'm going to fix you up anyway." She got up and left the room.

I smiled and told the guys in the room, "Now why did I ever think I could talk her out of something she wants to do?" We laughed. You could try to stop Angie from doing something, but it was only putting off the inevitable.

Angie got Libby Davis to set me up with one of her bookish friends. Teri was cute, almost as short as Angie, but had sort of a long nose. I mean, it wasn't ugly or anything, just a characteristic. Frank, Angie, Teri, and I went to a basketball game at the south side arena. I hated basketball.

Teri was quiet, but smart and witty. We went over everything superficial. When we were walking back to our truck, she put her hand around the small of my back, which was kind of nice. She gave me her number, but I never called her.

One day at school, I ran into Angie and Ben at my locker. Expecting to get a dressing down by the pint-sized girl for the failed date, she just smiled at me, "It wasn't there, was it?"

"What?" I asked.

"The stuff."

"Right, the stuff wasn't there."

After the couple had left, Frank and his girl showed up. I could tell they liked each other, I could see it in their faces. If you want to know if a girl likes a guy, watch her face, especially when the guy's not looking at her, but she's looking at him. Watch her face; what's it doing? Is she looking at him? You can tell a lot.

In March, we got the long-awaited list of charges from the school's disciplinary committee. Frank was furious as he read the letter to us in general meeting. I don't remember everything, but it had to do with the yellow pass riot, the fighting, and Ben's little escapade with Big Ears. There was a hearing date for next month. Frank went on to say that he got someone to represent us, a full-fledged law student from his society. He vouched for her, so we agreed.

We met with her up at the law school in one of these grand conference rooms, one that had real dark wood paneling. The law school was small, with most of the lectures being done via teleconference equipment from some law center in the south. All ten of us were seated at the table as Ms. Hightower walked in. We were stunned. She was tall, had blonde hair pinned back, a smart business suit and one critical feature: Ms. Hightower was breathtakingly beautiful. We couldn't decide if Frank hired a lawyer or Miss America. But let me tell you, this woman came to the party with the shotgun loaded.

She slammed down her briefcase, opened it and took out some papers, then sat. "Okay, I have read the complaint and your files." Then she looked up at us, "I'll be honest; there's not a darn thing I like about you guys. I'm not even that fond of Frank Davis. You formed an association to fight the bad guys, yet personally, from a legal standpoint, I can't tell the difference between you and these Mustangs. You threaten, you fight, and none of this looks good."

Ben made a feeble attempt, "Ms. Hightower, in our defense, we have had challenges ..."

"Mr. Holden!" she yelled, "Cry me a river, okay!" Ben slowly sat back in his seat as she recomposed. "But, Frank is a society brother of mine and Chloe Rankin thinks, for some reason I have yet to figure out, you guys are great. Anyway, all feelings aside now, they don't have much of a case here. Inciting a riot is the most serious charge, one you could all get expelled for, but I can get that one thrown out. I think they have some antisocial behavior charges you could get some punishment for, but I don't see you getting expelled for this nonsense. I'm not even sure why they even included Mr. Holden's assault thing as a charge; he was convicted and served time on that already. It appears to me that someone rushed this case to hearing without proper consideration. I will go over the evidence thoroughly. I'll be working with Frank on it but I will have you guys come in, one by one, and we'll go over proposed testimony. And don't make me repeat this; all crap has to stop, and now. Okay?" She got up and left.

We discussed the case on the ride home. We were generally happy with the lawyer; we also had to keep in mind that she was a friend of Chloe Rankin, and probably a total feminist. We made a pledge to start being more civil, right away.

Rose Russo had not seen me coming toward her, standing by her locker waiting for Jim. Apparently cutting off her escape, she found herself having to talk with me. "Hi, Rose."

"Oh, hi, Dan."

"How's it going?"

"Good, real good."

"How are all your dad's friends doing?"

"Who?"

"His fish, how are his fish?"

"Oh, pretty good I guess," she laughed, "He doesn't let us near them much."

"So, how are your sisters doing?"

She looked at me and smiled, and softened up. Maybe she saw I wasn't making her take sides in the Sharon thing or that I still liked her. "So, why the sudden interest in my sisters, you pervert?"

"Just wanted to make sure they were happy."

"Right. And they both have boyfriends by the way. You haven't seen my sweetie, have you?"

"Not since this morning. You love that guy, Rose?"

She nodded.

"I know the feeling," as I began to leave, I saw Jim coming. I guess I should have said knew the feeling.

In April, all in our best clothes, the ten of us filed into the hearing room on the second floor of the administration building at the school. There were not many people there; because of privacy issues disciplinary hearings were not public. We did notice one interesting individual sitting in the back: Bus Quint.

Under strict orders not to act up, Ben held off all urges to run over there and bust Quint right in the chops. We were all seated at the defense table, two rows of five. The table for the opposing side had a single tall, thin woman at it. As the prosecution, Ms Hightower and the hearing official, a lawyer from the school's legal department, discussed preliminary issues and rules, I chatted with Ben. He seemed a bit nervous.

As my attention returned to the hearing, Ms. Hightower was true to form, "Your honor, of the three charges, one seems to be inappropriate to the case. Mr. Holden was already found guilty of assault and received punishment. I move that charge be dropped."

"So moved," the older man said without looking up. The presiding official was bald, overweight, and wore a brown suit that was too small for him.

The other side called as their only witness, Bus Quint. Bus went over all the issues and some extra ones as well. He indicated the Eagles started two fights with the Mustangs, we planted drugs in their storage barn and burned it down and we, although it was really two guys from Holy Cross, tried to start a fight with Fuller and him in the hallway at school.

When it was Ms. Hightower's turn, she got up and immediately started to take Quint apart like a cheap watch.

"Mr. Quint, do you know one of the Eagles, a Frank Davis?" she started.

"Yes," the mutt brother responded.

"Did you not strike Mr. Davis when he wouldn't pay you some money?"

"No, I did not."

"Mr. Quint, are there charges pending against you right now?"

"Yes, possession of illicit drugs, but it was …"

"It's a yes or no question, Mr. Quint. Why do you say the Eagles burned down your barn?"

"Because they did, that's why."

"Did you see them?"

"No. It's a hunch. We know …"

"Oh, a hunch is it, Mr. Quint? Well, Mr. Davis has a 'hunch' you smacked him in the mouth. Can we proceed today based on all our hunches, or shall we stick with what we know? Were you ever on the grounds of the Centura Orphanage?"

"No, I was never …"

"I have some witnesses who say you were. Do you want me to call them?"

"I might have been there once or twice. I don't …"

"What were you doing on the grounds of a restricted area, Mr. Quint?"

"I don't know … maybe to see a girl, or …"

Ms. Hightower was nothing short of amazing. Moving around the room like she owned it, she could raise her voice and be obnoxious, and then be quiet, humble, and polite. Words came out of her mouth at ninety miles per hour and at the same time she was always looking around the room. She was born to be a trial lawyer. "Were you present when these alleged fights with the Eagles took place?"

"Yes."

"When was the first one?"

"Several years ago, behind the dining hall at the orphanage."

"Your honor, I think we can eliminate this fight in the charges, since it took place outside the limits of the statute."

"So moved," the official said.

"So, how did the Eagles set up this second fight?"

"Sent us a message, and once they sent use a big box of cow manure in the mail."

Ms. Hightower suddenly stopped talking and just stood there. She turned around and walked toward our table. We got worried when we saw what we thought was a tear streaming down her cheek. Then we realized she was trying to suppress laughter, almost ready to break up.

The official spoke, "Ms. Hightower, go on."

"A moment to recompose, your honor," she spoke, but still staring at Ben Holden. "Okay," she whispered, "who sent the big box of cow poop to the witness?" We all just looked down toward the end of the table at Corky Wall, now sitting there with his head hung low. She walked down to him and whispered, "Was that you?"

Corky just looked up and pleaded, "Well, it was more like a little box."

"You're a genius. After the hearing, I want you to show me how to do that." Then, without skipping a beat, she whipped around and continued, "So, Mr. Quint, did the box of cow manure have a note in it signed by one of the Eagles?"

"No."

"Another hunch, Mr. Quint? When was the second fight?"

Quint stated, "Last summer."

"Were you there?"

"Yes, they called it; we were to meet them in the ball field near south elementary."

"Did you ever, Mr. Quint, stalk and follow an orphanage resident named Governor Viche to his orphanage room in Delk Hall, then strike him in the head, so badly that he later died from this wound?"

That question caught everyone, including Quint, off guard; you could hear a pin drop in the room. Quint sat there with his mouth open. The prosecutor lady was caught sleeping. When she realized what was being asked she tried to get up so fast she fell out of her chair and onto the floor. Before getting back up into a standing position, Quint uttered, "Heck no!"

Recomposed, the lady yelled, "Your honor! That was totally irrelevant."

Ms. Hightower, looking at her, shot off, "He answered 'no,' what the heck you worried about?"

"Ms. Hightower," the official growled at her, "keep it on track!"

Without hesitating, she continued, "What were you doing there, at the ball field, before the fight?"

"Getting ready for the fight. They still started it."

"So you went there in order to fight them? If you didn't want to fight them, why did you show up?" She looked at the official, "Your Honor, I move to dismiss this charge as well. Mr. Quint and friends went there to fight. Whoever started it, both parties engaged."

"I disagree. No one but your clients are charged with fighting, Mr. Quint is not. Unless you can get the witness to indicate the Eagles did not take part in the fight, there are no grounds for dismissal. Do you have any more questions for this witness?"

"I do not."

"The witness is excused. Prosecution, call your next witness." Quint left the room.

"We wish to rest, sir," the thin lady said.

The official gave the prosecution a dirty look, "Excuse me, don't you have anything to add about the yellow pass riot?"

"The prosecution is not prepared to pursue that charge, your honor."

"Okay, that one's gone too, Ms. Hightower, call your first witness please."

"Your Honor, may I have five minutes?"

"You may have five."

She walked over to the table to take a breath. The hearing official drank some water from a glass on his desk.

Ben leaned toward her and whispered, "What the heck was that?"

She smiled, "Trick question. But it worked. I had looked at the prosecutor; she was not paying attention, so I sprung it on him."

I asked, "But he answered no, what good did it do?"

"Let's say you were on trial for breaking a street light. So I ask the question, Mr. Kelley, did you pick up a rock, throw it at the light, and break it? Let's say you didn't pick up a rock, let's say Davis handed you one. See? You could say no to that question, still be guilty of the crime, but not commit perjury. We don't know which part of my complex question he was answering no to. So, what mistake did the judge make?"

Frank Davis smiled at her, "He forgot to have the question and answer struck from the record."

"Right. That's why I started back on Quint so quickly. It's on record now, and it lets Quint know we are on to him." She winked at us, "I told you guys I'm good."

She had Frank, Ben, and me all testify. Carefully going over all the incidental issues, she proceeded through the process leading up to the fight. However, during the follow-up, the other side got each of us to say we were present, and participating in the fight.

After I sat back down, the hearings official barked, "I need both sides up here." Although it was supposed to be off the record, we could all hear the clown as clear as day. "Ms. Hightower, what's going on?"

"The charges against my clients are complicated …"

"There's only one charge. No one is now charged with burning down a barn, or inciting a riot, or starting a fight. Your first three witnesses have testified they were present and participating in the fight. Fighting is the charge. Are any of the rest prepared to testify differently?"

"Not to my knowledge, your honor."

"I'm calling this off. We'll take a short recess while I prepare my bench decision."

As the official left the room, Ms. Hightower returned to the table. "We're gonna take a rap on that fighting charge, but I don't know how to get out of that. I think I know how we can, eventually. We should get a light penalty, only Holden has previous charges."

The official returned; we stood. He read, "I find the defendants guilty of the charge of disturbance fighting. I now order said defendants to one month at the detention center. I also order them to immediately terminate any work-study job residence and return to the orphanage as of 9 a.m. Monday morning next. After moving back in, you will immediately, that same day, report to the detention center for incarceration. If any of these orders are not met, said defendants will suffer immediate suspension from school for an indefinite period. That is my ruling." He banged the gavel and left.

We all sat in Lisa's office, dejected and silent. Ms. Hightower was seated at Lisa's desk. Lisa sat on the desk. We were stunned.

Ms. Hightower said, "Good gravy, we got hosed on that one. Boys, that clown was way out of line. He just wrote a check his butt can't cover."

"What do we do now?" Ben asked.

"We can appeal this. The next level is the superintendent of schools, who I assume is in bed with Mrs. Popover, but then it goes to the Department of Education in Atlanta. This is a travesty." Then she got serious, "Only problem is, the quickest I can get this considered is two months; you're going to have to abide by the ruling."

Ben rubbed his eyes and said, "I'm not so sure we can do that, Ms. Hightower."

"Whatever you decide," she responded, "I do want you guys to know, I'm with you all the way. They went and got me mad now."

Our dejection and silence continued on the ride home and to our conference room. We were all seated, all the Eagles, Libby Davis, Angie, and Rose.

Clyde was the first to speak, "Well, I got news for you guys. I'm not going back to the orphanage, or any detention center. I'll go back to the barn or out into the wilderness."

"Me too," Corky added, "and I'm not going back into the walls."

Al Myers, "I'm in graduate school. They can't put me in the Irish Fort. My professor in the math department said he'd adopt me, let me foster with them at their house, or at least fake it. Before the adoption order can get approved, I'll be eighteen and it won't matter. I'll sleep on the couch in the math department before I'll go to Price Hall.

Frank Davis added, "I'm eighteen already, but to move out I need an approved residence, and I don't think anyone is going to have much pity on me right now. I can't get into my house yet. And I got my sister to worry about."

"No you don't," Angie spoke, "Libby's going to be staying at my house. She'll sleep in my room until my brother goes to college in the fall, and then she'll have her own room. My parents already agreed."

"Milt can't let us stay here," said Clyde, "They'll stop his work-study contract if he harbors us, and he needs the help. I also hope you guys know they'll put us in separate rooms, on separate floors, in separate wings at Price. No way are they going to put us together, and then we'll be at the mercy of Quint's thugs. And as you remember, he's the guy we just accused of murder."

I decided to change the mood, "Yea, Rose's sisters asked me to stay with them; I'll be sharing their room." I had to duck as a flock of couch pillows, paper wads, and other items began flying at me, thrown by all in the room.

I didn't say anything at the meeting, but there was no way I was going to abide by the ruling. I was no longer interested in school, or in this town that hated us, and it was beginning to look like there would be no Sharon in my life anymore. I no longer wanted to do this stupid charade of becoming a dutiful electrician and serving my beloved society. There needed to be some answers first. Why did things happen with Sharon and me like they did? Why did my parents leave a four-year-old boy in a snowstorm out on the prairie by himself? Why do we have to be afraid of thugs all the time? Why did we have to threaten someone to get a dang slice of pizza? What the heck was going on?

The plan started to come together that very Tuesday night. Ben was going to contact The Range and hopefully, Holy Cross for assistance. Empire was going to go down to the orphanage and get what plan they had for us. Clyde was going to talk with Milt Frazer. Since most of us were not going to pass spring quarter, school was out for us and I was appointed to go meet with Diane Win and get the facts on what was going to happen after the suspension. Cork was sent to find out anything on the status of the Mustangs, who by the way had been very quiet lately.

I skidded all the way up South Shore Drive getting to the school that morning. The snow was relentless even though spring was close. On my way to Win's office, I ran into the eye pleasing Cheri.

"You're gonna be late for class, sweetheart," she greeted me.

Walking right past her, I said, "I'm gonna be a lot later than this I fear."

Spooking Diane who had not seen me standing in her doorway, I asked, "Got a minute?"

She then held an index finger over her mouth, signaling me to be quiet, "Sure, Dan, let me just finish this report, have a seat." She was writing on a pad, and then turned it around for me to read. It said, "Quiet! My office is bugged. Pretend you are going thru with the detention."

I was confused but made up a story, "Well, Diane, don't know if you heard, but I got thirty days in the joint; we all did. I just wanted to see how my funds would be handled and if my money would be safe."

She kept writing but spoke, "No problem. Your work-study funds will end since you won't be working on the farm, but your balance will be safe in your account. All your classes will continue in there, via satellite however." Then she pushed the paper at me again, "If you're suspended, all you guys will be cut off from stipends. Balance will be safe."

"So, what should we do?" I asked.

She wrote, "Go to the woods, Holy Cross will take care of you."

I nodded. I wrote on her pad, "Thanks Diane!" Feeling naughty, I then added, I can get conjugal visits you know. She stood up, shaking her fist in my face but laughing.

"Kelley, you're a trip!" she said as I left her office.

We all met back together that evening and went over our intelligence. Ben reported that he finally had a meeting with Holy Cross, well, one of them. Giving Ben some coordinates on where to meet them, he said they would be happy to help. He told Ben to get all the camping gear we could carry on our backs. He also gave us a name of a soldier at the Army warehouse on the base.

"I called the guy at the base; he wants all our sizes, coats, boots, pants, and four thousand dollars." Frank made a face but Ben went on, "We're taking it out of the club account, we have a lot of money in there and this is what it's for. Bo, can you get all the sizes together. Frank and you will take a truck up there tomorrow and pick up the stuff. The guy told me to get good knives, those are at the sporting goods store up on North Shore, and they're another grand. Frank, get those on the way back." Frank nodded.

Clyde said that Milt wants us to clean the place, make our bunks up with the blankets covering the sheets and pillow, and then put all our valuables not taken in his safe. He was very positive and sure we would be returning after we get this straightened out.

The Mustangs were all but dead, according to Cork's report, saying the bank repossessed the gang warehouse from Quint's old man. Since it stunk so badly from the sewer backup, they decided to demolish it and sell the lot. Most of the members beat the drug possession rap because the police couldn't specify which member it belonged to. However, most members quit and no meetings were being held. Quint had been expelled from school and spent most of his time getting drunk with his dad. He was still considered to be a threat to us.

Ben finished by saying he had a proposed route to get out in the wild. He said that The Range will help us with that. After finalizing all the details, he stated he would go over it with us tomorrow. To get a jump on the truancy officers, departure day was set for Sunday. We all felt excited; the Eagles were mobilizing again.

Ben called Ms. Hightower and filled her in on what we were up to. She was already working on the appeal. Faxing us a "due process objection" form through Milt's office, she asked Ben to make seven copies and have them filled out by each of the guys who did not testify. He then faxed them back to her. She said she could handle everything else without us.

Our excitement continued to grow when Frank and Bo delivered the stuff we ordered. We unloaded ten fully equipped Army packs. All the fabric material was a dark forest green, the same color as the outfits worn by the Cross members I saw picking the fight with Quint that day. Each pack contained a compass, a fire starting device, a canteen, a mess kit, first aid kit, sleeping bag and pad, a poncho, half a pup tent, and one of those handheld multipurpose tool things. The mess kits weren't the usual Boy Scout aluminum variety, but rather a heavy metal. Each of the packs had an attached hand shovel, and since we figured we didn't need ten shovels, he said one guy without one could carry a larger super first aid kit he got at the sporting goods store. The knives were the coolest, almost the size of Roman swords, they were very heavy. He had also purchased ten, top of the line, hatchets, each with a blade on one side and traditional hammer head on the other. Frank said he spent about twice his budget, but we all forgave him.

Then ten large paper sacks were brought in, each containing waterproof army boots, a heavy coat, hat, and two pairs each of heavy shirts, trousers, underwear and socks. The underwear was dark green, and we all decided to use those, making sure they were laundered ahead of time. Much to our surprise, the shirts contained an inside pocket lined with rubber and sealable, so we decided to use these for our handhelds and ditch the compasses.

Corky, giving us an example of his high spirits, announced, "I only need two pairs of underwear because I wear them for a week at a time; then I turn them inside out and get another week out of them."

To this, Ben added, "Cork, ever wonder why you don't have a girlfriend?"

After laundering and packing, leaving out the outfit we would travel in, we put the packs on our backs. We were concerned about how heavy they were, but decided we would just have to build the muscle over time.

Al Myers wasn't going with us, and no one held any grudges. In fact, Ben thought it might be useful to have someone back in the mainstream looking out for us. His department chair filed a petition to adopt and told officials his foster child wouldn't be going to any detention center. Having a lot of weight at the college, administration reluctantly agreed. The professor actually rented a house from Milt Frazer, just north of the dairy barn, where Al would be living.

Before our final club meeting Friday night, Ben, Frank and I went over to Angie's house to say goodbye to Angie's new sister, Libby Davis. Angie's family was just as cool as she was, all short, all with that sharp sense of humor. Every Friday night after dinner, they would clear the table and each would do a skit of stand-up comedy, even mom. They were a scream. When it was time to go, we all gathered at the front door.

"This doesn't seem much like you, brother," Libby told Frank, "going off into the woods."

Frank said something that really got to me, "Yes, I've had my doubts. But it's this guy," he pointed to me, "Kelley may need me, I don't want him going off alone."

"For what," Libby responded, "he might need a lawyer to negotiate with a bear?"

Angie's dad gave Frank a hug, "Frank, don't worry about your sister. Today I have a new daughter."

Libby hugged me, with tears in her eyes, "Dan Kelley, you take care of my brother. Oh, what the heck, you've been doing that your whole life."

At the meeting, with just the Eagles, Ben went over our plans. "We party tomorrow with girls, everyone out by midnight. We leave Sunday morning, at four. We walk to the creek bridge, the one that leads to where Delk Hall used to be. The Range will pick us up in a couple of vans and take us down by the waterfront, east of here. There, we'll catch a fishing boat that will take us all the way around the school peninsula, across the bay, under the bridge to the base gate, then through North Lake, to the western shore. It's near a place called Candlelight which is a small group of buildings used by the Park Service during the summer. It's deserted now. There we will walk southwest to our rendezvous with the Cross. Any questions?"

Clyde raised his hand, "Seems like the long way around. Why don't we strike out on foot; south through Saint James?"

"Thought of that," Ben responded, "It's shorter by distance, but actually more walking time. Besides, that area is either empty farm fields or short grass prairie, no trees, no cover. We could easily be spotted from a helicopter. Pack light. A pair of sneakers may come in handy. Bo got us some power bars; take as many as you can, no telling when the next hot meal will be."

Saturday we slept late. We went out to the grove, by the far pasture, and practiced throwing hatchets. Murdock was deadly with his, but most of couldn't get ours to stick. We supped with the farmhands then returned to our quarters to meet the girls.

Our Saturday night was more of a wake than a party. Girls with puffy, red eyes sat around moping and hanging onto departing boyfriends. Going away parties are interesting. The going away people expect tearful but happy faces, wishes of good luck, or "I'm happy for you." But oftentimes people are crabby, or even dislike you for leaving. I grew weary of it and went to my cubicle to repack my gear. I was sitting on my bed, writing in my journal, when Angie came in and sat next to me.

I tried ignoring her, an almost impossible feat with Angie, when after a few minutes I looked up to see this giant tear running down her cheek. "Angie, what's wrong?"

"Oh, nothing," then she put her arms around me, "Promise me you'll take care of Ben. I'm afraid something's going to happen to him out there."

I pulled her off, looked her right in the eyes, difficult as it was with tears and snot running down her face, and said, "Ben Holden is my all-time favorite hero; I won't let anything happen to him. I promise to look after him with my life. I'd jump in front of a train for Ben."

But that just made her hug me again, "Dan Kelley, that stupid French girl made the biggest mistake of her life the day she let you go. Why didn't I meet you before that blockhead boyfriend I got now?"

"Yea, why don't you drop old Lard-butt in the lake, come back and marry me? Be with a real man for a change."

"Be careful, Kelley, if he ever breaks up with me I'll be at your doorstep, with my suitcase." She let me go, kissed me again, then clenched her fist and slugged me right in the jaw. For Angie, that was a sign of affection. She left. Rose never said goodbye.

I was up at three; so were most others. Nobody talked much. We donned our new gear, made up the beds, and carried our packs to the study room. Al Myers was there to give us each a hug. After assembling, we helped each other lift packs on, and then silently filed out. I stuck my favorite cow herding staff through a loop on my backpack.

It was dark and cold out, but our new clothes were quite warm. As we walked through the barnyard, we spotted old Milt Frazer standing there. He yelled, "I expect you back by harvest, you low life pansies!" We all waved to him, but he didn't wave back. Milt no longer had dairy, had no real excuse for being up at four on a Sunday morning but to see us off. Waving to us would have been too much emotion for him. You couldn't expect a lot from some people, you had to take what you could get.

By the time we got to the bridge, The Range members were there with vans running. It was only a drive of a few minutes down to the waterfront, although their loud music on a Sunday morning was a bit annoying.

Their tattooed leader told Ben they had contact with Holy Cross and to let them know if we needed them. He left us with the only emotional comment he could muster, "Ya know that judge? If ya change your mind, let me know, and we'll go up there and beat the crap out of him."

The fishing boat was already there, idling next to the pier. The young captain waved to us. As we carried our packs down the pier, a bright red sun appeared in the east. It was the prettiest sunrise I had ever seen.

We took off as our last man stepped on board, but didn't get to enjoy the cruise that much as the captain wanted us in the fish hold for the first part of the trip. He was worried about the Navy patrols spotting his boat with more crewmembers than he had life jackets for. It was uncomfortable; we couldn't sit down and it smelled like stale fish, but we could handle it. It seemed like forever, at least an hour, before we passed under the bridge to the base and he allowed us up on deck. The once clear sky was now cloudy and the wind had a bit of a chill in it. We made our way into North Lake, passed by the beach where I once took Sharon, and finally came upon the far west shore.

Corky started working on our sense of humor as he gave a speech he read in a book about the invasion of Normandy in World War II, "Boys, boys, when we hit those shores, when the lead is flying, in case of the worst, I want to thank you for the opportunity of serving with you. When you hit that sand, for those of us left alive, I want you to push forward, all the way to Berlin!"

The captain let us off on an old wooden pier. Ben was the last to disembark, thanking the captain and handing him some money. When we all got on shore, Ben asked us to jog to a tree line about one hundred yards away to get the kinks out of our legs. It looked so much like playing army as kids that we were in stitches before we got to the trees and found the river.

We formed into lines of two, with Corky on point, and started walking. We walked, and walked, and walked. Just when spirits were the highest, it started to rain. Stopping for a brief lunch, we donned ponchos and ate power bars. Then it was back to marching.

Our plan to follow the bottomland along the river to keep under tree cover turned out not to be a very good idea. With the rain, the ground became muddy and walking became difficult. But we kept at it, most of the afternoon.

The clouds thickened and when it became too difficult to walk anymore, Ben suggested we make camp. We figured we could move to ground that was a little higher since we wouldn't be moving. We set up tents, and got one fire going for a few minutes before the rain put it out. All of us must have walked all day without taking a drink, because it was only then that we discovered we had forgotten to fill the canteens.

For several hundred years after The Chaos and the land becoming uninhabited, rivers like this would have been poisonous. However, flowing water for centuries since then cleaned them out. We simply dipped our canteens in the river to fill them.

We set watch shifts of two men each; the rest of us just pulled ourselves up into the tents, ate another power bar, and tried to sleep. Sleep was difficult as the rain pelted our tents and the sound of running water unnerved us. This sure wasn't like sleeping in the grove. I got up a half hour early for my watch, only most of the guys were already awake. It was only four in the morning when we decided to pack up and start marching. We were already wide-awake, we couldn't get any wetter; and with everything wet there was no use even trying for hot coffee.

About a half hour into the march, to make matters worse, the rain changed to sleet and snow. We didn't even stop for lunch; we just ate as we walked. It was becoming increasingly slippery, guys started falling down, and some of the guys were sneezing and coughing. All of us were dying to say this was a bad idea; we could be sleeping in a warm, dry cot at the Irish Fort. But, good old fashioned orphan stubbornness refused defeat.

In late afternoon, the sky almost becoming black, point man Corky held up his hand to stop us. He reached behind and flipped out his hatchet into his right hand. Ben motioned me to grab my staff and join him. I flipped the staff up into throwing position and I followed Cork's finger as he pointed to the higher ground.

Two shadowy figures walked along the horizon, and then suddenly stopped, one raised a hand, "Eagles? Don't throw the axe. We're Holy Cross."

We could all hear the air rush out of Holden's chest.

CHAPTER SEVEN

"I thought there were supposed to be ten of you, did you lose one?" one of them spoke.

"No," Ben responded, "we left one at home."

"What are you walking down there for; it's a lot easier up here on the grass?"

"We didn't want to get spotted."

"Wait, we'll throw you down a vine." He threw down a long vine and tied his end to a tree on the top of the bank. We all climbed up, one by one, until we were all standing on the higher ground. Our hosts wrapped up in long fur coats, similar to those of mountain men of the old west, appeared kind. Although their faces only peeked out of coat hoods, I recognized one of them as the guy who looked up at me and winked while starting that fight with Quint. "I'm Matt, this is Corky."

Ben quickly ran down our names, adding that we had a Corky as well.

"I thought you guys were only truants. Why are you worried about being spotted?" Matt asked.

"Helicopters," Ben responded.

"Only the military has those; they won't give a darn about you. Well, we can chat later. I've never seen you guys before but I bet you've looked better."

"Yea," Ben said, "we're a little wet, cold, and tired."

"Let's go straight to the caves. It's about another hour but will be worth it." He then pulled out a handheld device, "Potter?" he spoke into it.

Some static came out of the device, then a voice, "Potter here."

"We're coming in with nine; put the stew on the fire."

We started a slow walk, in our same formation only with Ben and the two from Holy Cross in front. We did follow the river, but walking up on the short prairie grass was much easier. Ben kept looking up, however, still worried about being spotted. Our spirits were a little raised, so we had the stamina for the walk.

Finally, we came upon a group of rocky hills, not extremely tall but certainly standing out on the rolling prairie. Matt led us between two big hills where we came to a cave entrance. We slowly filed in; only one at a time could fit through with packs. The short hallway was dark, but we soon came out into a big, bright cavern. The large stone room was brightly lit by a big fire in the middle; a lone figure stood stirring a big pot. Most importantly, the room was warm and dry.

Matt instructed us to change into dry clothes, scrape the mud off our boots and store them near the entrance, and give them our wet clothes. They said they had a "drying" cave next door and would hang stuff up for us.

Finishing up, we stood in line by the fire as Potter filled up our mess bowls with the most wonderful stew we had ever eaten. It was some kind of fowl, but contained vegetables of sorts, most I couldn't recognize. We drank a hot, green tea. I think most of us had seconds and thirds, easily draining the big pot. After supper, we washed out our mess kits and spread them out on a large rock for them to dry. We pulled out sleeping bags and spread them around the cave. Some of the guys lay down immediately and a few were snoring within minutes. Finishing their chores, Potter left for the drying cave while Matt and his partner sat down on a rock near Ben and me for a chat.

"Warm cave," Ben commented. We couldn't get over how the stone ceiling glowed in the firelight, illuminating the whole area.

"It's vented," Matt responded, "Never start a fire in an unvented cave; go to sleep and you won't wake up."

"You guys are kind of a mystery," Ben went on, "not much is known about you."

"That's the way we like it," Matt said, "You guys, on the other hand, are kind of famous."

Matt's sidekick, Corky, didn't say much. His face was weathered; he had the beginning of a faint moustache he was trying to grow. He had a big grin on his face, like he liked living in the outdoors like this.

"I was wondering about your Catholic roots. What's the religious connection?" Ben asked.

"Oh, we're not all Catholic, maybe a few of us. Our two founders attended Holy Cross elementary school on the south side. We used that name to throw people off, making them think we were a good parochial club. You see, we had our enemies in the past, just like you. We were pretty paranoid back then. You will learn that a lot of the stuff we do is to create diversion. For instance, we don't use last names or ever report our numbers."

"We're also pretty curious as to why you're helping us like this."

"Let's just say you remind us a lot of ourselves. We were Delk Hall residents as well. Fuller and Quint were not around but their nastier older siblings were. We knew Big Ears, though; I heard after you threatened him he hasn't been back to the orphanage since. That gave us a lot of respect for you, Ben. No, we don't want anything from you. Someday we may need a hand with something and we'll ask you guys for help."

"I don't know if we took the right path," Ben began to get a little sad, "I'm not sure if fighting our enemies was such a good thing. Did I improve these guys by leading the charge or did I just get nine really good friends kicked out of school? We have military service coming up and no degrees. Did I just get all of us killed as infantry men in the war with Mexico?"

"Standing up to your enemies, Ben, is honorable. Someday Quint could have easily killed Frank Davis, or even some others. You don't know what they would have done. Somebody had to stand up to them. It's too bad us teenage schoolboys only know how to settle things with our fists. We admire your will to fight; we just don't really think much of your style."

Ben got a little testy, "What did you mean by that? We trained and everything."

Matt held up his hand, "Whoa, big guy, nobody's doubting your bravery. It's just that you guys go straight at them, face up, and heads up. Quint is desperate now. He isn't going to be standing there next time with his fists up; he's gonna have a gun or a club on him. Will your next charge be as successful, Ben? My suggestion is that you learn to come at them from an angle, not to stop their blows with your faces, but to redirect them, make them slide off."

"The fight was called. You guys started one too. If called, we will fight."

"That's my point," Matt pleaded. "Ben, tell me, what would have happen if you hadn't shown up for that fight?"

"What? That would be worse; that would be cowardly."

"But what would have happened?"

"Well, you tell me. You guys called a fight with the Mustangs and didn't show up."

"So what happened to us?"

"Well, we were all wondering the same thing."

"Who won the fight, Ben?"

"There wasn't one; no one won."

"Who lost the fight, Ben?"

The question got to Ben; he sat, thinking. I saw it right away and a big smile came on my face. Holy Cross Corky got it too, as he smiled and winked at me. Then, slowly at first, a smile broke out on our big leader's face.

"Well, you didn't lose. You weren't there. You keep your strength vague to throw people off. You knew the Mustangs were afraid of you. You knew they would have everyone there at the fight field." Ben looked up and laughed, "And that's when you guys snuck around behind them and burned the barn down!"

Matt laughed and looked at his friend, "You can lead a horse to water, Cork. And Ben, don't forget the sewer backup in their clubhouse."

"How did you pull that off?" Ben was excited now.

"Easy. We got one of the town's large pumps out of their storage facility. We drove it down there, threw an intake hose in the sewer, and ran the outtake hose up to the second floor. We started the pump, it's a diesel so it pumped all night, and we loaded poop into the clubhouse. Heck, throw up some caution cones and some flashing yellow lights, and people passing never gave a thought that it wasn't set up by the town workers."

"Such a wonderful job, but you got no credit for it."

"That's not our style. The important thing is that the Mustangs are out of business."

We decided it was time to conclude. Matt said, "Oh, we'll stand watch tonight, you guys sleep." As we drifted off, I heard Ben still chuckling from that story.

The cave was pretty homey, but it didn't have everything. A latrine was set up about twenty yards from the cave entrance. I was surprised how fast we could use the facilities when it's cold and windy.

Not being sure what time it was when I woke up, I just laid there thinking how nice it was to be out of the weather. Our hosts were already frying eggs and some sort of bacon-type meat on a smooth stone griddle on the fire. Holy Cross Corky brought me a cup of coffee and I sat sipping and listening to the laughing and joking from the guys. Clyde stopped by my bed and told me because it was still snowing and Bo Schlitz was still nursing a bad cough, we were going to stay put today. We ate and ate. Matt and Potter cooked steady for over two hours.

"So you don't fear being discovered?" Ben asked Matt.

"Naw. The town has no charges against you, the military could give a flip about you, and the truant officers won't go outside the city limits. I think you'll be surprised about how little people care about us. The dirty orphans are out of their hair. That's all they care about. Let the wolves eat them is what they think. While I think Mrs. Popover and the high school assumes you are scum, the people at the college are much more rational, try and foster that ally."

"Okay, guys," Matt said out loud to all of us, "fess up, who the heck burned down Delk Hall?"

We all looked at Clyde but, for the first time, he adamantly denied it. Holy Cross did as well, prompting Matt to say, "I think the darn thing just burned down. Good riddance."

The Eagles did the cleaning up, letting our hosts eat their breakfast. We then sat around, talking most of the day. We got the feeling that Matt and at least some of the Cross were a little older than us, but not by much. Facing a lot of the conditions we had, it seems they slowly, one by one, slipped out of the orphanage and into the woods. Most were officially listed as runaways, a term convenient for the orphanage administration. They just wrote that word on your record and promptly forgot about you. There was no accountability.

They did know a lot about us; more than we ever thought. While most of the high school thought we were gangbangers, at least we had some integrity with certain groups.

"Ben," Matt asked, "what's the story behind your mental illness? We had all assumed you were faking it, even though you were quite convincing at times."

The big guy, probably because the atmosphere was so calm and relaxed, became surprisingly honest, "I was scared." Suddenly, the whole room hushed as our leader confessed to us. "It's the truth. I've never told anyone this before. I lied to my friends here; said I did it to keep out of detention. My parents abandoned me; as a kid I figured it was because I was bad. I was a big, fat kid. I got beat up a lot. I had nightmares, almost every night. As you all know, for an orphan there is absolutely no one to turn to. I did what we all did, learned on my own to fight back. So, what's even the biggest, toughest kid afraid of? A crazy person. Murdock, you saw it when I turned away that thug that wanted Frank Davis' money. Here's this big, tough guy who got spooked by my psychotic episode. That's how I fought guys. It wasn't until these guys here rallied around me that I felt safe, safe enough to drop the act." Ben sat with his face in his hands.

Bo added, "I just cried a lot."

Frank, "I had my face used as a punching bag."

"I hid in a barn," Clyde added to the list.

I said, "I just took abuse."

Corky Wall, "Clyde Hastings dated a dairy cow."

As the cave echoed with laughter, Clyde pulled his axe out of his backpack and said, "You little sawed off runt, here's a date with Mr. Hatchet!" Then he chased the now running Corky through the cave entrance and out into the snow.

We woke at 3:30 the next morning, were all packed up and marching by 4. It was in the brisk 30s and dark; however, we all had winter gear so we were fine. The temperature rose with the sun and it turned out to be a nice day. Matt suggested we try splitting up to avoid detection. We walked in groups of four, with groups a few hundred feet apart. Matt directed us with hand signals when in view. The Holy Cross philosophy, as evidenced both by what they said and what they did, appeared to be one of stealth. Holy Cross Corky, my unit leader, quoted some old Chinese philosopher with, "Be unseen rather than seen, if seen then avoid, if struck redirect strike, harm rather than kill." Empire Murdock, walking with my group, added, "If all else fails, beat the living crap out of them!"

Our walk in the dark consisted mostly of prairie. By sun up we hit the trees. Two hours later we were in the deep woods. At a clear, bubbling creek, we stopped to rest, all following Ben's order to always empty and fill canteens when at a water source. All had wide-eyed grins. It was such a good feeling, out here, no chore time, no standing in line for chow, and no stupid moron bully calling you a pig. As Matt had said, "It's just me and the Mother," meaning Mother Nature.

Elk, deer, even some rabbits walked right past us. It was odd; they never took off running. Daddy elk snorted at us but continued walking in the opposite direction, not more than ten feet from us.

"What the heck?" I said to Cross Corky, "Why aren't they afraid?"

Cork shrugged his shoulders. "Well, I have a theory. We don't hunt over here. We're on the other side of the Saint James River, and I think they know that. "

We lunched at that river he had mentioned. Being springtime, the level was high and I had no idea how we were going to cross. We shared some of our power bars with our hosts since they had no food left after we devoured it back in the cave. Even the river water was clear and drinkable.

I walked up to Matt, "How we going to get across that?"

"We have two canoes hid below. It will take a while; I'm sure Cork and I are the only two who know how to use one. We'll have to ferry you all, can only take one guy and one pack at a time.

After eating, Clyde and I sat on the riverbank for about an hour as Matt and Cross Cork ferried the others over. Clyde could barely contain his excitement about our choice to leave. He said it was like the tree grove, only about ten times better.

Finally getting into the canoe, we held on tight as they took us over. I could tell my captain, Matt, was getting tired. The water was rough and bubbly. Finally across, through thick forest, we ascended two hills. Coming down the second we walked into this magical place.

It looked like something out of a Paleo-Indian museum exhibit. People sat by campfires; grass and leaf huts were scattered about. A single long, log structure stood to one side. The people were smoking meats or scraping on animal skins. It was Old World stuff, pioneer stuff. As we got closer we saw some of the people were female.

Walking into camp, everyone got up and crowded around us. Both sides exchanged two long lists of names, but there would be no way to remember any of them. We all felt welcomed. A guy, who I recognized as the one with Matt that day at school, greeted us with, "Hey, it's the fighting Eagles. It's about time you guys dumped that depressing place."

One female asked, "Did the truant officers follow you?"

"Yea," our Corky laughed, "but we dumped them back there in the river. They're taking a raft home."

Matt took us to the long, log house, saying we were going to be staying in there until we got on our feet. It was a long, narrow one-room structure. Although equipped with a wood stove, we would eat with our hosts until we became more efficient with our cooking skills. A newly-dug latrine was a short jaunt into the woods. They had built crude wooden shelves behind the beds for packs and personal items. Baths took place in a spring, about one quarter mile south of us, and we were to go in a group. Matt warned, “No long walks in the woods alone; this isn’t Frazer’s farm.” The place was rude and crude, and we all loved it.

Matt told us survival training would begin tomorrow morning at 6. We would split up in groups of two, and do a quick two or three-day course on each of the subject areas. After finishing all of them, we would decide on specialties and continue more intensive training into the summer. This way we could have a club expert in each area, but still be able to survive if we found ourselves split up.

Ben wanted to call Angie and check on Libby, while Jim needed to call Rose. Matt said he had a secure phone in “the cave.” There was a small, unvented cave nearby which they used to keep their special equipment dry. He said they had a computer satellite connection as well.

I asked Matt, “You have power out here?”

“Sure,” he said, “up on that hill there. Go up and introduce yourself to Paul.”

Clyde and I took a hike up a small hill to find a small wooden shack. It was constructed out of boards and nails, unlike our log home. We saw a windmill and a small solar panel spread out on the south side of the hill.

We met Paul storming out of the shack, throwing his hand tools on the ground and using language I’d rather not repeat. A puff of smoke followed him.

“You must be Paul?” Clyde asked.

“Oh yea, sorry. I’m a little involved at the moment.”

“What you got going here, Paul?” I asked.

“A big mess, I think.”

Waiting for the smoke to clear, I walked around the side of the shack and noticed several severe problems with his set up. I came back and looked inside the door. “Oh, no, no, no,” I said.

"I keep shorting out somewhere," Paul said, "I can't find what I'm doing wrong. Can you tell?"

"Paul," I said, "I think it would be faster if I told you what you're doing right. Not much."

Clyde explained, "Paul, meet Dan Kelley, electrician."

"You're an electrician? Wow! Help please."

"Buddy, you got the wrong gage wire all over here. You got inside wiring outside. The thickness of the insulation is all wrong. What shape's your breaker box in?"

"Well, I kept tripping the breaker, so I ..."

"Don't tell me."

"So I used a bigger one. That's not good, is it?"

"That's a fire, Paul. Can you get some stuff for me?"

"In a couple of days. Here, I'll write it down."

I shut it down, rerouted through the correct fuse, and replaced the outside wiring with what he had laying around. When the stuff got here, I could put all new wiring on and new breakers.

I became curious, "Do you have a club president, or something similar. Who's your leader?"

Paul said, "We don't have one designated, but organization-wise, I guess Matt fits the bill."

"He's a good guy," I added.

"Yea, kind of quiet, though."

I thanked Paul and he was very grateful for my help.

We had some dried soup with a broken seal, which was bound to spoil soon, so we just made it for supper by ourselves and had a meeting. We got a good fire going and our log house became cozy. We loved just having the fire and candles as our only light, making it rustic. We rearranged the beds to give us some more space around the fire. We brought in stumps to use as chairs. We sat on those and the closest bunks to the fire to have our meeting and eat.

Ben had some advice, "Well, guys, these people saved our lives. Let's do what odds and ends we can to help them out. And they are going to teach us how to live out here, so when they say we start at six, we're ready at 5:45."

All of us agreed this is where we wanted to be. Angie had reported to Ben no one came looking for us, but we were officially listed as suspended. Ben had also called Milt who had a very interesting fact to report. He said the truant officers did come to the farm but only met him at his main entrance. They weren't allowed to come on to private property. They could only grab us on public property, so they just had to rely on his good nature to tell them the truth. We all knew that Milt didn't have anything remotely resembling a good nature, so he told them, "Last I heard, they were catching a flight to New Orleans." But Ben made a note of their inability to come onto private property because that was a fact that may come in handy someday.

Jim Donovan reported all was well with Rose Russo and said, "Kelley, she said her sisters were disappointed you didn't decide to move in with them."

I laughed, "You see? Those girls know who the real men are."

The next day, Paul already had the stuff he needed, so my partner, Bo, and I used the first day to rewire the power station. We put in a new breaker box, replaced some of the storage batteries and then cleaned out that dirty shack. This ended the power disruptions and Paul and Holy Cross were very thankful.

The next few weeks flew by. We received our mountain man generalist training.

Unfortunately, our first session was not very pleasant. I didn't take extensive notes on this session because, well, I sort of found it difficult to write about. I don't mind hunting. I did shoot an elk on the first day, but I did it in the spirit of survival. Under the guidance of an experienced butcher, I also butchered a deer. I did not like that either but learned just to learn. I simply refused to skin an animal. Bo and I obtained enough knowledge to get by if we were stranded, but after those three days I just deferred those duties to someone else. Empire and Clyde decided to specialize in those skills and I certainly had no problem with that.

Our next session was my favorite, horticulture and gathering. Bo and I took off to meet our instructor, a person named Marie. When we approached the designated area, we saw Matt talking to a female. Rather, they were arguing. We couldn't make out what they were saying and as they saw us approach they quieted down.

Matt started to walk away and hissed, "Bo and Dan, meet Marie, my wife!"

We walked up the girl, she was obviously flustered, and so I joked, "Trouble in paradise?"

She just threw up a hand and said, "Sorry, we were arguing. I love Matt but sometimes he's just pigheaded."

It was a very good day. Figuring that all the ladies were spoken for around here, like Marie, it was still nice to be back amongst them. But these weren't your typical north Centura girls. Certainly the fresh new clothes styles, the shiny hair, the smell of perfume didn't exist here. But I found their toughness just as appealing. Marie had a long sleeve plaid shirt on and army green pants. She had high cheekbones and hair pulled back, work gloves that were too big for her, and she was much too skinny. Thin but certainly not wimpy, I could see she must have been strong and a look of steely determination on her face.

First, we walked over to a small clearing, freshly tilled, and ready for planting. She said when we returned for planting, she would show us how to put vegetables in. We then collected some of those special roots we'd had in our soup the first night. She showed us what the plants looked like above ground, where to find them, and how to harvest them. Surprisingly, some of them could be used as field spices, if caught out alone somewhere. Marie asked me not to take extensive notes, that these were secrets they didn't want everybody knowing.

Apparently done with the fun stuff, we spent the afternoon peeling and washing roots.

We spent the evenings in common meeting, going over our experiences during the day. Sometimes a Cross person would attend and lecture. I was struck how old nose-in-a-book Frank Davis was so into all of this. Those who had taken cooking already practiced by making suppers, some of them horrible, but we all had to learn.

Holy Cross Corky took Bo and me out in the forest for our wood training. We went over conifers, softwoods, and broadleaf hardwoods. Walking around, he pointed out identifying leaves. He chopped off pieces of each variety, had us smell them, even taste them. Showing us summer and winter woods, he went over those that put off the least smoke. "No need ever to chop anything down, there are always plenty of fallen branches which are already dry."

During the afternoon, he showed us how to build a campfire, and how to modify our setup depending if we were in a cave or out under the stars. He showed us how to do a wind blocker, and how to set a fire while it was raining. "Don't make your fires too large. White people are bad at this; Old World Native Americans made 'proper' sized fires."

Matt covered heat and cooking stoves. Stone constructed ovens and stoves took a lot of time to build, so he just took us around and showed us what they had already constructed. We were surprised to see large, fully functioning stone stoves they used to bake bread and even pizza in. All were wood fired.

The next day, Matt went over cooking. There was baking, frying, and cast iron pot campfire cooking. Finally, there was the old style Boy Scout method of just holding stuff over a fire. He managed to give us an extra set of cast iron cookware for our cabin. Dutch ovens were extremely versatile, almost essential on a foray into the forest.

Another Cross gentleman, an older person, took us fishing on a lake about a half mile to the southeast. Being uninhabited for so long had been good for finding food in the country, because we harvested buckets full of fresh fish. Of course, the afternoon was spent cleaning and washing the fish, not my favorite. Bo and I smelled like two fish by the end of the day.

Teaching us the working and tanning of animal skins, a skill that took years to develop was not even attempted by our hosts. "We can show this to you later, if you want, it takes a long time and either the chemicals are dangerous or the animal brain method too disgusting. This is a skill for a lifer out here. We have ways of obtaining clothes, shoes and coats," Matt told us. He did let us watch some of the folks stitching buckskin shirts and pants.

While saying it was important to keep our heavy field packs, Matt began substituting natural materials for our army issue gear. He gave us botas for our canteens, leather bags to carry things, and either strips of natural leather or vines for belts and straps. Ben got all done up one day and looked a lot liked an ancient frontiersman. By the beginning of full summer, we were all looking like mountain men.

Ben Holden and Jim Donovan, as time went on, were beginning to fear the loss of their girlfriends if they didn't pay a visit. When asking our hosts if it was too soon, Matt and his Corky came up with an interesting fact.

Matt spread out this old map of Centura Township. "It appears," he began, "that back in the days when Thompson and the town were starting up, Milt Frazer's grandfather, or maybe a great, and some of the other farmers, made homestead claims. Not unlike the Old World state of Virginia, old man Frazer's claim extended from his current homestead, west and then south, to the limits of the township. As you may recall, Virginia once extended all the way to the Mississippi River. So Milt's land now, extends from here, all the way west and then south to the Ice River, here. To the edge of the township."

"So what?" Ben asked.

"So, the truant officers can't go on private property. They can get an arrest warrant for a kid's guardian, who is in charge of the kid going to school, but they can't arrest a kid. They can only take him back to school. Milt's not your guardian, the orphanage is and they already lost you. They can't arrest Milt and they can't go on his property. You got a clear shot back up to Milt's farm if you want it. Besides, you are not even a student, you're expelled, and I'm not so sure they can do anything to you at all. Anyway, the Ice River is northeast of here; as soon as you cross you are on Milt's land."

Ben called Milt who even offered to bring the girls down to the Ice River in his truck. Ben asked him to get some stuff we needed. The school put no more money in our accounts but couldn't touch them at all, so we could use them for purchases. Ben ordered some field glasses and some summer wear for us.

We decided a small excursion was needed. Ben, Jim, Clyde and I would hike down, Ben and Jim could cross the river and talk, then we would all camp down there, coming back in the morning. We found it to be quite a short walk. We had been much closer to our old home than we imagined. Upon travelling from our first cave dwelling to where the main Cross camp was situated, must have been in a southeastern direction.

Upon our arrival, we found out the Ice River, opening out onto Lake Michigan to the east, was not really a river at all, but a long, narrow bay to the big lake. One could walk over it; throw a few logs in the shallow water and someone could drive a truck over it. While waiting for them to arrive, I pulled Jim Donovan aside.

"Jim, could you ask Rose, not in front of Angie, if anyone important has been asking about me or wants to get a message to me?"

Jim put his hand up to his face, “Hmmm, like maybe a cute girl with auburn hair and dreamy eyes?”

I blushed a little, “But not in front of Angie, okay?”

“Don’t worry, Kelley, I’ll get the scoop.”

As they went across the river and walked toward the truck, I watched on Matt’s binoculars while Clyde and I stayed on the other bank. I first saw the little pint-sized girl run across the prairie, jump up on Ben, and both fell to the ground. Rose was there too. They all milled around the truck, then cloth sacks of goods were unloaded. I also spotted Ms. Hightower there as well. Seeing enough, Clyde and I walked back to the south to look for a camp.

By the time Ben and Jim returned, several cloth bags slung over their shoulders, Clyde and I had a raging campfire going and meat already grilling. Clyde stood up, “What’d Hightower say?”

Ben lamented, “Well, we lost the appeal to the Super, but she figured we would. She has filed a formal appeal with the Department of Education and should be hearing from them soon.

Later, after we finished eating, I asked Jim, “Jim, any word?”

He patted me on the shoulder, “No, sorry Dan, nobody asked about you or had a message for you.” I went off to do dishes by myself, wanting to be alone. Just maybe I should get use to the feeling.

Since Ben and Jim were the primary beneficiaries of the trip, they said they would split the watch and for us to sleep. I spent a restless night.

We were eating breakfast when Matt’s wife, Marie, walked into camp. She had another guy with her, a big guy with a rifle slung over his shoulder. She said they had taken two or three days and walked down to the beach on Lake Michigan. I thought it kind of weird, her being on an overnight with another guy. I had to remind myself these were our hosts.

A few days later, Cross Corky brought me out to a field to go over firearms and canoeing. Fortunately, firearms used in hunting had become more humane. The laser coil rifles shot an electromagnetic light beam. The discharge didn't actually put a hole in anything, rather, if the light beam traveled through a skull, it short circuited the animals neural discharges and caused immediate and painless death, or so they say. It might not even affect the creature at all if it passed through a non-vital area or the distance was too great. It would cause burns if used too closely. He showed me how to handle, fire, and recharge the thing. Although safer, they took a lot of energy to recharge and they were heavy. Cork told me it was essential that any size group carry at least one if going out into the wilderness.

As summer had rolled on, the Saint James River had become much calmer. Holy Cross Cork then had me out on the river learning to canoe. I picked this up pretty easily. Finally, we just cruised a little and chatted.

"Where would we end up if we just drifted down?" I asked.

"This river runs into the neighborhood called St. James, then out into the big lake."

"Have you ever been to this St. James place?"

"Sure. It's not really a separate town, sort of a suburb. You've probably heard of a bunch of weirdos or homeless people living there. Not true. There are some communal farms, but nothing really weird. That's where Thomas Pine was from. Well, that's where his family was from, before they died and he went to the orphanage."

"Have you heard of Thomas Pine?" I asked, suddenly perking up.

"Heard of him? I know him."

"The one who wrote *Living in the Woods*?"

"Sure. What do you think got us all out here? It's like our bible."

"Where is he? Is he nearby?"

"Oh gosh, he's probably two or three days march from here now. He goes way out in the summer."

"Can you take me there, Cork?"

"I was wondering when you were going to ask. I saw his book on your bunk back in the log house; that's a big clue if you brought only essentials. Sure, when you're done with getting all the vegetables in, we'll go out and check him out."

I was so excited I couldn't stand it during the next week, when Marie and I finished the planting. She told me Pine was the greatest. My Eagle friends were not so thrilled with the venture, but knew there was no talking me out of it.

Corky somehow got word to Pine that we were coming. He was going to send his student in residence, probably a philosophy student from the college, to meet us at the end of day one of our march. Matt made sure I had everything I needed for the trip, including my toothbrush. "A toothache out here is as deadly as a broken leg," he used to say. Our packs were heavy but certainly not as bad as that army one. I grabbed two staffs, a blunt one and one I had put a metal point on. Corky brought the rifle.

We headed straight west, at four in the morning on departure day. Everyone was still asleep. Holy Cross Corky and I went through forest for the longest time, and then hit some open meadows. It was glorious out here. We passed all kinds of game. Most would just lift their heads, look at us, and then continue grazing. Marie had packed some sandwiches for us and we ate on the walk at about eleven.

Cork was an encyclopedia of knowledge, "See those rocky hills right over there, that's where we'll be wintering, those of us who do. A series of great caves there." He spoke between bites of his sandwich. "See these trees here, orchards. We'll raid them in the fall." The he pointed straight ahead, "Low, wet, soggy ground coming up. We'll go around."

Past the swamp, we ran into heavy forest again. He was following some sort of trail, but a good deal of it was difficult walking. Coming up to a stream, we sat, exchanged water, and washed up. I didn't give a darn about school just then, I wanted to live here.

We pushed on, all through the afternoon. He said, "Dan, I usually like to stop by four or five o'clock but since its high summer, we'll go until six. I know that daylight is much longer but it's not a good idea to stop and try and get camp set up in the dark. Always give yourself plenty of time."

Soon I saw Cork look at the GPS dial of his handheld, then looked around, and said, "I think we're where we're supposed to be."

We went right to work, Cork got stones and wood for a fire while I gathered some roots. We were carrying some leftover cooked meat, so we threw it all in our pot for stew.

"Do you know Pine's sidekick?" I asked.

"Yea, Jim Candolene. He's pretty knowledgeable, but a little unreliable. I hope he gets here."

We cooked, ate and drank our tea. We then gathered logs and rocks and built some crude walls around our campsite. We got more wood and stacked it nearby to replenish our fire. It was getting dark when we heard, "Corky!"

Jim Candolene came out of the shadows, packs and gear much like ours. He was tall and skinny, had long hair and a weathered face.

"We have a little food left, hungry?" Cork asked.

"Naw, I got hungry about four and stopped to eat. Sorry I'm late." He plopped down on the ground next to us, removed his pack and gear. We all introduced ourselves. Jim looked at me, "Dan Kelley; heard of you. Welcome to the wilderness. I slept late so I'll take watch tonight; you guys sleep. But first, I got some fine wine here," he pulled out his bota. "Care for some?"

Cork put his hand up and shook his head, I responded, "Never touch the stuff." So we sat and talked and Jim drank. About half an hour later, after putting a log on the fire, Cork pointed at Jim who was now snoring away.

"So much for standing watch," Cork whispered, "the guy shouldn't drink out here; it's too dangerous."

After he sat back down, I asked, "Cork, what's your family story, all orphans have one?"

"Oh, I'm not an orphan, I have a mother," he replied.

"I thought you grew up in the orphanage?"

"I did, social services took me."

"I'm sorry, Corky. You must have some bad feeling toward her?"

"No, not at all, I see her all the time. We get along fine."

"I don't understand."

"It's complicated. You see, my mom's a … well, a harlot."

"A what?"

"A woman of the evening."

"A dancer?"

"Well, she did that for a while. But she's a prostitute. She's retired now, but living in a shelter. We used to live up on the strip, near the main gate to Thompson."

I threw another log on the fire and apologized, "Sorry, you don't have to talk about it if you don't want."

"I don't mind at all. You have to know my mom. She tried, tried very hard at times, but she really wasn't very good at being a mother. She cried when the social workers took me away for the last time, but she knew it was best. We lived in a trailer and things were pretty bad, I mean with her being so poor. I used to tell people mom was divorced, I didn't tell them it was only after ten minutes." Then Cork and I started laughing; we couldn't control it. "In a sick sort of way," he added, "it is kind of funny."

I tried to muffle a chuckle, "Do you know who your dad is?"

"We got it narrowed down to two or three, soldiers at the base," now he was laughing too.

"Is his name, John?"

"I don't know. He don't write much."

I slowly drifted off. Every few minutes we started laughing, and then quieted again. I was suddenly shaken by Corky about two in the morning. I took the watch until five while he got some sleep. I had to walk around, in a circle around the fire, to keep awake. The night was clear and crisp. I had the rifle on my shoulder. About four thirty, I started heating up the leftover supper.

After we ate and used the facilities behind the bushes, we woke Jim and started off. Jim estimated about a six-hour hike. We were quiet. I started to practice what I was going to say to Pine. By midmorning, the heat was becoming intense.

"Do you want to lunch?" Cork asked.

I shook my head, "Too darn hot anyway. If you don't mind, I'd rather keep going." Jim didn't look too well; he was sweating and drinking a lot of water.

The butterflies in my stomach were peaking as we walked up to a crystal clear lake. Jim stopped and pointed to a grove of very large trees. "Kelley, there's sort of a trail, there. The grass is kind of a pain but no trees grow on it, must have been some sort of Old World freeway or something. Only about a quarter mile you will come to a cliff. That's where Pine is."

"What if I don't see him?"

"He'll find you. My camp is just on the other side of the lake there; we'll be there. I need to take a bath and eat."

Corky waved to me, "I'll go with the bathing beauty here and stand guard while he washes the stink off. I don't want some bear mistaking him for a dead carcass or something."

As my mates walked off, I took a deep breath and started walking. Cork had taken the rifle so I made sure to check that both my staffs were attached.

It wasn't a long walk by any means. When I got to the cliff, it turned out to be only a ten-foot drop-off. Hearing rustling behind me, I pulled my pointed spear out and stood at the ready. Then, coming out of the bushes, I saw him.

"Don't shoot," his deep, loud voice boomed through the woods, scaring the heck out of me as well as several wild fowl nearby, which flapped into flight. He laughed, "I'm not going to rob you. Of course, if you have a lot of money on you, then that's a different story."

A very tall, robust man approached. Long, sandy gray hair came out of everywhere on his head and face. He wore highly bleached buckskin, matching shirt and pants. His face was amazing, what you could see of it. The forehead was wrinkled and the bushy brows eclipsed dark, stern eyes. Although his mouth formed a smile, he had a hard, weathered face, the kind that came with living outdoors.

"Mr. Kelley is it?"

"Yes, father, Dan is my first ..."

He stopped in his tracks about ten feet from me. "What did you call me?"

I blushed, "I'm not sure what to call you: father, teacher, doctor?"

"How about Tom?" he came closer, holding out his hand to shake mine.

"I'm Dan Kelley; I wanted to meet you so ..."

"Yes, yes," his booming voice interrupted me, "Dan Kelley, you're here with that pack of hoodlums from Centura. I know about you, more than you think. Obviously, you know who I am or you wouldn't be here. Care to sit?"

We sat on two large rocks as he continued, "Gosh, this is a great summer. The rains have been good, there is plenty of food all around and I do feel one with the earth. So why did you want to meet me? Were you interested to see if this modern day ape man really exists? Wondering if I swing by grapevines? Well, I don't have a pet monkey." He laughed wildly, scaring yet another set of birds.

"No, sir." I was amazed with this man. I guess I had been expecting a very holy man who spoke in parables and proverbs. Expecting a prophet, I was in the company of a wisecracking, hairy, forest dweller.

"Good," his smile fading, "now I want to tell you why I wanted to see you."

"You wanted to see me, sir … I mean, Tom? I had no idea you wanted to see me."

"I know. Dan, I need a new student, I'm afraid I need you a lot more than you need me."

"Why? I thought Candolene was your student."

"Don't get me wrong, I love Jimmy, but he's been with me a year now. I think I'm at a wall with him. Jim's lost, lost as a person, lost in that stupid alcohol he drinks. They got to him."

"Who?"

"Them. That wretched society machine we got operating in Centura, those self-perpetuating morons who want to mass-produce plumbers and chemists and soldiers. I'm on the faculty, Dan, at the university. Do you have any idea how many doctoral candidates we have in philosophy right now? One! And he's draft age. The master's program has three. Pickin's are slim."

"Tom, I don't know a darn thing, other than your book, about philosophy. I took the intro course in seventh grade."

"I heard about you, Dan. You have qualifications."

"I'm an electrician."

"It's not the field you're in; it's the character." He leaned forward, "You look and wonder and are curious, Mr. Kelley. You have a lot of questions. You can both question God about why he puts clowns like Bus Quint in the world and yet see heaven in a young French girl's eyes. And I'm not trying to recruit a disciple, nor am I feeling sorry for the poor orphan boy. This is all for purely selfish reasons. We need thinkers, Kelley, there aren't many left!"

The old boy was really adamant. I didn't know what to think, what his expectations of me were. But after he told me to at least try it, I reluctantly agreed.

"So," he said, standing up, "are you any good with those spears or just pretending, 'I proud warrior?'"

"I'm not bad," I said.

"Okay. I know where some big fat geese live."

We went down the cliff and walked out into some marshy area. Pine slowly followed behind me, tossing small stones in front of me as he went. Suddenly, two big geese flew up; I recoiled and let one fly. It was a pretty straight trajectory, bopping one of the geese right on the head, knocking him out. I breathed a sigh of relief, hoping to gain some Pine points.

Tom was good with the rather large stone oven he had built on the edge of the cliff. We did a good slow roast on the goose, after cleaning it, for a good three hours. While we cooked and ate, we talked, mainly about current events, all my problems in Centura, the war. While we ate, Tom said his read on the slumping economy during the war build up was a sign of social disapproval.

"What are we going to do if we win, take some of their land? We have three quarters of a country now we can't populate. This is what we just don't get. This is why I'm so pessimistic. There is absolutely no rational motive for fighting this thing. The only real reasons for doing so are those inappropriate ones rational people have been complaining about over the millennia. Whether for financial incentive or maybe it's a national pride building thing, we just seem to have to fight one every so often. Your fight with the Mustangs had more credibility."

As the sky began to darken, I said my goodbye and headed back to camp with Jim and Cork. Pine told me to meet him the next day around noon.

I decided to get there a little early, to impress my mentor, a decision that turned out to be fortunate. About eleven thirty, I was walking back to the cliff on the trail when I ran into a figure, back turned to me, looking at something in the grass. Suddenly I saw that it was a female, one named Diane Win. And, wow, she wore this little green dress, only more like a long top. It was very short and, well, shall I say top-revealing. “Working on a tan?”

I startled her, she yelled, “Gee!” and ran behind a tree, slowly peeking around the side of it. “Dan Kelley? I thought you were coming at noon?”

I turned to the side out of politeness, “Sorry, Diane, I didn’t expect to see you here, or like this. Do you know Tom too?”

“Know him? I married him. He’s my husband, why do you think I’m hangin’ around the woods dressed like this?”

“Wow, that’s great. I mean, you being married to him and all. I am sorry.”

“That’s okay. I’m sorry too. It’s sort of a newlywed thing. Can we talk later? I’ll stop over.”

“Okay. Oh, Diane, I’m also sorry about the conjugal visit crack I made as well.”

“Okay. No problem.”

“I just don’t know what to do?” I felt naughty again.

“I told you no problem.”

“No, I mean I don’t know what to do with these pictures I just took with my handheld.” I took off running only to catch a glimpse of an acorn whizzing by my head.

Tom was sitting by his stone oven when I approached. Sitting down, he was looking at his handheld computer. “I’ve got some reading for you to do. We’ll talk about them this winter. I’m transmitting to you the names of some books to read.”

I just looked at him, "Aren't we being a little excessive here?"

"These are pretty basic."

"Some of my friends might be interested in some of this. Will our sessions be formal?"

"There's no college credit for any of these. It will be lecture, discussion, or you lecture me. Nothing formal, any friend you want can attend, it's a learning thing."

"I met your wife," I sort of blushed.

"Just now?"

"Yea, I apologized. I think I saw more of her then I should have."

Just then Diane came walking over to us. She was dressed in more appropriate pioneer attire. We just sat there, looking at her, both with grins on our faces."

"Both of you shut up!" she pointed her finger at us, "And Kelley, you come here and give me a big hug." I stood and we hugged. "It's good to see you again."

"Diane," I asked, "did this marital relationship have anything to do with you encouraging me to take Intro to Philosophy?"

"You never know." She laughed, "I was the one who told Tom the most about you. His Holy Cross spies did the rest. I was at school just a few days ago, no word on your appeal yet."

We talked for a few hours, mostly about our situation, which led Pine into a discussion about problems with the educational system. Finally, Diane bid us farewell and headed back to the couples camp to prepare supper.

After she left, Pine said, "Dan, come with me a minute." We walked north, through a grove of trees until we came out in the open near the northern cliff of the hill we were on. "There it is."

I looked out in wonder to a wide expanse of prairie, extending for miles, to see a herd of grazing bison, probably numbering in the thousands.

"My gosh," I gasped with my mouth dropping open. "I didn't know they came this far east."

"This is the first summer I've seen them this close, I saw them two years ago but about two hundred miles out. They haven't been in Illinois in over twelve hundred years. They've come back."

I returned to my camp, ate a great supper cooked by Candolene, and we got to sleep early. The next morning, Cork and I got an early start back, and found ourselves back to making a decision on what to do for the winter.

CHAPTER EIGHT

Although it was still early August, our preparations for winter were commencing in camp. As crops came from the garden, the washing and sacking of vegetables was almost continuous. Marie, Bo, and I spent hours picking peas, beans and beets. They were placed in leather sacks to be hauled out to the wintering cave. Jarring would take place out there.

Murdock and Corky left with a group of Holy Cross to the cave to begin pemmican production. This was a process used to preserve meat. Heavy game meat was dried, ground, and mixed with fat and berries that could be stored without refrigeration.

As harvest continued and the month of August came to an end, Marie invited me to a harvest picnic. One Sunday afternoon, I walked out to a tiny meadow in the middle of the forest. I was surprised to find her there alone.

"Where's everybody? Am I early?" I asked her.

She looked a little put off by what I said and replied, "Just us."

I sat down on a blanket she had spread on the ground with sandwiches and potato salad for two set in the middle. "That's fine," I said. "We still have a lot of stuff out in the garden, any reason why we're celebrating now?"

"I'm going back to school next week," she said, "so I won't be around to help finish. I'm a nursing student at the college. This is only a summer thing for me."

"I'm sure everyone will miss you." After I spoke I became a little confused because the look on her face told me it was something she didn't want to hear.

She managed a weak smile as she pulled out a bottle of wine, "I have a good cheap white wine here. Care for some?"

I was getting uncomfortable now. I thought about seeing her with that other guy in the woods and now this. "Marie, I'm sorry, but do you think this is right?"

"We're having fowl, and it is white wine."

"No, it's not that at all. I don't drink, but that's not the problem. I mean, do you think me and you should be out here like this?"

She was becoming exasperated, "Are you dense or something?"

"No I'm not dense. What about your husband, Matt?"

"My husband? Matt's not my husband. He's my brother!" She started laughing hysterically.

"Your brother? But he introduced you as his wife."

"He always calls me that when we argue. He always tells me when I nag him that people will think we are married. Oh man, I can just imagine what was going through your head all this time. I should have borrowed Diane's little wood nymph outfit and worn that out here; that would have blown your mind."

Dan Kelley, the big know-it-all with the ladies, had to sit there and pull his foot out of his mouth. After I stopped laughing, I asked, "So, you wanted to be out here with just me?"

"I wanted to be out here with just you, yes," she smiled.

"Well, I'll skip the wine and have some of that iced tea, if you don't mind."

We ate and drank and laughed most of the afternoon. Every now and then, she would break out into giggles about my little misunderstanding. I walked her back to her hut and she asked me to write emails to her over the winter. I said yes. I asked her if I could kiss her; she said okay, so I did.

During the remainder of harvest, we all took turns lugging sacks of vegetables out to the winter cave, about a three-hour walk from where we were. We all kept busy, jarring and smoking meat. Later in the fall, the jarring of wild fruits began. While we counted as many as twenty Holy Cross members milling about, only Matt and HC Corky were going to be staying over the winter. With Pine and Candolene, it turned out to be a group of thirteen. Most of the Cross folks were returning to school or jobs in the town.

The winter cave complex was amazing. This was a rather extensive cave, with three entrances and many tunnels leading to different larger chambers. Our main chamber, where we would be sleeping, was vented and the Cross had constructed a fairly complex stove/heating fire combination. Water was supplied inside, via a bubbling brook. A latrine was dug near one of the other entrances that could be flushed out periodically. We built wooden gates to put in the two distant entrances to keep the critters out, while we hung a huge animal hide rug over our main entrance to allow for air draft into the sleeping chamber.

Paul, with materials from the military base, constructed a small wind/solar power system near the top of the hill. I wired it in, running a cable down. It didn't produce enough power for lights or appliances, but we could use it to run a ham radio and to charge handhelds and rifles. The cave was ideal for storing produce, maintaining a constant temperature above freezing. Of course the sleeping chamber was much warmer with the fire.

Potatoes and firewood were next, putting all of us to work for over a week of chopping fallen limbs. They had planted thousands of potatoes near the cave in the spring that needed harvesting as well.

The whole process of preparing for winter was a great time. We worked hard, ate hearty food, joked and laughed. Clyde, Corky, and Bo kept us all in stitches with practical jokes and these little comic sketches they came up with. Most of the dark humor was aimed at the orphanage staff, Big Ears in particular, the Mustangs, and of course our love lives. Bo did a perfect Angie with Clyde as Ben Holden, Bo shaking his finger and yelling at Clyde.

With the potatoes sacked and moved inside, all jarred vegetables and tomato sauces stacked, and as much firewood as possible dragged inside, Bo and I followed Marie's instructions in digging and drying edible roots. They tasted pretty rough raw and were mainly used in stews with the stronger tasting pemmican.

I had never seen us so content.

The fall was lovely; leaves by the millions blew through the woods. All those who were staying for the winter had moved out to the winter caves permanently by now. One of our enjoyments was going into the woods or on the prairie. Small groups of four or five would depart, hike for a day, make camp at night to sleep and then return the following day. All sustenance was collected on route since the forest was filled with food this time of year. Frank Davis and Clyde Hastings loved the excursions and would go on as many as they could sign up for. Matt made sure that either he, HC Corky, Jim Candolene or Tom Pine was a member of each party.

One day Pine, Diane, Jim and I departed on a foray to their honeymoon suite, where I had first met them, to retrieve some belongings. It was warm and breezy that day, perfect weather for a hike. All four of us remained silent most of the day, deep in our own thoughts. Upon arriving at Candolene's old camp, we got a fire going and Diane and I started to cook supper. Pine and Jim wandered around the camp searching the grounds. They didn't go too far because they had the rifles.

"Hear anything on your appeal?" Diane asked me.

"No, Hightower said they assigned a prehearing negotiator to the case, he'll be flying up from Atlanta sometime to talk to her."

"How does it look?"

"I don't know. Hightower is so confidant all the time, it's hard to tell if she's trying to talk us into a bright outcome or trying to talk herself into one. I'm paranoid when it comes to decisions affecting our well-being."

"Do you feel you were in the right?" she queried, which I took to be a philosophical question.

"I think so. I think even the fighting was justified. I know it's illegal, it's harmful, but the circumstances required something nobody was giving us. Clyde doesn't have to grow up in a barn; Frank can take the bus home without getting clocked. I don't think we started the fight; it came to us. I can ask someone where I can eat supper without being told to go through the garbage cans in the vending room. Ben had to threaten a guy to find out where a pizza parlor was! Maybe that's just life. Maybe this is just my station in life, but I know one thing. Nobody would slap around Claire Popover or take her money without feeling the wrath of the town council. That stuff doesn't happen to 'them.'"

"What if you lose the appeal?"

"Then I become a full-time woodsman."

"What if you win the appeal? What then?" she smiled.

"I knew that was coming. That is a trick question, Doctor Diane. I just don't know. I'll become an electrician. I had enough credits for my associate's degree before I got kicked out, but the school didn't confer the degree yet. I know I'll try to find Sharon and see if she'll give me another chance. Then the military I guess. I'll become one of the marching ants."

"Is that what you want?"

"I don't know. I keep getting thoughts in my head that I need to know something else before I can be happy, and I can't put my finger on it. And it's all weird. I feel that answers are needed but I can't even put the questions into words yet."

Pine and Jim came walking up to us. "Honey, I'm home," Tom said sarcastically.

"I'm thrilled," Diane shot back, "another half hour, then we can eat."

"Kelley," Jim said, "let's get some stuff over at Pine's stone oven, on the cliff. We'll be back in a jiff."

As I got up, Pine told Jim, "Stay with him. You got the rifle."

We walked the short distance to Pine's thinking camp. Jim retrieved a cooking pot Pine had left there, unwashed from his last snack. "What a pig this guy is. I'll get some leaves in the grove over there. Stay put." He walked out of sight into the trees.

I squatted down and looked out past the cliff. You could see for miles from here. Then I saw the cutest thing. Two, jet black bear cubs came tumbling past me, in a pretend fight. They were surprised to see me but weren't scared. They looked at me in wonder, sniffing and coming closer. I heard Jim rustling in the trees behind me.

"Jim, come here. You have to see this." Now I had never seen bears this close before, maybe at the Centura zoo. I had only read about them in books. I was talking to them as they ambled closer to me. Suddenly, a feeling of instant dread hit me when the two-word question popped out of my mouth: "Where's momma?"

I slowly reached behind and retrieved my staff, then stood. Turning around, I discovered that it hadn't been Jim rustling behind me. Momma bear stood there, on her hind legs. She was taller than me by a foot, and, unlike the Mustangs, she had come ready for the fight.

A roar came out of her mouth that shook the whole woods. I knew there was a drop off behind me and that I had retrieved the round end spear instead of the pointed one. As she came running at me, I took off running at her, with my only chance being to go for her throat. Not more than a few feet from her, I hurled the spear with all my might. Ducking her head at the last second, the blunt spear hit her square between the eyes and bounced straight off. I jumped out of the way as she fell forward, the ground shook a bit when she landed.

Suddenly, Pine appeared at my left, rifle up in firing position and aimed straight at her head. Then Jim came in on my right, assuming the same posture.

"My gosh," Pine gasped. "I've never seen one that big."

"Is she dead?" Jim asked.

"No," Pine responded, "probably just seeing stars. Okay, everyone, back up slowly." We backed up into the trees as momma bear slowly started to sit up, and then all three of us took off running back to camp. Pine showed no mercy on Jim, "I thought I told you to stay with him, you moron!"

"I was cleaning your stupid pot."

"And we could have spent the rest of the day cleaning Kelley up, that was stupid, Jim!"

We came running into camp as Diane stood up, "You guys see a ghost?"

Pine replied, "Yea. Time to go, honey. Get your stuff."

"I spent an hour getting this meal ready," Diane protested, but saw the fear in all of us, so she complied.

I think we had been walking for two hours before the adrenaline wore off. Pine kept talking about it, "You should have seen Kelley running at that bear, honey! My first thought was 'Kelley, don't, this ain't Bus Quint.'"

Diane asked me, "You okay, honey? Do you need anything?"

"Did anyone bring an extra pair of underwear?"

We walked all the way back to the winter cave that night.

The next day found Bo and me gathering more roots, this time with Empire Murdock walking around us with a rifle. Matt had used the incident to announce to all that morning that we were getting lax with our safety measures. Black bears were not usually this close in because the absence of humans and the abundance of natural food didn't force them to. Plus, he said she wouldn't have charged me if she was sure I wasn't going to harm her cubs.

We built a big fire outside the cave entrance that night while Tom Pine took the floor. Pine had me come up and stand by him while he did a mock ceremony, "To Dan Kelley, whose bravery is only out matched by his stupidity, in the spirit of her highness, Mother Nature, I do hereby bestow this honorary Native American name of 'Great Bear.' While we cannot deny your bravery, we do have serious concerns about your IQ score. For he who puts himself between bear cubs and angry mother, is a total idiot."

I shook Pine's hand, "Thank you for this honor, sir." As I took my seat I thought, if a guy had poor self-esteem, he could never survive this crowd.

Tom looked out at us. "What are we doing here? I think that's the oldest philosophical question I know."

"But first, what about me? Some of you have told me some wild tales about my reputation back in civilization." We greeted Pine's words with sarcasm, of course, and he just stood there and smiled as we booed and called him a fake. After we quieted down, he continued, "Of course you heard the one about me doing live animal sacrifices. I never have; I only hunt. Then there's the one about me being a mystic. I wish that were true. I think the most hurtful of the lot is the rumor that I am leading a cult. It is the most hurtful because I had some responsibility for the mislabeling. I, outwardly, do not appear very religious, although privately I am a very devout Christian. I chose not to advertise that part of me and that is one area where I have received some criticism. To me, spreading religion is a duty for other people. Both my religious and agnostic peers at the college question me on this. They say that if a person is religious then the definition of the word requires that one spread that religion. But I do want you to know that I live by religious values.

"I studied philosophy, got my Ph.D. this spring. When I tell people that, I generally get two different responses. One is, of course, 'Why the heck would you want to pursue such a totally useless profession?' The second being, 'Wow, you must be wise. Tell me, what's the meaning to life?'" Pine got some laughs from the crowd. "You can imagine their dismay when I fail to answer either question. But first of all, they've got it wrong. I studied philosophy, I studied philosophers, thinking, and how others think. I am not a philosopher, yet, anyway. *Living in the Woods* is a book I wrote only on preparing oneself for thinking. Most of the pure philosophy is from others. But that is what we do at first, to grasp a basis. It is a lifestyle book, lacking a better description. And all this brings me to you guys, or us guys.

"What similarity do you guys share with the founders of this country?"

We all looked around at each other. A little of the Eagle sarcasm was sprinkled among the answers.

"We have a similar life style," one guy yelled out.

"We cook on a campfire," another said.

"We have to hear this Kelley and the Bear story for the rest of our miserable lives."

"Religious freedom. Freedom of the press."

I raised my hand, "We both came from a place where things weren't too good, to a place offering more hope."

"Correct," Pine said, "and I know guys, soon we may realize we'd be better off if that bear would have eaten Kelley. But that's an argument for a later time. But he was right on with his answer. I hope to show you, sometime soon, that turning around the situation back there in Centura and being successful out here are dependent on the same thing.

"Now, our American dream was one of optimism and that hard work will pay off, was it not? Technology helped us fulfill that dream. But something went wrong. Back before the mini ice age, we had a practice called foreign aid. This is where we sent millions of dollars in materials to other countries in exchange for their friendship. This practice had mixed results. We found that even with all of our benevolence, people still hated us. Any reason why?"

Frank Davis easily handled this one, "We didn't, and some say still don't, have a healthy respect for evil in the human race. Other cultures had it; they were wise enough to look a gift horse in the mouth because they had been deceived much in their lives."

"Correct," Pine continued, "and with the effects of our Blue Solution, they liked us even less. It is true. With all our optimism, charitable nature, and technology, we couldn't be saved when the climate change and the plague hit us. We will talk of these things more in the future."

One day before the snow fell, Al Myers made a visit, bringing along Rose and Angie. While Ben and Jim Donovan were spending time with the girls, Al briefed us on what was happening.

He was surprised at how the school backed off their negative stance toward him as a student in response to the Department of Mathematics' ranting about our case. His chairperson has had unwavering support for Al and has publically criticized the administration for "treating our sons so poorly." An article, with a byline that included all members of the math department, in the paper contained the sentence, "Stray dogs get a better deal from the pound." Frank Davis added the president of his law club recently texted him, saying they planned a similar article.

He said that Diane Win and student body president, Lisa, were keeping the fires lit as well. Lisa recently won a second term, beating out a dejected guy named Marv Greene. Greene had been losing some steam as more stories like the one with Sharon started to get out. Some of his groupies were talking to the press.

"I talked to Hightower," Al continued, "Her meeting with the negotiator from the Department of Education is next week. She said she was ready. She couldn't tell me when a decision will be made as the negotiator has to give his opinion to an administrative law judge who will decide to hear the case or not."

"Any other things going on?" I asked.

"Milt has been nice. He told me to tell you guys to come up through his fields if you needed to work for some money. He said he'll pay you out of his own pocket. We still have a few friends, guys."

"Oh, I almost forgot, in the gossip area," Al went on, "do you guys remember a girl named Monica, the one who worked the desk at Delk Hall? Rumor has it, she has a bun in the oven and Matt Fuller is the father. Of course, he is denying the whole thing. She has to move up to that home for unwed mothers, up on the school grounds, by the little kids' orphanage."

We had a hearty campfire supper that evening, sitting around and talking. Then Angie surprised us with a diamond engagement ring from Ben, who had used time that afternoon to pop the question. All of us guys showed no mercy on Ben, even announcing that we guessed this made Angie president of the Eagles. All visitors left around eight.

Tom Pine met with our group late that night. We were down to just Ben, Clyde, me, Matt and Holy Cross Corky. I know that Empire and our Corky said they had trouble understanding Pine and would "leave philosophy to the eggheads." Tom didn't seem to mind, even telling us he had expected it.

"I start off tonight with a story as retold by the famous, Dr. Eknath Easwaran, an old world holy man," Tom began, "I'm not sure who wrote it originally, it's from India.

"Once there was a student, long ago and in a faraway place, who wanted to learn meditation to gain inner peace. He knew he must make a journey to the mountain and learn from the great master. He had just bought a new bull that day at the market and, filled with worry about its care, left it in the barn of his most trusted friend.

"He then travelled to the high mountain, climbed it, and saw the great master. 'Father, I want to achieve inner peace.'

"The master replied, 'Then go down into this cave for a night, meditate on the Supreme Being, then you will be granted peace.'

"The student did so and the next day the master yelled down to him, 'Hey, come up and tell me how you did.'

"The student came up, frustrated, 'Sorry, Father, I have failed.'

"'Then go down for two nights, meditate on the Supreme Being, then you will be granted peace.' So the student did.

"After two days, the master yelled down into the cave, 'Come up.' The student did, but reported a similar failure. 'What bothers you, son?' the wise man asked him.

"'It's my new bull, Father. I cannot stop thinking about him.'

"'Then go down again son, and meditate on your new bull.' And so the student did. The very next day, the master, worried about his student, yelled down into the cave, 'Son, are you okay? Come up, now.'

"'I cannot,' replied the student, 'for my horns are too big to fit through the door.'

"Now this little story can mean many things. To me, it means that often times what rules us is what is on our minds at the time.

"We have, without a doubt, made great strides in biochemistry and neuroscience. We now, for example, have phenomenal brain imaging techniques and unique ways of measuring changes in the biochemistry of the brain to detect certain mental illnesses. It's not foolproof.

"But don't get me wrong, I think they are onto something and are just having some trouble figuring out individual variables with these illnesses. However, I like to look at those psychological theorists of old, those who developed their insights before biochemistry came on the scene. They based observations on how people acted.

"This brings me to balance. Tell me, why do we shiver?"

"When we see Rose Russo in a bikini," Holden commented. We all hit him.

Frank Davis said, "When we get a chill."

"Correct, Frank," Pine said, "Unlike your crude buddy here, you are smart. Now, what is a shiver?"

"Body movement," I responded.

"And what does movement create?"

"Heat," I said.

"True, and that's balance. Our bodies physically try to maintain a balance for normal functioning. As you see with a shiver, we can often explain many other physical behaviors in us. When we get a bug, what happens? We start running a temperature. Why? The body is raising the heat in an attempt to kill the bug. Some people are taught, at the onset of the slightest body temperature increase, to cram themselves full of aspirin to 'cure' it, when in fact, they are trying to cure the cure.

"Some psychologists have even transferred this phenomenon to the behavioral world. We tend to act in ways which keep us alive. As biological organisms, we tend to use what we learn to cope, to increase our chances of survival. Certain behaviors help insure this survival and our chances to procreate.

"Some of our most common behaviors can be attributed to this. For instance, yawning is believed by some to provide a way for a leader, before we acquired speech, to signal his tribe that it was time to rest. Facial expressions, the basic ones, are universal among the entire human race and have the same meaning in any given language. Dreaming, according to some, is a way of solving everyday problems. Sleeping has even been considered an adaptive technique in that it keeps us off the street, and out of the woods, at night when predators roamed about.

"Research has shown that when mentally ill people cannot see reality due to their illness, they make one up. Thus, delusions, false and crazy beliefs, and hallucinations, seeing and hearing things that are not there, can result.

"We act in ways which keep us safe. When we hear a rustle in the woods at night, it's better for us to think it's a predator than windblown leaves. If we're right or wrong, we're still safe. It's our way of preparing ourselves for a threat. In Kelley's case, he was right."

We woke up the next morning covered with snow, thus forcing our decision to move into the caves for the winter. The additional two-inches of snowfall that same afternoon proved it was a good decision.

Cave life turned about to be rather pleasant. We had the fire and stove going most of the time and plenty to eat. We had to admit, however, that we still relied on civilization as we had stockpiled spices for cooking and, of course, coffee. We ate like pigs and soon had to start boxing and defense training workouts to fight the calories. Obtaining water for hygiene activities was a little bit of a chore. We had to heat up water and carry a bucket over to the brook in another area. Mixing the hot water with the cool spring water in a raised canister, we could take a passable shower. Baths directly in the spring were a bit nippy. We agreed to keep just one man on watch, Ben making us all swear not to fall asleep. After all, just one guy near the cave entrance was enough to keep an eye out for critters sneaking up on us. We decided on four-hour watches as catching up on sleep was no problem in winter.

We had a few problems. Certain atmospheric conditions, we figured low-pressure areas, messed with cave's ability to draft out the smoke from the fire. We had to keep an eye on that. Our power generating system also broke down a few times. Someone had to climb the rocky hill to fix it. Since Paul was not around, it usually turned out to be me. When the weather was bad, Corky Wall scaled it with me.

But life was good. We had long talks by the fire, not always about philosophy. We still had handheld computers we could work on. We found that by going out on top of the smoother hill next to ours, we could get cell phone contact with civilization. The guys could call their girlfriends and we could also download needed web content to work on offline back in the cave.

While we had to ration our vegetables and fruits, meat was certainly not a problem with plenty of elk and deer around. After the ground froze, hunting was not that difficult. But one day Pine got to thinking about those buffalo and raised the possibility of a hunting excursion out on the endless meadows west of us.

Pine, Matt, Empire, Clyde and I set out on the great hunt. We could even see a small bison herd from the hilltop, probably about a two-hour walk from us. Walking out on the prairie was a most wonderful experience. Not an automobile could be heard, not one man-made building seen, and no other people to put up with. Every now and then, we could see a plane lifting off from Thompson but it was too far away to be heard. Our heavy clothing proved useful in the crisp, cold air. The snow was smooth and without tire tracks of any kind.

Judging our distance from the small bedded-down herd, we stopped on the other side of a slight rolling hill with the animals on the other side.

"How many do we want?" Murdock asked, removing a laser rifle strapped to his back.

Pine replied, "Only one, that's all we can carry."

Empire then slowly scaled the tiny hill, stopping at the top and laying down. He aimed the rifle. These special hunting rifles didn't make any sound when firing so we couldn't tell when he did. A red laser light beam could be seen if conditions were right, but he had the barrel pointed down the other side and we couldn't see it. Finally, he lifted his head. "I think I got one."

Pine yelled up at him, "Okay, scare the others, and make them take off."

Empire jumped up and down, yelling. "Oh, oh," he said.

"What?" Pine yelled.

Empire turned to look down at us, "They're running this way!"

"Good golly!" Pine yelled, "Come on, guys."

We ran to the top of the rise to see about eight of the big creatures galloping toward us. But with all of us yelling and screaming, they turned and headed north. One animal lay in the snow beyond them. We waited a few minutes until the rest were out of sight, and then approached our fallen bison.

There was a small grove of trees close by, so we dragged some wood over and set up a small camp. Clyde made us some hot tea and, while Matt and Murdock did the butchering, we sat and talked.

"Those things are huge," Clyde said to Pine.

"Yea, the scientists think they're even bigger than the ones in the twenty-first century, before the ice age."

"How did they survive it all? I was under the impression that everything in the northwestern states froze to death."

"Somehow some of them moved south," Pine explained, "and lived in small packs in the high grassy meadows next to the Rocky Mountains. Of course, after it warmed up, they moved back north and prospered. After they reach adulthood, they have no natural enemies. Air Force pilots, flying low enough, reported seeing herds of them, but I never had any idea they were this far east."

Clyde stood up, rifle lying across his shoulder, "I love it out here. I'm not going back."

The animal was much more than we needed. We put the best meat in these animal skin sacks and slung them over our shoulders. All of us carried some. Pine said that he usually liked to bury anything he couldn't harvest but our shovel only scratched the frozen ground. So we piled snow on the carcass and left it. "Well," Pine said, "the wolves will thank us."

"I think they came to thank us in person," I said, everyone turning to see a small pack of wolves, sitting patiently on the next rise past the trees. I looked through my field glasses at them, "Boy, they sure look like dogs."

"They are," Pine spoke, "those are feral dogs. Their ancestors are house pets left by people in the run south a thousand years ago. Look at their patience, the way they are waiting until we leave the area. All of the human isn't out of them yet, pure wolves are nasty looking and may have tried to run us off. Good eye, Kelley."

As we lugged the heavy sacks back to the cave, Clyde and Empire walked out in the lead.

"I think we should turn around, Murdock, and head west, then keep going," Clyde joked.

"I agree," Empire added, "I think we should go live in North Dakota."

"Yea, but we'd better pack an extra pair of underwear for that trip. It could take us months to walk there."

"Yea and we should bring Kelley with us, in case we run into any imaginary bears!" They both laughed.

Pine put his hand on my shoulder, "Kelley, nobody is ever gonna believe that story."

That evening, Pine spoke to us again, in the cavern down by the brook. This time only Ben and I attended.

"I want to continue tonight by finishing up on some general things and then moving on to our particular situation," he began. "It has to do with how we see things and how what we know depends a lot on how we were brought up, our culture. I will start with some general conceptions. We all know what prejudice and stereotyping are, right? And I think we can all agree that these are bad things?" We nodded. "But keep in mind what we talked about last time, how we often act in ways that increase our chances of survival. Let's look at those dogs we saw this afternoon. I knew those were dogs and not wolves, but I've seen how pure wolves look and act. I was stereotyping, was I not? Was this a bad thing? I think not in this case. Now look at Kelley and the bear again."

"So," Ben smarted off, "this is a 'hypothetical' situation?"

I snapped at him in good humor, "Ben, you dolt!"

Pine continued, "Kelley had never met this bear before. He didn't know her name. But Kelley 'pre-judged' her intentions, did he not? Of course with other humans, these threats no longer exist, so our negative prejudices are no long valid. But is it not easier now to think about how these now negative traits of humans began?

"All three of us had some sort of similar origin. Ben's folks left him on somebody's doorstep. Kelley's folks, for some unknown reason, had taken their four-year-old out on the prairie in winter. My parents died from natural causes so my case is a little different, but like it or not we were all left out there. Can you just imagine how this has affected you and continues to affect how you learn things? In your more recent years, did either of you experience anything in your lives that you didn't understand or had just come to realize?"

Ben raised his hand, "I have. Last Thanksgiving, Angie and I wanted to see this new movie. I thought getting to the afternoon show would be less crowded and even cheaper. So I said let's go to the one o'clock show. But she said that's when her family ate Thanksgiving dinner and since we were eating with them, we could go to the evening show. So, I told her let's eat at six, then we can make the afternoon movie. She had a fit. She said but that's when we eat! I still didn't get it. There had never been any particular time to eat Thanksgiving dinner at the orphanage. You got turkey at noon as well as at six. What's the big deal? I never knew the custom. It was the same with Christmas and birthdays, some of us don't even know when our darn birthdays are!"

"Lisa's dad didn't want me to park Milt's farm truck out in front of his house," I went next. "Lisa told me the neighbors would 'look down on that.' I couldn't believe that. It was the only form of transportation I ever had. Were people in his neighborhood actually looking out their windows and saying, 'Gee, look at that dirty truck, I sure don't think as highly of that guy as I once did.' Who the heck does that? But that brings up another problem, Tom, we have to learn all their stuff but don't they have to learn ours as well? You know my school record. I'm not resistant to learning anything. Our parents are dead; does that make us more of a threat?"

"Can't you see, Kelley," Tom went on, "that yes it does! Can't you see what I'm trying to say here? You are a threat. You're a threat to Colonel Dubois and what he wants for his daughter. You're a threat to Lisa's dad for the same reason. You're unnatural, you had no structure as a kid, and you're poor. Orphan kids, on average, don't do that well in school. They all become farmhands or work on fishing boats on Lake Michigan. Even Bus Quint and Matt Fuller see you as a threat. They don't even have your particular misfortune and they're more stupid than you are! They have to beat you up and keep you down because they're threatened by you. They had to do what you did to the bear because they are afraid you are going to kill them, make them even worse than their miserable selves are now. "

Tom was even sweating now. I had never seen him this worked up. "But it's not their problem, Dan, and that is the most troubling part of this. It's your problem. You have to deal with it. Bus and Fuller are never gonna get any less stupid. Lisa's dad isn't going to change his mind about you parking in front of his house. People, wolves, and bears attack us or are unkind to us for one reason only. We are a threat. You have to work around this, you, Ben, and all three of us. We need to *think* and we have to *excel*!"

Frank Miller woke me at four that morning for my watch. I knew right away that I shouldn't have gone on that hunt yesterday; my back was killing me from hauling that meat. Miller disappeared under his blanket without a word. I got up to find a half-cup of very old coffee next to the fire. I poured it anyway, and then took my seat next to the cave entrance. I pulled aside the skin to see it was snowing and blowing very hard. It kind of reminded me of that dream when I looked out the window of that helicopter taking me to Thompson.

I sat thinking about Tom's lecture last night. I could see his point. When Marie told me that she wanted to be with only me on that picnic, I doubted her. I compared it to Sharon saying how she liked the way I looked in my running shorts. Sharon was full of crap and I guess I thought all girls were. I had to resolve Sharon somehow, or that girl was going to haunt me for years. Thinking of Pine's talk, I tried to figure out what I may have missed, what part of culture kept me from missing some sort of clue to her disrespect for our relationship. It couldn't have been the old Betsy Barney prejudice; Sharon had denied any such feelings. If Sharon was shallow, how could she put on such an act? If she wasn't shallow, how could she switch off the old love light so fast? If that were the case, how could she make me feel so good?

I sat on that rock the rest of the night thinking about these things.

CHAPTER NINE

By the time the others began to wake up, a full-blown blizzard was raging outside. Being warm and comfortable, we decided to do nothing constructive that day and declared it "birth day." Since some of our birthdays were in doubt, and those who did know when they were born had never practiced celebrations, we were pretty flexible as to when we had a party. Usually, it was on a day when we just felt like it.

I remembered a day back in Delk Hall. I was watching a morning satellite talk show originating from Miami Beach and in the background a lady had a sign that read "Today is my Birthday." She had not even written her name on it, just that fact. I remember feeling confused. I didn't understand her motivation.

We ate Matt's new invention of homemade wheat cereal for breakfast that morning, and it turned out to taste pretty good. A couple of summer Holy Cross members had hiked down the day before with some milk. Later that day we grilled up our big buffalo steaks and had them with baked potatoes and jarred pears. We had so much smoke in the cave that Holy Cross Corky went down to one of the other entrances and opened the doors. He stood watch down there until the smoke blew out through the cave. We spent the rest of the day playing cards or mock fighting with our staffs.

Matt was really good at staff fighting. He showed us how to fend off a direct blow, not by taking the full force of it, but by redirecting it and allowing it to glance off.

I think our best birthday present was sitting around the ham radio set in the evening as Milt Frazer made a rare call. The United States and Mexico announced they had signed a treaty ending the war. It was more like they had called off the war since it had actually never started. Of more importance to us, it was also announced that all new military drafts were suspended until they decided what to do with the buildup of troops they already had. This probably didn't get us out of the service forever, but gave us a little breathing space to get things worked out with the school. All the Eagles knew that we were going to have to decide soon what we were going to do. Some members didn't want to return, while some wanted to finish school. It was beginning to look like this might split up our group.

I was the only one to attend Pine's next lecture several days later. Since it was just the two of us, he grabbed one of the rifles and we went up on the smoother hill. Snow still covered the ground, but a bright afternoon sun warmed us.

"Spring is slowly getting here, Dan," he spoke.

"Yes it is," I responded, "Our potatoes are almost gone and some are even going bad now. I'm a little tired of the cave as well. It will be nice to get outside more."

"Do you like this life?" he asked.

"I do. I do love it, but I also need a trade. I've been thinking of getting an apprenticeship and getting that done. I need to be able to do something. I sort of want a family someday."

"I was hoping, since school has been so easy for you, that you would want to continue with that."

"Oh, I don't think I'll ever be totally out of school. But I can do that during nights and weekends while I work in the day. I like psychology a lot, and philosophy, but I still like electricity. It's a 'hands' thing; it's like living out here. I feel so productive out here, like the things I do have a direct effect on my life, like you said in your book."

"Sounds reasonable. Speaking of psychology, today I want to look at threats a little more closely. I hate to keep using the bear example, but you perceived something when you saw those cubs come stumbling upon you. You knew that momma was going to be close. Another example is the war with Mexico. Their troop buildup on the border was only a threat, but we couldn't take a chance on calling their bluff. Attacks are usually preceded by such a move.

"And this brings us back to perceiving threats, which I mentioned last time. Now, did the Mustangs ever approach all you guys face to face, tell you they were going to beat you up, and then do so?"

"No," I replied. "But we assumed it. They roughed up Frank, and Clyde, and, I think, killed Gov Viche. We heard second hand of their intentions. We filled in the lines, with what we knew we had every reason to believe they would, so we took it to them."

"And I'm sure they would have as well. I do not doubt your perception. Now, let's talk about this in relation to fighting evil. Do you think the Mustangs were evil, and that they wanted to wipe out all orphans in the world?"

"No. Individually, I think they were just bad. They had character flaws. The only way they could feel like they had integrity was to put on this tough guy act and pick on weaker kids. We were just easy targets. But we tapped them on the shoulder and reminded them that we weren't going to allow that. I think they were actually stunned, at that first fight in seventh grade. I was sure they weren't expecting us to show up. Ben knew they wanted to 'jaw;' that's why he told us to just charge them. I know a lot of people have criticized us for fighting them, Holy Cross included, but isn't it a funny thing how the attacks stopped?"

"Gosh you are an easy student to work with; you make this so easy for me. Well, you are right in your analysis. Now let's talk about a related subject. Have you ever been socially embarrassed or had your pride hurt?"

"Well sure, who hasn't?"

"In any event, it's like you talking to Rose Russo for half an hour on some serious subject and then she suddenly tells you your fly is open. You lose pride; you become embarrassed. It's not because you have a mortal fear of exposing yourself, but that you lose credibility, seriousness. Now how does this relate to street fighting?"

I was beginning to take a little offense with this lesson. "We had to fight them to save our pride. Yes, I know. So we've been told."

"And don't you think they had to fight you for the same reason? Don't you think they would have eventually won? They were older, bigger than you guys. There was always ambush."

"What are you trying to say?"

"That it's time now for other tactics."

"I know. Holy Cross told us, not in so many words, that it was dumb to face them head on. We were using what we knew at the time, which is all we had in our arsenal. We started a fist fight because that's all we knew."

"But it's important to think about what you were fighting against, what both of you were fighting."

"A perceived threat?"

"Yes, but a threat to your existence. You were both scared about one another because civilization was scared of both the Eagles and the Mustangs, and they passed this on to all of you. Orphans and street rowdies don't do well, or so they say, and we need farmhands and janitors to keep the town going. And you guys were showing spirit, you organized, and those are dangerous things here. 'Well, we can't have the farmhands thinking, can we? They won't be happy doing that job.' Their biggest mistake was not putting you in the orphanage, but giving you blue library passes. They should have sent you to the Irish Fort in fourth grade and left you there.

"And now we all sit around in these little pockets of humanity, all over the world, using all our technology and even the arts and religion, to do what? Recreate the past. They broadcast Old World movies on the satellite, and we listen to digitally re-mastered Old World music because that's the last time people had passionate lyrics or even played actual musical instruments. Look at Rose Russo's cute little sister; she's a majorette in a school marching band made up of six people carrying electronic synthesizers. The majorettes outnumber the band! And can you name one New World philosopher, present company included, who's worth a crap?

"Poor President Arthur, genius as she was, spent all her energy trying to recreate the Old World in an age when the rules no longer applied. We long for the return to the good old days, but we're never going to get there because it was the way we were living which led to their destruction. The Mustangs, the Eagles, and the New World are all threats."

For the next few days, the "sermon on the mount" didn't sit too well with me. I was getting weary with philosophy. Everyone was giving us some righteous moral position and we told them our motivation. We got in a fight with some bullies; deal with it. Pine had a lot of good points, but I had deeper questions.

A few days later, Angie came down for a visit. The whole group liked this girl; she had us in stitches most of the time. One day Ben Holden had an important call with Hightower so he ascended the hill next to the cave to assure a good signal for his call. We walked out of the cave to see little Angie standing on a rock with a blanket draped over her head for some unknown reason. Bo Schlitz approached her and they broke out into their best Shakespearean characters.

Bo started, "Oh maiden, we come searching for the leader, Benjamin, have you naught seen him?"

"Alas, great Benjamin is not here," Angie came back, "for he is high yonder, on the mount, seeking guidance."

"From whom does he seek counsel?"

"The great priestess, Hightower, is giving him divine guidance."

"More divine than thou? Is not the fair maiden his betrothed?"

"Be-what?" she laughed

"Are you not to marry the great Ben? Is he not at the core of your heart?"

"He is at the core of my nose at present. I shall not marry before he showereth, because Ben stinketh. In fact, all great men of this cave stinketh. That's what I thinketh."

Angie left us laughing, as usual. And that night, there was a line for the shower.

The next day, after Angie had left, Ben called a meeting of just the Eagles. We met on the mount. Al Myers made arrangements to stay over a few days to attend.

"Hightower is meeting with the negotiator next week," Ben started off. "She's still unsure how long this will take. The negotiator will give his formal opinion to the judge hearing the case. The judge will then rule in the school's favor, rule in our favor, or hold a hearing in the matter, then make a ruling. A hearing means more testimony, more witnesses, and more time. It could take nine months to a year, worst-case scenario, before this is resolved. We could all be in the army by then. She said if it goes against us, she can always file in federal court, so more time still.

She said her confidence is high, but she's not even a lawyer yet so how does she know?"

"We can hide in the woods from the school," Corky Wall added, "but I hope you guys know that they'll send the army after us if we're drafted."

I added, "Our street fighting days are over according to Hightower, Pine, and just about everyone. So fighting our way back into society is not an option."

"I'm not going back," Clyde said, "win or lose. Oh, I'll probably finish school if we're reinstated, but my days on the streets of Centura are over. The place has kicked my butt ever since I was six years old, my dad before that. Cork, Empire and I have been talkin' about trying to make a run west, maybe out to the Mississippi River, and try and make a go at this wilderness thing."

"Somebody breaks an ankle out there, Clyde, and you're dead men," Frank Davis brought us back to reality.

"I know, Frank."

Ben asked, "Do we need to take a vote on what we're going to do?"

"I would like to hold off on that," Frank Davis answered, "and I will explain. First of all, I'm sure our immediate plans depend on this suspension decision. There's no real reason to decide right now; it might not even be smart to do so. Quite honestly, I don't want to see this family break up. I want to ask you guys for time to come up with a plan that may benefit all of us while still keeping us together. I'm meeting, albeit only via email right now, with two law student nerds and one of the most trusted law professors, to devise something. This is the same group helping Hightower with the school case. Let's let this thing play out, get our decision, then I need you guys to listen to my plan. I have something in mind that may meet all our needs."

Bo Schlitz added his touch of humor we sorely needed, "Davis is going to be a lawyer for sure; he actually used the word 'albeit' in a sentence!"

We all agreed. Then we all laughed and joked. Humor played a major role in the Eagle psyche. There were times in our lives when we had little else.

Tom Pine noticed right away that I was growing tired of the philosophy lessons. He asked me what subject I wanted to discuss next. I said I wanted to discuss issues with my parents and Sharon Dubois.

His first reaction was, "You know, Dan, when philosophers are drawn to the art to get personal answers, philosophy turns to psychoanalysis. But maybe it's good to talk about relationships at this time since we can relate it to human relationships in general."

"I'm sorry," I said. "I can tell you are painting the big picture with your lessons, but I got a couple of small pictures in front of me and I can't see around them. It's like your man and his bull story. I can't come up and see what you want me to see because my horns are too big to fit through the door."

Then he threw me a curve. He asked me to make a list of everything I didn't know about my parents and Sharon Dubois and bring it to the next meeting.

If spring had a choice on when it was to arrive, it couldn't have picked a better time that year. It hit with a vengeance as well with unusually warm days and mild nights. We were running around the forest like wild animals in no time. Some intense spring thunderstorms kept us near the caves at night. The Cross even began to shore up their summer camp.

One Saturday afternoon, Matt and Paul took us for a hike down south a ways. Not more than a hundred yards from the spot we camped that night Milt brought Hightower and the girls down for that visit, just on the south side of the Ice River, was a small horseshoe-shaped ridge. In between the twin ridges lay an area of intense forest not more than a couple of acres. The rock at the closed end of the horseshoe had a fair-sized cave containing a water source near the far eastern wall. The only problem we noticed was that it was not vented. Paul was of the feeling that we could use this area as both a summer and winter camp. He suggested, and had plans already drawn up, to put up a three-sided log structure and attach it to the face of the ridge where the cave opening was. This would allow us to build heat and cooking chimneys while still having the insulation and water source the cave provided. The location would also put us closer to the schools and next to Milt Frazer's land

There was no need for a formal vote on the matter since it seemed to meet all our needs and would remain a viable alternative no matter how our case turned out. We all agreed to start on the next Monday and while we were walking back, I caught a suspicious twinkle in Frank Davis' eyes. I was thinking my old best friend was up to something.

On Sunday, we threw our fears to the wind and had a large noon meal at Milt Frazer's. He picked us up right across from the Ice River and took us up to the farmhand chow hall where Milt and his wife gave us a civilized meal for a change. We made sure to hit the showers before we sat down to eat. After telling Milt of our plans, he just quietly spoke, "Okay, you guys are gonna need some stuff."

That next day, Milt brought down a caravan of vehicles carrying bricks for chimneys, tar paper, a small front-end loader, two farmhands and three members of The Range. With all of us, and some of the Holy Cross, we had an old fashion group barn-raising. Paul, who we found out, was a civil engineering student, set up the work teams and walked around like he was General Patton.

Milt stayed that first day. The old farmer in him came out a few times. Out of earshot from the others, he whispered to me his feelings about our Range workers, "Those guys are kinda weird, aren't they?"

We clear-cut a trail into the worksite. At first we started cutting trees with axes. When we figured that would take too long, Milt sent a farm worker back home for some chain saws. We thinned what logs we could use from the interior of the horseshoe, but soon had to go out into the woods for decent sized timber. We fashioned a stone foundation from rocks lying around, laid two chimneys, and then started placing logs. We build it the old fashioned way, cutting notches where the logs came together. Sensing another time-wasting venture in cutting planks for the roof, Milt made a run to the lumberyard for finished ones. We had to dig and build an outhouse until we could come up with a better idea.

By the end of the workday Friday, we stood in front of our new finished home. It was crude, and certainly not up to any construction code, but it was the new Eagles' nest. We moved in the next day. Building an outdoor cooking area in front of the log section, we grilled steaks and had a party. It was a total treat, shelter enough for any kind of weather yet out in the forest with birds and rabbits milling about. I think we sat in front of the campfire that whole night, telling stories and planning our return.

Pine had moved down to the Holy Cross summer camp. Spending some days and nights in his apartment in town with new wife Diane, he visited us often. One evening we met for our next discussion.

"I'm afraid I didn't do very well on my lists, Mentor," I told Pine. "Well, I didn't do well on one of them. With all the work we've been doing and my almost complete lack of knowledge about my parents, I'm afraid it would be easier to tell you what I do know about them. I know I had a mom and a dad. I know, for some reason only known to God, we were out in the central plains of Illinois Territory. We were in some type of vehicle. For yet another unknown reason, they left me and I wandered out in a snowstorm and got lost. My next memory is waking up in a helicopter bound for Centura. It took a few years before I could appreciate the fact they were dead and their bodies never found. That's the sum total of my weird childhood."

"I don't know how we can go any further with this subject, Dan," Pine lamented. "Fate's a cruel mistress at times. Until we get some additional information we can only make guesses. What about Sharon's list?"

"I got a lot, a lot more than I ever dreamed of. She was a beautiful, loving girl who knew how to take care of her boyfriend. She was an inspiration to me, the center of my universe."

"Get back to the list now."

"Wow, I got a lot here. I don't know where she was born. I don't know when her birthday is, or where she lived before here. But I know it was a warm place because this is the first place she played in snow. I know little about her parents. I don't know her favorite color, what religion she is, who her favorite movie actor is, what's her favorite food, her favorite book or author, or where she stands politically.

"I never saw her cry, not once. She was always happy, smiling; she never told me why. I guess I was just happy she was."

"What do all of these things have in common?"

"Well ..." I paused, thinking, "They're things that didn't matter to me."

"From what you tell me, she said and did all the right things. Do you think she knew she was doing that?"

"I don't know."

"What were her hobbies?"

"Fixing things up, decorating, interior design. She was in the interior design club."

"She liked the way things looked?"

"Yes, or liked to put them in a state where they looked good to her."

"Did she ever say what she liked about you?"

That one threw me; I had to think a long time on that one. Tom Pine was leading up to something, but I wasn't sure what. "I don't know, I had a good sense of humor, she said she liked the way I looked. She thought the Eagles were boldly facing adversity, not in so many words, but I think you understand. I guess that's it. What's the big deal? Can't she just like me?"

Pine didn't answer my question, "What did she call you?"

"Danny. She always called me Danny, not sure why."

"When did she fall out of love with you?"

"My first clue was when she put the ring in my pocket at her door at the end of our last date. That's what I can't figure out. That's why I doubt she was ever really in love with me. She can't turn it on and off that fast; no one can. Did I say something wrong during the evening?"

"It might possibly be something she can turn on and off real fast, but I doubt it. And I think she did love you at one time. But even if you said something stupid that night, she would have acted mad or at least went home and thought about it. While you guys didn't go together an extremely long time, it was intense, and certainly something neither of you would make a snap decision to end. So next time, we need to go over everything that went on that last night, what you did, what you both said, and so on. Try and remember exactly how she said things. Okay?"

Even though many of us were now eighteen and the truants had no right to formally return us to school or detention, we were still rather nervous about going into town. So we sent Milt in to pick up our solar/wind power generator from the utility company. Although they were making them much smaller now, we still needed a flatbed truck to haul it down. It was expensive. It and all the materials Milt bought for us were draining our club banking account. Plus we had some expenses we weren't expecting.

We had some problem with the roof leaking; finally figuring out it was where the wooden roof of the log structure met the stone above the cave opening. Al Myers "appropriated" some special sealant from the Chemistry Department, and with a little flashing we stopped the problem. Then we found when running both fireplaces on cold nights, the chimney draw was messed up, smoke got into the cave and just stayed there. Paul and some guys ran some hot air duct tubes down the center of the cave, installing a blower, which allowed us to vent it out the ceiling of the log structure. So we had that expense as well. Several of the guys made a small clearing on top of the south ridge of the horseshoe while Paul and I set up the generator.

Our friends supplied us with a lot of odds and ends from yard sales and excess equipment giveaways at the base. We slept in the log structure on cold nights, on beds of canvass bags stuffed with straw. With so much wood around, we also had a fire going outside most of the time, cooking inside only in the foulest weather. The arrangements worked out well as far as keeping us together.

One weekend in early April, we got the call. The verdict was in. Tom and Diane were bringing Ms. Hightower down on Saturday morning to present it to us. No one would give us the slightest hint about what it was, evidence of Hightower's love of the dramatic. We sat out by the fire on Friday night, none of us uttering one word.

Saturday morning found us all out sitting around the fire and sipping coffee. Tom, Diane, and Hightower came walking in, their faces uncharacteristically blank. Of course, Ms. Hightower couldn't just come out and announce the verdict; she had to go over the whole process, step-by-step. Her love of keeping us anxious and on the edge of our seats was a hidden cost of *pro bono publico*.

Hightower looked like the average farmer's daughter in her jeans and tee shirt, up until she opened her mouth. "Well, some good news, but not out of the woods yet. First of all, for the seven of you who did not testify, the charges were dropped."

A sigh of relief came over those seven, but it was no consolation for Ben, Frank and I.

"The judge goofed on that one," she went on, "In fact, he goofed a lot. Not allowing you guys on the stand and his statement to 'put an end to this' did him in."

Frank questioned, "But he asked you if any of the seven had anything different to say, and you said no."

"Wrong, Frank. He did ask me that, but I said 'not to my knowledge.' Just because I represented you didn't mean I knew how you were going to testify. Any one of you could have said you weren't there and, if Bus couldn't specifically identify you as being there, you would have gotten off. It wouldn't have worked for all of you, but since they couldn't say exactly who was going to say what, they had to let you all off. But things get better.

"The penalty was too severe. I presented all the nuisance fighting charges ruled on in the last five years and even the worst offender got a week in detention. He could have justified Holden's month sentence because he had a previous charge, but he didn't mention it in his ruling. Of course we never did get to that point.

"His next goof was ordering you back to the orphanage. He had no right to do that, not at this point."

"We were work-study students, receiving federal money. Why couldn't he do that?" Frank asked.

"True. And you were on an orphanage approved off-site work-study agreement, one that provided room and board. But that's not the point. Who does the orphanage belong to?"

"The town!" Frank exclaimed.

"Right, if the police had filed charges against you, a district judge could have ordered you back there. But as usual, the police just broke up the fight. They never arrested you. The school had no authority to tell the orphanage what to do.

"And finally, his biggest goof was ordering you guys suspended if you didn't report to detention. He was 'pre-supposing' you wouldn't show. He couldn't do that. He could order you to detention, but he could go no further than that. If you had not shown up, the school would have had to form a disciplinary board to hear that charge. He was finding you guilty, and announcing a sentence, for a crime that had not taken place yet. The suspension was illegal.

"So, I went back and forth with this negotiator. He kept telling me I still couldn't prevail getting the original thirty-day detention for Holden, Davis, and Kelley thrown out. So then I had to throw my weight around a bit. I reminded him that the length of that detention was excessive. And I said that I would file this puppy in federal court and tie up the school for years. I told him the people you guys send up to Thompson to fight this thing will have to buy a house here. It must have gotten to him; a formal decision came back, all charges dropped. You guys are to be retroactively reinstated in school, receive appropriate life-learning credits earned in you absence, and given over a year's work-study money, four hours a day."

We were stunned. We just sat there, still waiting for the attorney to end her speech, only slowly realizing that she already had.

Diane Win added, "Dan, I spoke to the graduate committee last night. Next week you will be issued an associate's degree, in electrical science."

We were still speechless until Frank asked, "So, what's the bad news."

"Bad, but not too bad. Popover wants to hold a hearing to go over this whole thing. I want to make it clear that she cannot reverse the decision of the Department of Education. But she can hold an open town meeting to discuss your status with the town. And we'll all be there, right in her face!" Hightower got up and started dancing around, saying "I'm so good!"

Ben and Angie slowly stood up, Angie hugging Ben. Then they went into the log house. Soon, Frank did the same, then all the original Eagles. We left Hightower, Ben, and Diane sitting and talking about the case.

As I walked into the great room, all began to move toward Ben, now seated on the dining table with his legs swinging in the air. He had his face in his hands. He was crying.

Angie kissed him, and then started for the door. She looked up at me as she passed.

"This is a meeting for Eagles only."

I said, "But you're just as much a member as the rest of us."

She stopped and kissed me on the cheek, "No, this is for the original ten." She walked out the door.

We formed a circle around Ben. He lamented, "I thought I had let you all down. I thought I ruined your lives with this club thing. I was afraid I'd doomed you all to hell."

"We've already been there, Ben," Clyde responded. "We've been to hell and back. We would have gone there again with you."

"We voted for you, nut job," Corky added.

"We were looking for some psychotic leadership, and we found it in you," Frank Miller said.

"You did the right thing, Ben," I said, "Some of us would be dead right now if we didn't do this. And you know it."

Empire added, "We fight, Ben; pure and simple. Somebody takes a swing at us, we swing back."

"You were good to us, Ben," Corky said, "Empire and me didn't do very good in school and stuff. You treated us as equals. You helped us. I just got a darn high school diploma for crying out loud."

We just stood there for a while, joking and punching Ben on the shoulders. Finally, Frank Davis said, "Okay, Mr. President, call a meeting for tomorrow. We got an example to live up to now. We did it. Let's show them they can be proud of the dirty orphans. Let's get to work on our future."

Angie took Ben and Frank Davis up to her house for dinner that Saturday night. They didn't come back so we assumed they stayed the night. The rest of us camped out in front of the fire. Even Hightower brought her sleeping bag. Jim Donovan and Rose slept in the log house. We stayed up until one in the morning, listening to Hightower talk about her experiences.

The next day, we had a day-long meeting with just the ten of us and Hightower, going over our plans for this town hall meeting Popover was going to conduct. This one seemed a little odd to Ms. Hightower. She told us it was not a hearing in any way except the Town Council President had authority to question people under oath and, with a majority vote by the entire council, also had authority to make recommendations to people with authority, the police, the utility company, and so on. She said we needed to have an all-encompassing strategy to include what we were going to do for jobs, or to remain in school, or where we would be living.

Then Frank Davis revealed his plan. It was to be top secret, so secret they didn't allow me to take any journal notes, put it in my computer, or write it down later. I was given a major assignment that I had to work on, and that was all I was to be concerned about.

CHAPTER 10

Ron's Electrical accepted me for my apprenticeship. Ron was the guy who I helped back in Delk Hall. He was a master electrician with all that was needed to certify me for a journeyman's license. Most importantly, he worked mainly on the south side for Milt, the orphanage, and some of the private residences. He had no other employees so I soon became more like a partner to him. He would often let me work on jobs alone, only coming by afterwards to sign off on my work. I worked most weekdays and took satellite classes in the evening. These consisted of a couple of general studies courses that could be applied to a bachelor's degree later on.

To the question of who really ran the Eagles, my answer was of course, Angie did. One night she started throwing a fit about the "facilities" we had for our frontier village. "I know you baboons don't mind squatting on some rock somewhere, but Rose, Libby, and I are getting a little tired of using that stinky two holes in the ground you guys call an outhouse! Plus it's cold on the rear. I'm sorry, but we're civilized. We don't take to zoo life like you animals. You also don't wash your clothes enough. Now that you're getting jobs and going back to school, shave and shower, monkey men!" We got her hint.

Paul brought a friend out with a rig to drill a well for water. We built an addition on to the log structure and installed showers, several toilets, and washing machines. Burying a pipe that ran out the west end of the horseshoe ridge, we connected to a septic system far away from, and well below, our water source in the cave. We had enough power to run the water pump, water heater, and the washing machines, but would have to wait to use the dryers until we got another power source. We heated the addition with a wood stove.

After paying my dues to the club, I used some of my money to buy a truck. I talked Milt out of one of his fairly new vehicles which he sold to me for a song. I used part of the remainder of the money to start on my electrical tool collection.

One day I took Ben and Murdock in my truck to see the leader of The Range. "Wheeze" was his name, and a more colorful character could not be found. We took Murdock because the neighborhood was kind of dicey. We found Wheeze, so named because he had severe asthma as a kid, with his head stuck under the hood of an old truck. Not having a shirt on, whatever skin wasn't covered with grease was completely covered in tattoos.

He greeted Holden, "Hey Bennie. Good to see you again. How's the little wife?"

"Angie's fine, Wheeze," Ben responded.

"She still slapping the heck out of you?"

"She's cut down, only doing it once a week or so."

"That's one classy broad you got there, Ben. I always liked that little powder keg."

"I'll pass along the compliment, Wheeze. How's your lovely wife doing?"

"Mean as heck. She hit me with a board last weekend. Man, did that ever hurt."

Unfortunately, he was probably telling the truth. Ben went on, "Sorry to hear that."

"No big deal." Wheeze stood up and stuffed a wad of chewing tobacco in his mouth. He could have been Mrs. Popover's poster child for her campaign against the south side. "She's mad at me right now. Says I don't take her out enough. We don't get into some of the finer establishments ya know." He looked at Empire, "Murdock, how goes it?" Then he looked at me, "Kelley, heck, I haven't seen you since that Mustang beat the crap out of you. Gosh, those were the days, huh?"

I responded, "Yep, I sure miss those good old days. I like your sword."

We looked down to see this medieval knight's sword leaning up against the truck. It must have weighted a ton.

"Ya like that? Bet I could cut off a few heads with that, huh? My wife got it for me for Christmas. What can I do for you guys?"

Ben explained, "We've been out of touch for a while. We're looking for Bus Quint and Matt Fuller. Any idea where they hang out?"

"What do you want with those two clowns?"

"We have a need to know their whereabouts."

"There's probably no need to keep tabs on them; they're mainly out of action. Most of the old Mustangs are either in jail or left town. Fuller sort of drifted north. He mainly hangs out with the jocks now. He's a small timer, a thug. He used to push eighty-year-old men around for their retirement checks and beat up little grade school kids. But, I guess you guys know about that. Heard he knocked up some girl so he's ducking her. You know that little burger place, where they used to have those dances, up by the schools?" I knew the place well, that's where I took Sharon on our first and last dates. "He's usually up there most evenings. Fuller's not a threat, he's too stupid."

"And Quint?"

"I'd leave him alone. He's dangerous. He drinks too much. He'd put a knife in your belly."

"I appreciate the information."

"No problem," Wheeze said. "I tell ya, Holden, you're handling this all wrong. The Range could whack those two guys for you in a heartbeat. I don't think any of my gang has committed a homicide yet, but we're in touch with people who have. No questions asked. We can do it cheap, fifty bucks a head and they could find Fuller and Quint floating face down in the lake."

"I appreciate the offer, Wheeze, but we'll handle it. Thanks again."

Wheeze returned under the hood, "Okay, call me if you change your mind."

After getting back into my truck, we all looked at each other and laughed. Empire asked, "Did his wife really hit him with a board?"

Ben smiled, "I've met his wife. And yes, she certainly is capable."

Ah, The Range, you had to appreciate the simplicity of their problem solving strategy.

Early one day, I called Angie to see if she had anything I could give as a gift for a baby. After she got done yelling at me for the short notice and the early call, she told me to stop by her house and her mom would give it to me. After stopping by Angie's and retrieving the buffalo style baby booties, I drove up to the YWCA apartment building for unwed mothers. I waited in the lobby while they called Monica. When she came down the stairs, I recognized her immediately. Her dark hair was shorter now and she had put on a few pounds, but that same sweet smile was on her face. When she saw me, the smile changed to a look of astonishment, almost like she was expecting someone else to be there.

"Danny Kelley?" she asked.

"Hi Monica."

"What are you doing here?"

"I was hoping to talk to you for a minute."

"I have to get to class."

"You have forty minutes. Here, I brought you something."

She seemed to grow a little less paranoid, sat down beside me, and opened her present. "Oh, how nice, boy booties for a baby girl."

"Oh, sorry," I said, "I didn't know what it was."

She smiled, "No problem. She won't know the difference. Thanks, Danny. I'll get them washed and I'm sure she'll enjoy them."

"Can I see her?"

Monica took me to the nursery and we looked through the glass at her sleeping baby girl. Fortunately, the Fuller family resemblance was not apparent.

Monica suggested we take a walk outside. We walked out toward the east, through the jagged rocks on the barren ground, looking out over Lake Michigan. Often, when I was in the little kids' orphanage, I used to look out at all that water, wondering what was on the other side.

"What did you want to talk about?" her paranoid demeanor had returned.

"I'm afraid it's not too pleasant. You know, when I checked into Delk and you processed me in, you acted all sweet and nice. But suddenly, while looking at my file, you suddenly got all weird and started talking in short, snappy sentences. What was that all about?"

"I don't remember that."

"Just before you assigned me to the north wing."

"Oh, that," she replied. "You had a blue sticker on your health record. I thought you knew that."

"No, I didn't. What does that mean?"

"They did that in the fifties and early sixties; they don't do it anymore. It was for kids who were thought to be exposed to that Blue Solution, that stuff they used that caused the plague. It was once thought you guys had some genetic disorder, something with your immune system. I'm not sure how they knew who had been exposed, but we put all those kids in the north wing. We were told to do that."

How interesting. Had all the Eagles been assigned to the north wing of Delk Hall because of some stupid rumor? But that was not the important issue. I had a more difficult question to ask, "That night Governor Viche got hurt, you were on duty, right?"

"You know I was, you came and got me, remember?"

"Did you let Fuller and Quint into the building that night?"

"No! I already told the police that."

"I know what you told them. I just want to know why you lied to them." I really had no idea, and was just taking a shot in the dark. "You were pretty active in getting Ben Holden sent to detention. You were dating Fuller."

"Matt Fuller is a scum bag! Look at me here, stuck with a kid he wants no part of. I can't even finish college full-time; I have to work to pay for this place. He can go jump in the lake for all I care."

"Then say the right thing, Monica."

"It's not Matt," her voice began to shake. Tears started to stream down her face, "It's Bus. He said he'd kill me if I talked. Bus killed that kid; Matt didn't. But you can't rat me out, Danny. Buss will kill me and you know he will. You have to keep my name out of this, Danny."

I promised I would. I only needed to be sure. I gave her a big hug and could feel her body trembling. I left pleased with the information I had received.

Since I was in the area, I had made plans to take Marie to breakfast. She lived in a privately owned apartment building, not part of the university, and a few yards from where I had just been. When I knocked on her apartment door, the smell of bacon and eggs hit me.

"I thought we'd eat here," Marie smiled. I took the offer.

It was a tiny studio apartment, books and computers and all kinds of crafts filled the place. Marie was an interesting person. Her folks lived on the north side, her dad a high-ranking civil servant on the base. Her brother, Matt, also attended college but lived at home. She asked me if I would come for dinner at her parents' house next weekend.

"Your parents don't mind you dating a southsider?" I joked.

She laughed, "I don't think a person can be judged on what side of town he grew up on."

Marie was solid. She was different for me. Oh, she had all the female charms any guy could ask for, but she had something I can best describe as strength of character. She didn't like living at home, so she got her own place. She needed money, so she worked. If she was bored, she did something. It was like, for the first time in my life, I was dating a grown up.

I worked that afternoon, but got off early. I returned to get cleaned up and then met Tom Pine, just south of the horseshoe ridge, near a small stream. We had planned a dinner and lecture that evening, just the two of us. He put on a cast iron kettle of stew and put it on a slow simmer.

"This okay for supper?" he asked, referring to the stew.

"Just right. I had a big breakfast."

"So, do you recall that last date you had with Sharon?"

"Yep, I got my notes here on my computer. I couldn't really recall me saying anything stupid all night. I'm not sure what turned her off so quickly. When she first got in the vehicle, and we were driving to the dance, we got into a conversation about her parents getting on her for not babysitting enough. She told me she knew I liked to go out on dates a lot and asked me if I would be sore if she worked more. I gave her a long speech about that not being a problem with me, that we would see each other when we could."

"So you weren't sore at all that she told you she couldn't go out as often?"

"No. It's hard to explain. It was a time when my happiness didn't matter that much. I thought I handled it nicely. She even told me, 'Dan, you sure make it hard for a girl not to love you.' That sure sounded like she was grateful I wasn't putting pressure on her."

"Okay," Tom said, "now say that sentence again only fill in the pronouns with names."

"Okay, Dan makes it hard for ... No, more like, Dan makes it difficult for Sharon not to love Dan."

"Okay, what does that tell you?"

"That she loved me. It's a double negative, 'hard' and 'not,' right?"

"'Hard' is not a negative. Well it could mean she no longer loved you but is feeling bad about it."

"No way."

"Okay, just a suggestion. What else?"

"Well, we got to the burger joint and it was raining. No one was there."

"No one?"

Well, just a couple of cars. So we went to the movies instead. The only other thing is, she told me she loved me when she put my ring in my pocket. Those two things don't go together, Tom. One or the other thing was a lie."

"Any other thing that was 'odd' that night?"

"Oh, her dress. She wore this outrageous outfit, this brand new dress. I wasn't complaining; it was the sexiest outfit I'd ever seen her wear. But it was out of place. I mean it was cloudy and damp that night. I could see wearing that to a formal indoor dance, but why would she wear it to a rock and roll dance which would be outside on a misty night?"

"Interesting. So, you're sure you didn't see anyone else there, where the dance was going to be? What about the few cars that were there?

"Oh, Marv Greene's car was there, that bright green thing he lost in the fire."

"Marv Greene's car?"

"Yea, I remember Sharon telling me how her mom was promoting the guy to her, like he was some kind of rehabilitated champion. He converted from the Mustangs and said he was on the road to redemption and all that crap. I told her I knew the real Greene, a bum."

"Now go back to that first sentence we talked some more about. See anything else interesting about it?"

"Not really."

"I thought she always called you Danny."

"Oh," I sat thinking for a minute. "Wait, she called me Dan that whole night. I never picked up on that."

"I think you missed a lot of things," Pine said. "But don't blame yourself; you didn't pick up on them because you were incapable of doing so. I'm pretty sure she was no longer in love with you when you picked her up. I think she had already decided. And that outfit was not for you; it was for someone else who was going to see her at the dance. It's becoming clearer for me."

"Well, explain it to me."

"I'm just guessing, Dan. It will only make sense if you figure it out. Someone telling you is just an opinion."

"Well, then give me a framework for doing that."

"Okay, let me explain some things. There was this guy once, Old World, named Ivan Boszormenyi-Nagy …"

"Can you spell that for me?"

"Don't get smart. Anyway, Nagy was a classically trained psychoanalyst; he only treated whole families in a group atmosphere. He was a genius. He could not only analyze individuals, but he could analyze the things family members said to one another, their interactions. Anyway, he not only borrowed psychoanalytic theory to back up his therapy, but also from the existential philosophers. He once discussed something he got from Heidegger.

"Dan, think about this. Has there ever been anyone so close to you, that when they died or left you, it felt like a part of you died?"

"Well, I can think of some, Sharon for instance."

"Good. Nagy talked about two kinds of relationships people have, the 'functional' and the 'ontic.' Functional relatedness is like someone you know who merely interacts with you. Let's say it's the guy who fills the vending machines at the orphanage. You may say hello to him or even tell him you like a certain kind of chips in the machines, but if one day another guy comes and he stocks the machines as good as, or even better than the first guy, you have no problem substituting the new guy for the first guy. Your relationship relies only on your interaction with each other.

"On the other hand, ontic relatedness refers to those people I mentioned before in which part of you dies when they leave. Your relationship is based on much more than just conversation. In fact, the conversations play such a small part in your relationship that they often lose their significance. Sometimes you tend to even ignore them. This has its bad points, since someone suggested it's why battered women stay with their cruel partners. These people, after they leave, cannot be substituted with another. It's just not the same.

"You've done a great job in analyzing Sharon and yourself. But now try and think about your conversations and how they relate to the actions you two took in this relationship. You are beating yourself up too much over this thing with Sharon. She was a very young girl, Dan. I can see you being hurt by her leaving, but wanting her to spend the rest of her life with you is a stretch."

As we ate our stew, we talked about other things. Tom talked about how good marrying Diane had been. She not only inspired him to pursue his work and writing, but added great purpose to his life. He described it as, "… kind of like Angie and her insistence on building your shower/laundry wing on the log home, sometimes us guys need some motivation." We talked some more about how I felt that Frank Davis's idea for living out in the woods and having access to all the stuff civilization had to offer was ideal.

One morning I made a call to my old friend, Ms. Kowalski. The sailor who answered told me it was Mrs. Henderson now. When she got on the phone I teased her, "So, Mrs. Henderson, I see you finally forced that guy to marry you."

She laughed, "I gave him an ultimatum. If we women waited on you guys to make a move I'd be retired before the jerk saw the light."

"I want to do something with that Viche case, but I need you to help me."

"Can't help you now, Dan. My old boss took that case and locked it in his office. I'm not to go near it. My old boss got transferred and when the new guy comes in I'll try and get him to reopen it."

"I need to move quicker than that. Anyone I can talk to?"

"Gee, like I said, our supervisor's position is vacant. The next in line is the Navy Commander of the base here. But I wouldn't advise it."

"I have to try. What's his name?"

"Captain Richardson."

A lump suddenly appeared in my throat. That was Lisa's dad.

So I phoned Lisa, "Hello, Lisa, this is Dan Kelley."

She sounded like she was still sleeping, "Dan, what is it with you and that tribe of cavemen you live with. Have you ever considered that most people don't get up at three in the morning?"

"It's seven."

"I'm still in bed, for crying out loud."

"Really? What are you wearing?"

"Why don't you drive up here and see for yourself? I'm not going to describe it over the phone you pervert. So, I assume you didn't call to ask me out on a date?"

"No, I need another favor."

"Figures. What?"

"I need to meet with your dad. I need to ask him something."

"I don't think that's a very smart thing to do right now, Dan. He got some really bad news this week and he's acting strange."

"I really need this, Lisa."

"Okay. I'll see what I can do. Let me call you back."

"Okay, bye."

That day, Ron and I were working at an electrical box. We were talking with a linesman who worked for the utility. Nick was a friendly guy so I decided to just throw it out there.

"Nick, what would it take to get the company to hook up my residence?"

"No problem," he said, "Just fill out a request."

"I don't live in the township."

"You don't? Where do you live?"

I took out a map and showed him. He thought it kind of odd. "Out there? I didn't think anyone lived out there. But look, we got an underground line running out to the bank of the Ice River, here, at the end of Frazer's land. We put those in several years ago thinking the township was going to have more population, it shouldn't be a problem. In fact, I think we are required to provide power to any potential customer. We have power out to that forest ranger camp out in Candlelight. That's not in the township either."

"Does the township have to approve such a thing, or do you notify them or something?"

"Not at all. Like I said, I think we have to provide any customer power. We'd have to put in the poles and lines to go over that water and run it to a box for you. But you can take it from there. Just fill out a request."

It all seemed too easy. Ben liked the idea so he filled out a request and sent it in. Within a week, a power line crew came out, put in the poles, ran lines over to the other side, and Nick set up the box. Suddenly, we had electrified our camp and had plenty of power for all our needs.

Lisa had called me back and set up an appointment with her dad on a Sunday afternoon. She had been totally surprised that he agreed to do it without details. When the day came, all the guys wished me luck before I departed. On the drive up, to keep my mind off the butterflies in my stomach, I started to piece together what Pine had wanted me to consider.

The conversation I had with Lisa was a good example. For the most part, my interactions with Lisa and Cheri, the upper classman back in school, were flirting and teasing and just plain goofing around. I'm sure they met the definition of functional relatedness because we were not serious. I'm sure those two girls could get any substitute to flirt with them. But Sharon and I were different. Both being ontically related, it didn't fit that Sharon could do the break-up thing so quickly and easily and not be the least bit bothered by it. That's why I had trouble with Pine's large-worded gobble-gook theory. It didn't make any sense in real life.

When I got to Lisa's house, I pulled into the back parking area. She met me at the back door and asked me again if I wanted to go through with this. After I said yes, she led me to her father's study in the front of the house. She wished me good luck, pointed me to the large sliding doors, and then split.

As I slid open the doors silently, Captain Richardson was standing, looking out the front window. He had his arms behind his back, his hands clasped together. I wondered, remembering Colonel Dubois used to stand like that, if all great leaders stood that way. Being a Sunday afternoon, I also wondered why he was in dress uniform.

"If you're worried, Captain," I broke the silence, "I parked out back."

Without turning around, he responded, "That's the least of my worries right now, Mr. Kelley. Come in. Have a seat." Still not turning, he continued, "Do you know what happened to me this week?"

"No, sir," I knew better than to say 'huh?' to an officer ever again.

"I got passed over for Admiral, for the last time actually. I'll have to retire as captain. Know why?"

"No, sir."

"Because I was stuck up here at wonderful Thompson, I should have known when they didn't send me to Galveston Harbor to get ready for the war with Mexico."

"I'm very sorry to hear this, Captain." He didn't want me to talk yet, I could tell, so I let him go on.

"You know how many ships I got tied up at the piers over there? Seven, with the biggest one being a destroyer."

"I'm sorry, sir, that would make you Commodore Richardson, wouldn't it?"

He turned to look at me and smiled. I think he was just happy to see a civilian who knew something about brevet rank and military history. "I don't have a flotilla here, Mr. Kelley; I have a detachment of sea scouts. Most of my men are locals. They get up, drink coffee until noon, and then go home. We go out on cruises once a month, that's all the fuel they give me, for two hours each. We go up and down the shore and then we are back by lunch."

Then he got a little more serious, "But I lost a lot more than my Admiral's flag. Lisa's mother didn't even last one whole winter up here, before she left us." He turned around and sat down, facing me. "I also have my daughter pre-engaged to a cadet officer in the Army. If I admit something about this guy, can you keep a secret from Lisa for me?"

"Yes, sir."

"I never could stand the little arrogant jerk!"

I wanted to burst out laughing but bit my tongue.

"I thought I was doing the best thing for her. I thought I was being the best that I could for both her and her mother. But in many ways I had already lost them both; and now, no stars on my shoulder boards. Do you know what, Mr. Kelley? I don't think either one could have cared if I made Admiral or not."

I didn't know what to say, so I stuck with an old standby, "Commodore, I've made some mistakes, certainly none that could compare to the ones you say you made, but sometimes we just have to make the best decisions we can with the information we have at the time. You were doing what you thought was the best to provide for your wife and take care of Lisa's future. No one can blame you for trying, sir."

He smiled, "Very well put, Mr. Kelley. You are kind to an old sailor, even if I did make you park your manure truck in the back. Now, how can I help you? Whatever you need me to do I'll have to do today because I have a flight to catch tomorrow morning."

"Oh, where you going, sir?"

"To see if I can talk my wife into coming back to me."

When I left the study, I didn't see my old girlfriend anywhere around. She probably left the base, expecting Captain Dad to cut my head off or something. I drove back, smiling. All the events causing Captain Richardson to suddenly turn back into a human being took place at the right time in history. I now had the green light.

The next day I picked up Hightower and drove her to the base with me to get my medical records amended. It was quick. We spoke to the records administrator who told Hightower that since it was put in there so long ago and since she didn't know what 'intent' the doctor had at the time for doing so, that we couldn't remove that blue sticker. Hightower simple said, "You could take care of this in ten seconds and rip that right out of there, or I can let you know my 'intent' which is 'big fat lawsuit.'" The administrator ripped it out and handed it to me.

As I was reviewing both my paper and electronic medical records for any other mention of the issue, and there were none, I saw the results of some intelligence tests. When I was four years old, the results of a child IQ test showed me as "normal." Another test taken later in school showed my IQ score as one hundred and one. I didn't mean to be pompous but figured, since I got an associate's degree at eighteen, that my IQ would be higher. I would have to check into that.

The day had finally come when we, Empire, Corky Wall, and I, drove up to the burger joint to try and find Matt Fuller. Empire was complaining all the way up there. "Kelley, why don't you let me handle this? I could beat the living crap out of that guy and get your information much quicker. What if something goes wrong?"

"I need to do it this way, Empire. Don't worry. I'll call you if I need you.

We stopped in a parking spot that people inside of the restaurant couldn't see. I walked in and there he was, Matt Fuller, sitting in a booth alone, stuffing his fat face. The old butterflies started up again as I approached him. He had on his famous letter jacket.

"Fuller," I said as he looked up at me, "I need to talk to you."

"Kelley. I didn't expect to see you back in town. Heard you were living like a dog out in the woods. What's the matter? The animals throw you out, too?"

"In my office, please." I walked to the bathroom, wanting to get him out of earshot of any other people. He didn't get up at first, but then I saw him behind me out of the corner of my eye. Murdock was right; this was scary.

We stepped in the bathroom; he stayed well behind me. It was only a one-stall/one-urinal bathroom with a lock on the door. He looked under the door to the stall, and then demanded, "Give me your wrist watch." I handed it to him. He pulled the bathroom door open and threw it, and I heard it hit the glass window on the side of the restaurant. Then he searched me, pulling all my pockets inside out and pulling my shirt up to check to see if I was wired. Finally satisfied, he asked, "What the heck you want, another black eye?"

"No, I wanted to come clean with something."

Before I could finish, some small high school kid came bolting through the door and ran right into Fuller. Matt grabbed him by the collar, pulled the door open and flung him out. He slammed the door shut and locked it. My stomach was in my throat by now.

"As I was saying, I wanted to tell you something I had lied about before."

"So, say it, Kelley!"

"That night, back at the orphanage, the night you guys killed that kid. I just wanted to let you know something."

"We didn't kill any stupid kid at the orphanage. You already tried pinning that on us and it didn't work. What's this big secret you got?"

I had to physically restrain myself now to keep from trembling. "But you did kill the stupid kid. That's what I lied to the police about."

"You weren't even there; you were over in the stupid barn slopping hogs. That's what you told the police."

"If you'd shut up a minute, I'd tell you. I lied to them. I saw you kill the kid because I wasn't at the barn. I was hiding behind one of the lockers when you and Quint came in. I saw it was you,

Fuller, that did it. I was afraid to tell them because I was afraid you guys would kill me too."

"You're full of crap!"

"But now I'm starting to be bothered by nightmares. I have to go to the cops now. I'm getting all mental over this."

"You lied once. They'll just think you're lying again. It's no sweat off of me whatever the heck you say. If you saw it, which I doubt, you'd know that Quint hit that kid that night. I didn't even touch the dumb freak."

"Well, it was dark in there, so I guess ..."

"Don't guess nothing, Kelley, you stupid orphan! Bus Quint hit the kid. You couldn't have even seen which one of us did it. You bring this all up again and I will kill you! You and all your fag orphan buddies. Try me, Kelley."

"I didn't figure it was you, Fuller. You couldn't even take on some poor circus freak. I saw you at that first fight we had, you know, but didn't see you doing any fighting. And the next fight, you weren't even there. Were you sick, or hiding in the car with the girls?"

"I swear, Kelley, I'll split your head open in a minute!"

"We did send you that box of cow flop to your parents. Don't tell me your folks thought that was chocolate and ate some? Did your mom have a bite?" When all else fails, insult a guy's mom.

That did it, everybody told me Fuller was all talk, but that right hand came out of his jacket pocket and hit me right in the face so hard I flew backwards, landed on my rear, and slid across the floor hitting and knocking over a trash can. Fuller grabbed his hand in pain, flipped open the lock on the door, and left.

I just lay there, wiping the blood pouring out of my nose, and smiled, "Thank you, Mr. Fuller."

CHAPTER 11

It's funny how black eyes are perceived at different stages in life. In the seventh grade it's a purple heart, a navy cross. Boys let you have their seat on the bus; girls think you're awesome. At eighteen, well, it's just plain ridiculous. Our club president never fully agreed with my plan. Frank Davis thought it was just plain stupid. My boss thought it scared our customers. Only our muscle men: Empire, Corky Wall, and Clyde, thought it was a good plan. But, they understood my intent. I needed Matt Fuller to see me as weak, easily scared, and frightened enough to keep my mouth shut. Fuller could have pulled a knife out and killed me on the spot, this is true, but I doubted his resolve to do such a thing. I was going with my original hunch, that Bus Quint did the deed. Ms. Hightower had doubts, but she was trained to see things through strict rules of evidence, while I took my own approach and made assumptions based on how people acted.

Only my old friends Bo and Angie came to my medical and emotional aid. Back at our log home, Bo did his emergency medical technician first aid on me, cleaning my face and applying bandages. Angie stood by with hugs and kisses. Tom Pine came in, joining in with the rest of the guys gathered there to heap sarcasm on me. I let them get all their jokes in.

People started to slowly file out, going back to their usual duties. Finally, only Tom and I remained in the large room.

"Tom, somewhere along the line, you studied psychology as well, right?" I asked.

"Sure, master's degree in clinical psychology as a matter of fact."

"Really, why didn't you stay in that field, instead of ...?"

"You mean why did I give up a lucrative career in clinical psychology and go into a worthless occupation like philosophy? Don't worry, Dan, it doesn't offend me. I've been asked that a lot. I liked the subject but not the practice of it, that's the best answer I can give."

"So, you know about IQ scores?"

"Sure, I used to give some of those tests, and graded them."

"I was looking at my medical records the other day. I had taken two of them. On the kids' one ..."

"When they brought you here?"

"Yea. I got a four."

"How old were you when they gave it to you?"

"Four."

"That's normal. They probably did that when they brought you here to check on you. Probably checking to see if you suffered anything from exposure to the cold."

"Well, on the adult one I got a 101."

"Yea and it's probably gone down about ten points since you took that whack in the head. But that's normal again, what's your beef?"

"Well, and I didn't want to say this around anyone because it seems like I'm bragging, but I thought it would be higher than that. I mean I did get an associate's degree at seventeen."

"I'm not that surprised, but I see things a little differently. Frank Davis and Al Myers have high ones. Myers is probably close to two hundred. Myers gets A's on tests because he knows the material; you get them by reading through the book and memorizing all the best test answers. By the way, who was the first one to notice this, this thing about you being a little different?"

"Gee, I guess it was Bossard, back at Delk."

"Sounds about right since Bossard has it too. But what was Bossard?"

"What do you mean?"

"Bossard was a high school student. You see, that's what's wrong with our system. This is a problem we started when we began herding students into particular occupations. Like I said before, the country needs electricians and carpenters and painters. They picked Al Myers to be a mathematician because of his IQ score. But the high school misses people like you because there is no advantage in doing so. A high school student saw it in you, but it was a high school student who only saw it because he has the same thing.

"It was driven in your head, since you were just four that the only way out of your current existence was to do well in school. You learned how to learn. You taught yourself to speed-read and how to pass tests because the motivation came from your heart, not your head. The fact that you chose a hand skill trade is evidence of this. You memorized the definitions of the philosophical terms but you don't know their meaning. Bossard saw it, my wife saw it, Principi saw it, and, well, why do you think I picked you as my student? Certain parts of your life, Dan, are directed by an almost desperate passion. Playwrights call it ends-of-the-earth type stuff. And it's good stuff."

My black eye turned out to be not so black, and within a week most evidence of my fight was gone. Frank had us out in the woods putting up these huts in various places. I couldn't figure out why he wanted us to construct them in the places he did, but he said it was in his plan. They were like our log home back in the Holy Cross summer village, only smaller.

I was working on one of Milt's cattle water tanks, the kind that has electrical heaters in them to keep the water from freezing in winter, when I got the call. He took a break and I answered it.

"Hello," I said.

"Hello, Danny?" a female voice said.

"This is he."

"Hi, Danny, this is Sharon."

"Sharon who?"

"Sharon Dubois," she laughed, "Don't tell me you already forgot about me."

I suddenly realized that this was the very first time she had ever called me. "Oh, Sharon. No, I didn't forget you."

"I have the greatest news. Dad made general. We're moving."

"Wow, that's great. Where you going?"

"Atlanta. Headquarters."

"Wow, the capital. I thought you once mentioned he would have one more remote assignment before Atlanta and his generalship."

"I know, but he got sent to Texas last year for the war. I guess war speeds everything up and he got promoted early. He's the second youngest general in the last one hundred years."

"Neat. I know he was dying to get that. And, gee, Atlanta. When you get there say hello to the President for me."

"I'm not sure I'll see her."

Nobody seems to appreciate my telephone humor. "So, I guess this is goodbye?"

"No silly. I want to know if you'll go out with me. You know, for old-time sake. Just friends, of course. I'm going out with some of my favorites while I am still here. Got you all lined up."

I decided to be a jerk, "Gee, I don't know. You know how I feel about the 'friends' thing."

"Dan Kelley. Don't tell me you're still on that crap. Come on, I got this all planned."

"Sorry, kid, call it a date or nothing at all."

"For crying out loud, okay, it's a stupid date. Are you happy? I have you down for next Monday night."

"Naw, Monday won't work for me, I have a date," I didn't, "How about Wednesday?"

"I'm leaving Thursday morning. The plane takes off at seven."

"That's the only night I have open."

"Okay, Wednesday night. See you about six. I have to be home early, okay?"

"Okay. See you Wednesday at six."

As I switched off the call, I still wasn't sure why I had just said that. So I was just "one" of her favorites? I wondered how many there were. I regretted agreeing to this, up until that very night, when I thought it wouldn't hurt to try and get some answers out of her. I knew I no longer had any leverage; I couldn't yell at her and I couldn't tick her off. I had to be nonthreatening.

I stopped off at a car wash and got the truck cleaned up before I headed to the base. I still knew the way by heart. I stopped in her drive, taking a deep breath.

As I knocked on the door, I heard her mom yell, "Danny, come in, please." When I entered the kitchen, there was the classic general's wife: tight dress, high heels, makeup and jewelry.

"Hi, Mrs. Dubois. Congratulations to you and the new general. You're going to be in the high society now."

"Oh, thank you. I'm so glad for the general." Imagine calling your husband the general. "He's so looked forward to this."

When she bent down to take the cookies out of the oven, I had a wicked thought. I wonder if she had been having an affair with some airman, but broke it off when hubby made general? "Oh,

Mrs. Dubois, I almost forgot, "Madame Dubois, vous êtes très belle ce soir."

"Well, my goodness," she smiled, "Merci, Danny, tu parles français maintenant?"

I responded, "Un peu. Je sais que vous aviez voulu que nous nous séparions, Sharon et moi."

She shot me the meanest scowl I had ever seen her make, just as her daughter stuck her head in the door.

"Did I catch you two at a bad time?" Sharon looked a little puzzled, "Are you guys talking about me? I heard my name mentioned in there."

"No, dear," Mrs. Dubois put on a fake smile, "Danny here was just telling me how lovely I looked and how he was so looking forward to going out with you one last time." As she turned back to scrape the cookies off the baking sheet, she threw me another dirty look.

"Okay, Mom, see you later." We walked out the side door to my truck. Sharon giggled, "So what the heck were you doing flirting with my mom?"

"Don't you know any French?"

"Don't speak a word of it. But I know you, Danny Kelley." she laughed.

"I was just admiring her personality."

"Yea, I saw you admiring her 'personality' taking those cookies out of the oven," she laughed. "You and every other boy I've dated here have this thing about my mom."

You couldn't have convinced me two years ago that Sharon Dubois could ever get any better looking, but she sure had. She was awesome looking; everything was just, well, enhanced. Her hair was shinier, her skin smoother, her figure out of this world. One thing, her great smile, was just the same. I opened the door and she jumped in.

When we took off down the road, with her not sitting next to me but sort of halfway between me and the door, she chatted endlessly about dad's promotion. She looked great in that customary seat, with her shorts and tee shirt and that big bright smile.

"So, I hear you dropped out of society for a while?" she asked.

"Yea, had to go out in the woods and find myself."

"I heard about it. I knew you didn't start any stupid riot; it's not in your nature. I must say, life out there becomes you."

"What do you mean?"

"Your chest is bigger, your biceps, your tan is glowing."

I had not noticed that before. "Thank you. Been going out with anyone interesting?"

"Me? Oh, no, don't date anymore. After us I needed some free time, some time to babysit."

"No one?"

"No, why?"

"What about the guy you broke up with me to go out with?"

"I didn't break up with you to go out with anyone."

What a load of cow manure that was. "Marv Greene. Didn't you date Marv Greene?"

Sharon shot me a growling look, but the smile soon returned, "So, guess there's no use trying to keep that one from you. You must have heard about it."

"That didn't turn out too well, did it?"

Another sour look came my way. She turned back again, looking out the windshield, "Danny, I'm not going to answer that and I never want you to bring it up again, okay?"

As much as I was angry with her for breaking up with me, I knew that was a place I had no business going. I didn't wish that kind of thing on anyone. "Understood."

"Danny, one last thing about that. That creep had my yearbook picture the first night I went out with him. I only got five with the price of the picture, because we didn't like it. I gave you one and my mom one, and I got three left. Did you give him the one I gave you?"

"Heck no, I've never met Greene, never even seen him, let alone give him my picture. I still got yours in my wallet."

"You still have it on you? Why?"

"Never cleaned out my wallet I guess."

"Any ideas how he got one?"

"That only leaves one person."

Like most of the other dates with Sharon, I had no idea what we did. We got something to eat, I know. I didn't take her to the burger joint because Fuller might have been there, plus it held too many dear memories to return there with her as my "friend." She rambled on about her design projects as I looked at those lovely eyes.

She was different that night; I did come to that conclusion. I finally got it figured out. Two years ago, Sharon was a young, beautiful, charismatic girl with an air of innocence. Tonight she was a young, beautiful, charismatic girl, but she knew it. I don't know if it was because of Father Time or Marv Greene, but she had an air about her that was unfortunate.

Sometime later found us turning on to Perimeter Road and passing the stones one last time.

"Sharon, you always liked this little road. Why?"

"What?"

"Sort of metaphorically, this being your last night here and all, how is it descriptive of your life here?"

"Oh, well," she smiled, "I guess I would have to say it reminds me of my times here; the laughs, the very good times, my dates. This is the way I came home after my dates and stuff. The stones remind me of good times here."

"Those stones are machine cut you know? They're not naturally shaped. How can you tell them apart?"

"Well, who would want to do that? It's the fact that the stones are all alike that makes the road so cute."

I pulled off onto the little parking spot where one could park and walk out to the lakefront; we had come here a lot. We sat in the truck since it was dark.

"What are we parking here for?"

"Don't worry," I got a little ticked at her implication, "I just want to talk."

"Okay, but not too long, I have to be in bed early. So, whose truck?

"Mine, I bought it."

"Cool, you working now?"

"Yea, I'm an electrician, working for my journeyman's license."

"Does it pay well?"

"It's good pay. Are we going to talk about this superficial stuff all night?"

Sharon pushed across the seat, sat next to the passenger door, and looked out the window. After securing a safe distance, she turned to look at me, "What happened to you … out there?"

When I looked at her, in the dim glaze of a single street lamp, I saw that girl again. The girl I was still madly in love with. She could have taken out a club and beat me over the head with it and I would not love her less. I wondered if she knew that. "Out where?"

"Out there, in the woods."

I smirked, "I beat up a bear with a stick." She gave me an unbelieving look. Pine had been right; no one was ever going to buy that story. "I had a lot of time to think, to think of what's important to me and what's not."

"So, what's important to you, Danny?"

"You and I were."

She looked out the passenger door window again, and spoke without looking at me, "I broke up with you. I loved you, and then I didn't. So sue me."

"You didn't have any responsibility to the relationship, Sharon? You told me people get divorced all the time. Even then they have to go through marriage counseling. We didn't go out that long, Sharon, but we were intense. Well, at least one of us was intense. And one of us is still in love with the other and wants to know."

Her head snapped around quickly, "Did you just say you're still in love with me?" She then looked out the windshield. "That's not the way it's supposed to be, Danny. It's not supposed to turn out like this. We broke up, two years have passed, and you're supposed to be my friend now. Why couldn't you just be my friend? How come you never could?"

"I know I didn't ever tell you why, but only because I didn't know either. I couldn't bring it down to that level. I couldn't stop and chat with you in the hall, be in your group of friends. I would not be able to stand seeing that smile flashed at some other guy. It hurt too much."

"I guess I can see that now."

"So, help me out here, how come you called me Dan on that last night?"

"That's not true. I always called you Danny. I liked that name better."

"But the last night you did."

"No I didn't."

I let that go. "Oh, the outfit, the one you wore that last night."

"Outfit? I can't remember what I wore that night. It was two years ago."

"The nice white dress. Your dad got mad at you for paying so much for it, remember?"

"Oh, yea, that one."

"So who did you wear it for?"

"What the heck are you talking about? We went to the movies; I wore it for you. Who would see it in a dark theater other than you?"

"We were going to the outdoor dance. We only went to the movies because the dance got rained out. Don't you remember?"

Sharon got flustered. She couldn't keep it up any longer, so she just blurted out, "I wore the stupid dress for Marv Green, okay? Are you happy now?" She sat up and shook her finger at me, "But I loved you, Danny Kelley! Don't ever say I didn't. Okay? Pretty boy caught my eye. Okay, I admit it. But that was just the last one percent of the time we went together."

"Okay, I believe you," I said, mostly to calm her down. I wasn't convinced but Sharon did start to be more relaxed. I think she had even felt better getting the Marv Greene thing off her chest. I looked at her and winked, and she worked up a weak smile.

"You are one deep case, Danny Kelley."

"Sharon. Help me out again. Tell me, what girls like about guys. What did you like about the guys here in your life?"

"Gee, let me think," she said, putting her hand up to her chin. "You know, the only things I had going before Tom were little girl crushes. Tom was my first love so I'll have to start with him. Tom was totally funny, he kept me in stitches."

"Yes," I added, "he was on our cross country team. He would do these imitations of the different teachers and coaches."

"And he was kind of cute as well. You were cuter, a little less funny, but you had your moments. You always complimented me on my smile, Danny, but you made me smile. Now Marv, he was just drop dead gorgeous, but he wasn't funny at all."

I didn't care for my assignment in Sharon's hierarchy, but at least we were getting somewhere. "So what happened to us, all us guys that is?"

"Tom was great, up until his mom died. He got all weird about it and stuff, just sat there not talking all the time. You did the same, with all that stuff about school and the Mustangs and the draft. Plus, I had trouble understanding you. You spoke like those guys in the bible, you know, in parables. The fun ended. Marv of course, was a jerk from the start."

I had to hurry; I didn't know how long she would let me keep her out. Pine always told me to substitute nouns. She liked smiling and looking at us. Smiling or laughing? Stand-up comics made me laugh. We made her laugh. We were "entertaining?" She loved us until we quit being entertaining? I decided to try something else.

"Sharon, let me give you another one of those parables. Say it was back in time when you were the most in love with me. Let's say I was having all those troubles with the school at that time, and I had to run off and go live in the woods. Would have come with me?"

She perked up, a little annoyed, "Now that's an example of you being weird. I was a fifteen-year-old girl! I had a family. I was in high school." And then she floored me, "What did you expect me to do, follow you to the ends-of-the-earth?"

That's when it hit me like a ton of bricks, more like a ton of bricks falling from a ten-story building. It was downloading faster than my thoughts could process it.

Do you know how female friends, girls that enjoyed your company, but did not have any romantic feeling for you, always wrote "Luv ya!" in your high school yearbook? They didn't write "love you" because that would be a totally different emotion. Sharon wrote "love" in mine, but spelled the word wrong.

"You did love me!" I proclaimed.

Sharon said, "That's what I've been trying to tell you. You sure are dense sometimes."

"It's the ends-of-the-earth. It's a matter of degree. The ends-of-the-earth for me was some mountaintop in Tibet. For you it was the end of your driveway. You weren't allowed out of the yard yet."

She tried a joke, "And this is the gospel according to St. Danny."

I thought back to that time Tom Pine talked to me about ontic relatedness. Tom Crosby didn't "get all weird" when his mom died, he was grieving. I had become obsessed with my problems as well, but because Sharon was so attached to me, so much a part of my being, that I wasn't listening to her. In the ontic scenario, interactions lose their significance. This explained why I had imagined still being in love with her, even if she had beaten me with a club.

But the interactions were all poor Sharon had. Tom and I and whoever else weren't attached to her soul, so when we stopped entertaining her, she dumped us and moved on. It didn't matter to her, her smile continued, because we could be substituted. She had no trouble eliciting these emotions from the next guy; she didn't even have to try hard. We provided a function for her. She loved us the way she loved a perfectly decorated gym for the prom!

A total smile came over my face as I started the truck and took off.

Sharon tried another joke, "Now why am I getting the funny feeling that this date is over?"

As I tore down Perimeter Road, I thought about Sharon's totally inadequate offer for me to be her friend. It was similar to Tom's letter jacket. He didn't dislike the coat; it was still a good coat. The coat meant nothing to him without her in it. He couldn't substitute what it meant to him symbolically and once again wear it for warmth.

I pulled into her driveway, stopped and hopped out. A kind of astonished Sharon got out of the truck and followed me to her door. Not only didn't I have time to explain my moment of insight to her, I doubted she was at a point in her life to understand it.

Sure, I wanted to yell and scream at her at times, but it wouldn't have done her any good, or me any good. She would have to learn this lesson from someone else.

I pulled her close and kissed her, long and hard. As we parted, she said, "I did love you, back then."

"More than any other boy, or so I've been told."

"But you do understand now, that I did love you?"

"I know," I said.

"I don't really understand why you suddenly feel so much better about the whole thing."

"I know." I ran my hand down along the side of her face, turned and walked back to the truck. After getting in and starting up, I backed out. Sharon decided not to run inside right away like the last time I was here, but instead walked out in the middle of the drive way and waved to me. I waved back. Now I had but just one more thing to do.

***

He walked back to the truck with no further explanation. As he was backing out, Sharon waved to him. She couldn't tell if he waved back or not because the headlights were shinning in her eyes. Then he drove off.

She turned and walked to the house. There went one boy who Sharon could never figure out.

She heard her mom packing in the kitchen, "Sharon, that you?"

"Yes," she responded. When she walked up to her, she saw something in Sharon's face that put her on guard. "Mom, what did Danny tell you, in French, just before we left?"

She looked down into the box she was packing, "I already told you."

"Mom, did you forget I took French in junior high?"

"Well, you flunked that class if I recall."

"Well, some of it stuck, enough so I knew what he said. Mom, did you give Marv Greene my yearbook picture?"

"I might have."

"Why?"

"Sharon, Danny was no good for you. I know he was cute and funny, but look at his background, dear. He was a fad for a while but he's really going nowhere. Your father and I could both see that."

"You don't think he had the right stuff?"

"No."

"Do you think Marv Greene did? Boy, Mom, there was a great pick!"

"I didn't know that at the time, Sharon."

"You didn't know Danny, ever."

"I'm not happy with your tone at all. Maybe you had better go to bed. I'm waking you up at five. We need to be on the tarmac at six thirty."

She walked up to her room, flopped down on her sleeping bag and sat with her knees pulled up to her chin. Coherent thoughts were hard to come by. Suddenly, she felt drowsy, and sleep and peace were all that she wanted.

She pulled herself up and walked over to the window to close the sheet her mom had hung as a makeshift curtain. As she looked out into the large grassy courtyard for the last time, something caught her eye.

Sharon couldn't make it out very well. At the far end of the courtyard, she could see the end of the runway and part of the little road going around it. She thought she saw a vehicle out there; it kind of looked like Danny's truck, but she couldn't be sure. She reached into a paper bag wastebasket and pulled out an old pair of opera glasses she had intended to throw out. She looked through them, but they were inadequate.

Sharon could only see a stopped vehicle, the left side door was open, and its driver was out walking up and down, as if he were looking for something alongside Perimeter Road.

CHAPTER 12

I was up on the ridge, at seven the next morning, as the large Air Force cargo plane lifted into view along the northern horizon. It rose steadily, heading west, until it started to make a slow turn to the south. Continuing to rise, higher and higher, it came around to the southeast. By the time it passed just south of straight up, it was too high to even read the insignia on the tail fin. Not being able to see anyone waving out a window, I blew it a kiss.

"Kelley," I heard from below, only to look down and see Rose Russo coming up the side of the ridge. She was having a hard time of it, I heard her complaining, but finally approached me. She greeted me, "Just checking to see if your heart was still in your chest, or flying south on that plane."

"No," I laughed, "it's still where it belongs."

She sat on a tree stump next to me as I continued to work on the power generator. "So? Jim's not here, Rose."

"I know," she said, still a little out of breath, "He went fishing or something, early. I'll never figure you guys out, why the heck you like so many steep hills and why you get up so darn early.

What makes you think I was looking for him? Maybe I wanted to talk to you."

I looked at her a little astonished. Rose was a beauty for sure. She wore a yellow sweatshirt, shorts, and her dirty, rock climbing tennis shoes. Her hair was a mess, probably just got up, no makeup, but it didn't matter with her. Even at her worst, Rose looked good. I was beginning to think it had to do with more than her looks.

I confided in her, "Well, sorry, you just haven't done too much talking to me in a long time."

"I know," she said. "Looks like Sharon got off okay, huh? Any hard feelings?"

"No, we worked a lot of things out last night. No hard feelings, well, maybe just one. Tom Crosby once told me that she left us when we needed her the most. I guess I can't ever forgive her for that. I returned a verdict of guilty, but commuted her sentence on account of ignorance."

"So, what part did you work out?"

She sure was getting a little personal. "May I ask why, after two years, you're suddenly taking such an interest in how I feel?"

"I wanted to apologize," she did appear sincere. "I know I haven't talked to you about it much."

"Or not at all?"

"Okay, not at all. I'm not good at those things. I think we all got a little dose of reality when Sharon dumped you. I think, or should I say I know, that Jim thought I was going to do the same to him. I'm sorry. I just didn't have any words for you. I wouldn't have been able to handle it myself, let alone help you with it."

I sat down next to her, "I thought it was because you were friends with Sharon."

"No. In fact, I saw some things I doubted about her from the start. See, you guys see girls who have showered, washed their hair, put on makeup, and ironed their clothes for you. We're already pretty phony before you get us out the door. But we have sleepovers with each other, don't forget. We go where the real crap comes out."

"Do you think Sharon was shallow?"

"Never cared for that term, Dan, no one is intentionally shallow. Sharon liked fun. Girls can still like or even love a boy and still want fun."

"So how does a girl like Sharon and one like you differ in your motivation?"

"Sharon wants fun and I want Jim Donovan. I can't say it any better than that. She loses sight of the guy because they're a dime a dozen for her."

"Rose, what do you think ..." We were interrupted by Angie, walking up the same hill and cursing every rock she stumbled over. She had her outdoor clothes on, army pants and combat boots. She got to the top, panting like mad.

"You and your stupid forest! Kelley ..." she stopped to catch her breath, then caught sight of Rose. "What the heck you doin' up here with Rose, you pervert?"

"Arguing, actually," I teased. "She just told me the reason you're so short with such a big mouth is that your parents are first cousins and I disagreed with her."

Angie was so out of breath she couldn't even put up a good come back for me, she just laughed. "I don't even have the strength to bust you in the chops, Kelley. But hey, there's this guy out by the bridge. Says he's your brother. Jim, Donny and Bennie are bringing him up here now, to the log house. They tried to assure him you didn't have a brother, but he was pretty persistent. He rode a bike all the way out here. Ben's gonna have Al run a check on him while you and Empire talk to him. Ben thinks he might be a Mustang or something. It is creepy, Dan, the guy looks a lot like you."

I sure did want to continue my discussion with Rose, but that was out of the question now. I went down to see what this guy was up to.

There was indeed a bicycle parked in front of our log house. When I entered I saw the guy, seated and talking to Empire. Both of them stood up when they noticed me coming in. The guy seemed nice. I didn't see any family resemblance in him, but he was a decent looking guy, a little older than me perhaps, taller. He looked strong and fit. He had a folder of papers sitting in front of him on the table.

"Hi, I'm Dan Kelley," I shook the guy's hand.

"Pat O'Dea," he greeted me, looking me up and down. We all sat.

"I hate to wreck your visit, but I've never had a brother," I said.

"That's what I came to see you about. I had one once, but lost him," he said, appearing sincere. "I am a little worried since getting in here. Your friends checked me for weapons and asked me many questions back there at your river crossing. I was beginning to think you guys were a drug cartel working out of the forest."

"No," I said as Empire and I both laughed, "We got into a little jam with some of the criminal element a while back. It's mostly cleared up now, but we're a little paranoid some loner may try something. I'm sorry about that, but you can imagine what we thought when you told us your story. I'm an orphan, Pat, always have been. Where you from?"

"South Carolina."

"That's a world away from me. Never been there."

"I'm originally from Illinois Territory."

Both Empire and I sat up and paused a moment. Now I was becoming paranoid. "What part?"

"Near Old St. Louis. There was a civilian settlement there at one time. My little brother was born there."

"So where did you lose your brother?"

"My parents decided to go on some wild excursion, never found out why or where. We got caught in a freak snowstorm. Mom and Dad went off somewhere and never came back. I was in our vehicle with my brother. Then I lost him."

Murdock and I were staring in awe by now. Empire started to say, "Dan, that's …" but I held up a finger, stopping him. I didn't want to say anything just then and give it away. "Pat, what were you guys out there for?"

"Like I said, don't know."

"How did you get out of there? How did anyone find you after the storm?"

"I walked. After the snowstorm stopped, it became clear and sunny, melting a lot of the snow. I started walking, three, maybe four days. I knew enough to walk back in the direction we came from. I finally ran into some pirates."

"Pirates?"

"That's what I called them. They were treasure hunters. That's what the settlement in Old St. Louis was set up for, treasure hunters. The company outfitted and funded these search parties, but some of the guys were rogues. Some kept the treasures they found for themselves. They were looking for buried bank vaults mostly, covered over and left in the Old World chaos. I asked them to take me back up there to look for my family, but they wouldn't do it. They took me back with them to Old St. Louis."

"Why didn't you look for your brother?" Empire asked.

"I did. The next morning I looked all over. I was six years old, guys, give me a break." One could almost tell that the guy had been going over some grief all these years, over his inability to find his family. He must have been scared to death.

I said, "Pat, let's say that some of this story makes sense to me. But what you told me so far is either information available in the public record or could be made up. What can you tell me that no one else would know?"

He looked me right in the eye, "My brother's name was Danny. He had to go out and pee. While I was holding onto the collar of his coat, he slipped out of my grasp and down into a ravine. I never saw him again, until ten minutes ago."

I almost fell out of my chair. I couldn't talk for a few moments. Then I looked at Empire, "What's for lunch?"

"Elk burgers," Empire responded, almost speechless as well.

"Can you throw on a couple of extras and tell the guys my brother will be joining us for lunch?" Empire left the room. "What was dad's name?"

"Well, I was born Patrick O'Dea, Jr., if that's any help."

"So that's my last name, O'Dea? Wow, talk about a Celtic soul brother. At least that doctor at the base got my ancestry right. How the heck did you find me?"

"I became interested in finding out about the family in high school. I have a lot to tell you, although many things are still unknown to me. I assumed you had frozen to death, but one day I was online and reading about the orphanage up here. I was looking for O'Deas in the listing, having no idea you didn't remember your last name. Then I looked for Daniels, and saw you listed in the official records, only under birth place it had 'undetermined.'"

"So I was born in Old St. Louis?"

"Probably. A midwife delivered you. Dad didn't file for a birth certificate; that place was pretty frontier. I'm sure the company that ran the place had records there, but the river flooded one spring and all the records washed down to the Gulf of Mexico."

"Where were you born?"

"Memphis, eighteen months earlier. By the way, did you mention lunch of some kind? I've been peddling that darn bike out here since four this morning."

We ate lunch around the campfire, all the Eagles, the girls, and many of the Holy Cross. It turned into an event with all eyes and ears on Pat. The poor guy could barely eat.

Pat was now a geophysics major at the University of South Carolina in Columbia. The company at old St. Louis sent him to an orphanage in Memphis. He said when the orphanage there burned down he was sent to one in Chattanooga that burned down as well.

I looked at Clyde and said, "Yes, those orphanages sure have a problem with that." Clyde just looked up in the air and started whistling.

Pat eventually got adopted by a nice family in Columbia and has been there ever since.

He told us dad was raised near Mobile, Alabama, but was probably born somewhere in the Florida panhandle. Growing up on a farm, his parents died when he was in his teens. He was an expert at odd jobs and a total handyman. He did two years in the Navy, then moved to Birmingham and worked at an apartment complex there. He married our mother there. Pat never found out much information about her. After a time working in Montgomery, they moved to the Black Belt region of Mississippi where he farmed. After working in Memphis for a while, they went up to try their fortune in the Old St. Louis camp. With his extensive knowledge on repairing things, they even made good money.

"He did just about everything there: he was a repair man, a mechanic, even took care of the company's beef cattle herd," Pat went on. "He had the strangest way with cows; this strange call for them, sorta like 'Saa boss' he would say, and they would come running toward him."

Patrick the first, according to his son, was an avid reader. He barely recalled once how excited dad had gotten over something he had read. Soon talk of an excursion to the north began. He remembers the day dad brought home this vehicle that Pat could only describe as "looking like a tank that floated on water." He said mom argued with him about it.

In any event, the family took off on this adventure into the wilderness, searching for something young Pat had no recollection of. Pat also said that he and I got a big kick out of the adventure. He had no idea how long the whole thing took but that it seemed like weeks.

He spoke of the sudden snowstorm, and dad was driving when they suddenly confronted a high hill right in front of them which dad almost ran into. He stopped, started to back up when "the vehicle broke and we were stuck." He recalls us all sleeping there. He said in the night how dad came back from outside, got mom, and they both went out. They never came back. He said then I woke up, had to go to the bathroom, and the rest was history. Our parents were in their early thirties when they died.

"This is the most incredible hamburger I have ever eaten," Pat exclaimed, "This is elk?"

"We go for the fresh stuff," Clyde said.

"So tell me, Pat," Bo asked, "what did you expect Dan to be like?"

"I had no idea," Pat responded, "but it looks like he turned out okay. He sure made some nice friends who like good food."

Angie couldn't resist, "Actually, Pat, Dan's a moron. We only let him hang out with us because we feel sorry for him. So, how did you find us here?"

"I first went to the base to do some research on rescues done that year, then to the orphanage. They said the last they heard, you guys were on Frazer's farm. I went out there and one of the hands there told me where you guys were holed up. He even loaned me a bike. He didn't tell me it was four miles out here!"

I took Pat in my truck to return the bike. I apologized for the bumpy ride over the prairie grass since there was no road. We then went up to his motel just outside the base to get his stuff. On the way I told him our whole story here. I told Pat the helicopter must have somehow found me wandering around in the snow and had actually picked me up while he was in the vehicle.

He told me he had wanted to see the site, but the military wouldn't take him and he didn't have the money to purchase a charter. Plus he had to fly back to Columbia in the morning, as he had to be back at his summer job.

At the campfire supper that evening, he gave me photocopies of all the hard copy information he had collected while here, and then transferred all the electronic data from his handheld to mine. I gave it to our two spies, Corky Wall and Al Myers to look over. We exchanged contact information, and promised to keep each other abreast of our discoveries regarding this mystery. I took him to the airport to catch his flight the next morning.

As we stood waiting for the plane to board, Pat said to me, "I was hoping to take you back with me, we'd have to share a room and all, but I was worried how you might be living. I can see you are doing fine and have a lot of friends looking out for you."

"I sometimes get angry with them, mom and dad," I confided, "for leaving us out there."

"I've been through that as well," Pat said, "but at the times I have been mad with them, something pops into my head. It's almost like an argument against me being angry. It's almost like an argument dad would put up in his defense. It's crazy, I know, but I got some impressions from dad that maybe you, at that time, were too young to process. Whatever crazy notion motivated him to make such a journey, he was driven by something, something bigger than us all. I can't explain it, but it was like he was driven by a desperate passion."

At the late night campfire that evening, all kinds of thoughts kept racing through my head. We all sat around. I could tell we were all thinking about this new mystery. Very few of us spoke, save Angie's course remarks about this or that. Finally, after Ben threw another log on the fire and sat back down, he spoke.

"You know, this thing isn't going to go away."

Pine added, "I think there's only one thing to do."

"Yea," Ben said, "we're gonna have to go down there and have a look around."

Corky, Clyde, and Empire suddenly perked up. Then Al Myers made a statement, "Ya know, Dan, the stuff your brother gave me; it's got the GPS coordinates where that helicopter picked you up."

There was no need for a vote; we were going. Frank Davis gave his warning on the dangers we faced: predators, heat, thirst, exposure, and only a slight possibility of rescue if one of us got hurt. Ben started making plans with the group. Clyde, Ben, me, Empire, and Corky Wall were definitely going. We talked Al Myers into going for his scientific knowledge plus his state-of-the-art, six thousand dollar, handheld computer. Tom Pine and his wife wanted to go. We also asked Holy Cross Matt to go because he been out in the wild much longer than any of us. Empire suggested we get Wheeze from The Range to go for his knowledge of old vehicles. Frank Miller was left in charge while Frank Davis would be involved in working on our case with Hightower. Ben suggested we go soon, since it was late June and still close to the summer solstice, plus we had our hearing with the township in September.

We decided to break up into two sections of five each, with each group carrying a set of cooking utensils and three rifles. Each group would put one person on watch, making two people awake at all times. While eating, sleeping and campfires would be in two groups, we would march and defend as one. We packed as light as we could, using animal skin pouches and botas. The whole group, including those who were not going, met the night before we left. Ben pointed out the route that he and Al had come up with. We would skirt west of Old Chicago and then straight down. Al pointed out that collapsing underground structures and tunnels still occurred in the old populated centers. These also, at times, exposed skeletons which would be nice to avoid. Of course these problems could occur in any area but with less frequency on the outskirts. Ben figured we could do twenty miles a day in good weather.

The possibility of using horses or all-terrain vehicles was discussed. Of course, none of us knew anything about horses and we would probably have to abandon all-terrains at the first river we came to.

Frank Davis, of course, had to review the grotesque with us. "Dan, I don't want to make too much of this, but also want you to know some things. Of course, if your parents wandered off and succumbed to the elements, there might be a couple of skeletons lying around somewhere. If they met their fate due to predators, it could be a pretty gross scene." I nodded. Frank continued, "I think we need to brainstorm some possible motivations for this journey they went on, noting Mr. O'Dea's almost fanatic mood prior to the trip. I was wondering if it couldn't have been some sort of religious experience."

Ben agreed, and then added, "A pilgrimage?"

"Nothing really religious connected with that part of the country, is there?" Clyde asked, "I mean this isn't exactly the Holy Land."

"How about some sort of vision quest?" I added, "Native American style?"

"Maybe St. Patrick was going to run all the snakes out of Illinois," Matt joked.

"Perhaps an Old World connection," Frank said, "ancient relatives or a homestead."

Al Myers added, "You know, I confided in some of my most trusted professors at the college and all agreed this is a pretty ridiculous adventure."

"How so?" Pine asked.

"That it's not worth the dangers involved. Their question was why would anyone do this with 98 percent of the data being discoverable from satellite scans and photos from a seat in a secure lab here? I didn't really have an answer for them."

"I think I do," Tom said, "We're basing this on a fourteen-year-old hunch here, and I don't know if such a thing is going to show up on a telescopic photo."

We discussed the possibilities for a while, until Ben announced that we should get some sleep. We all knew that finding out whatever led to this O'Dea family outing would depend on finding what was left of that vehicle. Before going to sleep, Frank had us all sign some papers he had been preparing for our case with the town. It was a bunch of "party of the first part" legal stuff that I barely read before signing.

We woke at four in morning, and awaiting us was a full breakfast cooked by Angie and Bo Schlitz. We formed in ranks of two around five. Angie, dressed in those oversized army pants, worked off her nervous energy by making sure all our packs were secure on our backs. She was not a big fan of these excursions, when Ben would take off to the unknown, but saw the uselessness in arguing about it with him.

Ben had me in line next to Wheeze from The Range. I took it as a compliment because Ben wanted someone with a little tact walking next to him. I had been getting the feeling, however, that much of the impression Wheeze put out came from the same motivation Ben Holden used in his crazy person routine. As Angie approached us in line, she and Wheeze got our spirits in good shape for the long day.

"Well," Angie said, "if it isn't Sleazy Wheezy." Leave it to Angie to call the most likely candidate for committing a capital offense a sleaze. But that was Angie, with a charisma exceeding Sharon's, she could pull it off.

"Hi, darling," Wheeze responded.

"How's the wife?"

"Mean as a mad dog on a Monday. Still engaged to the big guy, huh? You are gonna come see me, before you get married? You know, be with a real man one last time."

"Ya keep promising me you'll get divorced, Wheeze, but you never do."

"My wife once said, 'I'll never be a divorcee again, but I could be a widow.'"

"When she say that?"

"On our wedding day. It was part of her vows."

The pair had us all roaring with laughter, until Ben had to make his ceremonial announcement, "Okay. Today, the Corps of Discovery II goes forth to find St. Patrick of the Prairie, to explore this mystery and any others we stumble upon. We stick together; of course if we come across a hungry lion, we offer him Kelley. Ready? Forward ho!"

Our band slowly walked out of camp, laughing and joking. Although Pine was the oldest, he and everyone conceded that Ben was the leader of this expedition; this was an all-Eagle thing.

We were headed southwest, and soon came upon ground very few had been on in the last one thousand years. The landscape was hilly and wooded. With Corky on point, we bypassed the low damp areas and denser tree groves. We were headed to a campsite, actually. Tom Pine had told us of two wandering types who lived out on the plains. They were not Holy Cross; rather, Matt had referred to them as "Independents."

We stopped at noon, but with such a big breakfast only a few snacked on pemmican bars or fruit. Within twenty minutes, we were on the move again. While our handheld computers could get GPS data straight from a satellite, we needed the proximity of a signal tower to receive internet and email connections. The further we walked, more of us noticed these connections disappearing.

"Hey Wheeze," I asked, "Did you ever finish high school?"

"Naw," he responded, "quit when I was sixteen, never did care for it. I'm now takin' a class to get my GED. My wife's on me about it."

"How did you avoid the truant officers?"

"Are you kidding? My old man had done time for armed robbery, none of them truants wanted to stop by and have a chat with him."

"Gee, I always thought the laws were pretty specific."

"Ya know, Kelley, sometimes you philosophers can't see something standing right in front of you. The law is clear, but the situation has to do with the enforcement. Laws are used when the good people want something done for themselves."

"You guys also helped us out a lot, helped us build our log cabin, and helped us in that fight. How come? You guys had the stuff to pound the crap out of us anytime you wanted to."

"You asked us. You were in trouble and you came and asked, and nicely. You treated us with respect, as equals. Few ever did that. And speaking of that fight, we did most of the damage, yet you guys got all the blame for it. And not once, in all those hearings and stuff, did you guys finger us. That kind of stuff is pretty sensitive with the guys, Dan. We don't forget stuff like that. You have us over; you share your food with us. Wheeze smiled. "Now I'm even getting a little misty. Okay, Kelley, enough of this sweetie stuff. Shut up or I'll take that staff off the back of your pack and bash your head in with it!"

We spent the afternoon marching and singing songs. Some of them had some spicy lyrics, and our poor female, Diane, just shook her head and smiled. We must have been quite a sight. Once a herd of deer just stood there, looking at us, as if thinking, "I'll just never understand why they think they're the master species."

It was only about four in the afternoon when we approached a grove of trees with about five different fires going and smoke everywhere. Out of the trees walked the two oddest fellows on the planet followed by two, rather strange females. I once thought that The Range members were on the edge, but these characters had gone over it. The guys were dirty and unshaven, and the females not much better. I couldn't tell if they were drunk or had been sampling the local mushroom crop. They acted like people who had been working with oil based paint in an enclosed space.

"Greetings, Brother Matt," one yelled after seeing our Holy Cross friend. "Have we got something to show you guys?"

We walked over in the trees to see an old army personnel carrier. "We're gonna take you guys down to Big River in this thing. Save ya some walkin'."

Ben pulled out his topographical map and showed it to him. It was obvious that formal education had eluded this fellow most of his life in that he looked at the map like he'd never seen one before. Finally, he said, "Here, see?" Ben then sort of backed up, from the odor no doubt.

"What's it run on?" Ben asked.

"Ethanol."

"How did you get that way out here?"

"We made it."

Diane Win whispered under her breath to me, "I wonder how much of it they drank today."

"You guys joinin' us for supper? Deep fried field mice, just gut 'em and throw 'em in the grease, a real treat."

"You know," Ben said, "we got some stuff that will go bad if we don't cook it tonight. So, we'll just cook ourselves. We'll be in that grove yonder."

They told us to be ready by six in the morning, and then we walked over to trees in a grove about one hundred yards away from theirs. A stream of cool water flowed nearby.

We set up camp, sharing a few jokes about our hosts. We didn't have anything that was going to go bad right away, but Ben thought it wise to avoid what they were having. We set up fires and made a stew with pemmican and some of the potatoes we had carried.

"What's the Big River?" Cork asked Ben.

"I think it's the Illinois, from what I can tell. It's a good offer though, that will cut about forty miles off our walking."

"If the bongo brothers don't drive us straight into the Big River," Diane added.

My watch was at two in the morning, which suited me just fine since I had always loved that time of the day. I started brewing some coffee, making sure it was weak to conserve our coffee supply. I looked at the adjacent tree grove, all the fires still going like mad. I wondered if the alcohol they were brewing was going to blow up.

Right at six our hosts were spotted driving their truck over to our camp. After getting out, they seemed a little more clear-headed.

One of them offered to Tom, "Maybe the little lady would like to sit up front with us, sure would be more comfy for her."

Pine looked at Diane and teased, "What do you think, honey, wanna ride up front with the fellas? It sure would be more comfy."

Diane shot him a dirty look and began climbing in the back of the truck.

We began to regret their offer as soon as we got on the road. By the road I meant the bare ground, since there wasn't a road. It was so rough and bouncy I didn't think we could last the day like that. But as the trees thinned out and the wide-open prairie began to unfold before us, it became tolerable. Pine was seated up against the cab, with Diane and then me by her, in the open-air truck bed. Diane was giving her husband the business.

"Little Lady?" she sneered, "Good thing Angie isn't here, she'd box that guys ears shut. Little Lady? I don't know about this marriage, Tom. Where do you dig up these characters?"

"Same place I found you dear, under a rock."

"I mean really. I thought Kelley was weird," as she elbowed me, "but these two? Can you see in that back window, dear? Are they drinkin' all our gas?"

"Personally," Wheeze added, "I like 'em. They make me look good."

These guys didn't like to stop, either. It was well after noon when we approached the river. Our hosts didn't even get out; they just talked through the window to Ben.

Diane informed us, "I don't think I have any kidneys left!" and dashed off into the bushes. As Ben returned to the group, the two drove off in the truck.

"These guys made a crossing downriver a little ways from here. It was a month or so ago, so I hope it's still usable. They said they would try and pick us up here on the day we plan to be back."

We marched down and found the crossing. After getting on the other side, Al Myers set our course to the coordinates of my helicopter rescue. It was south by a little east. So we marched.

The landscape excited us. The grass was shorter than I expected, a mixture of native prairie grass and some other grass that looked like regular domestic lawn grass. Herds of elk and deer roamed the scenic view, most of them paying no attention to us at all. At about six, we stopped to camp in another grove with a water source.

Matt had always drummed into us to stop, set up camp, hunt if required, get fires going, and supper cooking all before sundown. Messing around in the dark was dangerous and foolish.

Empire and Wheeze went out hunting, but didn't take long to return with big elk steaks. I grilled them on open flame, along with fried potatoes in the Dutch ovens. Then we all sat around eating and telling stories.

I felt so good, so alive. I loved this life. And this wasn't just some backyard campout; we were fifty miles from the nearest two-car garage. After dark, the sky was lit up with millions of stars. It was not difficult to count half a dozen shooting stars in just ten minutes. Not having a watch that night, I enjoyed my seven hours of uninterrupted sleep.

We got up early again and ate leftovers. Matt indicated that it was efficient to heat up leftovers for breakfast. We were on the march well before five. With the weather being so good, we felt an urgency to get as far as we could before we ran into any thunderstorms.

Suddenly, Cork stopped and yelled, "Oh no!" Matt instantly put his rifle up into firing position and ran forward. Then we heard Cork laugh, "No worries, I just stepped in some animal flop." He was wiping his boot on the grass as Matt warned us to keep our eyes on where we were stepping. We continued, but Cork's episode repeated itself with several of us during the hike.

The problem with early July, however, was the heat. By midday we could feel it. Drinking water every chance we got proved wise. Near the end of the fourth day we came to a small river, not too wide across but fairly deep. Clyde swam the river, and then I tossed over a rope tied on to my staff. We hung a taught line and pulled ourselves across. We pulled packs over with another rope. It took a good hour getting all across. Since it was close to seven, we decided to make camp on the other side and take advantage of the water source. We were approximately two and half miles from our goal.

Matt noticed some storm clouds in the western sky, so we found a high spot out of the riverbed and set up our pup tents. With two of us having half a tent apiece, we quickly put them together. Corky and I were tent mates. Seeing several fallen tree trunks, we pulled some over and constructed a low perimeter around the tents. We set watches and the group, in pairs, started going downstream for baths.

I cooked supper again only because I was getting nervous and needed something to keep my mind occupied. Corky and Clyde kept pulling trout out of the river in buckets. I fried fish and cooked the last of the potatoes, using melted deer fat we had gotten the night before. It was probably not a healthy meal, but we were on vacation.

Matt finished up with the cooking while Cork and I went down for a bath, taking one of the rifles. The water was a bit chilly so it was a speedy process.

The fish were so good we easily consumed the lot. My filleting technique wasn't the most efficient, but we had so many nobody complained about the waste I left with the bones. After washing out our metal mess kits in the river, people began crawling into the tents and were soon snoring away. I listened to Corky snore for about an hour and I decided to get up and go sit by the fire.

It never did rain as the clouds, passing to the east, stayed south of us. I must have fallen asleep, as Diane woke me for my two o'clock watch. She gave me her rifle.

"Who's on guard with you?" she asked.

"Wheeze," I responded.

"You sure we should let that guy have a gun?"

"He's okay."

So my gangbanger companion and I took our watch. I had the edge of the riverbank while he took the open ground side on the south. About three thirty, I put water on to boil as people started to get up.

Then I heard, "Kelley! Backup, please." It was Wheeze, standing about five yards out in front of the camp perimeter, his rife up in firing position. I slowly stood up and walked toward him.

Out in the grass I saw a wolf, teeth showing and a low growl coming from the animal. Behind it stood about five more, all of them watching the leader. Wheeze was in a stare down.

"You must be havin' a bad day, Poochie, because you sure picked the wrong guy in this tour group," Wheeze talked to it. I had seen the feral dogs back up north, but this was the real thing. It was skinny, and dirty, and had breakfast on it mind. Wheeze continued, "Try it! I'll put a hole in your noodle the size of a grapefruit." The wolf raised a paw, as if to take a step, but held it up to see how Wheeze would react. "You got the wrong guy, fella, I don't care. One more step and we'll be havin' fried doggy for breakfast!"

Just when we thought Wheeze was going to blast it, the wolf lowered its paw, turned around, and starting running away, the others following. It stopped every few yards to look at Wheeze. Then they disappeared over the hill.

When we turned around, the whole camp was up, and gave Wheeze a standing ovation. He smiled, made a perfect bow, and said, "Thank you. It's all in the attitude."

"It must have been a female, Wheeze," Clyde yelled, "You have that effect on women."

"I know," Wheeze responded, "I've seen that mood in my wife, several times."

We packed up quickly and formed to march. Although Matt gave us another safety talk about the possible perils, the wolf event picked up our spirits and sense of excitement. So, despite sore legs, we started off refreshed.

The two and a half miles seemed like they took forever to walk. I marched along side of Diane.

"A penny for your thoughts," she spoke.

"I'm so nervous, I don't know what to expect."

"That's what's keeping me going," she smiled.

The ground was all so similar, nothing but rolling hills and low spots. Tree groves were spotty and scattered. Every now and then, we would see a lone tree, standing out on the prairie. My heart was racing a mile a minute. My hands began to tremble.

We came in from the west of our GPS target. Seeing a group of fruit trees up on a hill to our east, we climbed a sharp rise and came to the edge of a rather steep drop off. We gathered at the top, looking down on a vast landscape of more of the same type country. Getting nauseous now, I watched Corky and Clyde stumble down the steep decline onto the prairie below.

The two dusted themselves off, looking about. They looked west, then, as Corky looked east, he suddenly stopped dusting and muttered, "Oh my good gosh!"

Clyde whipped his head around in the same direction, and then looked up at us, "Kelley, you'd better get down here."

I was down there before the large group knew I had left. I went down on my behind and slid. Standing up at the bottom, I looked over to the east. There, amongst a patch of tall weeds, sat a vehicle. It was well camouflaged in the overgrowth. A large, army green vehicle with a boat-like bottom sat there. It had been headed right into the incline. It was facing north.

"It's here," I gasped as the others were scaling down the cliff. "The dreams were true."

Although it was about a hundred yards from us, I was there in an instant. The boat bottom had a top on it that was similar to a tank, only with a windshield on the front. It had two large tires on the front, both flat, with a halftrack set up for the rear wheels. Wheel wells were cut up into the bottom. One of the tracks was broken. The windshield, the side windows, and the rear windows were all intact.

As the others began to gather behind me, I heard Wheeze gasp, "What in the world is this? St. Patrick, what in the heck were you doing out here in this thing?" The nickname for my dad had stuck, ever since Matt had joked about it the night before we left.

"Seen anything like this before?" Ben asked Wheeze.

"Yes," Wheeze laughed, "only in a picture. You guys know what this is? This is military. They didn't make many of these. This is unbelievable. We have another mystery now, how he got it. Your dad couldn't afford this, Kelley." Wheeze looked at some numbers carved into the metal.

"When was it made, middle forties?" Ben asked.

Wheeze responded, "Just as I thought, this is a UXU, experimental. No, Ben, more like early forties or even late thirties. But even at fifteen years old, this would have been out of Patty's price range. This is an amphibious vehicle, water jets probably in the rear, must have been how he got across rivers in it. You guys sure he wasn't still with the military?"

"Pat said he was discharged years before," I reminded him.

Wheeze slowly walked around it, cutting weeds away with his knife as he went. Al Myers turned to Cork and gave him his handheld.

"Here," he told him, "walk out to the southwest, over there. Walk until these cross hairs meet the X on the screen. And don't drop it!"

"Empire," Ben said, "go with him. Bring a rifle."

They trotted off, traversing a small ditch in the field.

We watched Wheeze walk around the vehicle, a big smile on his face. He came around on our side again and scaled a ladder attached to the side. Climbing up, he tried the driver's door. "Just what I figured, seems rusted shut." He climbed higher and looked at the top.

"How'd he power it?" I asked.

"He must have had a solar converter, there's half of an unfolded solar panel up here. The other half must have blown off. Perhaps that was what he and the wife went out after. This thing must have taken a lot of power, though. He could probably only get five or six hours running time out of it before he had to stop and recharge. On cloudy days I bet they just had to sit." He climbed back down.

"Now we gotta get in there."

"I don't know how we're going to do that," Ben said, "I would hate to break the blade of a good knife on that."

Wheeze put his backpack down on the ground and retrieved a small crowbar. "Here we go."

"You pack a crowbar?" Diane asked.

"It's more of a weapon, actually." He smiled at her, then climbed up and started prying on the door.

Al had me turn around to see Corky and Empire out about a hundred yards in the distance, jumping up and down. "Mark it!" Al yelled.

"Dan, that's where the helicopter picked you up." He walked me over to the edge of the ditch. "This is where you most likely fell in. There may have been water in this ditch if it rained at all before the snow started. The water probably had a layer of ice on it; the wind blew you down to where they are. That helicopter found you by dumb luck, only a hundred yards or so from the vehicle."

The guys returned, leaving a small stick stuck in the ground in that spot. Al took his computer back and punched in some data.

"Kelley, look at this date."

I looked at the screen, "Monday, September 3, 3055. So what?"

"Isn't it odd? That's the date they picked you up. I know winters come early up here, but do we usually get blizzards on Labor Day?"

We walked back to the group. Most were sitting on the ground as Ben got things going. "Okay, let's set up camp. There's no wood down here so three of you go up in that orchard and throw some down. At least one rifle goes as well." He assigned everyone something but Wheeze and I, probably knowing my mind was too preoccupied at the time.

"Kelley," Wheeze yelled down, "bring up some tent poles." He climbed up to the top of the vehicle and as he pried on the door, I stuck a pole in the opening. He slowly worked his way around.

"We'd better change places; this thing is gonna pop in a minute."

I climbed back down on the ground as Wheeze took my spot and continued to pry. Then we heard a loud pop and the door swung open. Wheeze then jointed us on the ground, "Go ahead, Kelley. It's your home. Go check it out.

Ben objected, "Cork, why don't you go in first. You know, in case there's something, or someone, in there."

I understood that Ben might have feared my parents had returned, went back in, and expired.

But soon Cork yelled out, "No one's home."

I scrambled up the ladder and sat in the pilot's seat. The small cabin was musty but was in good shape after sitting there for fourteen years. The driver's control panel consisted of a mass of small, black screens, a radio transmitter, and a steering wheel that looked more like one would see on an airplane. Four foot pedals appeared at my feet.

The cabin was small, but cozy. It contained two small racks for beds on each side in the back, a small food preparation area and some storage shelves. What looked like two small sleeping bags were on the floor between the beds. Cork was in the back, looking around.

Al Myers climbed up the ladder and went up on the roof to check the condition of the solar unit. Wheeze followed him and stood on the ladder and looked in, I asked him, "These screens are blank, any way to get them on?"

"No, those are probably digital gages. No power, no gages. I'm sure this thing has an operations computer, but we can't turn that back on either."

Al Myers formed a search team of him, Diane, and me. We went through the whole compartment. In a storage compartment, in front of the passenger seat, I found what looked like to be some sort of supply list and some manuals on the vehicle. I found no other papers, titles, registrations, pictures, or books. In the back, Diane found clothes, some canned and instant foodstuffs, a laser rifle with no charge in it, and the usual utensils someone would bring on a camping trip. She found a young boy's sweatshirt with

"Junior" written on it and gave to me. We made a thorough search of every nook and cranny. We found nothing to indicate where they were going or why.

Frustrated, Al pounded his fist on the dash, "Darn! If I just knew where they were going."

"I think we're looking too closely." I pointed above his head.

There, attached to a sun visor on the roof of the cab, was a scrap of paper with the words "It's here" written on it. Below the words were GPS coordinates. Al exclaimed, "Eureka!"

After exiting the vehicle, we found a full camp set up and dinner cooking on the fires. Two search parties were just returning, both with the same news: no lost half of the solar panels, no bodies, and, worst of all, no water nearby. I gave Wheeze the operating manuals I took from the vehicle.

As we ate supper, we brainstormed again.

"Any chance of getting under the hood of this thing, maybe we could get it running?" Ben asked.

Wheeze said, "We probably could, but I would like your permission not to."

"Why?" Ben asked.

"Well, several reasons. Even though it has an electrical engine, it must have some sort of lubrication, which is probably mud by now. We turn that over and we'd crack it. The same can be said for the lube in the transmission and axels. Plus, the battery is probably melted by now. Besides, we need new front tires, a rear track, and something to jack it out of that hole it's stuck in. The engine compartment is sealed on these things and if I pop it the moisture will invade. We won't gain any advantage in getting it started now; we couldn't move it. I'd like to come back here someday, with some vehicles and all the tools, jacks and parts we'd need to bring it back."

"Well," Cork added, "I think it belongs to Dan and his brother. It's up to him."

I said, "I don't even have a memory of the thing, but maybe my brother does. I just wish we had found a solution to my mystery."

"Maybe we have," Al spoke, "Those coordinates we found, the spot is exactly one point eight three miles from here, due north. We must have walked right by it coming here."

I remember waking up at four, and turning over. I saw Al Myers lying next to me, and was startled when I saw his eyes wide open. "I got it!" he exclaimed.

"Got what?" I asked.

"I been thinking about what I could have missed, been thinking about it all night. So I don't know if I was awake and thought of it, or it came in a dream. There was a reason old Patty didn't have a written log. Wheeze mentioned it, the operations computer, I'm sure it has a hard disk of some type! Patrick might have kept a verbal record, a recorded log." Al jumped up and started getting dressed. I did the same.

"But Al," I asked, "how can we play it? That computer must be fifteen years old, that disk isn't going to fit in anything we got."

"I know. I'll have to take it back with us. I can do it in the lab at school."

When we got into the cab, it was too dark to see anything, so we came back down and made the coffee. As soon as the sun started to peek over the horizon, Wheeze joined us back in the cab. He read from the manual and Al had me go under the dash. Al said he was too nervous for handwork.

"Where is it?" I asked.

Wheeze responded, "In the middle, there should be a small panel door."

"I see it, how do I open it? There's a tiny knob here with some writing near it."

"What does it say?"

"It says, 'Turn here to open.'"

"Well, that might be it. Good thing we got a trained electrician here," Wheeze joked.

"Okay, it's off."

"Is there any printing on a small black module? What does it say?"

"Ah, can't make it out. Okay, it says 'Made in Japan.'"

"Kelley, knock it off!" Al scolded me.

We all knew from history class that Japan didn't exist anymore, but Al wasn't in the mood for any jokes right now. Scientists have no sense of humor.

"Okay, there's a clear plastic type wrap around all the circuits."

"Rip it off. There should be a black box, no bigger than a credit card, with three wires leading into it."

"I see it. The wires are attached to three tiny plugs."

"Okay, don't pull the plugs out! Every computer company has their own types of connections to keep someone from using other equipment. If we leave them here I won't be able to fabricate copies. Take a small pair of wire clips and cut the wires, leaving as much on the plug as possible. Then just pull that black box out."

"I got it," handing it out to Al. He carefully put it in his waterproof pocket as I put the panel door back on.

Back in camp, we soon found out that there was not much for breakfast. We snacked on the last of our pemmican bars. Now we had no food and very little water.

"We're going to have to get back to that river before long, guys," Ben said. "But I think we're done here. Let's go take a look at St. Patrick's destination and see what this was all about."

Wheeze shut the door to the vehicle and sealed it with some waterproof tape he had brought. Nearly everyone took pictures; Al got one of me standing next to my old home. We packed up, lined up, marched off, climbed the ridge and headed for the coordinates on Patrick's note.

As we started off, Wheeze leaned over to me and whispered, "Kelley, where the heck's Japan?"

Again the walk was short, but seemed like it took forever. The land was lousy with game, and growling stomachs reminded us of our hunger. About a quarter of a mile away, Al pointed at a rise in the prairie, "There, there it is. See those three trees?"

As we walked, the group was in the grip of a nervous feeling about what was to come next. We yelled alternatives out loud. We listed every strange phenomenon in any apocalyptic novel we had read, play or movie we had seen, and strange urban legend we had heard. Al said, "Clyde, turn on the environmental data recorder on your computer, I want an independent recording of all conditions here."

The wind suddenly picked up and the three trees, Myers guessed oaks, swung back and forth. They stood alone on the open prairie with no companions for several miles in any direction. Other than the almost imperceptible rise in the landscape, there didn't appear to be any remarkable characteristics about the spot. The grass appeared somewhat taller and more lush but not incredibly so.

Al and I were on point. As we slowly walked the last few feet, Al had his computer out and it was buzzing with excitement. "How accurate is that thing?" I asked.

"Are you kidding?" he came back, "This one is better than what the farmers use. I would say it's correct within a fraction of an inch." Al looked down at the computer screen, stopped, and backed up, moved to the right and left, then exclaimed, "This is the spot."

Al and I looked around. Save for the remainder of the group about one hundred feet away and already stopping to kneel down and rest, we came to the same unfortunate conclusion: there was nothing here.

All of the special events we had anticipated drained from us so intensely; you could almost hear them hiss like air escaping from a punctured tire. There was no unicorn here, no albatross circling above. There were no pyramids, monoliths or obelisks about. We saw no Greek gods, Roman gods, nor Native American deity. There was no evidence of a recent spaceship landing. We didn't see any locusts or frogs. No burning bush, pillars of fire, four horsemen, or bright stars could be seen. There was no stairway to heaven. We didn't see any meteor impact craters, headstones, slings or arrows. There were no three witches stirring a pot.

The prairie looked like it had since leaving the forests south of Old Chicago, save for the three large oak trees, almost bending over from the now fierce, southerly wind. The rest of the group now had to shift their backs to the south to keep from getting blown over.

Undaunted, Al Myers went about his work. Leaving me standing "on the spot," he proceeded to measure the distance between the trees, even calculating the angles of the points of the triangle they formed. He squared, and then cubed the distances, mumbling something about the Pythagorean Theorem. He took core samples from the tree trunks and some leaves for tissue analysis.

Ben had Empire and Cork form a search party. They circled the spot going out to about a one hundred foot radius, searching the ground.

Al took tissue samples of the grass in various spots. He did a soil sample on the spot, reporting ph, nitrogen, potassium, and potash to be within normal limits for land east of the Mississippi River. He took additional samples to take back with him. He did a scan of the ground near the epicenter. He took atmospheric measurements of humidity, barometric pressure and wind speed. He had Clyde hold up his computer to get backup readings of those.

We noticed a small herd of buffalo, about twenty of them, coming from the south and heading right toward us. Then, at a distance of about half a mile, they made a sudden turn east.

"Think they spotted us and want to avoid us?" Empire asked.

"No," Tom Pine answered, "their eyesight's not that good. More likely they picked up our scent."

Al checked the magnetic fields for irregularities, also radiation levels. After the search party rejoined us, Al reported, "Okay, I don't see anything significant here. Those trees on high, dry ground is rather odd but not unheard of. I'd estimate they're about fifteen years old. There are some indications of an old foundation or line of stones down in the ground here. It just might be a foundation of an Old World homestead but it looks more like just normal rocks."

"How deep are the rocks?" I asked.

"Five or six feet," he said, "I guess we could dig'em up. There is no evidence of either burial vaults or skeletons."

"Gee, going that deep would take us until midnight."

Al, almost apologetically, said, "I'm sorry, Dan, the place your father gave his life to get to doesn't seem to contain anything I can see that is out of the ordinary. Of course, these additional tests and our computer hard disk might yield something later. I can also get satellite photos ordered for this site, now that we know where it is."

"We can't stay here long, Dan," Ben added, "We're out of food and have little water left. We had best be getting back to that river soon. But it's your call, buddy."

I sorely wanted to camp here and spend a few hours digging around. Then I looked around at nine tired, wind-beaten faces and saw that they had had it. Most everyone was laying down stretched out in the grass. My friends had been too kind in helping me with this adventure and I could tell the excitement had worn off. "No, I can't see what else we can do by staying here. Let's go."

Having the strong wind at our back was actually helpful now, as it pushed us along on our trek straight north to the river. A couple hundred yards out, I turned into the wind and looked back, asking myself, "St. Patrick of the Prairie, what the heck were you looking for?"

CHAPTER 13

The wind died down as we approached the river. We crossed it straight north of where we had been. Our more lofty thoughts returned to camp life, and we set up as quickly as we could. Fires were started, roots gathered, and our thirst quenched. The area was crawling with pheasants and our hunters soon brought in several. The buffalo herd that we saw earlier must have left the area, as we never saw them again. We also got a few clothes washed and our packs reorganized. The roots were a little different than I was used to up north. I mashed them up with a little water and made something similar to potato pancakes. They were quite bland, but with enough red pepper and oregano I made them edible. We were going to spend the remainder of the day resting up and getting some food prepared.

As I fried up the vegetables, Marie popped into my head. Boy, a soft and warm female would be nice to snuggle up against right now. I thought about her a lot for the rest of the trip.

We stuffed ourselves and talked of our adventures. The pressure appeared to be off, and our jokes and pranks soon began to return.

When Diane got up and asked Tom to escort her downriver to take a bath, I interjected, "You know, Tom, I've learned a lot from you this past year. I want to return the favor; I'll go down and guard Diane for you."

Diane laughed but scolded me, "Dan Kelley, you just sit back down and stay there. And I don't want you anywhere near me for the rest of this trip."

After they left, Ben told me, "Looks like it's going to be a high protein diet from here on out. Not much out here this time of year except meat."

"It would be nice to have some pemmican for snacks," I added, "but it would take a day to dry and another to make it. Of course, that wouldn't help us in the fruit and vegetable department."

Ben told me, "I'm sorry things didn't turn out as expected, back there, with your dad and all."

"I think in some ways it sort of did. I know I had a lot of this mystery stuff and details running through my head, but there were a few times I could almost feel him being there. It was almost like he wanted me to complete his journey. I did, but I didn't have his knack for perceiving what it was he was looking for. I wonder if I ever will."

"And then again, maybe that wasn't the most important part of this trip."

I ate the last bit of my questionable side dish. Right then, on that spot, I named my new culinary invention "St. Patty's Patties."

We continued to eat and talk throughout the day. With the exception of our guards, we all drifted off and were snoring like dogs.

The next day, we soon returned to the same route we had walked down. I expected the walk home to be tiring and frustrating, but we had a ball. The jokes, the laughs, and our songs with the distasteful lyrics soon returned. We took a few side routes, going by lakes and other natural sites of interest. Once we spotted antelope in the distance but never got close enough to bag one for supper. In the evening, we stretched out by the campfire and watched glowing sunsets. I had never felt more alive than on that walk home.

I saw things out there, well, more like felt things. I could almost picture ancient Illini Indians dancing or bearded men laying down railroad tracks. One night, I told Tom Pine that Abraham Lincoln had probably peed right on the spot he was sleeping on. He thanked me for that historical thought.

While walking along with Matt we began talking.

"So, Kelley, how do you like my sister?" he asked.

"Great. She's a wonderful girl."

"Are you guys getting serious, or what?"

"Oh, I don't think so. I'm not sure she likes me that much."

"Really? That's not what she thinks."

"Are you sure? I can't tell."

"She's hard to read a lot of the time. We call her 'old poker face.' She made you breakfast once, didn't she? If she's cooking, she's nuts about you."

Late one afternoon, after arriving at and crossing the Big River on the day we anticipated, we discovered our glue-sniffing friends were nowhere to be seen. We waited until eight the next morning, and then decided to take a more northeast course straight home rather than to swing up north to their lair. That day was the hottest, and felt the longest, of any. We made it to the big cave where we had spent the winter but camped out in front of it.

We only had a walk of a few hours that last day and finally came strolling into the horseshoe shaped ridge and home. Everyone was around. Little Angie came running at Ben Holden so fast she jumped up on him and knocked him over, again. Rose and Jim were there, Frank and a new girlfriend along with Libby. Finally Marie came out of the log house, looking better than ever.

None of the women would have too much to do with us until we had long showers and clean clothes. So how did we spend our first night after camping out for the past two weeks? Well, in front of the fire outside the log house, of course. We had to go over all the stories, twice.

Life got back to our old, comfortable routine. I sent Pat Junior his old sweatshirt, copies of all the pictures, and a long letter describing our trip and our findings. Al took dad's hard drive and all the samples into his lab at the college and started working on them. I think Al was way more frustrated with the trip than I was, since he was the technology officer of the team and so far his technology wasn't putting out any answers.

Frank Davis brought up this crazy idea of getting a wheat crop planted. He knew it was late in the season, but wheat grew quickly. Anyway, he said it would help his plan if we just had some growing. We talked Milt into coming down and tilling a couple of acres in one of the meadows and putting in some wheat. He cursed us most of the time he was there, saying the ground needed much more attention than we were giving it. Plus, we had to shore up our river crossing by throwing some more logs in the Ice River for him to drive his tractor and planter over. But old Milt put in the crop and even came down to check on it several times.

Life went on as September, and our hearing, soon came about. Ms. Hightower met with all of us the night before. She exuded the same confidence she always had, which made us worry more about a possible negative outcome.

She explained, "This is a funny deal here. I'm sure it's the total creation of the President of the Town Council, Mrs. Popover. This is not really an administrative law hearing like we had with the school. We are not dealing with any crimes here, but the council can pass resolutions limiting you guys or even running you out of town. She does have the authority to administer an oath, so no fibbing out of any of you on the stand. She can call witnesses, question any of you, and you can question the council as well. It's not formal rules of evidence, but she has enough knowledge of proper procedure not to allow any crap in either. The council has six members and the President can only vote in case of a tie. They can pass, and enforce, any matters regarding the township.

"Now, Frank and I have a good, solid plan, and we're going to try to impress the six council members, even to the point of going after Mrs. Popover a little. We don't want her to get an opportunity to vote because we know where that will go, we need at least a four to two vote to go against her wishes."

We all showed up at the hearing in our new suits. I couldn't believe Hightower had talked us all into buying suits. Having never owned one, I didn't know the first thing about buying one. I took Marie with me to get mine, remembering Ben's advice of "Whenever you need help with a problem and no one around has any experience, always pick someone who cares about you." Marie couldn't be at the hearing but told me to call her the instant a verdict was in.

We all sat in the grand chambers of the town council as the room began to fill. Ben and I sat at the table, with the other seven Eagles sitting right behind us. Two empty places were saved for Hightower and Frank Davis, who had not yet arrived.

Then, tears began to well up in my eyes as our support came in. First there was an immaculately dressed Mr. Bossard; he leaned over the rail to shake all our hands. Milt, cursing the constraining necktie he was wearing, and Mrs. Frazer came in. Diane Win-Pine came in, flashing us the "V" for victory sign. I almost fell out of my chair as Lisa Richardson and a fully uniformed Captain Richardson burst through the door, the latter waving to me. Mrs. Kowalski-Henderson followed them. Wobbling in with his walker was Doctor Principi.

Following were Matt, Paul and many of the other Holy Cross, Rose Russo, Angie, Libby Davis and her new parents. Ron, my boss, joined them.

We were shocked as Matt Fuller came in escorting Bus Quint and his father, both obviously intoxicated as they stumbled to their chairs. Clyde Hasting leaned forward and whispered to Ben and me, "One word out of that clown and I'm jumping the rail and breaking Quint's jaw." Empire got up, walked to the back of the room and spoke to two police officers standing there.

Finally, wearing a brand new suit, in walked Wheeze, arm in arm with his wife; the rumors about this wife of his were all true. She was at least six foot six; she was big framed and had a look on her face meaner than any man I had ever seen. She paused before sitting down and glared at Quint. Clyde soon returned, "On second thought, I think I'd rather let her have a go at Quint."

But our moods dropped about ten points as the doors opened and in came Frank Davis, pushing Ms. Hightower in a wheelchair. Her face and neck were swelled up and red, her ankles looked puffy as well. He pushed her up to the table. Frank was beside himself. "Well, this is great. The famous attorney here, who by the way is allergic to peanuts, goes out to a restaurant last night and guess what's in the dish she orders? What else, peanut oil! I'm going to have to ask for a delay, guys, sorry."

Poor Hightower just shrugged her shoulders as her eyes watered.

Finally, the council and Mrs. Popover filed in and took seats at the front table. The council president, ignoring the plight of our attorney, began speaking about the rules of the meeting, going over what Hightower did the night before. As I looked around the room, it was funny to see five or six people on the other side of the hearing room and standing room only on our side.

"Your honor," Frank stood up after she had finished, "our representative is obviously unable to speak today. I would like to request a delay."

"Mr. Davis," she said, letting us know what we were in for, "I'm sorry, but I've waited at least three months to get this special meeting arranged. We are going ahead with it. Do the best you can. I'll give you five minutes to get prepared."

A lone city attorney came rushing in and took his seat at the table beside ours. He had a handful of legal-sized papers and was trying to organize them, obviously unprepared.

Frank was livid. He paced up and down in front of the table. Hightower felt bad, we could all tell, as she wrote on her pad, "Frank, you'll have to do it."

"I'm no trial attorney; I told you that! This is crazy. I got the futures of nine guys here."

She wrote a second note, "You're the best we got."

After reading that, Frank took a deep breath. He knew he was our only shot.

Mrs. Popover jumped right in, "Okay. I've got some serious concerns about you boys. We all know your history well. You are brawlers, you have a history of insolence with the orphanage, there's that riot at the school, and at least an alleged connection to the burning of an orphanage hall. I would also like to discuss your present situation, and the term 'vagrancy' comes to mind. You have no permanent addresses. Although your post office box has you listed at Mr. Frazer's farm, you do not live there. Some of you have terminal degrees in subjects that would prepare you for work, yet you have no jobs. Those that have jobs are not registered or licensed with the township. I wanted the school to handle the problem but they failed to."

"I beg to differ, your honor," Frank turned it on, "but the Department of Education has acted and has returned a decision to drop all charges, have they not?"

She ignored him, “How do you wish to proceed, Mr. Davis?”

“I would like to call some witnesses, but first I have a few questions for the council.”

“Go on.”

“First of all, we all know about this fight you speak of. Was a police report filed on this fight matter?”

“Yes,” Mrs. Popover responded.

“Were any charges brought against any of the men seated here?”

“I asked the police to charge this out and they …”

“I’m sorry, your honor, I didn’t know this was an essay question.”

We could hear Hightower sigh as she wrote on her pad, “Watch it!”

“No,” Popover gave in, “no charges were filed.”

“Was a fire marshal’s report filed in the case of Delk Hall?”

“Yes, and no, no charges were filed.”

“Do I really need to go into the decision regarding the riot?”

“No.”

“Thank you, your honor. I would like to call Mr. Bossard to the stand. I would like to discuss some of the orphanage conditions please.”

Mr. Bossard did a wonderful job of pointing out such things as the dining hall closings, Frank and Clyde’s run-ins with the Mustangs, and the orphanage’s liability in not providing adequate security. Frank then called himself and testified how Fuller and Quint tried to extort him. He followed with me telling the story of the Governor Viche incident. I noticed how the three gentlemen in the room, who were connected with the incident, began to fidget in their chairs.

After I sat back down, Frank said, “Your honor, I would like to call Mrs. Henderson of the Naval Investigative Service.”

After sitting down in the witness chair and being sworn in, Mrs. Popover asked, "Mrs. Henderson, by whose authority are you here today?"

"My commanding officer, Captain Richardson."

The good captain stood up and spoke loudly, "That's me. Any problems with that?"

"Oh, no," Mrs. Popover knew how important the military commanders were to the town, "The council recognizes the prominent captain. Okay, go ahead, Mr. Davis."

"Mrs. Henderson, you investigated the death of Governor Viche, an orphanage resident, did you not?"

"I did."

"Were there any chief suspects?"

"Yes, Matt Fuller and Bus Quint were investigated."

"Are those two gentlemen in the room today?"

"Yes," she pointed to them.

Frank turned around so the town council couldn't see him, raised his hand to about chest level, and then made a gesture like he was shooting a pistol at Fuller and Quint. This gesture showed a side of Frank we never saw before. His anger regarding the treatment he and his sister were subjected to at the orphanage was starting to come out. "What is the status of this case?"

"It's a cold case. It was never forwarded to the city prosecutor."

The city attorney finally woke up, "You honor, I object to this questioning, Fuller and Quint were never charged in this case. They were only suspects."

Mrs. Popover surprised us, "I'm fully aware of what a suspect is, Mr. Wiggs. Appropriate weight will be applied to such status."

Frank continued, "Mrs. Henderson, did you coordinate the taping of a conversation at the Party Burger, in Centura, between a Mr. Dan Kelley and Mr. Matt Fuller recently?"

"I did."

"Do you have that tape here today, to play it?"

"I do."

Wiggs was wigging out, "Your honor! This is highly illegal, this is ..."

"This is not a court, Mr. Wiggs, as this tape relates to orphanage conditions, I will allow it."

The tape caught everyone off guard. There were audible gasps in the room as it was played. When it got to the parts in which Fuller said, "... Quint hit that kid ..." and "Bus Quint hit the kid ..." everyone perked up. Of course his threat on my life didn't help his case either.

After it was played, Mrs. Popover, regretting her decision to play the tape, looked at Mrs. Henderson, "You know this will never stand up in court. Where did this conversation take place?"

"In the men's room at the burger joint."

"And where were you, Mrs. Henderson, in the men's room?"

"Yes, your honor, in the stall, standing on the toilet."

Gasps and groans filled the room. I quickly turned around to see that Fuller had fled the hearing. Quint's dad was passed out snoring, Quint himself in some sort of state of shock.

Frank smiled. "Thank you, that is all." We had done it, we didn't get Quint convicted but we now had it in the public record. Mrs. Henderson had brought Gov in from the cold.

Frank didn't hesitate, "I now would like to discuss our current status, your honor."

Mrs. Popover composed herself. We weren't out of the woods yet. "Mr. Davis, you have no permanent address, you have no place you are living which has a structure, no utilities, no ..."

"Beg your pardon, your honor, we have electrical power, we have a building."

"What? How did you get power out there?"

"Called the utility company, asked them to hook us up."

She held up the hearing while she called the utility company. She talked for several minutes, and then returned to the questioning. "Mr. Davis, well, you do have power, but you never asked the town if it was okay."

"I asked the utility. They're under the auspices of the Public Utility Commission, not the town, and they don't seem to have a problem with it."

"You got that power hooked up to your 'structure,' Mr. Davis?"

"Yes, your honor."

"Is it up to code?"

"What code?"

"Town code."

"Don't need to."

"And why not?"

"It's not in the town. It used to belong to the federal government, but not anymore."

"I don't know how to address this because nobody has done this before. But you don't have an address!" She was starting to pull her hair out. "You can't have a residence if it's not in the town, but …" she just stopped, sat there, and looked down.

"You honor, if I may explain. I have here, copies of a recently filed limited liability company, LLC, articles of organization and operating agreement, hereafter to be known as the Eagle Company, Limited. This sort of incorporates us."

"Okay, Davis," she yelled, "I got you now. No such paperwork was filed with this town."

"Don't have to." Frank was smiling now.

"Let me guess, because it's not in the town?"

"Correct, your honor, you're getting good at this. But no, we were on federal ground and filed the LLC application with the U.S. Department of Commerce. It has been approved. I would also, before you ask me about the town again, like to say that I have here, with copies for all the council, a document from the Department of the Interior, approving our application of land acquisition under the Homestead Act. We have shown intent to live on and develop four square miles of land, designated as on the document, and do so for a period of five years, thereby granting us full ownership of said land."

"And I suppose this limited liability company is your proof of income?"

"Yes, the ten of us will be farming, raising organic produce, raising cattle and a small logging operation, sustainable logging I assure you. We also have a contract with the college to hold natural philosophy seminars there with certified faculty."

Mrs. Popover kept trying, "Mr. Davis, there's no road out there, how will you get access."

"But we will have one."

"When?"

"When the town puts one in."

"I wouldn't count on that."

"Oh, but, your honor, I must object to your statement. The town lands were surveyed when they built Thompson. This survey was conducted in a manner consistent with the rules of the 'metes and bounds' survey conducted in the 1800's after the Louisiana Purchase. All section lines were set aside for future roads. Now that you have people out there, you have to put a road in. We can drive on the open prairie if you want the mud all over your town streets. We don't mind, but people will complain. Oh, and the bridge. You can put that in as well. Your road will officially end in the exact middle of the Ice River. You put up half of it; we'll do the rest."

Mrs. Popover just sat there with her head in her hands. Then she looked up, "Mr. Wiggs?"

The city attorney was sitting there, looking through our papers. He finally stated, "This all looks good to me."

Mrs. Popover then took a large stack of papers, presumably the sanctions she developed against us to have considered by the town council, and threw it in a wastebasket under her table. She then laughed, threw her hand up in the air, and said, "You know what? I'm going to adjourn this thing before you guys make me build an airport. The issues against these boys are dismissed without prejudice. I'm gonna go have a drink." She pounded the gavel. There were cheers and sighs of relief from the gallery.

We all stood up as Frank laid down right on our table. "That's it! No more trial stuff for me. I wasn't built for this." Hightower was smiling.

Ben Holden said, "Guys, you know Hightower did all the work on this case. I say we all thank her, but in the usual and customary Eagle manner." Poor Hightower had to sit there as we all passed by, the humor pouring out of us.

"Great speech, you stupid mute."

"Way to go, fat face."

"Let me call the Guinness people, imagine, a lawyer that can't talk."

"Nice job, peanut brain."

"Don't tell me you're gonna charge us for this?"

"That's easy for you to say."

Poor Hightower just sat there, shaking her fist at each one of us as we passed by. We started walking to the exit, momentarily held up due to the crowd filing out before us. Quint was having trouble getting his dad to his feet. After doing so, Empire stood at the end of their row of seats, blocking their exit.

"Okay," our big guy said to Quint, "it's all over now. No more hearings, no more legal stuff. And you're not gonna drag my brothers into it this time. This time it's just you and me, bub. Quint, I've stood by and watched you smack around my friends for the last six years. There's no more Eagles, no more Mustangs. We're gonna go at it, man on man. I'm gonna knock the ever-lovin' crap out of you. You're gonna need a hundred yards of piano wire to sew your head back on."

As the two police officers started to approach us, Ben whispered, “Oh my gosh.”

“I can’t say I’ll do it today,” Empire continued, “the police are here and all. But every time you come out of a liquor store, or out to get your mail in the morning, I may be there. You’ll never know when, but be prepared to fight. This time I’ll be ready for you.”

Quint did the only smart thing; he stood still and silent, waiting for the police to get there. They quietly put handcuffs on Empire and led him out. We all followed.

Out in front of the town hall we were greeted with cheers from the crowd. When Angie saw Empire being led out in cuffs, she shrieked, “Oh no, you guys got Murdock arrested? We need him!”

The police officers led Empire over to their car. But suddenly, all three were laughing and they took the cuffs off. Empire came strolling back to us, but Angie grabbed him by the arm. Ben, Angie, Murdock, and Libby Davis went back in the building.

Our guests all shook our hands and were leaving as our four friends returned.

“Where’d you guys go?” Clyde yelled at them.

“We got married,” Angie said, wearing a smile bigger than her tiny head.

“What, without us there?” Jim Donovan asked.

“Especially without you guys there,” Angie came back, “Gosh knows what you clowns would have done in there.”

Best man, Empire, came out as well, joining us all. He announced, “Okay, feast and party guys, let’s go back to the forest. Let’s go back to our land.”

We were soon all at the log house, getting out of those awful suits. The fires were lit, the steaks were grilling, and Angie and Ben were dancing. I called Marie and filled her in; she was very happy for us. Soon back in my buckskins, I looked out the door at the group, noticing that two were missing, Empire and Al Myers. I knew where Empire would be.

Out beyond the south fork of our horseshoe ridge, was a smaller hill with a bald top. With no trees, it gave one a totally awesome view of the forest to the south. I saw Empire, standing up there, a rifle slung over his shoulder. I approached him from behind.

"So, why did the police let you go?" I asked.

"Hey Kelley. Oh, the cops? No, they were in on it with me," Empire laughed.

"I didn't think you were kidding."

"No? Good, maybe Quint didn't know it either."

"I must have missed something."

"I know. Quint and me are a lot alike, Dan. You're the big thinker; Bus and me are just ignorant cavemen. I just talked to him in language he could understand. I knew the cops could never get that murder charge to stick. That's why they helped me; they felt bad about it too. So I sentenced Quint. Every day, for the next five or ten years, hopefully, he'll be watching for me, never sure if I'm behind some car in a deserted parking lot."

"And you won't be?"

Empire looked at me and smiled, "Hey, Kelley, I said I was ignorant, not stupid." He put his arm around me and we walked back to the group.

As we approached, Ben, his new wife seated next to him, read a text message he had just received from Hightower. He read from it, "Dear fellas, I want to thank you for your gracious sendoff at the town hall. This is something I'd expect from a group of low life, dirty, stupid, moron orphans. If I added up all your IQ scores, it would equal that of a fairly bright tree stump! Your parents left you guys on someone's porch because they possessed something you guys don't, common sense. And I did all this pro bono? You underemployed, undereducated, baboons have yet to pay me a dime for anything. I take the bar next month, and when I get my license, I'm doing all the legal work for you that Frank can't handle. Then I'm overchargin' your sorry butts and squeezing out every last nickel you got. Then I'm gonna individually wring each one of your scrawny necks. Love, Hightower, Esq."

Ben laughed, "Oh, there's a P.S., I was never more proud of Frank and the rest of you as I was this afternoon. I really love you guys, but don't tell anyone."

We ate and laughed and talked. We must have gone over every "Oh, remember the time we …" story that we could remember.

Finally, near sunset, Angie stood up and took the floor. "Okay, I went over this speech about a hundred times already, but only about once without crying. But today is not a time to cry. I'm sorry about the sudden wedding thing today. I promised my parents a religious ceremony, and we'll do that for them, but I had to make the move today. You guys have been telling me all afternoon what a great guy Ben is and how he took care of you and all. I'm lucky to have him. But you guys took care of him too. No one could say a bad word about Bennie in front of Empire. He and Corky were so close I thought they were attached. So I'm thinkin' there must be something good about Ben. Then, one day …" She had to pause as the water was building in her eyes. "One day, Dan Kelley told me … he told me … he said that he would jump in front of a train for Ben. Of course, with the number of black eyes Kelley had over the years, you have to question that boy's judgment." A few laughs could be heard. "But that day I realized, with that type of loyalty, a life without the Eagles would never be in the cards for Ben. That day I knew if I was ever going to marry Ben, I'd have to marry all ten of you clowns. You're a matching set. You're some of the most fowl, stinky cavemen who always need a shave, I have ever met. But you're my fowl, stinky cavemen who always need a shave. And tonight …" The tears were rolling down her cheeks now. "Tonight I have the best husband, and the nine best brothers-in-law a girl could have." Diane gave her a tissue and she blotted the tears away. "Okay, no more crying. Tonight is my wedding night and Benny and me need to go!"

We all applauded the happy couple as they headed for their honeymoon, in the long log hut we had spent our first months with Holy Cross. Darkness was slowly overcoming our campsite as the guys started to head in, to get ready for dates or whatever. Marie was working tonight or I would have joined them. Soon, just Diane, Tom, and I sat by the fire.

Diane asked her husband, "Tom, you guys need to have one of your talks, want me to leave?"

But I objected, "Diane, would you mind staying? I'd like to talk to you too."

Pine said, "You never did talk to me too much about your last date with Sharon. How did that go?"

"Oh, okay," I answered, "I sort of wrapped it up into the ontic relatedness theory you told me about and explained it away. I'm not sure if I was right or not, but I got it all rationalized."

"Those are just theories, Dan," Pine acknowledged.

"How did it come out according to you?" Diane asked.

"Do you know what I used to think? Diane, I've always considered you in the great looking female club."

"Hey," she responded, "I'll stay here and talk to you all night if you keep saying those things to me."

"Well, what is it you girls do, metaphorically of course? Do you have secret meetings and decide which boys' heads you were going to screw with next?"

Diane laughed, "So, do the Eagles, in their secret meetings, sit there and discuss the same thing about girls?"

"No."

"Dan, I was an adolescent not too long ago," she went on, "and I work with them now. Girls like to sightsee too. Did you know, by the way, that Lisa Richardson was and maybe still is, madly in love with you?"

"How do you know that?"

"I worked with her on your case. I can tell."

"Yea, but she had her army man as a fall back. I couldn't look her in the eye without seeing his shadow."

"I know, and she knew. She said you had scruples and that she didn't. She blocked you out because she knew she could never be at her best for you. She would only be good for kisses behind the bookshelves."

Pine asked, "What did you get from Sharon, Dan?"

"Four months of bliss, a feeling I can't adequately put into words even two years later. And still, after all that time, Sharon has no concept of such a thing. Two years from now I will be a blur, a note in an old yearbook to her. She had in me a guy obsessed with her every breath, and in a while, she won't be able to tell me apart from Tom or Marv. I may forget her, but I sure as heck don't want to ever forget that feeling she gave me."

"You are one deep cookie," Diane continued, "I've heard some weird stuff come out of you. And don't forget I married a philosopher; weird stuff is coming up at our house every day. You appear quiet to girls, Dan, and they think that's cute. But your mind is always working, way so for someone your age. You had to grow up fast; you were thinking adolescent thoughts in the second grade. When you two were dating, you were a man already and Sharon was still a little kid."

"Did you expect some sort of reconciliation on that last date?" Tom asked.

"No way. I'd already given up on that. Sharon left me two years ago, in the carport, outside her door. Even her moving didn't have the effect I expected. She'd already flown off, somewhere else. She was in why-can't-we-just-be-friends land."

"And you didn't want to be?"

"I couldn't get in! I didn't fit into the culture there."

"What did you expect from that final time together?"

"Here comes some more weird stuff, Diane. I wanted her to recognize that we shook up the world, that this thing we had blew our socks off. I wanted her to say, 'This time I ran into something different.' I wanted her to give a tip of the hat, not to me, but to what we had. I think experiencing this is about the best thing someone can do with their life."

I grabbed another log and put it on the fire. Suddenly, out of the dark, Al Myers came walking toward us, carrying all sorts of bags and papers and an assortment of odd utensils. Diane suddenly knew it was time for her to go. She got up and kissed me on the cheek, then said to her husband, "Good night honey, don't stay up too late." She left.

Al sat down in her spot, a lot of stuff dropping on the ground all around him. He looked weary.

"Late night in the lab?" Tom asked him.

"Yea," he sighed, "a late night and not a very good report."

"What did you find out?" I asked.

He pleaded, "Dan, can't we go over this in the morning? I got all your stuff back. I'd rather not talk about it now."

"Al, you know as well as I that if I don't sleep, you're not sleeping, until you tell me."

He looked at me, saw the determination in my eyes, and gave in, "Oh, well. Where do I start?"

"What did you find out about the trees?" Tom asked.

"They're oaks," Al short of smiled, "I don't mean to be glib. The samples say just about that, normal oak trees, let's see …" he looked through some papers, "… oh, here, sixteen point eight years old. No diseases. The tissue samples of the grass look normal. The extensive soil samples show pretty much good, black, Illinois dirt. The dirt on the 'hill' didn't have quite the nutrient level that the dirt I sampled on another part of the prairie did. Magnetic tests and radiation samples normal. The satellite photos show nothing weird. I had a problem with the atmospheric stuff."

"What problem?" I asked.

"Oh, no problem with anything being out of the ordinary. But my wind speed indicator is all messed up. It didn't take right. I had it on. I checked it for proper operation, but its way off. Wasn't it exceptionally windy there?"

"Oh my gosh," Tom said, "It was a terrible wind. What does your thing say?"

"Well, it reads 4.78 miles per hour, out of the northeast."

"No way!" Pine exclaimed, "That wind was out of the south, at least at 35 or 40 miles per hour. I remember the stupid thing. We could barely stand up. What happened? That's a totally top-of-the-line computer you got there."

"I know. I can't figure it out. All my other measurements are okay; just that one is odd."

"Odd is an understatement," Pine sighed, "Well, Clyde got backup, I'll check with him."

"What about the disk?" I asked.

"The disk contains it all. We pumped a little juice into it and did the readings. This is what took the time; we had to apply every old program we had to make it come out legible. There are some highlights. Mr. O'Dea jumped around a bit. I don't know if he had those coordinates when he started his trip, but it sure didn't seem like it. You guys traveled here and there, you went in one direction, then stopped and went in another. Several times actually. I plotted a map for you, with coordinates and dates. You were out there for at least five weeks before … you know … before the end.

"There was an excellent record of the status of the vehicle, power coming in the solar panel, amount of juice in the batteries, engine speed, gear ratios, fuel consumption, all that. We got inside and outside temperatures, humidity. There are even wheel traction reports."

"What about the audio journal?" Pine asked.

Myers put down all his charts and graphs and looked at me. He sighed, "There lies the bad part of the report. He did have an audio log application and he did utilize it. But when we listened to it, it was a scrambled mess. We couldn't even tell if it was a human voice. We found the software we needed to print out an English version, but it was gibberish. It didn't even form words, not even good hieroglyphics."

"What happened, Al?" Pine asked.

"We aren't sure. It might have been the magnetics in the disk housing, it might have been exposure to the elements, or might have been something wrong with the disk reading arm. I'm not sure. The guys are still working on it, but so far nothing's worked. I'm sorry, Dan, I let you down on this one."

"You didn't let me down, Al," I consoled him, "This one might have been beyond us."

Pine and I sat silently as Al picked up his papers, charts, graphs, formula books, programming guides and his million-dollar computer and slowly walked into the house.

"Boy," I said, "we must hold the record for getting so close to something but never reaching it, don't we?"

"I'll say."

"I just can't seem to solve this thing!"

"Maybe that's the point."

"I'm not so sure we could even describe it as a 'thing.'"

"I felt something down there on that hill, and I think you did too. Maybe it was beyond our perception."

"But even a philosophical explanation has to be based on a scientific fact or at least some sort of observation. We can't show any; we don't even have a hallucination to point to. I can't believe all of Al's gadgets didn't pick up something."

"I can."

"Why then?"

"Because they weren't designed to measure such things; I'm going to go out on a limb here, and I think that right now it's the only way we can look at this," Tom went on. "I don't think Patrick O'Dea was some nut job or that he put his family in jeopardy for no pressing reason. Maybe he wasn't sure what it was either, but he was looking for something. Patrick might have based it on superstition or even faith. He came up a little short but his son completed the trip."

"But his son has nothing to report."

"He can report that not all formulas are written yet. You can't calculate the sum of the squares of the remaining two sides if you're not sure it's a triangle you're looking at."

"What do you base your theory on?"

"Only Patty's preparation and whatever genetic influence he passed down to his descendent. We keep focusing on some observable fact when it's the people searching we should be concerned with. I don't know Mr. O'Dea, but I know his second son."

Now it was Pine's turn to throw another log on the fire. It was totally dark out by this time. We just sat there until we heard Clyde, in the log house, singing as he was getting dressed for his date.

Pine yelled to him, "Clyde!"

"What?" Clyde yelled back.

"On your computer, those readings we asked you to take, you know, the ones Myers was taking and we asked you to back up. He screwed up on the wind. Look on yours and tell me what you have."

"Okay, hang on. Well … let's see … okay, here it is. A light wind … out of the northeast … at 4.78 miles per hour."

Tom Pine and I just sat there, with our mouths open, staring at each other.

CHAPTER 14

So that was pretty much how things went. Sitting on this hill here at this time, now that I'm twenty-five and look back on things, I still don't know what to make of some of it. I had always hoped that someday I would reach an age where everything was sorted out, but I'm beginning to doubt that such an age exists. I wanted to catch you up on a few things, since I haven't had a lot of time to give proper attention to my journal, with the military and babies and all. The six or so years since Al Myers gave me that report on my dad have been interesting.

I'm sure it's not a big surprise that Bus Quint and Matt Fuller were never charged with any crimes. Ms. Hightower sent a transcript of the town hall hearing and my tape to the prosecutor's office. Although they wanted to question Quint, he and his old man skipped town. The Feds told us that they were thought to be in Mexico. Since that country had never renewed their extradition treaty with the U.S. since the war, they doubted we would ever see the pair again. They're probably down there now, drinking tequila and eating tacos.

Fuller is still around. He got married, had another kid, and then got divorced.

Frank Davis's idea of forming our limited liability company turned out to be a blessing. We now owned, pending meeting all the requirements of the Homestead Act, four square miles. This included the land our log home occupies, the section next to it, and the adjoining two sections west of those. The southwestern section contains the cave system we used that one winter. We automatically became the landlords of the Holy Cross and their summer camp. Although they all have permanent residences in Centura, we charge them rent of one dollar a year for those few huts and campsites they use in the summer.

Most of our land is forest, although a large prairie meadow is located right in the middle. Here we have our vegetable growing grounds and a forty-acre wheat field. We fenced off a portion of the grassland and use it for a pasture. We have since added a barn and a chicken coop. Most of our produce is used by us, but we got certified as organic gardeners and sell vegetables and fruit to some stores in town and the commissary store on the base. We have a small herd of cattle and some chickens which we use all of now, but hope to be in a position someday to sell some on the market. We also do a little logging in the southeast section. Milt Frazer has been very helpful with loaning or selling us old farm equipment.

The town finally put our road and bridge in, although reluctantly. Some of the guys built log homes on the property. Ben and Angie's was the first. Clyde and Cork built one out in the southwest corner of the land, out by the caves. These new homes, however, had electricity and plumbing and all the modern stuff.

I finally got my electrician's license but my work on the property limits me to doing it part time. I do only custom work, for people I know or get referred to. Since I did so much of that background reading for Pine that one winter, I took several challenge exams in philosophy. Passing most of those and taking a few more courses, I got an associate's degree in philosophy. This certainly did nothing for my income; I just wanted to do it. I started taking courses toward a bachelor's degree in history, but only a few at a time. I can't help it, I still like electrical work.

Many of us started to fulfill our military requirements, staggering our time to keep the property functioning. With Captain Richardson's help, I got into the Navy and got my electrician's rating. I went in at age twenty.

I was loaning my truck to Marie while I was gone, so she drove me to the airfield at Thompson. I remember our parting; it was difficult. I didn't really have a commitment for her or anything and didn't know what to say. Then she floored me, as she had a way of doing, by saying, "You don't have to say anything. If it's meant to be, you'll come back to me. If you don't, I'm selling your truck!"

Boot camp was a walk in the park. Orphans do well in boot camp; we had been sleeping in dorms and showering with about twenty guys since we were four. Many other guys couldn't take it and had to be discharged. For my boot company sports team, I threw the javelin in competition and came in first in the all-camp finals.

I got assigned to a ship docked in Savannah, Georgia. It was a guided missile cruiser and I got into some advanced electrical and electronic stuff that really helped my career. I finally got to visit the emerald city, Atlanta. It had too many people in it and I got claustrophobic. I went to visit my brother and his family. He was really lucky to get adopted.

My one-year tour on the ship was rather boring as far as seeing the sites go. We rarely sailed and then it was usually up and down the coast. Once we went to the remote base on Long Island; it reminded me a lot of Thompson.

I remember one time I had a few days off and got the urge to drop in on Sharon and see how she was doing. A few days before, I called General Dubious in Atlanta to see where she was. I had to leave a message and the clown never called me back. His wife must have thrown a fit. So I called the professionals, Al Myers and Corky Wall. In ten minutes, Corky called back and said she was at some private interior design school in St. Petersburg, Florida. So I decided not to call or anything and would just drop in on her.

When I got to the bus station in Savannah, I had an hour to wait. I was people watching when I spotted a very young couple, probably around eighteen or so. The boy, a new military recruit, was leaving for somewhere and the girl was there to see him off. I concentrated on their faces. Then I saw it, that look, you know the look they make when their partner is not looking at them. I saw that big smile on her face. It was a bitter/sweet smile, because he was leaving, but it was there. I knew that smile.

And then I suddenly wondered what the heck I was doing. Sharon was someone better off left in the past. I guess I had really hoped to go see the old Sharon but now realized her famous smile was from a time and under circumstances that didn't exist anymore. I took a cab back to the ship.

We went on another voyage, this one around Florida and into the Gulf of Mexico. I started a series of emails to Marie; she wrote back. We would discuss nearly any subject; it didn't matter. I so looked forward to getting her next one that I was becoming preoccupied with her.

When we got back from that cruise, we sat in port for months. I don't know if the Navy was trying to cut expenses or what, but I was bored silly. My days consisted of checking in at the electrical shop, making my rounds, and then returning to read a book for the rest of the day. Nearing the end of my one-year rotation, I put in for inactive reserve duty at the Thompson Navy piers. Since they had so much trouble getting people to go there, I was approved.

Before I go on about myself, I wanted to update you on the Eagles. Somehow, I thought the old gang would be together forever. Reality isn't often kind.

The first one to leave was probably the one most fanatical in keeping us together. Frank Davis got into law school at the age of nineteen. After graduating and passing the bar, he worked as a case investigator at Hightower's practice in Centura. It didn't take him long to realize that the kind of law he wanted to pursue didn't exist in this town. He applied, and got into a firm in Daytona Beach, Florida. The day he left was one of the saddest in my life.

He set down his bags, walked up to me, and stuck out his hand to shake, "I'm Frank Davis." just like he had done in the boy's john at Delk Hall the first day we met.

I shook it, "Dan Kelley."

"You new?" he asked, and then we broke down and hugged. He promised to visit and did keep his shares in the LLC. A big part of my heart left that day.

Empire Murdock left us as well, in another way. Empire had mainly worked on the property since the town hearing. He graduated high school and started college, but gave up on it. He helped Corky and Clyde set up their guide and hunting business. When his military time came around he went into the Marines, a dream of his.

After boot camp, he was stationed in Mobile as a Shore Patrol officer. One day he drove his partner to a sleazy bar where an officer was in a fight with a guy over some love triangle thing. His partner went into the establishment and left Empire sitting in the jeep. Then a drunk driver came barreling down the street and ran into the jeep. It exploded and Empire died instantly.

They sent his body back. Captain Richardson arranged for a full military funeral. After getting all the appropriate permits, we buried Empire on that little bald hill, just south of the horseshoe. I put his old rifle in the casket, so he could stand guard duty. We renamed it Empire Hill.

Jim Donovan and Rose Russo never got married. They went together a long time. They got engaged, broke up, got engaged again, and broke up again. One day she fell head over heels for a dashing young fighter pilot at Thompson. They got married and she travelled with him all over the place. Last I heard, they had two babies and he was flying commercial planes out of some airport in the south.

Jim drifted in and out of relationships while he got his degree in political science. He did his military time in a reserve unit and never got called up for active duty. He ended up in Atlanta, working for some lobbying firm and got rich. Marrying some model, he still lives down there now.

Clyde Hastings and Corky Wall had never lost their love of the outdoors or living in the wild. Their hunting and fishing guide business remains moderate, but they enjoy it immensely and also work on our property.

Ben and Angie live in their log home just west of the horseshoe ridge. They can't have kids but both say they have one each to take care of. Ben, a management major, runs our business and both do labor for the LLC. Angie still offers to give me a fat lip at least once a month and on some early mornings I can hear her yelling at Ben for this or that. She's still everyone's little sister.

Bo Schlitz had some problems. Bo had always been quiet, reserved, and shy. He worked as a paramedic part time as he went to nursing school. One day he came home from the college, upset and frustrated, and announced that he was quitting the program. He became friendly with a girl and would go out a lot. We first noticed him coming home very late and then sleeping until ten or eleven the next morning. Having an unwritten rule that if one didn't work or go to school, that person had to work for the LLC. Bo started ignoring his duties here and would be gone for several days at a time. Ben put Corky on the case who reported that he sighted Bo and girl at a nightclub. He said the girl was all of fifteen years old if she was a day. Ben did his surrogate fatherly talk with him which only lead to Bo getting upset and moving out.

About a week later, the police called us to say they had Bo in custody, and that he was taken to the jail because he was exhibiting odd behavior in the street. It seems that his girlfriend and another friend had taken his debit card, emptied out his bank account, and left him without anything. We called Tom Pine right away to come up and see him, and he reported that Bo had suffered some type of psychotic break. We took him to the psychiatry service on the base.

After spending about a month and a half as an inpatient, Bo was finally discharged and is back with us now, working on the property. He still takes a lot of medications but is doing better. We all cursed ourselves for not noticing the signs earlier.

Quiet Frank Miller became a pretty good writer. He writes for several publications in the south but does it via satellite from our big log house. His most famous work to date is a book called *Living on the Prairie*, which is the life story of Patrick O'Dea and our story of trying to solve the mystery. He took out the copyright in the name of our company, therefore allowing us all to share in the profits.

After obtaining a Ph.D., Al Myers serves on the college faculty here in Centura and writes as well. His most famous scientific paper is entitled "O'Dea's Riddle," a totally scientific look at the phenomena in central Illinois. He did this for two reasons: (1) to keep it in the scientific arena; and (2) to stimulate think tanks around the country to try and solve it. Above all, we didn't want it relegated to the group of mythical legends including such things as the Old World's Bigfoot or the Loch Ness monster.

Al reported getting a number of attempted resolutions in the beginning, but the number decreased over time. He never received a solid theory on its explanation and characterized all of them as being things he had guessed during his analysis. He let me read some of them, there was one interesting scientific explanation of some sort of geological force being located in that area. However, most of the responses came from psychological, theological, or philosophical circles. How was one to verify or compare any of these explanations? Did one consult Freud, the Bible, or Occam's razor?

Big Ears was never seen again. Mr. Bossard is an undergraduate instructor at the college. Lisa's army officer got his first assignment at Thompson. They got married and after three months got divorced. Marv Greene left for college in the south and never came back. I see Mrs. Henderson every now and then. Marie's brother Matt is an employee of our LLC.

Paul, the Holy Cross member who I helped with the solar power generator, became a contractor. He pulled a similar stunt to ours and made a Homestead Act land claim, only he chose the land directly east of ours, along the coast of Lake Michigan. On it he built high-end log homes. He not only had me do all the electrical, but he even bought our logs. He is on his way to being a millionaire with the sales and now lives in one of his fancy homes. His firm also built us a machine shed and shop for our farm. He ended up marrying Libby Davis.

Wheeze is still around. He did finally get my dad's old vehicle back to town. My brother and I agreed to go into a three-way partnership with him if he could salvage the old thing, get it up here, restore it, and then sell it. He got his hands on this old flatbed trailer and an auctioned-off tractor. He put these old balloon tires and an old lifting crane on the bed, and, with another vehicle to haul fuel, he took off with those two very weird guys we ran into out west and Clyde and Corky. They had a heck of a time. It seems after they finally lowered the thing on the flatbed, they blew out the tires. They came back, got some more, and then returned. About two-thirds of the way back up here, they ran out of gas and had to make another trip for that. I'm not sure what they did at that big river, Clyde just shook his head and told me not to ask. It took them nearly two months.

Wheeze took another year restoring it. He had a lot of offers for it but they were all from down south, but they all dropped out when they found out how much it would cost to ship it down there. We finally ended up donating it to the college who put it on display in the lobby of the history department, mainly because Wheeze's wife wanted it out of the driveway.

Tom Pine and Diane Win live in town. Tom became the youngest ever Chair of the Philosophy Department at the college, although he struggled with dwindling enrollment in that major. They still come down on Saturday nights and join us around the campfire for our philosophical debates. Not all of the remaining Eagles attend every week, except me of course.

After landing at Thompson upon my return, I called Marie. It was my most spontaneous conversation.

"Hi, Marie."

"Hi, a … Dan?"

"Yep."

"Where you at?"

"At the airfield."

"Which one?"

"Thompson."

"You're back? Let me come and get you."

"I need to ask you something first. Will you marry me?"

"What?"

"Will you marry me?"

"Are you drunk? Can't you wait to see me before asking something like that?"

"Tell you what. If you will, come and pick me up. If not, sell the truck and I'll take a cab."

"Okay."

She was there in ten minutes.

She said, "Yes." When I asked her why, she said, "I couldn't get a good enough offer on the truck." I fear that exposing her to Angie was not a good idea.

So, we got married. She wanted a log home as well, with a backup heating system but with a fireplace and wood stove for atmosphere. Paul built it for us, just west of the horseshoe ridge and just south of Ben and Angie's cabin. She now works as a nurse at the orphanage where I grew up and on our big garden as well. We have a baby girl now and a boy on the way.

We never did figure out the riddle of our wind speed discrepancy down on the prairie. Not only did two independently operating computers get it wrong, but both got the exact same incorrect measurement. Neither of our guys said anything about it in their writings.

Al Myers insisted that we not mention that it felt very windy on that day. He knew that he would be asked for a wind speed measurement and he didn't have an accurate one. Science is a wonderful thing and explains a lot, but without the data it's lost. He could envision a group sitting around and laughing, "Oh, so they thought it was windy on that hill. Doctor Myers needs to refer this case to that guy who can bend spoons with his thought waves." Al would be guilty of sounding crazy. I explained it away as just one of those things. Tom Pine explained it as just one of those special things.

***

"Ppppffffttttt!"

I look down to see my baby girl awake now, sitting in her portable cradle, and giving me her best Bronx cheer. "What's the matter, you don't like my story?"

She smiles up at me and then repeats it.

"Critic," I accuse her.

Just then a butterfly comes floating into her view. Her eyes get big and her mouth forms an "O" shape. She grabs at it, but it's too fast. Now it's almost playing with her, teasing her as she tries to grab at it.

I lean down to her, "You know what that is, honey? Do you know what that look on your face is? That's ends-of-the-earth type stuff, and that's great stuff."

I pick her up and we slowly walk down the ridge to our cabin, smoke pouring out the chimney. "Mom's got dinner on. After we get something to eat, we'll go for a walk out on the prairie. We'll put you in your papoose and all of us will go. We may take the metal detector and search for hidden, Old World treasure. Or we may go and look around with just our eyes. It's always good to go for walks out on the prairie, sweetheart, you never know what you'll find out there."

AUTHOR BIOGRAPHY

David J. Kirk, an honorable discharged veteran of the Unite States Navy, earned his master's degree in personality psycholog from Rhode Island College, Providence, Rhode Island, in 1980. H worked as a counselor and then began a career with the U. Department of Veterans Affairs. He was assigned to the V Medical Center, Detroit, where he graduated from the agency personal management training program and continued in HR as staff recruiter and employee relations generalist

Transferring to Milwaukee, he was assigned as a supervisor recruitment specialist. David was next promoted to assista director of human resources at the agency's medical center in An Arbor, Michigan. Shortly after that, he was promoted to th position of Regional Human Resources Manager, Central Regio Ann Arbor, a corporate level office which oversaw medical cente in the entire Midwest.

He then transferred to the VA Medical Center in Fargo, Nort Dakota, as the Human Resources Manager and retired in 200 David then became an instructor at Rasmussen College where h taught psychology and sociology for four years.

An avid writer since 16 years old, he enjoyed elective colleg courses in creative writing, poetry, and drama. He has written ov a dozen poems and the short stories "Stranger on the Beach" an "Blue Men." After completing *Particular Stones*, he is current finishing up his most recent novel, *In the Big Flood.* He als enjoys vegetable gardening, fishing, book discussion, geograph science, and philosophy

David lives with his wife, a college nursing instructor, Logansport, Indiana. They have two children. He continues wi his writing career.

Learn more about David's work at www.djkirk.net